Bring Me Home

by

Sonnet Harlynn

Brooks Falls, Book Two

Bring Me Home

COPYRIGHT © 2024 by Sonnet Harlynn

Cover Art by *The Wild Rose Press, Inc.*

The Wild Rose Press, Inc.
PO Box 708
Adams Basin, NY 14410-0708
Visit us at www.thewildrosepress.com

Publishing History
First Edition, 2025
Trade Paperback ISBN 978-1-5092-5765-2
Digital ISBN 978-1-5092-5766-9

Brooks Falls, Book Two
Published in the United States of America

Dedication

To my incredible support system, to my dear friends,
you are everything.

Prologue

Jade

The drumbeats of soggy earth under my boots, the cadence of my heart, the words, the words, the words. That was all I heard as I ran across the lawn, tears streaming down my face, my vision blurred. Blood seeped through the gauze on my shoulder, though the pain of it paled in comparison to the ache in my heart.

A canopy of trees cast shadows of images dancing in the night's darkness, surrounding me like a haunting. Like a cage that I couldn't break free of fast enough. I had to get out. I ran, his words chasing me, gaining on me as I wound down the mountain in my Camry.

Hateful words reverberated in my mind, over and over, stabbing deeper and deeper with each thrust of his knife. A searing pain, a final blow.

Rain pelted on my windshield and lights blinding my vision from the rear-view mirror. A black SUV, a man with black eyes, followed close, gaining with each hairpin turn. I squinted. Paranoia, fear, I didn't know. Now, I felt lost and alone, just as I had always feared I would be in the end. And it was true, I'd finally lost everything.

Pain twisted and knotted in my guts. Nausea crept, clawing its way to my throat. The acid burned, and I knew I just had to hang on. I had to get out. I clutched my stomach and willed myself to keep moving, only a little longer. *Down the mountain, just get down the mountain.* And then? I didn't know.

Chapter 1

Jade—Seven years later

The trip had been bittersweet. Bitter because now that I'd once again uprooted my life to return to the home I'd left, I was no longer sure that it was the right idea. But it was also sweet. Brooks Falls held all my formative memories, both good and bad. The bad ones were awful, but the good ones were earth-shatteringly wonderful. And I'd felt it all the moment we passed the town sign— *Welcome to Brooks Falls, California, Gateway to the Coastal Mountains*. I'd rolled down my window, the sweet smell of pine trees awakening memories I'd locked away. The feel of his warm, rough hands against my soft ones as we lay in the bed of his truck, surrounded by evergreens and staring up at a thousand stars. I'd inhaled deeply the second we'd hit the base of the mountains, remembering the curative properties of the air up here.

I pulled forward and stopped at the entrance of my childhood home when I got to the large steel gate that hadn't existed before. I wasn't sure what I had been expecting, but it wasn't this. The home I'd left, the one that had abandoned me long before my eventual departure, had been nothing more than a place to sleep. And it had barely been that.

I looked beyond the gate and took the rest in. It was clear that my father, Brooks Falls' infamous Nathan Greene, had been successful and he'd wanted to flaunt it.

In his successful, but ultimately fatal, bid to become the man he always thought himself to be, he'd built what had been important to him. The rest he'd destroyed. Namely, his family. I stared at the house and exhaled a long breath.

It shouldn't be me standing here, making these decisions. I had never wanted it and Nathan hadn't wanted me to have it. The attorney that contacted me reminded me of that fact when he informed me that my father had left me exactly nothing. News that hadn't surprised me considering we had no relationship. And when the attorney told me that my father had no final will or testament, something else that didn't surprise me, he explained something known as intestate succession. It was a law that determined who would get someone's crap in situations like this. You know, the one where your estranged father dies and leaves nothing to anyone, and all his estate and assets defer to the child not serving time in prison. Yeah, that was me. Thus, by default, I had become the not-so-proud owner of his bunch of crap.

During the time it took for me and my business partner to decide that moving to California actually made good business sense, I'd been mid-signing paperwork to take over the old Greene property.

I looked in the rear-view mirror when I heard the vehicle approaching. Dust from the road floated in the air around the large, white truck as it neared. I glanced at the clock on my display. The builder was on time, and I was thankful for it. I wanted this to get done quickly for many reasons. But the primary reason was the less amount of time I spent in this hellscape that Nathan had created, the better. And even though I'd signed a lease for a small apartment that was close to the town center, I wanted us to get settled and back in a home as soon as possible.

I rolled down my window and punched in the code that the attorney had given me, before throwing my hand out of the window and waving for the builder to follow us in. The gates swung slowly open with a muted metal-on-metal screech. My body tensed as I pulled forward and immediately, I felt pressure on my chest.

My heart raced and my head spun as I surveyed the land I grew up on. *Nothing* was like I remembered it, except the trees surrounding the property.

Evie, my business partner and best friend, rustled next to me, rousing after having spent the last few hours quietly napping in the passenger seat. She sat up, rolled out her neck, and peered out the window. I heard a sharp gasp before she whispered, "What in the Pablo Escobar is this?"

Evie whipped her head around, her long, black hair flying around her. "This is. Jade. It's." She stammered out the words, her verbal struggle mimicking my mental one. "This is like something straight out of Narco's." She pointed to the house; her brow knit tightly together as she waited for my response. And what did I say when I was just as horrified as she was?

The truth, I supposed. "Uh, yeah. That's basically what it is, Vee."

Evie winced and shot me a weak smile. "Right. Sorry, that was rude."

I shook my head and looked back at the house. "It's okay. I mean, look at this place," I gestured to the house. "You're not wrong. This is ridiculous." And it was. One hundred percent. It was a far cry from the ratty trailer that I'd grown up in, which had always been parked in the center of our family's beautiful property. But this house? It was imposing, lavish, and entirely out of place in Brooks Falls, which was actually fitting for Nathan Greene, who'd always been a pariah.

It was also gaudy. A hacienda-style mansion, complete with tall, tiled archways surrounding a courtyard that was overlooked by a large, open rooftop balcony.

"Whoaaa!" I heard a quiet voice from the back of the car. "Is this our new castle?" Lex asked, her voice pitching the way it did when she was over-excited. How the kid went from dead asleep to fully awake in the span of five seconds, I didn't know, but I guessed it had something to do with the sight before us. The one that had us all confused.

"No honey, this is—"

"Look mommy, a fountain!" Lex screeched.

I had seen it. It was hard to miss. The center of the fountain held statues of a man standing between three nude women, two of whom were holding water basins, and one who was bent down in front of the male statue. And the entire extravagant display was front and center of the house entrance.

"Woooooow." Evie snorted, darting her widened brown eyes back and forth between me and the fountain. "That is quite the display."

As we neared, I realized just what I was seeing. I stopped the car, not wanting to get any closer. "Lex! Don't look at that!" I shouted as I glanced around for a parking spot.

I stopped nearby and put the car in park. Evie and I both sat quietly, looking ahead, our eyes fixed on the fountain.

"Is that a…?"

"Yup," I answered, cutting her off.

"And is she?"

"She is." I cut her off again, slapping my hand over my face. I felt the heat creeping up the back of my neck until it made it to my cheeks.

Evie leaned in and whispered, "I've never snorted anything. Unless you count nasal spray, so I can't say for sure. But, um, is it even possible to snort a line off someone's, ya know, 'The Colonel'?" She did air quotes and waggled her brows.

"The who?" I asked through a wheezed breath, now realizing that I hadn't been prepared at all for this day.

"You know, someone's *El Presidente*," she said with an accent and a salute as she tipped her head downward.

"Oh my God, Vee." I shook my head at her, gasping out a small, but unexpected laugh.

Evie snickered and leaned in closer. "I'm talking about a penis, sweetie."

I turned to look at her, my face nothing but dead-panned annoyance. "Uh, yeah, I got that."

She giggled and shrugged one shoulder. "Just making sure." She pushed my arm; her playful nature always lightened my mood, and I was especially grateful for it in that moment.

I took a deep breath and squared my shoulders, looking over at the builder, who was already walking around, surveying the property. "Okay, are you girls ready?" I asked, turning to the back seat.

"Yeah!" Lex shouted, her whole body bouncing in place.

"Um, I don't know about ready, but I am curious

about some things." Evie tipped her head toward the fountain, her eyebrows raised.

I scrunched my nose. "Gross." I frowned at the stagnate, green film on the surface of what water remained.

"Well, it's gross right now, but it'll be pretty once you restore it. And maybe remove the people."

I looked away, avoiding eye contact with my friend before clapping my hands together, trying to sound as hyped as I could.

"Let's go!" I opened the door and hopped out. Lex jumped out of the car and slammed the door behind her before she made her way to the abomination that was masquerading as a fountain.

"Oh hell no," I muttered, turning toward Lex and cupping my hands around my mouth to shout. "Honey, do not go into that thing, okay?"

"Okay!" Lex hollered back as she continued to bound forward.

Evie and I headed toward the tall man, who was now facing us with a friendly smile. I stopped in front of him and offered my hand. "Hi, I'm Jade Greene. Thanks so much for meeting me here."

"Nice to meet you, ma'am." He took my hand and gave it a gentle handshake before he introduced himself. "I'm Andrew West. I'm the one who's been emailing you about the house. You can just call me Drew," he said with a singular nod.

Before I could get another word in, he looked over to my side and smiled that smile that I'd seen a thousand times when men spotted Evie. "And you are?"

"Hey, I'm Evie Nakamura, the best friend, the business partner, and overall general advisor," Evie said with a half-smile and a flip of her hair.

I scoffed and rolled my eyes when she turned to scowl at me. Evie was definitely more than confident, but she also wasn't wrong. She had a part in every decision I made. She was a true friend who loved me, but she was also a shrewd businesswoman who knew exactly what it took to be successful.

"Very nice to meet you, Ms. Nakamura," he said with near-perfect pronunciation.

She waved him off. "You can just call me Evie."

Drew's eyes flashed, and I knew it was time to step in.

"And this is my daughter, Lex," I interjected.

His head whipped to the side and his face reddened a shade. "Yes, so nice to meet you all. Well, let's get down to it, shall we?" Drew motioned for us to follow and then turned to head toward the house.

"Yes, let's," I said, elbowing Evie as we moved forward.

"Ouch, what was that for?" she whispered.

I side-eyed her and whispered back. "You know exactly what that was for. I can't take you anywhere," I teased. "Stop being cute to the general contractor. He has a lot of work to do *and* he's the best in the area!"

"I didn't do anything!" she replied in a softer yet somehow harsher whisper.

"You don't have to do anything," I reminded her. "You just simply have to be your gorgeous self and men drool all over you."

Evie snorted and rolled her head back. "Right, like your pin-up look repels men. You know men hate curvy red-heads with more tits and ass than they know what to do with."

"Oh, please! I—" I paused, my eyes landing on the side of the house. My heart sped up, and all I could hear was the violent pounding in my head.

"Shit," Evie muttered. "Are you—"

I put a hand up. I needed a minute, or so I thought. Honestly, I hadn't considered this part. I'd been so busy making preparations that I hadn't had time to deal with the rest.

I felt a warm hand grip my shaking one. My head snapped to look at Evie, whose eyes searched mine the second she met my gaze. I huffed out a short breath and squeezed her hand, holding on tighter as I turned back to process the sight before me.

It hadn't been visible before, but I could sure see it now. Nearly the entire north side of the house had been blown out. I swallowed hard as I surveyed the damage through the huge hole in the house. Shattered glass and the melted, charred remains of some kind of equipment were scattered all along the inside. I stared, stupefied and suddenly too aware that this was the place my father had breathed his very last breath.

Any child who'd had a normal upbringing would've been gutted. But I didn't know what I was feeling, aside from the inescapable loss that I was accustomed to. I inhaled and looked away. The fact was that I had lost my father long ago and that feeling, that pit that I had lived with for my entire life, was nothing new.

"Ahem." I looked up, the sound pulling me back, away from the dark place that I was spiraling down into. "Ms. Greene, I, uh…" Drew's voice trailed off as he twisted his lips and looked to the side before shaking his head and turning back to me. "Ma'am, I didn't realize. I—" he stammered. "I'm so sorry. Do you need a moment?"

I looked down at mine and Evie's hands, still securely fastened to one another. I lifted my head and shot my friend a warm smile before I released her hand. Turning back to Drew, I gave him a curt nod and a thin-lipped smile.

"Thank you, but no, I'm fine. Let's continue on," I said quietly, before twisting my body around to search for Lex, whom I spotted playing near the fountain. I breathed out my relief. I hadn't once considered what we would be walking into, and if I had, I'd never have brought Lex here. I was suddenly very grateful for that horrendous fountain, which somehow seemed easier to explain than the remnants of an explosion.

"I, uh, loved the ideas you sent me," Drew said, and I turned back to face him. He pointed to a large window off the main entrance. "I was thinking that we could open that up even more and get you that wall windows room you mentioned. And over here." He pointed to the open grass area next to the house, where the original barn was, still standing after all these years. "We could install the garden and waterfall pond feature, along with the trellis leading up to the—"

I cut him off, realizing I hadn't been clear enough in my emails. "I want to tear it down."

Drew cocked his head to the side. "The historic barn?"

I shook my head and gestured toward the house. "No," I answered. "That's actually a piece of my family's history that I'd like to leave as is. But everything else can go."

Drew cleared his throat and his eyes darted to Evie before he replied. "I'm sorry, Ms. Greene, but I don't understand."

"You can call me Jade," I said, hardly recognizing the monotone sound of my own voice.

"Okay, Jade." He tip-toed into the words thoughtfully when he told me, "Ma'am, this is a two-*million*-dollar house."

"Yes, it is," I responded, looking around, my lips curling as I scanned the house, finally feeling something.

"Well," Drew went on. "It's just that, uh, financially speaking, you would be losing all that money by tearing this house down." He tossed his hands up and shrugged. "Now, obviously it profits me nothing to tell you this, but you'd be better off selling."

I shifted from one side to the other and fiddled with my hands. It was all too much. I hadn't been ready to see this place again, let alone like this. I inhaled and readied myself to speak when Evie jumped in.

"She's not selling," Evie said with a finality in her voice that welcomed no further discussion. "Jade wants it gone, and the real question is whether you can make that happen."

I pressed my eyes shut momentarily, so utterly relieved that Evie, who'd had zero previous knowledge of my plans, had my back.

Drew jerked his chin back like he'd been smacked. And that was the thing about Evie. She may have looked unassuming, but she was a total boss and when she spoke, people listened.

"Okay, understood." He ran a hand through his hair and adjusted the collar on his shirt before focusing back on me. "So, I didn't prepare for this. When I surveyed the house a few weeks ago, I took into account everything we'd discussed as add-ons or renovations. I apologize for the misunderstanding, but I think I'll need a little more time."

I nodded and sent a small smile his way. "Of course. I'm sorry I hadn't been more clear." I gestured to the house. "To be clear now, I don't want anything near as big as this house. It's just going to be me and my daughter, so I was thinking of something two stories, three bedrooms, an office, and two and a half bathrooms."

Drew was tapping out notes on his phone and repeating what I'd told him when Lex called out to me.

"Mom, look, there's a frog in the fountain!"

I spun around to see Lex standing on the edge of the fountain, leaning forward, reaching toward the center.

"Oh, Lex, no! That water is icky!" I shouted. "Move back!"

At my words, Lex turned to look over her shoulder, throwing her arms up as she tipped backward.

"Lex!" I screamed, lurching toward her, my arms outstretched. Lex shrieked right before she hit the gravel with a crunch, and my little girl's cries filled the air.

****

Bram

"Jameson! Taylor!" Sheriff Riler poked his head out of his office. "An ambulance was just called to the Greene property, need you to find out what's going on over there." He retreated back into his office, mumbling something about "shouldn't be damn anyone on that godforsaken piece of land."

I straightened in my chair, the hairs on my skin standing on end upon hearing that name. The Greene name was all too familiar, one I'd never forget. But the place? I hadn't been there in a very long time. And even then, it hadn't been nearly long enough.

I pushed against the desk, rolling backward in my chair until I could see Cameron, who had also rolled away from his cube to look at me. I raised my eyebrows in question.

Cameron shrugged and then stood up from his seat. I inhaled a sharp breath. He didn't have a clue and he couldn't. I pulled out my phone and tapped out the quick text to the last remaining connection I had to the Greene syndicate.

Me—*Greene Property?*—

I hadn't been to Nathan's property in years; despite it being the one blemish on our quiet town, everyone steered clear. And me especially. That shithole had ruined my entire life and countless others. And I had no desire to go back, not now, not ever. Thoughts flooded my mind and my lungs thickened with the sludge of it all, the suffocating, debilitating memories. Ever since Nathan was said to be dead, the Greene property had been abandoned and even before that, it had gone dormant for years, with Nathan doing a much better job of covering his ass. I had been so close, too.

Cameron grabbed his shit and headed to the door. "You coming?"

I cracked my neck, shifting it back and forth, trying to work out some of the stress that had suddenly taken hold of me. I was a carefree guy, and I liked it that way. I kept my life simple, so stress was not something that I took on easily, but the Greene place? That place held all my bad memories, all my stress, and all my fucking regrets.

"Comin'," I grunted as I snatched up my own shit, stuck my firearm in its harness and grabbed my radio.

"When was the last time you went there?" Cameron asked as I shifted uncomfortably in the passenger seat of his truck.

"Been a hot minute, that's for sure. Not since Jules." The mention of Jules's name roiled my guts, digging up feelings I'd long since buried. Failure, shame, loss. All of it, the source of my unending pain. Pain that I would relive, over and over until the day I died. It was just the way it had to be. As far as my friends knew, I was all easy-going and casual smiles. Only one person really knew all the darkness I had inside and I'd fucked him over, too.

"Shit. Heard Nathan died, don't know who has the land now. Wonder what the hell is going on there?" Cameron mused, steering his truck down the dirt road.

"Who fuckin' knows, could be any number of things with the way that man did business. Could be a break in gone bad or someone looking to score whatever that waste of space left behind."

We turned down the path leading to the open gate. The ambulance was already at the scene. I scoped out the area, noticing a large truck with the words "West Construction" on it and a black Mercedes SUV parked in the driveway. Cameron looked unconcerned, and why wouldn't he be? He was just as in the dark as everyone else, and it had to be that way.

The ambulance was parked by that insanely stupid-looking fountain that looked more like it belonged at a French chateau than a house in Brooks Falls.

We got out of the truck and headed over to the ambulance.

"Hey, Bram," Sierra, one of the EMTs, called me over. "How ya doin' handsome?"

Ah, Sierra. She and I were on a bi-annual hookup schedule. When she wasn't seeing someone, I'd provide the service of keeping her fit for duty for the next guy she found, and she'd provide the service of keeping me laid between women.

I lifted my chin to her and smiled. She was cute and fun, with a personality that was easy to be around. We never talked about anything too serious, which is exactly what I needed for a hookup. "Hey."

Sierra twisted her lips back and forth, trying to hide a smile. "Haven't seen you at all. I think it's time for the first one." She smiled at me with a row of perfectly white teeth framed by a mound of blonde hair that was held up in a tight bun.

"For sure, you know where to find me." I winked at her. "I better go check this out. Anything we need to know?"

"Yeah, anything that doesn't have to do with you propositioning my boy for sex preferably," Cameron put in, looking annoyed.

Sierra flinched, and I shoved him. "He's just jealous because no one propositions him for sex anymore."

It was complete bullshit, and Cameron knew it. The very notion that he would be jealous when he had a woman like Raven at home was foolish. Cameron laughed and rolled his eyes.

"Sure, man. I get it steady and good from the woman I love, but yeah, I'm the jealous one."

I managed to snort out some form of a laugh, but being here, hearing him say that, tore my heart in two.

Sierra rolled her eyes at him and then looked back at me with a grin before she sighed. "Anyway, no, nothing crazy happening here. Just a kid messing around on the fountain. She fell backward and probably broke her elbow, but we're mostly concerned about concussions. Hodges is checking her out now while I get the stuff to move her. Poor kiddo, she was bawling, but she'll be okay. Her mother is there with her if you need to get a report."

"All right, I'm gonna go get this done. I'll talk to you later."

"Sure thing."

And she was definitely that—a sure thing.

"You get the report and I'll fill Riler in," Cameron hollered to me as he walked back to the truck.

I made my way around the ambulance and saw a black-haired woman sitting beside the little girl. She was slender, but her body was covering the girl, so I wasn't able to get a good look. I put my hand gently on her shoulder and she jumped.

"Whoa, hey. It's okay. I'm Deputy Taylor with Falls County Police Department. I just wanted to come over and chat with you, get an idea of what happened. We'll just make a quick report, no big deal."

The woman stood up and turned slowly, her brown eyes wide as she looked me up and down. Her head darted from side to side and if she didn't look a certain way, her behavior would've raised the alarm.

I put my hands out and tried to relax my face, reassuring and calming. "Nothing to worry about. I'm just here to check on you and your daughter," I said with a soft smile. "It's just standard procedure."

"Lex, honey, I've got your bear. Look, she's right here."

That beautiful voice came at me from behind, pummeling me and going straight to my dick. It was like a goddamn song as it floated through my mind, unwinding all the bullshit and getting down to the soul. I was still staring at the black-haired woman when I was passed with a whoosh.

And then, I was struck. Wild copper hair, so long it reached the small of her back that led to curves. So many curves, and long lean legs. Jesus, no. No fucking way it could be her. She had been thin, rail thin, and her hair had never been that long. I ran my hand through my hair, along my jaw, and then tugged on my neck, a ball forming right in my throat. I leaned around the black-haired woman so I could get eyes on the little girl on the floor. She was seven, maybe eight years old. And the minute I saw the kid, I knew for sure. It was like looking back in time, taking a trip right through memory lane to the part of my life that had been good.

That voice, that feeling, the electricity that surged in her presence and sent me straight to my knees. There was no other way to explain it.

"Jesus," I murmured as I took a step back, wanting to run out of there like the coward I was and always had been.

The black-haired woman still stared at me, looking just as stupefied as I felt.

"Vee, can you go get her blanket out of my car, please?"

"Uh, uh, sure, yea," the woman stammered, still staring at me, moving slowly as I watched her back away to the SUV. A fucking Mercedes?

"Taylor." Sierra's voice cut through the mix of my emotions. "This is Ms. Greene, Lex's mom. You can talk to her to get her report." Sierra touched the back of the woman's arm. "Ms. Greene, do you mind talking to

Deputy Taylor while we continue to check out your daughter?"

Her entire body stilled and stiffened as the air shifted from panic to fear. She had been bent over her daughter, wearing short cut-off shorts and a white tank-top, just like that girl I used to know. Had she even changed? Oh, fuck yeah, she had changed. She stood up, the color draining from her face when we locked eyes.

At that moment, Cameron came to my side.

"You get the report?" he asked, but his words fell on deaf ears.

Her hair fell down the length of her body and the wiry copper strands whipped around as she turned to face us. Shit. My entire body went wired. Ms. Greene. *My* Jade Greene. I looked her up and down as if I hadn't traveled her body with my hands a thousand times, as if I hadn't been imagining her every second of every fucking day for years.

But this Jade Greene? This was a version of her that I'd never imagined. She had been beautiful before, but now? Fuck, she was a woman. Her skin was perfect and flawless, as it had always been, with freckles dancing lightly over her pale cheeks. Her body was something else entirely, more curves than she'd ever had before, with a slim waist that led straight up to full tits. Holy shit. Those piercing green eyes were framed with a ton of wild and wavy copper hair that made her look like she had just walked off a windy beach on one of those social media model accounts. Christ.

"Jadey," I said in a breath. All of my breath expelled from my lungs, just gone.

Jade looked between Cameron and I, searching us both as she bit her full, pouty bottom lip. A lip, that in that moment, reminded me of only one thing and it wasn't sweet, and it definitely wasn't professional.

"Mom, Mom! Can I have my bear now?" The little girl cried, and Jade jolted, then pressed her eyes shut. Mom? Jade was a mom. My Jade had a fucking kid.

"Of course, honey. I have Bramble bear right here." She held out the bear to Sierra, who was talking to the kid. "Vee, can you stay with Lex while I do this?" Her voice was tremulous.

Her friend nodded and gave her a wary look. "Yeah. Are you okay?"

Cameron cleared his throat and announced. "I'm gonna, I gotta—"

"Yeah, you go do that man," I told him, not really wanting to hear what he was pretending he had to do. I felt his eyes on us as he disappeared into the background.

"I need to give you a report?" she asked, her eyes facing the ground.

"Jadey." Her name fell from my mouth like it was meant to be there the entire fucking time. I reached out to touch her, and Jade watched me in horror as I extended my hand. Her entire body jerked back, a reminder that she wasn't mine and we weren't meant to be. I'd stolen what wasn't mine to have, taken that something sweet for myself for a little while. I stilled. Fuck. This couldn't be happening. "Tell me what the hell you're doing here."

Her head shot up and her face twisted. "What do you mean, what am I doing here? I'm here to sort Nathan's crap. " She straightened her shoulders before leveling me with a look, and then her words. "And I'm staying." Jade jutted her chin out, the attitude reminding me of that scrappy girl I'd fallen in love with all those years ago. And I wanted nothing more than to take that face in my

20

hands and kiss it, lose myself in that sweet mouth.

"You're what?" I gritted out, half pissed, half something else that I couldn't quite put my finger on.

"Staying." She drew out the words with all the attitude she had always possessed and thrown only my way.

"You're staying?" I lowered my head closer, hating that no matter how close I was to her, it wasn't enough. "Here?"

She huffed out a breath. "I'll stay out of your way, if that's what you're worried about."

Fuck, if that's what I was worried about? I needed the woman out of here. She couldn't be in this goddamn town, but most of all, she couldn't be on this property.

I whispered, bending my neck down until we were face to face, knowing what I had to do. I bit back the emotion that crested when I got close to her, that part of me that wanted to say fuck it all and hope for the best. "I told you, Jadey, I don't want you here." I pointed to her SUV. She followed my finger with her eyes before her jaw fell open on a gasp. "Get back in that car and go." I pointed to Nathan's house. "And stay the fuck away from that godforsaken house."

Jade sucked in a sharp breath, like I had just scooped her up and carried her with me back through time and shattered her all over again. Those green eyes filled with moisture, and she bent forward slightly at the waist, wrapping her arms around her midsection, inhaling short, little breaths. Fuck. How could this be happening?

"You have a kid."

"I—"

I put my hand up to stop her from telling me something I didn't want to know. "You know what, never mind. I just want to get my report and get out of here. And then, I want you to get gone."

Her trembling hand rose to her head as she moved her hair away from her face. A few small tears dripped down her cheeks, and shit, I couldn't get sucked in. I had come this far and sacrificed so much; I couldn't throw it all away now. I clenched my fists shut, along with my heart.

Jade straightened her posture and in an instant, her face hardened. "She was standing on the fountain, and I was talking to the contractor."

I jerked my head back and blinked. "What?"

"On the fountain, deputy. She was playing on it. Do you need to take notes, or will you remember?"

She didn't wait for me to respond.

"Lex told me that she saw a frog and when I turned to look at her, she was about to jump into that ridiculous and disgusting fountain, so I told her no, don't go in there and she fell back."

"Jade—"

"I heard a crunch when she fell. I'm pretty sure she fell right on her elbow, but thankfully she avoided hitting her head. We called the ambulance and here we are. Did you need anything more form me, or are we done here?" She pursed those pouty lips in that same way she'd always done. So fucking beautiful, all that sass.

I tilted my head to take her all in, to take one last goddamn snapshot before I let her go again.

"Great, I need to get back to my daughter. *She* needs me." With that, she turned around and bent down to the kid, who was now being carefully loaded onto the stretcher.

"It hurts mommy. It hurts." Tears poured from the

little girl's eyes and Jade ran her fingers through her daughter's hair, cooing comforting words. My heart fell, bottoming out, ruined. It had been nearly nine years, and I hadn't forgotten. I hadn't forgotten a single thing.

They loaded into the ambulance, with Jade jumping in behind. I watched, waiting for her to look up. The girl who, at one time in our lives, only had eyes for me, didn't bother to look my way. I stared, ready to react, when she turned back to catch my eye. Instead, the doors shut, and she was gone.

Chapter 2

Jade—Fifteen years old

"Jules! Jules!" Dad hollered, his heavy steps shaking the trailer as he stomped down the hallway. The door to my room swung open and the cheap, light material hit the wall with a muted smack.

"Where the fuck is your brother?" Dad shoved into my small room, knocking over my laundry basket in the process. He didn't bother to clean it up, instead narrowing his eyes at me.

"Like I should know?" I sassed, looking back down at my biology textbook like I gave a crap and hadn't been daydreaming about cute boys just thirty seconds ago.

"Goddamnit, get your lazy ass up and help me look for him." Dad yanked the blanket off me and I watched as my book went flying into the wall. I didn't even flinch anymore. I turned back to him and wrapped my arms around my body, trying to hold on to a little warmth.

Fall nights in the mountains were cold for everyone, but ours were extra freezing. I only knew this because Jules was always arguing with Dad about insulating the house better. I think it was something he learned from Mom, who also used to complain about it, before she up and skipped town for some guy with a big city job.

"I don't know where Jules is." I threw out one arm in a quick sweeping motion, before bringing it back to wrap around me as soon as possible. "He does whatever he wants and doesn't exactly check in with me."

Dad scowled at the floor before he looked up, his beady, bloodshot eyes fixed on me when he commanded, "Get some clothes on and go find your brother, girl."

I scoffed my disbelief. "But I don't know where he's at," I squeaked.

"Then fuckin' look." He threw his arms up and leaned in. I jolted and frowned when a few drops of spit hit my face. "Got shit to do, kid, and that boy needs to be here workin'. I don't have time to run around looking for him. Go be useful for once!"

I tried really hard to hold back the eye roll. Because other than drinking and disappearing for days at a time, my favorite days, by the way, he didn't do much. I didn't know what work he was talking about, but I had sure never seen him do it.

"Take my truck and get lookin'." Dad tossed his keys at me, and by some miraculous act of reflex and hand-eye coordination, I caught them. And then I stared at them, because what was I supposed to do with these?

"You know I can't drive." I dropped the keys on my bed when what I really wanted to do was throw them across the room.

Dad snorted and shook his head. "Christ, kid, it's a few miles. If you get pulled over, you worry about that later," he said, like I was the unreasonable one.

"No," I replied slowly. "Like, I can't drive. I've *never* driven because, you know, I'm fourteen."

When Dad's red eyes got huge, I knew I'd gone too far and agreeing with him was my best bet for avoiding something worse than driving without a license.

"Okay," I sighed. "I'll go look for Jules." I picked

up the keys with one finger and jingled them.

Dad grunted, the fire in his eyes dying down almost as fast as it had lit up. He backed out of my room and turned to walk the short, narrow hallway until he was all the way out of the trailer.

Thirty minutes, and two unsuccessful driving attempts later, I was making that two-mile walk into town at seven o'clock at night. I had bundled up in an old coat that Jules had given me, but once the wind picked up, it went right through the fabric, and I might as well have been wearing a tank top.

I trudged along the side of the road until I got to my target neighborhood. I knew of only one place that Jules might be, so I took my chances and traveled down Cherry Lane, toward the large, gray house. And sure enough, my brother's bright yellow, 1970s Camaro was parked in front of the house.

My stomach fluttered as soon as I got to the gate of the white picket fence that surrounded the front yard. I tried to run my fingers through my hair, frowning when the knotted, wind-teased strands got stuck in them. Great. Not only was I drowning in my coat, but I looked like I had been transported here by a cyclone. I inhaled deep, pushed open the gate, and walked up the three steps to the door. I took one more really big breath, preparing to meet *his* parents while looking like a psychotic girl scout.

I pushed the doorbell and waited. A minute later, the door was opened. I wished that anyone but *him* would have opened the door. God, he was cute. My heart was pounding in my chest, and I felt my whole face radiate heat.

"I'm looking for Jules," I blurted out, hearing, and

hating, that I sounded like Jules's annoying little sister.

He raised an eyebrow at me, his eyes wandering up and down the length of my body. It wasn't in a way that guys looked at girls they liked. He was definitely not interested. No, he was probably wondering what his best friend's dorky sister was doing at his house?"

"And you are?" he asked, his sandy blond hair flopping to one side.

God, it was so much worse. He didn't even *remember* me. My brother's best friend, and the boy I'd had a crush on since I was twelve years old, didn't even know who I was.

I was humiliated. I wanted to turn around and run home. And if that enormous coat, and Nathan's threat of punishment, hadn't been weighing me down, I probably would have.

So, I sucked it up and powered through. "I, I'm Jade," I stammered.

His eyebrows shot up. "Jade? As in Jules's sister, Jade?"

"Yes, that's me." I threw my rigid arms out, feeling awkward.

"Damn. Okay." He smirked, and opened the door wider. "Come on in then."

I walked in, happy to be out of the cold, terrified that I was standing in *his* house.

When I got in, I just stood, waiting, not really knowing what to say next. He was sooooo cute.

"I'm Bram." He tossed out a hand. I looked down at it and then back up at him.

"I know," I answered the moment we made eye contact. *Idiot Jade, play it cool.*

"You do, huh?" he asked, dropping his hand. I

27

melted when a huge smile spread across his face and little dimples formed in his cheeks. I had to ball my fists just to stop from sticking my finger into one of them.

"I mean, I see you at school every once in a while." I shrugged, looking away and taking in the house instead of his cute smile. His house was really clean and looked like it belonged in one of the magazines they had at the free clinic my dad took us to once a year before school.

Rows and rows of family pictures lined the walls leading up the long stairway that doubled back at least once. The house smelled like apple cider and pumpkins, but also, it kind of smelled like pot, a smell I was very familiar with because of Dad.

"*You're* in high school?" He raised his brows with the question.

I sighed. I was getting so tired of this. Everyone still thought I was in middle school and even the people who knew I wasn't still treated me like a little kid. I wasn't that short, but I was gangly, and I still had a baby face.

"Yes! I'm in the ninth grade." I flipped my hair and rolled my eyes, trying to convince myself that it didn't matter what he thought of me. "Where's Jules?" I pushed. "I need to talk to him."

"He's up in my room." Bram motioned with his head toward the stairs. "Come on."

He started walking, but I didn't move. I was young, but not stupid. Jules had warned me all about the lengths boys would go to take advantage of a girl.

After a few steps, Bram turned around. "Are you coming?" He smiled at me, and his eyes were nicer than any eyes I had ever seen. Plus, his dimples.

I bit my lip and thought for maybe one whole second before I followed him up, taking in everything along the way. The hallway was dim, and I could hear rock music blaring, getting louder the more I ascended the stairs.

"Come on, your brothers in here." Bram pointed to a door in the middle of the hallway.

"What about your parents?" I whispered.

He shrugged. "They're out of town."

Then he grabbed my hand. *My hand.* And tugged me forward through the hallway. My fingers tingled, and I squeezed his hand tighter, then died a slow death when he turned back around to smirk at me.

Thankfully, Bram dropped my hand to push open the door. I flinched. The loud music and the smell of weed was a slap in the face. My eyes easily found Jules, who was sitting on a couch in the middle of the huge bedroom. A bedroom that had to be bigger than the entire living space of our trailer. I almost gagged when I saw my brother making out with some girl who I knew was one of the popular cheerleaders. He had a lit joint in one hand and her ass in the other.

"Oh my god, Gross!" I hissed, turning around to shove out of the room and back into the hallway, where I ran straight into another cheerleader.

"Uh, excuse me?" She narrowed her eyes and looked me over before she looked beyond me and asked, "Who the hell is this?"

I opened my mouth to give her a piece of my mind, but I didn't have a chance.

"Time to go, Beth," Bram told her. "My parents are on their way home," he said with a casual ease that was so convincing that I whipped around to search his expression. Bram winked and gave me a slight shake of his head.

"Oh crap! Lindsey!" Cheerleader number two

hollered into the bedroom. "Linds, look at me!" she yelled louder, probably trying to interrupt the disgustingness between my brother and Cheerleader number one. "Hey, we gotta go. Bram's parents are on the way home and if my parents find out I was here, you know I'm toast! Come on!" she screeched.

The girl shot up off my brother's lap, her eyes wide before she turned back to Jules. "Call me, baby," she whined, then grabbed a sweater and scurried out.

Bram and I were still standing in the hallway when I heard Jule's mutter, "Yo, what the fuck, man?"

Bram tipped his head toward the door. "Come on."

I wasn't sure if it was shock or the weed, but Jules stared at me for a few silent seconds. His eyes were red and mostly shut. "Jade?"

"Yep, it's me." I shot him a small smile and raised one shoulder. My stomach fell, and I looked down at my feet. I hated disappointing my brother. And with all the crap he had to deal with from Dad, and all the crap he protected me from with Dad, I didn't want to be the one to spoil his fun. Even if it was gross. "Sorry to—"

"What are you doing here, kiddo?" Jule's interrupted, his voice soft, the way it always was when he spoke to me. "And how did you get here?" At that question, his dimmed eyes came alive.

I bit my lip and looked up, knowing he would not be happy with the answer. "I, uh, I walked here?"

His eyes darkened and his jaw hardened.

"Dad made me." I rushed the words out, not wanting to be on the opposing end of Jules's anger. "He wanted me to drive, but obviously, you know, I can't." I swallowed hard, trying to keep back the tears that pooled when I saw that look on my brother's face. "I'm sorry,

I—" I threw out a hand. "He was really insistent, and I didn't want him to get madder than he already was."

"Dad?" he asked through gritted teeth. "Why the fuck did he send you to get me?"

I raised one shoulder tensely. "I don't know. He just said he needed you to do some work or something."

Jules's nostrils flared, and he shifted his gaze to Bram. "I gotta go, man. I'll be back for her tomorrow."

At that, I snapped to, and I straightened my spine. *Tomorrow*? "What? No, I'm coming home with you!" I demanded, and then shrunk back when Jules stood, towering over me, his features hard and unflinching.

"No. You're not. You're staying here, Jade. I'll pick you up tomorrow." He tipped his head to Bram, and they had some telepathic conversation that played out in a series of head nods before Jules turned on his boot and left me standing there, completely dumbfounded.

****

The mountains surrounded us and aside from a few scattered clouds, the sky was clear and the sun warmed Lex and I as we made our way through downtown Brooks Falls. It was a perfect summer day for reacquainting myself with the town and introducing Lex to her new home. We walked, hand in hand, as I took in the changes and familiarity of this place. Brooks Falls was just as beautiful as I remembered, and I was more than excited to show Lex where I had grown up. I wasn't feeling nostalgic; I just felt like I was finally home. We'd been here only a week, but from the moment I arrived, my heart knew it belonged here. And I rested in that knowledge, positive that I was no longer that dumb, love-struck girl who ran out of this town nine years ago. I was Jade freaking Greene, successful businesswoman,

Pâtissier, and mother.

Sure, I still carried the pieces of my past, *that* Jade Greene, daughter to Nathan, the blemish of Brooks Falls. Sister to Jules, my estranged brother whose path in life had only deepened the hole in my heart. And finally, I was Jade Greene, coward in love and reject of the town. Yes, these were all still parts of me, parts that I couldn't shake, even if I wanted to. They were the constant reminders of where I came from and why it had taken years to build me back up after *he* had spent years building me up, only to tear me down in the most heartless, hapless way. And when I ran from him, I ran from all of them and never looked back. And despite returning to Brooks Falls, I still wasn't looking back. I was moving forward and no longer running from the ghosts of my past.

"Jade? Oh my god, Jade, is that *you?*"

I spun around slowly, Lex in hand, to find the familiar face of an old friend. I instantly smiled, the spot in my chest warming at one single look. I truly was home.

"Oh god, it *is* you!"

"Renata," I said, barely believing it. Renata had been my best and only true friend in this place. And even though I'd left without a word, it was evident from the look on her face that she hadn't held it against me all these years.

We beamed at each other, and her eyes moved to Lex. Her jaw fell as she looked between Lex and me. "And who is this? Your clone?"

I laughed. "Yeah, basically. In looks and attitude. This is my Lex." I turned to Lex, who was also smiling wide, bouncing on her toes, looking just as excited about this unexpected reunion as I was. "Lex, honey, this is Renata, remember I—"

Lex bounced faster, and I pressed gently on her good arm to remind her to go easy. "Your best friend Renata that you told me lots of stories about?" Lex's eyes sparkled with excitement, the green centers coming alive.

"The one and only." I grinned, looking over at Renata, whose face had gone even gentler than before.

"My mom's told me about you! She told me how you guys used to jump on your trampoline and have sleepovers and go to the movies and make up dances together! I want to have a best friend one day like that too." Lex tilted her head to one side and asked, "Do you have a daughter around eight or nine that could be my best friend?"

Renata pressed her lips together, holding back a smile. And that was my Lex. The easy-going, social butterfly who wanted to befriend everyone, but most of all, she was all about making that one best friend. She hadn't found that in Charlotte, where we'd come from. North Carolina had been a lovely place, but it was never home, not really. and I, like her, had hoped she would find it here.

Renata laughed and looked at me, her smile warm and easy, before she bent down to Lex.

"I am so honored that your mom talks about me! We were the best of friends and I have so many good memories with her. And I do have one kid, but he's a boy."

Lex tilted her head and worked her lips from side to side. "Hmm, I think I could make that work. Is he a nice boy one or is he one of the mean ones that doesn't like girls?"

Renata stifled a snort and dipped her chin to look at Lex. "He's a very nice one. A special one!"

My daughter pondered again, before asking, "What kind of special is he? My mom says that I'm special because I'm nice to my friends and I also like to do charities. Is he that kind of special?"

Renata inhaled a deep breath as the light in her eyes dimmed and the smile she had been wearing went from carefree to earnest. "Well, actually, he is special in that way. But he's also special in the way that half of one of his legs is made out of metal."

Her sorrow was palpable, and it instantly stung my heart. And I felt the heaviness of my own regret. I had left my dear friend without a goodbye and now, to find out her life hadn't been as great as I'd always hoped it would be, touched places inside of me that had never fully healed.

I looked down at Renata and Lex and swallowed back the pain.

"He has a prosthetic?" Lex asked, like it was the most common thing she's heard.

Renata jerked her head back slightly and then looked up at me, her eyebrows raised as she searched my face, before turning back to Lex. "He does. It's on his left leg. He was in an accident a while ago."

Lex bit her lip and peered up at Renata. "Okay, but do you think he'll want to be my friend?"

I watched as the tension melted from Renata. Her shoulders sunk and her face softened. "I wouldn't see why not. It seems like you'd be a very good friend to have for my Liam. Did you say you were nine?" Renata asked with the lightness and ease of earlier returning to her voice.

"Not yet. I'm eight, but I will be nine soon!" Lex bounded forward on her toes, losing her balance, and falling into Renata, who caught Lex by her one good arm and steadied her. My friend giggled, and I breathed out a sigh of relief at her catch. It was no mystery how my kid had managed to break an elbow. What was a mystery was how this was her first broken bone.

"Well," she said through snickers. "So is my Liam."

That got my interest. "Eight, huh?" I asked, amused and also a little sad, that my best friend and I had been pregnant at the same time and hadn't been able to share it.

"Yep, he'll be nine in November! Now." Renata looked me up and down. "My god woman, where did you get that and how do I get there?"

Confused, I looked down at my clothes. Pulling the hem of my plain white tee out a little, I asked, "This?"

Renata barked out a laugh and shook her head. "Um, no. All the rest of what's under that. I'm saying you look incredible! You used to be a bean pole and now you look like one of those social media influencer models that wanna trick me into pants that'll make my behind look like that when we all know, it ain't the pants!" Her face turned a light shade of pink as she bit her lip and looked away. "Geez, sorry, I'm just in shock."

I laughed and waved her off. "It's all good. To be fair, I don't think I reached puberty until I was twenty-one," I joked, even though it wasn't that far from the truth.

"So, are you back, or are you just visiting?" Her eyes sparkled as she asked and it felt good, feeling like at least one person wanted me here.

"I'm living here. We just moved back and—"

"Babe?" A male voice broke through the conversation, and Renata and I both turned toward the man. My jaw dropped to the floor as I gulped back the surprise when it finally registered.

"Cooper! Come here, honey. Look who it is! You remember Jade Greene, right?"

I smiled brightly, sifting through memories of those two falling in love so young, of Renata and I planning dual weddings.

"My God, Cooper Daniels! Look at you two, still together. Married. A kid!" I was definitely squealing but the joy of seeing my childhood bestie still in love after all these years was something. Yes, a bit of sadness and my own loss came with it, but I didn't let it tarnish the joy I felt for them.

Cooper grinned, the corners of his eyes crinkling as he flashed a row of white teeth. "Wow, Jade Greene. Get in here!" He reached out his arms, and I gladly rushed in for a hug. "It's so good to see you," he said as I stepped back with a smile. "Ren's missed you for years, you know?"

I bit my lip, unsure of what to say. There was too much to say for a first-time reunion. Cooper searched my eyes, a gentle smile playing at his lips. I was about to end the silence when Renata covered his eyes with her hands.

"Okay, okay, don't look too hard, baby!" she teased, her voice playful and light.

He chuckled and turned toward her. "You know, babe, after all these years, I still only have eyes for you."

She tilted her head and beamed up at him. "I know, I know, but I can't get over—" She pointed to me. "How freaking *amazing* she looks!"

"Hmm, honey. Maybe you're the one with wandering eyes." He winked at his wife and they kept eye contact. Damn, they were cute.

"We got Liam's appointment in about fifteen minutes though," Cooper told her as he brushed a strand of hair from her face.

"Oh, shoot, that's right. I got so caught up!" Renata looked down at Lex, who at this point had pulled out my phone and engrossed herself in a game.

"We should go, sweetheart," Cooper told her gently.

"Yes, okay." She turned back toward me. "Darn it, Jade, I really want to catch up."

"I would absolutely love that." And I would. Renata had been so much more than a casual friend. She had taken care of me during a time when I desperately needed it, before that ass-hat stepped in and took even better care of me. Until he didn't.

Renata studied her watch and then looked back up at me. "Are you free this Friday? We could meet for drinks at Shea's."

"Oh, can I go?" Lex interjected with that bubbly energy of hers. "You can bring Liam and we can be friends!" she suggested.

Renata laughed, bending down so she was closer to Lex. "Well, Shea's doesn't allow kiddos, but how about your mom and I figure out a time when you and Liam can play. Does that sound good?"

Lex nodded and looked up at me, her green eyes wide and hopeful.

"Absolutely," I told Lex and Renata.

"Okay, I think it's a plan!" Renata dug into her purse and pulled out a card. "Sorry to give you a business card, but it's all I got right now." She shoved it into my hand.

"Text me and we'll make a plan!"

"Okay, I will." We both moved in for a hug without even thinking. "God Renata, I'm so glad we ran into each other."

She spoke softly when she released me from the hug, still holding onto me and squeezing my arms. "It is a breath of fresh air to have you back. I can't wait for Friday!" she said as she stepped away. "Talk to you soon!"

"Bye." I gave a short wave.

"Bye," Lex hollered, and beamed when both Cooper and Renata waved goodbye.

Lex and I stood side by side, watching them go. I was mid-thought when it hit me. And it hit me head on. The scent of espresso and baked goods. I sniffed the air, searching for the happy culprit, when I spotted it across the street; A quaint little cafe surrounded by a wraparound patio and a garden. I let my eyes wander to a yellow sign that had a large, round coffee mug with steam coming out of it and the word "Sunshine's" next to it. Now this place was new and thank God that a coffee shop had made its way into Brooks Falls. I tugged lightly on Lex's hand.

"You want some hot chocolate, kiddo?"

Lex nodded vigorously, and we crossed the street hand-in-hand before making our way up the steps.

"Welcome to Sunshine's," a woman called out cheerfully.

I gave a low wave and studied the place, paying special attention to the glass display case that held the baked goods. Instantly, hope spread. They didn't have anything that looked like what Evie and I could make. Even though the bulk of our business was in Los

Angeles, I wanted a local presence in my town. And this was exactly where I needed to begin.

Chapter 3

Bram

I settled onto a barstool, the noise of the crowd barely distracting me from the anxiety I'd been feeling ever since I saw *her*. My week had been one of the worst weeks I'd had in nine years. I needed a distraction, one that could get my mind off a fiery-haired and hot-tempered woman, with curves that I couldn't stop thinking about since I saw her. And to top it all off, I was supposed to get her to leave. Again. And I had not the first clue how I was going to do that. And shit, after seeing her, remembering what it felt like to be near her, I wasn't even sure I *could* do it.

Thankfully, it was Friday, the day the gang and I usually got together. Of course, the one day I needed a diversion, everyone had other things going on, so our usual get together at Shea's had been cancelled. I wanted to sit at home and drown myself in a bottle of bourbon, but instead I opted to take Sierra up on our semi-annual night of debauchery, hoping that maybe she would get my mind off Jade for a bit.

Sierra and I agreed on our usual—meet at Shea's, do a quick catch up, have a few drinks, and then go back to her place and go to town on each other before we parted ways until the next time we needed to scratch the itch.

"Hey man, what's up?" Jet tipped his chin at me

from the side while he was mid-chat with some blonde haired, big-chested woman. His next conquest, no doubt. The man had game plus constant opportunities to sleep with women, more than anyone I knew. Being a bar owner did that for a man, I supposed, and he freely took advantage, never getting wrapped up in anything too serious.

I jerked my chin all at up at him. But, and he'd already returned his attention to the blonde.

I felt a hand land on my shoulder from behind and I turned to find Sierra standing with one hand on her hip, her short blonde hair gathered to one side, and a huge grin on her face.

Sierra was cute, and she was the kind of person that I was always happy to see, but never dying to see. It was good when we met up, but she was out of my mind the rest of the time.

"Hey handsome, shall we?" She swept her arm out and pointed to one of the empty tables.

"Drinks first? Orrrr…?" I raised my eyebrows, thinking maybe we could skip the formalities and get moving to the part that would get my mind off Jade.

"Yes, please! After the week I've had, I need something large."

I smirked. "Something large, huh? I think I can help with that." I may have been twenty-nine, but I still loved a good boner joke.

She snickered and rolled her neck with an exaggerated eye roll. "Yes, that too. But I need to start with a margarita or something."

"Hey, you two, it's about that time, huh?" Rachel sauntered over, tossing a rag over her shoulder, and leaned in on the bar to face us. She was Jet's manager and an old friend. And Rachel knew the deal with Sierra and me. I'd told her about it, offering the same deal, one depressing and drunken night. She'd laughed in my face, and from that point on, took any opportunity to remind me that I was pathetic. But Rachel had also known me during a time when I wasn't such a piece of shit and that night, she'd told me that my dumbass belonged to one woman and it wasn't anyone in this town. She had been right then and if she said it today, she'd still be right.

"We need drinks, Rach," I told her.

"Hey, I'm gonna grab us that table before it gets snatched away and we're stuck drinking under the judgmental eye of the bartender," Sierra quipped with a grin before making her way to an open table.

Rachel threw the hand towel she'd been using to clean the bar top to the side and gave me her attention. "All right then, what are you drinking toni—" She stopped, her jaw agape, her big brown eyes enlarging as she looked beyond me.

I waved my hand in front of her face. "Yo, dude. You okay?" When she pressed her lips together and her eyes darted to me before looking back, I had no choice but to turn around and find out for myself.

It didn't take long to figure it out. I picked her out of the crowd instantly. The woman was hard to miss and as I scanned around her, it appeared no one had missed her entrance. Every eye in the bar seemed to be on her. My jaw ticked and that voice inside of my head, the irrational, foolish one that had long since blown his chance, whispered *Mine*.

I looked her up and down, taking her in like my first real breath in years. Her long, copper hair was tamed, flowing down to her waist, curled somewhat at the end in a way that made it look like flames. She wore an emerald, green dress that hugged every perfect curve and dipped down at the front, showcasing her full tits. Tits that had not been there when she left all those years back. A small pendant dangled between her breasts and sparkled under the bar lighting, drawing even more attention to her tits.

She was beautiful, but she had always been. It wasn't just her beauty that had necks breaking just to catch a glimpse of her. No, it was what had drawn me in right away, the first time I noticed her. Jade's energy was magnetic, and it was clear as day that she owned every room she walked in. She was somehow vulnerable and tough all at once, and she wore that attitude like a second skin.

The pit in my stomach was growing when I heard Rachel ask, "Is that who I think it is?"

"Yes," I choked out, unable to hide the effect this woman was having on me. I had come to Shea's to escape her and now, holy headfuck, she was here looking the way she did.

"Jesus, wow," Rachel whispered. "Is she back?"

"She is," I clipped out, growing impatient. I wasn't sure if I was irritated that Jade was here at all or that she had shown up alone, looking how she did. The hole in my stomach deepened at the thought of Jade with someone else.

From my periphery, I saw Rachel staring at me, when she dipped her head down to ask in a soft voice, "Have you two talked yet?"

I yanked my eyes from Jade and inhaled a deep breath. "We had a run-in about a week ago, but we didn't have much to say to each other. So, no, we haven't talked." Before she said anything that I definitely didn't need to act on, I added with a finality that was just one more lie to add to the list. "And no, I don't plan on it."

Rachel narrowed her eyes on me, her lips quirked to one side, scrutinizing me. "Not much to say to each other? Are you stupid or just plain dumb? And those are your only choices."

I tried to remain poker-faced, but lost the battle when Rachel lightly smacked my forehead, aiming a scowl at me. "Yeah, you're both. God, Bram, what the hell? You two were, like, totally in love. Sickeningly so!"

I scoffed, pressing my fingers into my temples. "Yep, the key word there being 'were'. And that was a long time ago. Things change," I put on, knowing neither of us bought it.

"Oh no! No way do I believe that what you two had just disappeared into a cloud of smoke after she left!" She tossed her hands up dramatically. "I mean, for real, once you and Jade became whatever the hell you and Jade were in high school, you were *off* limits. I remember this very clearly. The train straight teenaged girl species as a whole cried when you started hanging out with her." Rachel paused and scrunched her nose at me. "Except for me, I never wanted any of that." She waved her hand around me, gesturing to all that was me.

I chuckled, grateful for my friend's ability to keep things light, even if it involved tossing barbs my way. "Thanks, that feels good knowing you were disgusted by me then and now."

She winked at me, a half-smile playing on one side of her face. "Absolutely babe, you know I'll always give you the truth." She winked, before her attention shifted back to Jade, and as much as I tried to avoid it, I followed suit.

"It doesn't really matter what we were then." I said off into the distance, my eyes fixed on my beautiful Jadey. Fuck, *my Jadey*. I shook my head, shaking off the familiar moniker once reserved just for me. "We aren't anything now, Rach. She's got a kid and—" My throat closed and damn, I couldn't even bring myself to say it. She was living in that house. Nathan's house. A million scenarios played in my head, none of them good.

"And what?" Rachel asked, turning back to me.

I went to open my mouth, when I noticed the fucking train wreck happening in front of me. I snapped my mouth closed, and my spine straightened as I watched Sierra, who was sitting at the table she had claimed for us, waving to Jade and motioning her over.

"Ummm, what is happening, Bram?" Rachel asked through a barely stifled laugh.

"Fuck. Margarita lime, double for Sierra, and I'll take whatever Jet's been brewing back there lately. Gotta go." I pushed off the stool, my heart racing as Jade waved and made her way to Sierra. I froze mid-stride, unable to move as the nightmare played out in front of me.

When Jade arrived at our table, she and Sierra chatted easily with one another. Jade was all big smiles and animated features, a confident way about her that was as new as it was annoyingly attractive.

And I knew that I should be happy about this development. What better way to drive the woman out than throwing another woman in her face? But I couldn't deny how deeply I was drawn to her. My entire body pulled forward, hands tingling with the need to touch, to reach out and remember what it felt like to have her in my arms.

I balled my hands into fists and held them to my side, holding back, reminding myself that she couldn't be here. She couldn't be here. I'd say it as many times as I needed to until I convinced myself to do something about it.

My eyes were on Jade when I got to the table, but it was Sierra that spoke up.

"Bram!" Sierra announced as I joined the women.

Immediately, the air was sucked out of the room, and I felt the space between us grow tense, right along with Jade's perfect body.

"Remember Ms. Greene from the other day? Her daughter was the one who broke her elbow," Sierra told me, seemingly oblivious to the way everything had shifted the moment Jade and I were in each other's space.

Our eyes met and my whole world tilted. Jade's chest heaved as she inhaled a deep breath and the smile disappeared from her face. Her green eyes flashed before they dimmed, and her expression becoming impassive.

Sierra kept going, unaware of any of it. "She was just telling me about her daughter." She turned to Jade. "Lex, right?"

Jade pressed her lips together to form a tight-lipped smile before she answered, "Yes, that's right."

"I thought so!" Sierra turned back to me and continued on, seemingly unaware of the tension that filled the air. "She said Lex is doing good and recovering well," Sierra rattled, before turning back to Jade, who looked as wooden as I felt. "God, she is the cutest kid ever and she looks just like you!" Sierra gushed.

Jade sighed, her mouth relaxing into a warm smile. "Thank you, I certainly think she's adorable."

Sierra beamed, her eyes lighting up when she asked, "Do you want to have a drink with us?" I jolted, and I knew Jade felt it when her eyes darted to me at her side. Sierra continued, unaffected. "Or are you here with someone, too? I know you just got into town, but look at you." She ran her eyes up and down Jade. "I wouldn't be surprised if you already had ten dates lined up!"

And shit, I had been trying to avoid that thought. If every guy in town hadn't noticed her yet, they would now. Jealousy sprung up instantly, and I was suddenly that kid again, in denial, but fighting off assholes who wanted Jade.

Jade giggled, a sound that took me out of my reverie and back into the moment. "Thank you. That's really sweet of you to say and so thoughtful of you to invite me to join you guys." Jade swallowed hard at the words and shifted uncomfortably. "But I'm actually meeting a friend, so I'll let you get back to your date. It was nice seeing you both again." Jade gave Sierra a warm smile and then turned to face me, her green eyes piercing me with a glare, the sight of her knocking the wind right out of me.

"Nice to see you too!" Sierra grinned. "Tell Lex I'm glad she's doing better."

Jade smiled brightly. "For sure, I will. Thank you."

"Yeah, uh, me too," I added in, unsure of what else to say.

Jade's eyes glinted with fire as she gave me a cursory glance. I could feel her anger like a physical slap to the face. But most of all, behind her glares, I saw all that hurt I'd inflicted. And it felt just like that fucking day all over again.

****

Jade

How I'd managed to convince myself that I could live in this town with him was beyond me. It had taken nine years *just* to get back here. Nine years to get the strength to face my past and all the crap that came with it. But it took all four days for Bram to pulverize my resolve into a fine powder that would easily disperse in the wind, leaving nothing behind but a lovesick teenaged Jade.

And now that I was standing there, my second run-in with him behind me, I wasn't sure what I had imagined would happen when I got here. I also wasn't sure why I thought living with the love of my life in a small town would ever work. The last of it, the hardest bit to swallow, was how he had changed. I supposed I still pictured him as that charming, caring boy, the one who had always gone out of his way for me, the one who would never scowl at me and accuse me of being a terrible person. Yes, he had obliterated all that in one single day, but before that, he had been kind. No, he had been more than kind. He had been my everything.

What I hadn't ever let enter my mind was the idea that he would be with someone else. All these years later, surely, he had been a monk, right? I mean really, what did I expect? That he joined the priesthood and was all a sudden not that same boy that melted the panties off every girl with just one look?

I was half-right. He was definitely *not* a boy anymore. Oh no, he was all man. He was tall, like he had been when I left, but now he was brawny, so powerfully built that it physically hurt to look at him. In his uniform, he'd looked sturdy for sure. But tonight, in fitted jeans and a tight, black tee, he looked like absolute sin. Sin that

I wanted to commit over and over, until I was sent straight to hell. Do not pass go, do not collect two hundred dollars.

I strolled up to the bar, cursing myself for being early. I had Jules to thank for that. My brother had done his very best to teach me to be responsible, before he got swept away into other things. Things that I didn't want to think about right now. I sighed. Thoughts of Jules had a way of bringing my spirits down.

It had been nine years since I'd seen him too, but twelve since he had ceased to be the boy I once knew, the brother I loved. The one who had given me as much as he could from the nothing we had. I didn't know if I'd ever see him again or, after everything, if I wanted to.

All of these thoughts were bouncing around my brain like a pinball machine, so when a deep, booming voice pulled me out of the depressing memory lane I was spiraling to, I welcomed it.

"Hey gorgeous, what can I get you to drink?" I followed the sound, turning my head toward the voice. I stopped dead when I saw the man leaning into the bar, a sexy smirk planted on the familiar face. His hair was longer than it used to be. Thick, dark waves fell to his cheeks, highlighting what looked like a day's worth of stubble. I focused my gaze on his muscular arms that were covered in bulging veins and tattoos. He was hotter than ever, and he'd been a beautiful boy.

"Jet Bensley," I mused, feeling suddenly devious. "If it isn't the one who got away," I teased, tipping my lips up into a half-smile.

Jet raised his brows. "The one that got away, huh?" His gaze dropped from my face to my chest before he peered up at me through darkened eyes. "I think you're mistaken, beautiful. If I was lucky enough to land a woman like you, I'd never let her go."

I giggled, my cheeks warming, his flirty compliment the exact boost of confidence I needed. I shook my head, laughing at the man who'd once been the boy that claimed I was the only girl he wanted.

"It's Jade." I laughed. "Jade Greene."

He blinked slowly, his lips parting before a full grin spread across his face.

"Well, shit!" Jet pushed up off the bar until he was towering over me, eying me up and down. "No fuckin' way, no way! Look at you!" He sauntered over to the swinging door and exited the bar area. "Bring it in, babe." Two large tattooed arms stretched out toward me, and a shot of warmth traveled through my body. It was the welcome I didn't even know I needed.

I stood up, doing nothing to conceal the self-satisfied smile that formed on my face when Jet declared, "My god, you look even better standing!"

"Yeah?" I cocked my head back to catch his eye. "Well, so do you," I told him. It wasn't a lie; the man had always been gorgeous.

Before I could utter another word, Jet pulled me into a crushing hug, smashing me against his large, and hard, body before grabbing my shoulders and stepping away to examine from a distance.

"The one that got away, huh?" He quirked a brow. "Like you ever noticed me. The only girl I wanted was the one girl who didn't even see me."

I scoffed, dipping my head down and looking up through narrowed eyes. "Everyone noticed you, Jet. But you already knew that. You just wanna hear me say it!" I poked his chest, no longer thinking about anything but reuniting with an old friend. Jet intercepted my hand and pulled me back in.

"That's right, say it loud for everyone to hear." He squeezed me to him.

I laughed, feeling light. "You are a beautiful man, Jet Bensley," I muttered, my cheek pressed to his chest, my words coming out jumbled.

"There you go! She finally admits it!" He paused briefly and then pushed me away, still holding my shoulders squarely. "Fuck. Are you back for good, babe?" He shook his head. I supposed after the way I left, it would be hard for anyone to think that I'd ever return.

"I am," I said, right before he yanked me back in, smushing me back to his chest.

"No fucking way! Say it again, so I know you're not getting a guy's hopes up!" He pushed me out again, shaking his head, his eyes roaming my body up and down before he looked beyond me. His face tightened and his relaxed body tensed. "Aw, shit, forgot about—"

"Nope." I held up my palm. "I already saw him. It's, it's fine. I'm okay, really." I gulped back the anxiety that had crawled up from my stomach to my throat.

He continued staring past me until he was glaring. I didn't need to turn around to figure out what, or who, he was looking at and why he appeared so annoyed. Bram flirting with Sierra? No thanks! Her laughing at his stupid charms? Pass! The two of them kissing? Kill me now.

I placed a shaking hand on Jet's chest. "It's been a long time," I told him listlessly, my voice monotone, my heart cut off from things I couldn't afford to feel. "We've both moved on. That happens, you know," I said with a strained smile. "Anyway, we were kids then, foolish, young, and hopelessly—"

Jet cut me off to add an unnecessary "In love."

My heart stopped in my chest, falling to a depth I had worked hard to pull it out of. "No," I forced out through a tight throat. "Naïve," I whispered. "Hopelessly naïve." I shrugged, knowing the only thing hopelessly naïve was believing I could convince anyone I was over Bram. "And now we're"—I inhaled deeply, mustering the courage to admit the truth—"nothing."

Jet lifted one side of his mouth. I wasn't sure if it was pity or lust, or maybe both. "Well, I know you don't care, Jade," he scoffed, before leaning in close to my ear to whisper, "But in case you were wondering, he looks pissed."

I felt the pull of my lips before the feeling spread across my limbs. Was it joy? Maybe. Was it revenge? Possibly. Was it right to torture Bram? Yeah, probably. I shouldn't have cared. It shouldn't have made me this happy, but God, it did. And I felt the euphoria from the tips of my toes to the top of my head.

"Want me to kiss you and really fuck with his head?" Jet got closer; his lips were pressed firmly to my ear.

I swallowed, his offer bringing me right back to reality. While a kiss from sexy Jet Bensley was enough to make any girl tear her panties off and beg for a proper fucking, just the idea sent my soul sinking back into the same cavernous place that it could never escape. Not in nine years. Not now, not ever. I was tethered to that man in a way that I couldn't cut myself free of and I was terrified that it would always be that way.

I buried my head, letting the kindness of his arms hold me for just a little longer. "That's a sweet offer," I muttered into his shoulder. "I bet any other girl in this bar would take you up on it."

Jet sighed and gave me a squeeze. "It's bullshit." His words were harsh, but his tone was light. "I hate to admit it, but you always did belong to him. Even if he's a total jackass."

"Jade?" I heard Renata's voice from behind. "Am I, uh, interrupting something?" she asked, her voice suggestive. "Or did I just transport into Jet's high school fantasy?"

Jet chuckled before he let me go. I stepped back and turned toward Renata. "Nope, just saying hello to an old friend," I reassured her.

"Hey, Jet!" She placed a hand on her hip. "I'm an old friend. Say hello to me!"

"Hey, trouble." He smirked. "You just want to see Cooper and I go at it like old times, is that it?"

"Um, two sexy men fighting over me?" She raised her brows and flipped her long brown hair. "That's the dream, honey."

"You see this, Jade?" Jet hiked a thumb toward Renata. "She hasn't changed even a little. The woman still has it out for me," he told me with a false, disapproving shake of his head.

"That's right and don't you forget it." She winked at him and then turned to me. "Hey! Sorry that it took so long."

"No problem. Jet and I were just catching up." We leaned in for a quick hug.

"Oh, sure." She bumped my hip with hers. "I might skip town just to return for a catch up like that."

"All right, trouble," Jet interjected. "What do you ladies want to drink?" he asked as he threw one large arm around my shoulders. I wasn't going to lie to myself and say I wasn't absolutely, one hundred percent loving this. Even though the thing he'd always had for me was something I suspected he used just to make Bram angry. Regardless, it was a tried-and-true formula. I knew it worked, and the evil Jade, the one who wanted Bram to feel the way I was feeling at the moment, was happy that Jet was lavishing so much affection on me. And then there was the nice, pathetic Jade. The one who still cared for that ridiculous man and didn't want to hurt him. It was infuriating, that after all he had done to me, I still felt something.

So, I did the only thing that felt right. I wiggled out of his hold.

"I'll have a vodka soda," I told him.

"And I'll have red wine." Renata tossed her purse over her shoulder and glanced around the bar. "Yikes, I didn't think *everyone* would be here tonight. Then again, I hardly ever go out," she whined as she scanned the bar.

"Let's find a seat on the other side of the bar," I told her, hoping to avoid a certain someone and his date.

We found a spot far away from Bram and Sierra, and the rest of the night was great. Renata and I caught up for an hour straight. I filled her in on the details of my life that I was ready to share, which was almost everything, and she talked about her marriage to Cooper, which happened about one year after I left, and a few months after she already had Liam. The conversation never steered toward Liam's accident, and I didn't pry. I could see the pain behind her eyes, a sorrow that hadn't been there before. I supposed we had both been scarred in different ways.

When both of us started yawning, we decided to call

it a night. I'd successfully ignored Bram and Sierra for most of the night, losing track of them somewhere between my second drink and telling Ren about my business. We were walking out and saying our goodbyes when a tall, well-dressed man placed a hand on Renata's arm.

"Hey, I thought that was you." His tone was friendly, and when Renata turned toward the man, her expression brightened.

"Dr. Jacobs!" She grabbed the hand on her arm with her two hands. "What are you doing in Brooks Falls this late?" She asked.

The man's gaze darted back and forth between me and Renata before answering her with his eyes on me. "I'm with some friends over there." He motioned with his head to a booth in the back. "We come here to unwind every once in a while. To keep our sanity and all."

Renata's face, and tone, softened. "It's well deserved, that's for sure."

He shifted the conversation when he asked, "Is this your sister?"

Renata turned toward me, a huge smile spreading across her lips.

"No, we aren't sisters, unfortunately," I answered with a snicker. "I'm an old friend, just moved back to town. Ren and I went to school together. We were best friends," I said proudly.

"Oh, we *were* best friends? Nuh uh, girl, we just caught up and that bestie status has now been restored," she scolded me with feigned annoyance. "Anyway, Jade and I knew each other all our lives, before she got too big for this town and went and got famous."

I laughed at her. "I'm hardly famous."

Luckily, the man skipped past talk of my fame and introduced himself instead. "I'm Jake." He extended a hand toward me.

I worked my lips back and forth, trying to hold back the giggle that wanted to break free as I took his hand.

"Jake, uh, Jacobs?" I asked.

He at least appeared amused when he threw his hands out and announced, "It's actually Jacob Jacobs, but yes, that's really my name."

I grinned, peering up at him, my hand still held firmly in his. "Wow, I have never met another one! I'm Jade Greene."

He chuckled and dropped my hand. "Ah, so you know my pain!"

"I do indeed," I returned.

"Well Jade Greene, since you're new to town—"

I cut him off. "Oh, I'm not new to town. I was actually raised here."

"Okay." He eyed me. "Well, since you're new to the town as it currently is, maybe you need someone to help reacquaint you?"

"Oh." I fumbled for the words to respond. "Well, um, I." I cut myself off and glanced quickly in the direction of Bram. I couldn't see him, but somehow felt he was watching me.

Renata inhaled a sharp breath and clapped her hands together. "Oh, you should Jade! Dr. Jacobs is an angel and I mean, look at him," she said, waving her hand up and down the man's body, as if this entire night hadn't already been awkward enough without her showcasing the hot doctor like I was getting a prize from a game show. Except it was one of those prizes that you didn't want because the taxes on it were worth near as much as its value.

I snorted, making eyes with Renata, hoping our telepathic girl connection had stayed intact after all these years.

She pursed her lips, raised her eyebrows, and tilted her head at me with all the subtle attitude only a woman could answer silently with. Oh, she understood me all right. She just didn't care.

I shot her a terse smile before turning back to Jake. "Um, okay. Yeah, sure, that sounds nice," I said, giving in.

A big, toothy grin spread across his face. A face that I was just noticing was handsome in a non-obvious way. His eyes were a bit narrow and his nose was shapely, pointed, and pronounced, giving him a distinguished sort of look. He wasn't the type of man that I would normally be attracted to, but maybe that was for the best. After all, my type had never served me well.

Jake reached into his pocket and pulled out a piece of paper. When he offered it to me, I grabbed it, seeing right away that it already had his number on it.

"Do you just have these at the ready to pass out?" I teased, fighting the sneaking suspicion that this man was a player, just like every other man.

His gaze met the floor. "Well, I didn't expect you to call me out like that." He looked up and shook his head once. "But no. I saw you from across the room earlier. Wishful thinking, I guess," he confessed with a shrug.

My cheeks heated at the admission. "Oh, I'm sorry." I fiddled with my hands, realizing I hadn't the first clue how to flirt anymore. "That's very flattering and, well, it worked."

"Yeah." He shifted on his feet, before straightening

his spine. "Well, it was nice to meet you, Jade Greene. I hope to hear from you." He turned to Renata. "And good to see you," he said with a curt nod, keeping his eyes locked on me until he turned around to walk away.

Renata weaved her arm into mine and I could feel the glee radiating off her as we walked forward. "Oh my god, you are on fire! Wait!" She stopped, jerking us to a halt. "Please, please, *please* don't tell me, but is this how your life always is? You just walk into a room and the sexy vultures circle?"

"I—"

She put her hand up. "I said don't tell me, and I meant it. I love you and I've missed you oh so much, so I really don't want to be forced to hate you."

We said our goodbye's outside and solidified our plans to meet up again.

The night had been a whirlwind, so I welcomed the short walk to my car as a chance to unwind. The mountain air was crisp and relaxing, and I let it soothe my lungs. I clicked the remote to unlock the door and was about to pull the handle when a hand gripped my arm. I squeaked right before I froze completely in place. So much for those self-defense classes I'd taken in Charlotte. But it wasn't fear that stopped me dead. I could feel him. It was the endless bolts of electricity that fired through my body, sending bursts of emotion so thick, I could hardly think.

And I knew.

I knew instantly that it was him.

"Jadey." The gruff sound of his voice melted any shred of fear that remained and immediately my heart throbbed inside my chest, beating so hard and loud, it was all that I could hear. I whipped around, my attitude so diametrically opposed to what I was feeling.

"What are you doing running up on a woman like that?" I shoved a finger into his chest and leaned closer. "I almost pepper sprayed your eyeballs out!" I hissed, then ripped my arm from his hold.

Bram looked at my hands. Empty hands that were nowhere near a can of pepper spray. I rifled mindlessly through my purse to try and produce the damn spray, but I couldn't find it.

"Sorry." Bram grimaced and shrunk back a bit. "I didn't mean to frighten you, babe." I was jolted by his casual use of "babe" and the way it hacked at the hard shell I'd built around my heart. It was the only truly terrifying thing about the encounter so far.

"Well, you did." I snapped and took a shaky step back before I hoisted my chin in the air and narrowed my eyes on him. "Now, what do you want?"

I watched in shock as he squared his shoulders and set his jaw, before he asked, "Who was that guy you were talking to?"

Me mouth fell open, and I stared, eyes wide, into his baby blues. I studied them, sure I would find some small indication that he wasn't serious. He stared back, that unyielding expression of his taunting me.

I inhaled through my nose, each breath heavy, my chest rising with every lungful. My neck burned, the fiery sensation traveling straight to my cheeks. I clenched my fists and pressed them into my thighs.

Blinking several times, I asked through clenched teeth. "Are—" I shook my head, unfurled my fists, and sucked in the calmest breath I could find. "Are you—" I knew the breath did not have its desired effects when I sneered. "Are you for fucking for real?"

Bram jerked back as if my words had physically manifested as a slap to the face. The scathing, and unearned, expression he'd been wearing disappeared, and he hung his head.

"Look at me!" I demanded. He lifted his gaze, his rounded puppy eyes doing nothing to counter my rage. "You have no right." I stood tall, drawing resolve from my countless memories of betrayal. "Not that it even matters, but just a reminder." I raised my hand and gestured in the direction of Shea's. "You are on a date! And I'm sure the beautiful, sweet Sierra is unknowingly waiting for her jackass in shining armor to return and deliver her from any sliver of happiness she might carve out in this world!"

My vision blurred, and I began to tremble, the one-two punch of this depressing trip down memory lane, the final blows before the inevitable knockout. Trying to steady myself, I placed a hand on the door of my car. "I can't." My voice cracked and my heart raced as I fought to stay upright. "I haven't seen you in years." I threw a hand out, but my movements were stilted and awkward. "Years!" I screeched, finally buckling under the pain that surfaced. I shook my head, too far gone for games or pride. "*You* left me, *abandoned* me, kicked me ou—" I choked up, the image of his cruel face that day forever burned in my brain.

I thought I must've stood there forever staring back at that cold expression, trapped in the past, when Bram's soft "Jade," pulled me from the agony of my own thoughts. I stared back at him, returning to the moment.

"No," I whispered, shaking my head. "You don't get to ask me anything about who I talk to or what I do. You are nothing to me, Bram Taylor. You're nothing but an old, distant memory. One I'd very much like to forget," I lied. Oh, how I lied. I took my own heart and crushed it. Again. I didn't know how much more it could take before it was nothing but pieces. And I didn't want to find out, so I turned back to open my door, desperate to escape. Before I could even pull the handle, Bram's hand clasped around my arm and with so little effort, he spun me back around.

"Don't touch me!" I screeched, ripping my arm away. "Go back to your date!" I moved close and gave his chest a hard shove, but the man was sturdy, and he didn't budge. Instead, I fell into him. The nearness paralyzed me. Between the smell of his cologne and the warmth of his broad chest, it took everything I had in me just to keep breathing.

I clasped his forearms to keep myself from falling over when I felt his breath hit my forehead. My mouth went dry as I foolishly tilted my head back without even thinking what it cost me. And oh, did it cost me. I paid in full, forking over any good sense and bad memories I had. Suddenly, the only thing between us was a sliver of space.

Bram groaned and within seconds, closed the gap. I squeezed his arms tighter, digging my nails in, doing anything to feel closer to him. His hands landed on my hips and he was so gentle that I barely felt it when he grazed his fingers across the fabric of my tight dress. I closed my eyes, remembering how gentle he could be with me. The feel of him transported me to a simpler time.

"Jadey." His voice was muted and soft and the sound of my name on his lips sent waves of emotion through me. I liquified in his arms, giving up and giving in.

"You're more beautiful than ever and you were always perfect." Bram ran the tip of his nose down my cheek, pausing when he got to my ear. He nipped at it, and I gasped, urging him to keep going when I tilted my neck to one side.

"Fuck, you smell good," he groaned as he continued down my neck, stopping only to place a single kiss that sent thousands of shivers rolling down my spine, waking up every nerve in my body.

His head came back up slowly, nudging my chin up with his nose. Our eyes met. His were soft, and the flecks of gold at the center sparkled as he leaned in. My eyes fluttered shut when his lips landed on mine, and he pressed a gentle kiss to my lips. It lasted seconds before I couldn't wait any longer, the pleasure a bitter reminder that I'd felt nothing like this in a very long time. I ran my hands up his arms and raked them through his hair as I pulled him closer, needing more.

Bram obliged, groaning into my mouth as we both opened to one another, tongues dancing while hands moved everywhere.

"Bram," I gasped when he drew back and took a breath.

His eyes darkened, his nostrils flared as he stood there, staring at me like he wanted to absolutely devour me. My pussy clenched, and I squeezed my thighs together, hoping he wouldn't notice that I was losing control.

He bent down, this time grabbing my thighs and running his hands back along my ass where he gripped and then, much to my surprise, lifted.

"What are you doing?" I asked, giggling when he set

me down on the hood of my car.

"This," Bram growled, working his thumbs under the hem of my dress before he pushed up, exposing my thighs. He stared at my legs, the tip of his thumb rubbing the edge of my panties. I squirmed.

"Bram," I whispered, my voice pleading, the contact, or current lack thereof, too much and not enough all at once.

"Jadey," he growled, almost as a warning, an intimation that mimicked my own fears. But it didn't matter. I was becoming unhinged, sliding toward full-blown madness with zero brakes.

I knew it was over for me when without warning, he clutched my jaw with his hand and pulled me toward him, tenderness be damned. The man was well aware how I liked it, and he wasted no time in giving it to me.

And I went willingly, the feeling of his tongue sweeping across my lips so arresting that I opened at once. The smell of his musky cologne was nothing more than an afterthought to the way he felt against me, his solid arms wrapping me up, his hard body pressed against my soft. Our tongues met, his teasing mine as we explored each other once again, a reacquainting that felt less like a reunion and more like returning to the familiarity of home. Even if it was a dysfunctional one.

Bram pushed his center deeper into me. I felt the hardness press against my core and was grateful when he luxuriated in that position. He didn't wait too long before he ran one hand between my legs, skimming the outside of my panties, a maneuver that had me instantly dripping.

"Mmm, you like that, don't you, baby?" Bram asked as he caressed my pussy teasingly slow.

I lifted my hips and thrusted them forward, shamelessly trying to get closer to his fingers. "Yes," I gasped. "I like it. I want more," I demanded, unbothered by how foolish and brazen this all was. It had been a long time and besides, I'd always been stupid when it came to Bram.

He groaned, a deep rumble that I felt in my pussy. He slid one finger along the wetness, languishing on the outside of my folds before he entered with a single finger. I inhaled a sharp breath and shifted my hips up so his finger inside of me went deeper. I threw my head back, reveling in the feeling of him. Bram worked me with his finger, adding another, filling me more, and hitting the spot that he'd always known how to find.

My body moved with him and I ground into his hands, unapologetic in my desire. Our lips fused together. I whimpered and moaned into his mouth, and he groaned and growled into mine. He bit at my bottom lip, and I clawed at his back until the only thought in my head was the release that I was careening toward at the hands of the only man I'd ever loved.

"Honey," I pleaded, speaking into his lips. "Please, don't stop. Make me come, please. I need it."

"Come for me, Jadey," he commanded, keeping his momentum and adding a thumb to my clit. And that did it. It was all I needed. I spread my legs and rode his fingers as I looked up to the night sky, losing myself in the moment as shockwave after shockwave sent bursts of pure ecstasy throughout my body. I rode him harder, my pussy convulsing, moving until my orgasm waned and the high of it all turned to utter relaxation; It was a full body tranquility that I hadn't felt in more years than I cared to admit. I marinated in it, soaking it all up, letting my breaths ease naturally as I came down from the clouds.

"Come here," Bram said in a gentle voice as he pulled me into him, my head hitting his hard chest. He ran his fingers through my hair, starting at my scalp and running the length of my long tendrils. "Did you like that, baby?"

I leaned back, tilting my head to look at him, way too lost in the moment to admit I was being reckless.

"Mmm, yes." I smiled, my eyes hazy and near shut. He smiled back at me, the corners of his eyes crinkled with laugh lines, showcasing a life of laughter and joy. It shouldn't have affected me. I shouldn't have let it twist my insides up the way it did, but I couldn't help it.

Anger burned up any peace I'd managed to take hold of, incinerating my euphoria with a flicker of the flame he'd ignited with one simple smile. Smiles he'd been smiling for years without me, joy he'd been feeling all this time, forgetting me as readily as he'd let me go.

His blue eyes, those same ones that still held the power to render me speechless, searched me. But they were full of emotion, so different from the emptiness they held the last time I'd looked this deeply into them, on the night he'd obliterated me and sent me running. The night I'd never recovered from. Never recovered. Oh god, what was I doing? He would ruin me again if I let him. I barely survived it face relaxed, and I knew that I wouldn't survive it again.

I gathered myself, turning away from him to break the spell as I spoke into the cool, night air. "Let go of me," I said impassively, feeling that wall re-erect.

Bram released a puff air like he'd been suddenly punched in the gut, before he asked, "What?"

I turned to face him, finding my backbone, as I narrowed my eyes at him. "Move away and let go of me. *Now.*"

He shook his head and looked at me, bewilderment flashing in his eyes. His face fell as he assumed a tortured expression, maybe even more than my own. Bram took a step back, and I lurched forward at the sudden loss of his hands on me. I recovered quickly, launching off my car to straighten and smooth my dress with as much composure as a woman who'd just been finger-fucked by her estranged ex on the hood of an SUV, could muster.

"That was a mistake," he said, his voice dry, as if he had come to this conclusion on his very own.

My cheeks burned with the rage I felt. "Ya think? I'm pretty sure *I* was the one who just made that clear."

At that, Bram's face relaxed, and he smirked. He actually smirked and then took a step toward me.

"What are you doing?" I whispered, my voice annoyingly husky, oozing all that sex and attraction that I was trying so hard to restrain. I stiffened, the only defense I had against him.

"I think we need to talk, Jadey." His voice was earnest, and it caught me off guard. But he was right, we did have a lot to discuss.

I nodded woodenly, reluctantly agreeing with him. Because if anything was true, that was it.

"Yeah, you're right, we do. But not here and not now," I told him, my trembling voice exposing my defeat. "I need some time, Bram. I need time to get settled here, but more than anything I need to get my daughter settled."

Bram's soft features turned hard, and he dipped his head forward, lifting one arm and pointing down Main

66

Street in the direction I used to travel home.

"Get settled in *that* house?" he asked through gritted teeth.

I shook my head at him, the sudden change in his tone a reminder of how quickly he could shift his emotions on me. But I didn't have to explain myself, so I held my head up straight and said my piece.

"Bram, I don't owe you an answer to that question or anything else you'd like to know at this point. *You* threw us away. Dealing with you is secondary to everything I have going on right now. I have an entire life that has nothing to do with you and I'm trying to start that life here, but it takes time and energy." I lifted my chin and squared my shoulders. "Now, you should get back to your *date,*" I emphasized. "She's probably wondering where you went."

I didn't wait for a reply. I had to end this because I knew if I didn't, I'd likely end up in another precarious position and it wouldn't take much, nor would it take long. I swung open my door and got in. Bram never left or stopped watching me as I drove away. I glanced at his shrinking figure in my rear-view mirror, wondering what the hell I had been thinking coming back here.

****

Jade—Sixteen years old
Bram and I sat in his room, snuggled on his couch like we did most of the time we were together. We had become really close since last year and more often than not, I found myself staying at his house. Jules didn't usually stay, but he sure had no problem dumping me off there. I was fine with it. Dad had been acting even weirder lately, so I was happy to avoid him.

I shot up, eyes locked on the television, transfixed

by Anne Hathaway's disheveled and desperate Fantine, mourning the cards life had dealt her, having given everything up to care for her child. It was a love I'd never know. My eyes filled with tears as a hopeless Fantine belted the final words to "I Dreamed a Dream."

I was clutching the couch tightly, tears pouring down my cheeks, when two hands wrapped around my waist from behind. As much as Bram hated this movie, he was always sweet about this part, never questioning my tears or poking fun at them.

Bram let go of me with one hand and reached up to wipe some moisture from my face. When the song was finally over, I sat up and let out all the breath I'd been holding.

"Come back here, Jadey." Bram tugged my waist, where his one hand was still resting. With a deep sigh, and zero hesitation, I fell into him and relaxed in his arms. My back was to his front, a few tears still dripping down my cheeks, when I turned my head to the side and let the wetness soak into his shirt.

"My tissue paper," I teased.

And then, instead of feigning annoyance like he usually did, instead he ran his fingers through my hair, weaving in and out slowly, grazing my scalp with his fingertips.

"How was your day?" Bram asked, his voice soft and soothing.

I sighed, my limbs loosening as he stroked my hair. "Jet asked me out. *Again.*" The words came out dreamily, but not because of Jet. Bram's head massage had put me on cloud nine and my entire body was tranquil as I spoke.

Bram stopped moving but used his hands in my hair

to pull my head back so it rested on his shoulder and I was looking up at him. "What did you say?" he asked, his brow furrowed.

Bram was protective of me and did not like the idea of me and Jet, so I always treaded lightly around the subject. Jet was cute. Hot even, and popular. But something about going out with him felt plain wrong, so I'd declined both times.

The first time I'd told Bram that Jet had asked me out, he went off the rails about it, like Jet had committed some unpardonable offense. They'd even got in a fight over it, which was when I decided that I definitely wasn't going out with Jet for fear it would ruin their friendship and more importantly, my friendship with Bram.

I blinked up and fluttered my eyelashes. I didn't know why I was about to tease him when he was being so nice to me. But I was, because if I was being honest, I loved how it made me feel. I lifted one shoulder and sighed out the lie.

"I don't know, have to think about it."

It was all a provocation that he saw right through. He tugged my hair lightly and smirked. "Oh, yeah?" He tilted his head and narrowed his eyes at me.

I nodded and giggled. "Mmhmm."

Bram leaned down and whispered, his lips tickling my ear. "You're a liar, Jadey. And you know how I know this?"

A shiver raced down my spine and I jerked once in his arms, before I asked, my voice high and teasing, "How?"

Bram pulled away some and looked into my eyes. His arctic blues drew me in while he studied me. Another shiver struck, and I felt my cheeks heat.

"I heard him whining about you turning him down. Again." His scrutinizing expression relaxed into a lazy grin. Boy was he handsome.

"What?" I asked, curious and now paying attention.

"Yup, in the locker room after practice. Dude is used to getting any girl he wants, so I'm not gonna lie, it kinda made my day." He snickered.

I rolled my eyes at him, knowing he could also have any girl he wanted. I hadn't seen him with any of them, but that didn't mean he wasn't active. I was around him a lot, but not every second of every day.

"You both can get any girl you want. Except me," I joked, and I thought I felt his body tense. "Anyway, I really don't understand you two. You're best friends, but you also like to see each other suffer?"

Bram pushed my head forward again to continue sifting his hands through my hair. "That's dude friendship, Jadey."

Bram's couch felt smaller than normal, and I wiggled a little to get comfortable. Bram released a painful groan. "Are you okay?" I looked up.

He was looking away when he mumbled, "I'm fine. Get comfortable, but when you do it, can you not move around like that?"

I was fully melted into him and was about to ask, "like what?" when I saw the door opening from my periphery. Bram went rigid, before urging me off him by giving me a tiny push forward. I was mid-sitting up when Jules walked in, blinking away the sleepiness as I watched Jules's expression go from chill to fire. His eyes rounded and landed on the spot where I was sitting upright between Bram's legs.

I scooted all the way out, hoping I looked natural

and not like I was freaking out inside. It was a miracle he hadn't seen this before, because it wasn't out of the ordinary. The thing was, Bram and I really were just friends. This was how we always were, *except* when Jules was around. We had an unspoken agreement that we didn't touch or cuddle in Jules's presence.

When we were alone, we fell into a comfort with each other that made it all feel okay. But when Jules was around, it felt like we were doing something wrong.

"Hey, big brother," I greeted Jules, mustering all the normalcy I could gather. He ignored me entirely and turned to Bram.

"A word, *friend,*" Jules said, his voice strained.

Bram nodded casually, like nothing had happened. "Sure, what's up?"

"Alone," Jules clipped.

I didn't look at Bram as he slid off the couch and followed my brother into the hallway. They closed the door behind them, and I told myself to stay seated. *Do not eavesdrop, don't do it.* So, naturally, I got up from my seat on the couch, and went to the door to listen.

"Dude! What the fuck was that?" Jules's muffled growl was still piercing, and I flinched.

"What was what?" I heard Bram ask, his voice still even and calm.

"You know *what*, man," Jules clipped out. "I saw you two when I walked in. I'm not stupid, bro. So, I'll ask again, what the fuck was that?"

I shrunk back some and grimaced. Jules was pissed. And when Jules was pissed, he was not the kind of guy to mess with. He was big and strong to be sure, but more than that, he had been raised by Nathan, who had hardened my brother from a young age.

"Jules, she was fuckin' crying about that stupid movie again. Hysterical, like she gets, and it's always that one scene. It's like, I don't know, personal for her or something. I'm not gonna see her cry and do nothing about it, especially when it's more than just crying about a movie scene." Bram's voice lowered when he added, "Anyway, you know she's like a little sister to me. I felt bad for her."

I cringed at the term. Little sister. Not best friend. Not even regular old friend. Nope, little, sad, pathetic, crying like a baby, sister.

"Oh, is she? News flash, asshole, she *is* my sister and I have never, nor would I ever, hold her the way you were holding her."

"Jesus, man, yeah okay, but she's not my actual sister," Bram put in, sounding impatient.

"Just keep your damn hands off her, okay? And you know fuckin' well and good that she doesn't get certain things, and I don't want her too. Not now, not ever. If you go down that path with her, no telling what might happen."

Jules's voice had gotten lower, and his words had been issued like a warning. A warning that, even if I didn't understand it, I felt it in every part of me.

"Now that is clear, did you talk to your parents?" Jules asked, while I stood frozen in place, unable to move from whatever betrayal it was that I was feeling.

"They're good with it," Bram replied. At the sound of his voice, my body unlocked, and I ran back to the couch.

I waited, watching my movie alone, for fifteen minutes, before Jules walked in and sat down next to me. His face softened the way it always did when he spoke to me.

"Hey lil' sis." He bumped my shoulder with his.

"Hey," I said slowly, feeling him out. I did not want to be on the receiving end of my brother's wrath.

Jules tossed a bag on the counter. "Clothes, hygiene, money."

I jolted and looked at the large bag, then back up at my brother. "What?" I asked, confused. I'd only ever stayed at Bram's for a day or two and never really had to pack.

"You're staying here." Jules looked to the side and narrowed his eyes on Bram. "Dad is on a tear and I don't want you around him right now. You'll stay here a few days and I'll be back to check on you. *Often*." Jules emphasized the last.

I had never seen Dad "on a tear," so I didn't know what he was protecting me from. I did know that I was just fine not going home, so I didn't argue it.

"All right. Why aren't you staying away?" I tilted my head back to look at my brother. He presented as a big, tough guy, who was affected by nothing. But I'd grown up with Jules and I knew that he was capable of so much emotion.

Jules's jaw got tight, and he peered at Bram briefly, then watched the ground. "Will you be okay here?"

I nodded, realizing he wasn't going to tell me anything. "Yeah, of course," I told him.

"All right, I'll be back to check on you." He tugged a piece of my hair. "If you need anything, just call me, okay?"

"Okay," I answered softly.

Jules sent me a warm smile and made his way to where Bram had been standing at the door. Jules whispered something to him and then tipped his chin at Bram before walking out the door.

I stared ahead, thinking about my brother's words in the hallway. *She doesn't get certain things*. What things? *And I don't want her to*. Why?

My thoughts were interrupted when Bram spoke up. "Wanna watch the rest of the movie, Jadey?"

He walked over from where he had been waiting at the entrance of the door. I examined him, searching for any indication that what I'd overheard him say in the hallway, wasn't true. But his expression was unreadable, and I couldn't explain why it hurt the way he saw me, but it did.

"No, I'm tired," I answered, with a half-smile that I hoped would convince him that I was totally fine. "I think I'll just go to bed. Can I sleep in the guest room tonight?"

I knew that he had a guest room because he'd offered it to me before, but I always chose to sleep on his couch or in his bed, not wanting to be too far away. Until tonight.

"What?" Bram jerked his head back. "The guest room? Why?"

I looked away. Really anywhere but at him, hoping he would miss the hurt in my eyes. "I just need some space right now." I twisted my hands together, my nerves rising to the surface with the lie. "And it's only seven, so I doubt you're tired. Besides, if I'm in there you can call whatever girls over and you can live your life, especially if I'm gonna be here for days." I smiled weakly, trying so hard to sound light, but my words were laced with pain.

Bram pressed his lips closed and nodded toward the

door. "You know where it's at."

I sure did. So, I wasted no time in grabbing my stuff and hurried out of his room to make the five-step trek across the hallway to the guest room. I tossed my bags into a corner, collapsed on the bed, and absolutely lost it.

Hot tears poured down my cheeks as I did my best to hold back the violent sobs that wanted to wrench free. I pushed my face into the pillow and cried into that, letting it stifle the noise. I replayed his words over and over. *She's like a little sister to me.* I knew I was being stupid. I was his best friend's little sister, of course he saw me like that.

I was lost in thought when I felt a warm hand touch me. I jumped up and flipped around to my back.

"Jadey," Bram spoke quietly, his eyes gentle and welcoming. He reached out and touched my cheek, then nodded. "I thought so."

I pushed up onto my elbows, not bothering to wipe away my tears. "You thought what?" I asked through short puffs of air, trying to calm my crying and catch my breath.

He shook his head, but his eyes were still analyzing me. "You heard our conversation."

I looked away. "Yeah, part of it."

His hand landed on my cheek and the warmth of his fingers burned into me. "He doesn't have a choice, Jadey."

My eyebrows shot up, and I tilted my head. "What? Who doesn't have a choice?"

Bram narrowed his eyes and then paused for a moment, before he asked, "Why are you in here and why the hell are you crying?"

"I just wanted to give you space," I told him, with

more than a hint of pain to it. "I didn't want you to feel like you're always taking care of me, and I don't want to be someone else's little sister. Jules already takes care of me. I don't need you sacrificing for me too. If I'm going to be here, I'll be in here and I'll stay out of your way."

Bram scoffed. "Is that what you think?" he asked, his face twisted, like I was crazy for even suggesting it.

"It's not what I think, it's what I heard you say." I shrugged and gave him a failed smile that got lost somewhere between sadness and successfully saving face. "It's okay, really. I just thought—" I shook my head, the words stuck in my throat.

Bram reached out to interlace our hands together, and I let him. I felt good like this. "You thought what, Jadey?"

I hiked one shoulder to my ear and let it fall. "I thought we were more," I said, quickly adding, "I thought we were friends," when his eyes enlarged. "And what you said, well, I'm just hurt, that's all. I'll be okay, just go back to your room."

He pushed out a shaky breath while his head bounced slowly up and down. I watched in amazement as his lips quivered through the words. "And I'm trapped between not being a shit best friend to Jules and dealing with the fact that I'm closer to you than anyone else." His words leveled me, but he wasn't done. "Jadey, you *are* my best friend. But how can I tell Jules that? He thinks—" Bram paused and threw out a hand. "Fuck, I don't know what he thinks. I just know he's got it wrong."

I didn't blink, and I didn't move. Instead, I let his words weave their way in and bind to my heart. They created a cocoon around the crumbling world that I lived in and suddenly, I saw nothing else, I felt nothing else, but him. My best friend.

I must've sat that way for several minutes because Bram tugged my hand forward and said, "Hey." My gaze snapped to his and I could feel my sadness melting away. "I'm sorry, Jadey. Come back to the room. Please?"

"I, I." I struggled, unable to form words. But I could smile. And I did. I let out a breath with a small laugh and suddenly, I was beaming. It was probably that same goofy smile that he saw on my thirteenth birthday.

"Come back to the room, Jadey," Bram urged.

I gave in and let him guide me back, my hand in his. He led me to the bed, where I lie down next to him and stared at the ceiling for a minute, before I turned my head toward him.

"You know, you're my best friend too, Bram. I think that's why it so much to hear what you said."

Bram inhaled deeply. "Well, if Jules finds out that I've ditched him for his little sister, I'm positive he'll chop my dick off or at least revoke my bro card."

I bit my lip, trying to hold back my giggles.

Bram smirked. "Not funny, Jadey. He already thinks I've done something wrong with you and I'd be surprised if he doesn't chop my dick off just to make sure I don't."

"He won't chop your, you know, off. He's my protective big brother, but he also trusts me. If I tell him we are just friends, he'll believe me."

Bram scoffed. "Yeah, he'll believe you, but probably won't believe me. And, he'll think he has to protect you from me."

This was true. In Jules's eyes, I was still a kid who couldn't choose good for herself, even if I'd never done anything to prove that point.

I waved him off. "He'll get over it. Besides, it's his fault. He's the one who made me stay here and get close to you."

He squeezed my hand and scoffed. "Yeah, you can be the one to tell him that."

"Hmm. Or maybe we can keep it from him, for just a while." I giggled and then buried my face in his chest.

Bram pulled me in, just like he'd done a hundred times before. I was flush against his chest. He smelled so good. Not at all how I imagined most boys smelled. He smelled like clean laundry and a touch of mint. I dragged in a breath and then tipped my head back to look up at him. His eyes were fastened on me, and I got lost. I got so lost that when he found me, his lips were on my forehead where he pressed a gentle kiss. It was soft and his lips stayed on me for a while.

"My first kiss," I joked on an indulgent sigh that was way more dramatic than necessary.

Bram smiled on my forehead. "Really? I'm your first kiss? That's sad as fuck, Jadey."

I shoved him lightly and glared at him. "Yes. Unless kissing Michael Bralen in the first grade after an intense game of tag counts?"

Bram rolled me over to my back, so he was half-hovering over me. "I don't like that guy," he teased with a feigned protectiveness. He raised his brows. "Except, if we're making confessions, I have to tell you right now that I have a wife."

I threw my hand over my mouth in my own mock surprise.

Bram nodded casually. "Yup. Wendy Bancroft. We've been married for eleven years."

I used the full force of my weight against him, and

he let me push him back so now I was halfway over him. "We have so much to learn about each other."

Bram smiled the widest, brightest smile I'd ever seen. "Jadey, I like this side of you."

My cheeks heated, and I felt his words warm every part of my body.

We continued teasing each other and laughing for the rest of the night, until we both fell asleep, fingers interlocked, closer than we'd ever been.

Chapter 4

Jade

Lex and I sat in my car, parked in front of Nathan's house, watching the crew set up the equipment before the fun began.

It had taken less than two weeks to clear the house. Evie had some sort of businesswoman magic. She called it networking connections, and I called it sorcery. Potato, Po-tah-to. She had figured out a way to donate all Nathan's belongings to be auctioned off by an organization that kept twenty percent of the profits, while the rest was donated to a charity of our choice. Lex and I chose an organization that donated prosthetics to low-income families that needed them. It was something that Renata had told me about when Lex mentioned what we were doing with the money from Nathan's belongings.

Once that was taken care of, we were ready for demolition day. It was the day I had been waiting for. I had kept very little from the house, most of it the minimal number of mementos that I found, along with every piece of paper in the office and a small safe that I hadn't been able to open. The thing had been sitting in my bedroom closet, causing my anxiety. I didn't want to open it, but I knew that one day I would want to know everything I could about Nathan Greene and his business dealings.

For the past nine years, it had felt like a dark cloud hanging over me and I hoped that a little closure would help me move past that part of my life.

I pulled up to a parking spot right in front of Sunshine's and looked back at Lex, who was staring out the window.

"You ready, kiddo?" I asked.

"Uh-huh," she answered, her voice distant and her eyes focused on something else. I followed her gaze, grimacing when I saw what she was seeing.

"Ready for some hot chocolate?" I pitched excitedly.

Lex turned to me, her eyes wide and glimmering with hope. "Can we go to the park, Mom?"

My heart sunk and I sighed. "I'm sorry, honey, but it's too soon. You need to let your body heal." I watched as her face withered and had no shame when I laid blame by adding, "it's the doctor's orders!"

Lex huffed and hung her head.

"Everyone okay over here?"

I knew right away who it was. Bram's gentle voice couldn't be confused. My heart pulsated in my chest, and I felt it reaching for him. All those scattered pieces begging to be put back together.

I turned my head to the side to glimpse him from my periphery. And damn, was that a mistake. Standing tall in dark, slim-fit jeans and a retro Tom Petty and the Heartbreakers tee that hugged his muscular arms, he looked good enough to abandon common sense for. I released Lex from my hold, but kept her close. Clearing my throat as I stood up, I avoided eye contact with him.

"Um, yeah, we're fine. Lex is just missing home a bit, that's all," I told him as I smiled down at my little girl.

She studied Bram for a beat before she tilted her head to the side and asked me, "Who's that?"

My mouth was dry and my movements stiff when I answered her. "This is Bram Taylor, sweetheart," I said, gesturing toward him. "We, uh," I stammered before I found the right words. "We went to school together. He used to be a really good friend of mine."

Lex glanced at him and then looked back at me, her green eyes wide and a small frown plastered on her face. "He isn't a good friend anymore?"

"What?" I croaked out the question through a tight throat.

Lex's lip quivered before she inhaled a breath and inquired thoughtfully, "If you went to school together, why aren't you friends anymore? Did you stop bein' friends because you moved away?" Her eyes brimmed with tears as she waited for my response.

It was a loaded question that felt more like a landmine, so I tiptoed into my response.

"No, it wasn't because I moved away. We—" I stammered. "We just. We had a fight and stopped talking." I hurried out the words and grimaced when I saw a horrified look flash across Bram's face before he focused on Lex.

"We argued, sure," he told her. "But that's not why we stopped talking. After your mom moved, I lost her number and could never find her again to apologize."

I rolled my eyes, grateful that Lex was concentrating on Bram.

"I looked and looked," he continued, more lies rolling smoothly from his tongue. It was no wonder I'd been so easily fooled. "It's a good thing we have the internet now, so you can always find your friends and they can always find you."

He told her this, like we had been raised in the stone age and a strong Wi-Fi connection was all that had stood between us for years.

Lex straightened and swiped a few tears from her cheeks. "Really?" she asked, before peering up at me, her eyes wide, her expression hopeful.

"Mmhmm," I muttered, annoyed, but powering through for the sake of my daughter.

"That's so sad you looked for Mom and couldn't find her."

Bram nodded his agreement while I restrained my irritation.

"It made me really sad for all those years that I didn't get to your mom. But I can be happy again because she's back and I don't have to miss her anymore." He smiled brightly at her and god, he was charming.

Lex grinned broadly at his lines of pure horseshit. At least one of us believed him.

"Mom and I got bored, so we came to get ice cream!"

A slow smile spread across Bram's face, and his blue eyes flickered in the sunlight. Oof. I didn't want to feel it in my toes, but I did.

"Well, that sounds like a plan. Maybe I'll get some ice cream too," he told Lex.

"Really? What's your favorite flavor?" she asked, grinning as she awaited his answer, the drama from the past ten minutes nowhere to be found.

"Chocolate, of course," he replied with a shrug.

Lex's face lit up like they were the only two people in the world who liked chocolate. "That's my favorite too! With sprinkles and hot fudge and whip cream and sometimes a cherry. Mom likes bananas in her ice cream, and I think that's weird and gross." She pretended to gag and bowed over.

Bram chuckled and then winked at me. "Your mom has always liked bananas in her ice cream."

I rolled my eyes, more irked with the feelings this man could elicit in me, even when I hated him. I controlled the smile that wanted to form on my face, but couldn't stop the stinging that ran along my cheeks. Damn biology. It had been *nine* years. How in the hell did he still have this effect on me?

"Let's go get ice cream then," Bram said to Lex.

Lex jumped in place as my head jerked back. Wait, *let's*?

****

Bram

The kid was adorable. She looked just like Jade. I couldn't take it. An image of a young Jade flashed through my mind—Red, tear-stained cheeks and her vulnerable eyes staring back at me.

As her daughter went on about Nathan's house, fear and anxiety seeped into every inch of me. Jade was building a house on *that* land, and the woman had no clue. And unless I stepped up, she had no protection, and that wasn't an option.

"Sunshine's isn't the best place to get ice cream. You should know that, Jade." I shot her a look of disappointment and wagged a finger her way. "You remember Sweetie's, right babe?"

Jade skewered me with a look. "I think Sunshine's will be just fine. They have ice cream *and* they have coffee, something I desperately need."

Lex tugged on Jade's arm. "Mom, please? I want to go to the best ice cream place in town. Please, please, please can we go? Can we, can we?" Lex begged, and when I saw the look on Jade's face, I knew I'd won.

Jade closed her eyes briefly and inhaled before pinning me with a look. Her mouth was smiling, but her eyes were murderous. "You know what? Sure, *we* can go." She emphasized, her emerald eyes enlarging with the word. "Well, enjoy your coffee, Officer Taylor! Thanks for the suggestion." She grabbed her daughter's hand and made their way down the stairs. Lex craned her neck around, stumbling awkwardly, until Jade stopped and steadied the kid.

"You're not coming with us?" Lex asked, concern knit in her brow. "You finally found my mom and you don't want to see her more?"

Jade's expression dimmed as she looked at me through her lashes, her soft, pale features made more pronounced by the flaming waves of hair that framed her face. She looked like a fantasy come to life in a short sundress—a dress I was just noticing—that showed off her toned legs and arms.

"Of course I'm coming. Now that I found your mom, I'm not letting her go." I ignored Jade's snort. "Besides, your mom doesn't even know how to get there anymore."

"I haven't forgotten how to get there. It's not even a block away." Jade rolled her eyes and shook her head at me before turning to walk away.

I grabbed her wrist, and it was either a mistake or the best idea I'd ever had. An undeniable current hummed between us, stopping us both in our tracks. Jade stared at my hand wrapped around her delicate wrist and then looked back up at me.

"No baby, they moved it to the lake," I said, unable to stop myself from dropping that bomb on her. And I didn't even regret it.

Jade's lips fell open and the look in her eyes. Fuck. It was a look I'd seen a thousand times, one that had seared into my memory. It was pure anger, and god, it turned me on.

"The lake? Like our—" I smiled at the inclusion and Jade paused to reset with a deep breath. "Or the—" I was enjoying seeing her like this and I realized my smile had spread wide when she stopped again to roll her eyes. "Like Lake Chandler?" she finally asked.

"Yep, *our* lake," I emphasized. "It's a pretty busy place now. Not at all like it used to be. They've built a beach where you and I used to go and there's a dock nearby with rentals. Sweetie's closed their storefront five years ago and moved to a food truck that they park at the lake half of the year."

Jade worked that plush bottom lip between her teeth. "I don't know if we should go all the way to the lake, Lex bug. That's a long drive and—"

I still had her wrist in my hand, so I gave it a small tug. "Jadey." Her gaze snapped to mine and our eyes locked. "Come on, it's only ten minutes away. And it's even better now, babe. You should really see it again." I ran my hand along Lex's hair, baffling myself with what the hell I was doing. "And this one should see it, too. This is her new home after all. Let's show her all the cool places in Brooks Falls."

Lex hopped in place. "Please, mom? I wanna see the beach!"

Jade sighed, her resolve wavering just enough.

"Okay. I guess we can meet you there," she said through clenched teeth.

"Nah, I'll drive you ladies in the truck. It's better to take it to the lake than your nice car, you know that. It gets muddy up there and you don't want all that lake sand on your fancy SUV."

Jade scowled at me and was about to open her mouth, to say something feisty, no doubt, but Lex spoke up.

"A truck! I never been in a truck before!" Lex jumped up and down, sending that spot in my chest straight into a tailspin, spiraling down to my gut. It killed. It should've been me. All of it should've been mine. Jealousy burned like wildfire, the feelings that I'd tried to bury so long ago, surfacing like no time had passed.

"No? Your dad doesn't have a truck?" I asked, searching for answers that I knew I didn't deserve.

Jade's eyes widened and blazed with anger. "That's—"

"Nope, I never had a dad." The kid spoke over Jade with a casual innocence that hinted of no loss. "Come on, guys! Where's your truck?"

I pointed to the red truck parked ahead and Lex skittered to it. Jade turned her head away, avoiding my searching eyes. I touched her arm. "She doesn't have a dad?"

She turned to face me, pinning me with narrowed eyes. "No, Bram, she doesn't have a dad. She's Jesus and I'm Mary!" She threw her hands up and rolled her eyes back.

"Jadey," I whispered, my heart aching for different reasons now.

She leaned up on her toes and hissed, "Of course, she has a dad. He's just never been in her life. It was the way he wanted it, so that's always been the way it is."

"What?" I growled. I didn't understand it. I couldn't. This perfect kid and my beautiful Jadey. What kind of unworthy piece of shit wouldn't want them?

"This conversation is over." Jade leaned in, her face in mine. "And if you ever, freaking ever, ask my kid questions like that again, it will be the *last* time you talk to her. Do you understand?" Nothing about her tone was playful. I'd crossed a line, and I knew it.

I didn't have time to apologize because Jade broke out into long strides to get to her daughter, who was waiting for us. Jade's stony features mellowed when she looked at the truck. Our truck. The thing was so damn old that it should've been retired years ago. I'd poured more money into it than was financially responsible, just to keep the heap running. Just to keep the good memories alive.

I opened the passenger door and moved the seat to let Lex in. "You know how to get buckled up, kiddo?"

"Yep!" The little girl fidgeted in her seat while she clicked the belt in.

I helped Jade in by grabbing her waist and lifting her onto the passenger seat, the way I always used to put her in my truck. I let my hands linger for a beat, disregarding the death glare she was shooting me. I reached over, grabbed the seatbelt, and clicked it in, my arms grazing over her body, the touch electrifying. I pulled back and stopped at her ear to whisper, "Buckle up, baby."

Jade bit her lip, her green eyes searching. She was still, and I was close, feeling that hum of energy that buzzed between us. It had always been this way and years apart hadn't changed a thing. I was spellbound, and she was also locked on me. I didn't know how long we stayed like that or how we breathed through it, but Lex's voice broke the trance when she asked, "Ew, are you guys gonna kiss?"

Jade's hand sprung up between us, and she shoved me back. I was so shocked at the move that I gaped at her before I chuckled, amused at her reaction. Pleased at it too.

"No, oh, honey, no. Officer Taylor and I—"

"Jesus, call me Bram, Jadey."

She sighed and continued talking to her daughter, side-eying me when she said, "*Bram* and I are just old friends."

"You looked like you were going to kiss him, Mom. Boys are gross." She stuck her finger in her mouth and made a gagging noise.

Jade snickered. "You're right; boys are gross, especially this one." Jade smirked and tilted her head at me. I shook my head at her, wishing I could ask her how gross she thought I was the other night when she was coming on my fingers in a parking lot.

Lex talked the entire drive to the lake, boomeranging between topics, her energy mesmerizing and maybe the only thing different about Lex and her mother.

When we got to the lake, I was happy to find that our spot was free. Jade looked over at me, but I kept my eyes ahead as I pulled in. "Still here, right where we left it."

"Sure." Her tone was listless as she looked away from me and out the window.

I cut the engine and ran around to her side to open

the door while she was gathering her things. Jade skirted around me as I tried to help her out of my truck, avoiding my touch as if Lex's words had really sunk in.

I showed the girls to Sweetie's ice cream truck. It was situated right in front of the water, which sparkled and waved in the mountain breeze. The smell was fresh, the surrounding trees offering protection from the sun. The beach wasn't lengthy, but it was big enough for several families to set up umbrellas and chairs while they watched their kids play in the water.

"Look, Mom, it's a beach!" Lex pointed and then paused before adding. "It's not like Carolina beach, but it's really pretty."

Memories flashed through my mind like movie reels. Sitting on the bed of my truck drinking whatever cheap beer we could find in my parents' fridge. Late-night, moonlit dips in the cool water. We were young, and even though life had already started catching up to me, I was always optimistic, even then. We'd had each other and that had been everything I'd needed. I swallowed back the pain that wound its hands around my throat and squeezed.

"Yeah honey, I grew up around this lake. It was one of my favorite places to swim as a kid," Jade said with a shrug, her nonchalance an irritation that I suspected had been aimed directly at me.

I nudged Jade with my elbow. "Your mom and I used to hang out here all the time, didn't we?"

I raised my brows and absorbed Jade's glower with a grin. Lex wasted no time in inquiring further.

"Really? Did you swim? Because my mom is a really good swimmer and she looks just like a mermaid, everyone always tells her that. Also, she has the prettiest bathing suits and when I get older, I'm gonna have two-piece bathing suits too. Right now, I have just a one kinda suit, but I want one like Mom!"

My brain turned to mush as I pictured Jade in a bathing suit, surrounded by her gorgeous hair, those full breasts, and that ample ass spilling out of a bikini. Fuck. I turned to Jade. "I'll have to see what she's talking about some time, babe."

Jade glared at me and then whispered, "Not a chance in hell, asshole."

I chuckled and wiggled my eyebrows, before turning back to Lex. "Come on ladies, let's get ice cream."

Lex skipped to the ice cream truck while Jade and I lagged behind. We had limited time, so I jumped right in. "You know, I still want to have that talk, Jadey."

Jade scoffed and then threw her head back. "Huh, do you? That's nice," she clipped.

"Come on." We were just inches from each other, and the energy between us was enough to start a large fire. "I know that I've been a dick since you got into town, but fuck, I wasn't expecting to see you. It caught me off guard."

She stopped dead, slowly turning her head toward me to pierce me with her eyes. "Since I got into town?" she asked, right before she huffed. "Well, if that isn't the understatement of a century!"

I opened my mouth, but she spoke first. "No." Jade pointed a finger in my direction. "You've been a dick since you kicked me out of this town. And then, when I hadn't seen you in nine years, the first thing you tell me to do is to leave? Like, like you have any right? Like I even care what you want anymore? And now you want me to pretend that you didn't send me away, brokenhearted and running, only for you to try and do it all over again?"

Her words struck a place inside of me that had been buried in guilt. She continued. "You're unbelievable, Bram. Just unbelievable. I know that in your mind, I'm just trash, but I've made something of myself, and honestly, I don't care what you think anymore. And I also don't care what you want. I'm certainly not going anywhere just because *you* don't want me here." She threw her hands up. "Sorry to disappoint, but I'm staying, and I don't really give a fuck what you want. And that's just the truth. Deal with it."

Her words knocked the wind out of me and, for the first time since I'd seen her, I didn't know exactly what to say. I didn't want to dig or push or prod. All I wanted was to wrap her in my arms and tell her I was sorry.

My voice was nothing but a strained whisper. "I've always cared about you, Jadey. You have to know that."

She laughed, a humorless sound. "Do I? Do I *have* to know that? You have a strange way of showing just how much you care, Bram Taylor."

"Please. I just, I didn't expect to see you. And at that house. But it is good to see you." Fuck, fuck. I couldn't tell her. There was too much hanging in the balance. Too much that had to stay tucked away. It was for her own good, her own safety.

"Is it?" She was studying me, looking for something that she just wouldn't find.

"Yes, Jadey, it is."

She inhaled deeply and at that moment I was thankful for Lex, because everything wanted to come spilling out.

"Come on, you guys! This ice cream looks soooooo yummy!"

Jade shrugged and tipped her head toward Lex. "The girl needs her ice cream." She shot me a half-smile. It wasn't that bright, radiant smile that she used to give me, but it was a start. And with our history, we had to start somewhere.

Lex played in the sand with some other kids while Jade and I sat and watched. She was pretty handy with just one arm and damn, the kid was charming, easily making friends with any and everyone.

"She seems like a really great kid, Jadey."

Jade watched her daughter in the distance and smiled. "Yeah, she's pretty fantastic." She looked down and then back up at me, her eyes soft. "Besides Evie, Lex is all I've got." She laughed wistfully.

"Oh yeah? What happened to her father?" I asked the question, knowing I was crossing so many lines.

She inhaled a deep breath and looked into my eyes. "He didn't want anything to do with me."

Her words annihilated me. The idea that some jerk had left her, had left *them,* was like salt on an open wound. The irony was that I had done it first. Or second. Or third, I supposed. Who knew? Jade had been left and tossed out and forgotten so many times in her life, I wondered if she ever trusted anyone at all after that.

I knew that what I'd done was a devastating blow. I had made her promises. I made her believe that we'd have a life together, only to pull the rug out and send her packing.

"I'm sorry, Jadey. You don't deserve that."

Her eyebrows lifted, vitriol in her voice as she scoffed out the word. "Right."

"Listen to me. I know that I fucked up. I knew it then; I know it now." I hung my head and ran a hand through my hair. "I've re-lived that day every day for years. There's nothing I regret more."

She shook her head. "It doesn't matter." She continued with a shrug. "You don't matter to me anymore, Bram. Lex is my life and I'll do anything for her, to keep her happy and safe. I don't care what you did to me. It hurt me then, but my life has been so good, I never really thought of you. Or of us. I've moved on and I really don't want to talk about it."

Her words slashed through me, cutting to the core. The thought of some other guy giving Jade the child that I should've given her ripped me in two. But the idea that she didn't think about me anymore or care about me the same way I had cared for her all these years, was like acid straight to my skin, ripping away until only marred flesh remained. It melted and flayed and cut straight to the bone. I deserved all of it. I swallowed back the disappointment, the realization that I had really lost her. All of these years had gone by and there were still parts of me that hoped she'd come back or that we'd find a way back to one another when the time was right.

"Okay." I accepted her words and wanted to give in, to give up, but something in me just couldn't let go. Not again.

She turned away, but I didn't miss the single tear that fell down her cheek. I reached out and wiped it away. She sucked in a breath and bit at that bottom lip. That lush one that I wanted to suck into my own mouth.

"It hurts me, what I did, knowing I hurt you." I cupped her cheek in my face, and I swore I felt her lean in. "And as much as it hurts to hear you say that you haven't thought about me all these years, I'm glad that you're happy, that you found the family you've always deserved."

More tears fell down her face and splashed onto my fingers. "Jadey. Baby, why are you crying? You know I can't take it when you cry. I never could."

She shook her head. "You're confusing me. I don't understand why you're doing this." Her words came on the coattails of a harsh exhale of breath. "Do you take some sort of sick pleasure in this? In making me feel things for you that aren't good for me?"

Jesus, is that really what she thought? I grabbed her with both of my hands, her face pressed gently between my grip.

"Fuck, Jadey. No, never. All I've ever wanted was you. That was all. It's simple. From the moment I saw you standing outside of my house that first night until now, it's *always* been you, even when neither of us understood it." I didn't even try to stop myself; I just leaned in the short distance and placed a lingering kiss on her lips. Jade leaned forward into our kiss. Our breaths mingled, our lips pressed together, our hearts beating as one, and I felt it. She was still mine.

"Ewww." Lex's disgusted groans cut through the moment. "I knew he wanted to kiss you! Gross, Mom!"

"Shit," Jade whispered into my lips, then pulled away and recoiled entirely.

"I know, you were right. I should've listened. It was super gross, Lex." She pushed up from the rock and wiped dirt from her dress. "Well, you ready to go, kiddo?" she squeaked out.

"Yeah." Lex stayed in place, studying us, deliberating about something. "I've never seen you kiss a boy before. I've never even seen you hold one's hand, and I know that people do that when they like each other."

I stared at Jade, who kept her eyes locked on Lex as she subtly shook her head. "Well, I haven't met anyone good enough for us yet."

That was the wrong choice of words because Lex pointed to me. "But he is?"

"What? No! I mean, he is good enough for someone, but I don't—Well, we don't." Lex screwed her face up tight. "Lex, honey, Bram is good, but he's just my friend. That was a friend's kiss. We don't like each other like that."

"Okay." She shrugged her good arm, but her tone was skeptical. "I'm ready to go." Then she whipped around and skipped back in the direction of the truck.

"Great recovery, babe," I teased, as we both stood up.

Jade shoved me. "You shouldn't have kissed me."

I put my arm around her shoulder and leaned in. "You kissed me back, Jadey." I whispered softly into her ear, "And I think you liked it."

"Yeah, well, you always did think too highly of yourself, Taylor."

I let my arm slide from her shoulders to her waist. And Jade didn't say a single word. I grabbed onto her hip and pulled her in. "This isn't over, baby, not by a long shot. I don't want to be your friend."

She let out a sigh and said nothing else as her body melted into mine. And I meant every word that I said. I let her get away once, but it wasn't happening again.

Chapter 5

Jade

"You did *what?*" Evie's dark brown eyes were centered on me, scrutinizing my every expression.

Over dinner, my little loud-mouth Lex raved about our time at the lake with Bram, making sure to note that "Mommy's old friend" bought us ice cream. I'd hoped that it would end there, but I should've known better, because Lex was a talker and when she talked, she left no stone unturned, covering every inane, and not so inane, detail. She capped it off with gagging and squeezing her face together while laying it out for Evie.

"And then they kissed! It was so disgusting, and I told Mom that she shouldn't be kissing boys because they are gross." To which Evie craned her neck toward me, lips pursed, eyebrows raised.

"Oh, really?" She asked and then let it go. And I knew that we would be talking about it later—that later being as soon as Lex was in bed.

Now Evie was intent on finding out exactly what, because she already knew the who, had happened between me and Bram. I handed her a glass of wine and we moved to the kitchen, away from any listening ears in the bedroom down the hall. My apartment was much smaller than the house Evie and I had shared in Charlotte, and thankfully, this was only temporary.

I sighed and swirled the glass of wine in my hand. "He's like my Achilles heel, Vee. He always has been, since I was a kid. And today proved that nothing has changed. I'm still stupid. And you know what?" I took a sip and sighed out a long breath. "This is the precise reason that I never came back in all these years." I slapped my hand over my face and hung my head. "I thought that I'd be stronger this time, but I swear, one look from him and I'm that foolish girl all over again. Shit, Vee, how the hell am I going to live in this town with him?"

Vee opened her mouth, but I wasn't finished. "Oh, and get this! After he kissed me, you know what he told me? He said, 'I don't want to be your friend.'" I did my best impression of his deep, sexy voice.

Evie scoffed and jerked her head back. "Rude."

"No." I let out a frustrated breath. "It wasn't rude, Vee, it was a warning. I'm pretty sure he was saying that he wants *more*."

Awareness dawned, and she pressed her lips together. "I mean, is that so bad? You two were in love, weren't you? And clearly, something is still between you."

She didn't get it. "Evie, *I* was in love. I was so irrationally in love with that man that I didn't even see it coming. But looking back, I should've known. There were times he was available and then times he would disappear for 'school stuff' and I just never questioned any of it." I shook my head, reminiscing over my own stupidity. "If I hadn't been so blinded by love, I would've seen it coming."

"That was a long time ago. Maybe he's chan—"

I threw a hand up to stop her. "I don't want to hear

that. I need to live my life here like he hasn't changed. And if by some stretch of the imagination he's different, it still doesn't matter. We came here for two reasons: for our business and for Lex. I didn't come here for him and he's nothing but a gorgeous, annoying distraction. I need to just put on the blinders and keep moving forward with the plan."

"Okay, but are you really going to be able to do that?" Evie tilted her head, her skepticism evident in her features. After all, she knew everything about Bram and me. But she also had seen me during that time. Hell, she'd helped me pick up the pieces after he left me in fragments.

"I have to do it," I told her, my tone decisive. "The thing that gets me now is that all these years later, he has the audacity to act like this. After all he's put me through. If we have to live in this town together, I can't deal with this possessive, confusing, back-and-forth bullshit that he should've grown out of by now."

I took a sip of my wine, the sweet Riesling a welcome contrast to the bitterness of this conversation.

"Then you need to set boundaries and you need to do it sooner rather than later." Evie's knowing eyes settled on me. "I know it's going to be difficult, but the sooner you talk to him and lay it all out, the easier it will be to draw that line."

I pressed my eyes shut and inhaled through my nose. "I know, you're right. But I just need to be sure first."

Evie jerked her head back. "Sure? But I thought you knew—"

"Yes, yes." I waved her off. "I know *that*. I just need more time to figure it all out without him in my space, confusing everything. I would never be able to forgive him if he hurt us, Vee. It would be the final straw."

She took a deep breath. "All right. So then, how do you propose to determine his staying power?"

That part, I really didn't know. I already demonstrated that I couldn't be around the man without getting sucked straight back into his vortex. But how would I figure him out without being around him?

"I have no clue. Any suggestions? At this point, all ideas are welcome."

She sipped her wine and stared into it, as if the answers to all my questions were held in it. If only. "Maybe you should just sleep with him and get it out of your system."

"What?" I asked, my eyes bugged out of my head at the mere suggestion of it. It was the actual worst idea she could have pitched. And not only was it terrible, but it also just flat out could not happen.

"Yeah, seriously. For one, that man is H-O-T *hot*. If I didn't know your history with him, I'd question your sanity for not jumping those bones asap. He's like living, breathing art, hun. Like one of those Greek god sculptures come to life. All that muscle definition and chiseled abs." Her eyes widened in horror, and she threw her hand over her mouth. "But please tell me that his penis is not the size of one of those statues. I couldn't handle it!"

I put the glass to my mouth and peered meaningfully over the brim at her, my fluttering eyelashes telling her everything she needed to know.

"Oh?" Her brown eyes got even bigger, the golden rings around them sparkling with the knowledge as she clutched the shiny, black strands of hair at the side of her face. "How big are we talking? Like average? Above average? Obscenely big? Rearrange your insides big?" She leaned in, waiting for an answer.

I smirked, and Evie giggled. "Oh my god, that's the real reason you skipped town, isn't it? You were trying to get away from it!"

I rolled my eyes at her and giggled along, the alcohol finally loosening my tightly wound nerves leftover from the day.

"Well?" she asked, motioning for me to go on.

"I'm not telling you that!"

"Ugh. Blink once for average, twice for above average, thrice for obscenely big, and—"

I blinked three times and then smiled, my lips on the glass, preparing to gulp down some more liquid courage.

Evie squealed with delight and tossed her hands up. "Right, so like I said, *grind* him out of your system. That's the only way to go about it."

I snorted. "Vee! I can't. I would never be able to stop things with him once they got going. That's what landed me in Charlotte in the first place. He makes me stupid and reckless." I put up a hand, needing to make this point clear. "Trust me, I would love nothing more than to break the dry spell with him if it could be a one time thing. But it wouldn't be. We have way too much history for that."

"Okay…" She resigned with a sigh. "Well, that was my one good idea, so I don't know what else to tell you."

Since the good ideas weren't exactly flowing, I decided a shift in the conversation would be helpful in getting my mind off Bram, so I announced. "I got asked out on a date."

Evie's mouth fell open and when she gathered herself enough to speak, she asked, "What? By whom?"

I pursed my lips. The idea of being asked out

injecting a healthy, and needed, dose of confidence, during an otherwise confusing time. "A doctor that I met at the bar the other night." I flipped my hair. "He gave me his number," I said casually, before it dawned on me. "Wait! Maybe if I start dating again, that will set the boundary." I spouted my idea as if it was some profound epiphany, when really, it was just a logical conclusion.

Evie worked her lips back and forth. "That's actually not a bad idea. You'd be finally putting yourself out there *and* sending the message that you aren't available to Bram for *that*."

God, the very thought of dating made my stomach churn with nausea.

"You should call him then," Evie stated with finality. "Is he cute?"

"Yeah, he was cute," I answered as non-committal as one could possibly be.

"Soooo, not really then? Because that was pretty lackluster, J."

I laughed and threw out a hand. The thing was that Jake *was* cute. It was just that anyone stacked up against Bram was never going to measure up. "No, he was. He's not like some ripped model, but—"

She cut me off. "Got it. So what you're saying is that he's not Bram."

I rolled my head, trying to ease the tension and think before I answered, "No, what I'm saying is that he isn't exactly my type." It was a stupid thing to say because what was the type of someone who had barely dated? Oh, I knew what my type was. Sandy blond hair, blue eyes, ripped body, and an easy-going attitude that made everything feel right. I shook off thoughts of Bram and powered through. "*But* he is a cute doctor. A little polished for my taste, but do I really even have taste anymore?" What a lie. It was a lie that, by the dead pan look on Evie's face, I could tell she wasn't buying.

"Honestly J." Evie shrugged. "I think it's a good second place idea. Clearly in first place is my idea of jumping Bram out of your system. But, if you are hard-pressed for a plan B, I guess going on a date with a cute doctor works."

And I was definitely going with plan B, because being with Bram in any way other than friends or acquaintances was not *ever* going to happen again. Today was the last day.

****

I tossed and turned in bed that night, unable to close my eyes without seeing his face or imagining his hands roaming my body, without feeling his soft lips back on mine. I groaned and rolled over toward the end table where my phone sat. I needed a distraction, and if anything would get my mind off Bram, the handsome, hung hero from my new favorite romance series, could get the job done.

I had just unlocked my phone when an incoming text caught me off guard. I startled, jumping and dropping the phone on my face.

"Fuck!"

I rubbed the spot on my forehead as I swiped the screen, fully expecting to find a text about some discount from one of the many store distribution lists I was somehow signed up for.

Unknown—*Are you awake?*—

Oh great, a "U Up" text meant for someone else. Well, at least whoever used to have this number was getting laid.

Me—*I think you have the wrong number.*—

I watched as the text bubbles appeared and disappeared, until another text came in.

Unknown—*Is this a spicy red head with lips that I haven't stopped thinking about all day?*—

I stilled, staring at the words on my screen, re-reading them several times while my heart pounded in my chest at the very notion that it could be him. But how? How the hell could he have gotten my number? I tossed the phone to the foot of the bed like it was on fire. Then I stared at it like it was going to get up and attack me if I wasn't too careful. My phone pinged. I blinked, unable to do anything but observe the hunk of plastic in horror. It pinged again and again. I pressed my eyes shut, knowing that I needed to answer this, draw a line, and then go to bed.

Bram—*Jadey?*—

Bram—*I know it's you*—

Bram—*Please answer me*—

Damn. I tapped out the question, because I needed to know:

Me—*How did you get my number?*—

Bram—*might have called myself from your phone when you were getting ice cream with Lex <smiley face emoji>*—

I unsuccessfully fought a grin and then reveled in the moment, rolling around in the warmth I felt, like a dog in a pile of fall leaves. I squeezed my eyes shut and let the butterflies beat in my chest for just a little longer. When I was done, I reminded myself that this was Bram. The man could be hot and engaged, right before he would ice me out completely. And that did it. I snatched up my phone and tapped out my reply.

Me—*what do you want?*—

Bra—*mmm if I get to choose, I want you*—

I chuckled, marveling at how this man could make me feel this way with a few simple words. I knew I had to shut it down, so I made one final attempt.

Me—*K, well you can't have that, so good night then.*—

I thrust up my chin, proud of my frosty response to the man whose late-night attention was making my body all toasty and tingly.

Bram—*Mmmm, not so fast, Jadey. What are you doing?*—

Me—*I was trying to sleep*—

Bram—*Trying? Can't sleep, baby? Were you thinking of me?*—

I narrowed my eyes at the phone, hoping he could feel my annoyance somehow. Had I been thinking of him? Hell yes. Had I been obsessively replaying our short kiss over and over in my brain? Yeah, I had been. But he didn't need to know that.

Me—*Wow, someone is full of themselves. I could sleep if you would stop texting me*—

Bram—*When did I ever let you sleep?*—

Oh god. Oh my god. My clit pulsed at the thought and suddenly I was remembering quite clearly what the man used to do to me when he kept me up at night.

Me—*Stop. It's late and you are obviously horny. Go find a Katey. Night.*—

I tossed my phone again and threw my hands into my hair. Ugh, he was so frustrating.

Seconds later, my phone rang. I was going to let it go to voicemail, but my hands had a mind of their own and pulled me toward the phone. And I did what any sane, entirely over her ex, person would do—I dove like I was trying to catch the game-winning pass in the final ten seconds of the Super Bowl. I steadied my voice as I answered.

"What?" I asked, feigning irritation, when my heart was really saying, "yes, honey?"

"Jadey, you answered," he drew out in that sexy, always relaxed voice of his.

"Yes, well my phone was ringing, and you would have woken up Lex if I didn't answer," I lied.

"Shit. Sorry, babe."

I sighed, both loving and hating that he kept calling me that. "What do you want, Bram?"

"Wanna talk about that kiss today."

I fell back onto the bed and fought the curling of my toes at the memory of our kiss. "There isn't much to say. You kissed me and you shouldn't have. There, conversation had!"

He chuckled, his arrogance both irritating and endlessly sexy. "Mmmm, you leaned in, baby."

I scoffed at him. He was still the confident boy he always had been.

"I so did *not* lean in."

"Jadey." He groaned. "You leaned in so hard I thought you were going to fuse yourself to my lips."

I snort-laughed. "Shut-up!"

"Ay, I'm not complaining, babe. I'm only disappointed that it didn't last longer."

"Bram, what are you doing?" I asked, sobering up and forcing myself out of the moment, knowing that I could easily get snared in his charms if I wasn't careful.

Silence sat between us as I waited. I was pretty sure that he was about to hang up when he said to me, "Tell me what you're wearing, Jadey."

My mouth fell open. Yeah, he was definitely horny. I remembered this. It was years ago, but I knew his games. "Excuse me?"

"Shit, babe. Just tell me. Put a man outta his misery," he whined, and I enjoyed knowing I was still capable of torturing him.

I held the phone away as my smile spread, before I heaved out an annoyed breath and gave in. Just this one last time.

"Cheeky, black lace panties," I practically purred.

My heartbeat sped up as my fingers tingled with excitement. I hadn't forgotten that Bram was an ass man, specifically, my ass, even when I barely had one. Now, I really had one, and I didn't miss the opportunity to rub that fact in his face.

I heard his heavy breaths through the phone. "Jadey, baby. Fuck. What are you wearing on top?"

I answered immediately and truthfully. "Nothing."

Oh, this wasn't good. My body was getting worked up and my head was starting to feel fuzzy. I was forgetting everything important and only remembering what he could do to me.

"Don't. Don't do this to me," I begged, foolishly showing my hand, admitting to him how much power he still had over me.

"Do this to *you*? Are you insane, Jadey? Have you seen a mirror lately?" he asked, his voice deep.

"What?" I didn't want to let myself believe him. Or buy into his charms, which I knew came easy for him and cost nothing for him to give, to me or any other woman he wanted something from.

"You're a fucking knock-out, baby. You always

were, but now——" He released a throaty growl that woke up all my girly parts. "Remember how we managed while I was at school during the week?"

Did I remember? How could I forget? This man was capable in person. He had always been very in tune with my body. But over the phone, he was still a god. The things he said to me, well, they made me blush even now.

"Yeah," I pushed out breathily.

"You want that, Jadey? You want me to tell you how I want you to do it, babe?"

Oh hell, I was screwed, in more ways than one. *Say no, say no, say no.* "Yes," I whispered needily.

"Fuck, you're just as needy for me as you always were."

I whimpered, part disappointment in myself and part defeat in that I was totally helpless to stop this.

"Touch yourself, Jadey."

"Bram." God, I was pathetic. My attempts to restrain myself from him were feeble at best, non-existent at worst. Especially when he was reminding me what it felt like to be with him. Or any man, for that matter.

"Take your hand and put it between those gorgeous legs and tell me how wet you are for me."

I didn't really need to check. I already knew. The second I started thinking about Bram, it was like a torrential downpour in which my vagina was ready to single-handedly repopulate the earth.

"I am."

"I know you are, but I want to know how wet you are for me."

I inhaled and ran my finger along my pussy, and I was powerless to stop the moan that released from my throat.

"Fuck, Jadey. Are you doing it? Are you touching that wet pussy for me, baby?"

"I'm so wet, honey. My fingers are covered after barely even touching the outside of my pussy."

I heard a soft grunt and some rustling around.

"Did you take yourself out?" I asked, more brazen than just a few seconds ago. But the idea of Bram's hard cock being worked in his hand was enough to break any resolve I might've had.

"Yeah, baby. I'm stroking myself, thinking about how wet you are, thinking about my fingers inside of you, my mouth on those beautiful tits."

I mewled, completely losing control of the sounds coming from me. "More, tell me more." Oh lord, was I begging?

"Do you have a toy?

"What?"

"I want you to get your vibrator, Jadey."

"I, I don't—" I started to murmur.

"You trying to tell me that a single woman doesn't have a vibrator?" he asked, his tone skeptical. "You had a vibrator when we were together."

I turned toward the nightstand and opened the drawer.

"You getting it?" he pressed.

"Yes," I admitted, reaching in and grabbing onto the silken, purple toy that I had no problems locating blindly.

"Good girl."

His familiar words of praise sent shivers down my spine, and I fought the urge to slip right back into the dynamic we'd always had. Instead of answering, I whimpered.

Bram moaned before he gave me my instructions.

"Run it along the outside of your pussy, just like I'd run the tip of my cock along you to get myself wet before I slid inside."

I did as I was told, too overtaken by lust to give a damn that this was a terrible idea.

"Are you doing it?" he asked.

I croaked out a nearly inaudible "yes".

"Good," he said gently. "Now slide it inside of you, but do it slowly, Jadey."

I closed my eyes and started to push the vibrator inside of me, the entire time imagining Bram hovering over me, working himself in. I let out short gasps of pleasure, and Bram groaned, cursing quietly on the other end of the phone.

"Is it in?" he clipped, his voice now labored.

"Yes," I sighed out as my body melted into the bed.

"Are you thinking of me?" It sounded like a question, but I knew better. It was a command.

Yes, always, because it's only ever been you. The foolish words were at the tip of my tongue, but I still had some presence of mind to hold myself back. "Mmhmm." I let the sound vibrate past my lips.

"Now start fucking yourself with it, but don't touch your clit yet," he demanded, then growled. "Goddamnit, Jade, I should be the one making you feel this good right now."

"You are," I told him in a moment of weakness.

I wasn't sure how I knew he was smiling, but I just felt it. That irresistible smile that knocked the wind right out of me.

I moved my hips, taking the toy, just like he told me to.

"Are you stroking yourself?" I asked and instantly

110

knew that, at least tonight, I was done for. I couldn't believe the words that had just come out of my mouth.

"You know I am, Jadey. Now give me that filthy little mouth." His voice was deep and his tone bossy. This was the Bram that no one, except for me, ever saw. I used to tease him, joking that he was the horny version of Dr. Jekyl and Mr. Hyde.

"You want this mouth wrapped around your cock, honey? This tongue licking up and down your balls and sucking you until you come down my throat." I had officially lost the battle. I'd convinced myself that I'd live to fight another day, but what was the harm in surrendering to him just this once?

"Oh yeah, fuck yeah. You want to taste me again, don't you baby?" His voice was throaty and strained and I could tell he was getting closer.

"Ye-Yes!" I stammered. "I want that so badly."

"Play with your clit and if you keep it up with that dirty mouth, maybe I'll let you come."

His challenge urged me on. After all this, I needed to come and would do anything to get it. "I wish you were here next to me so I could watch you stroke your huge cock until you came all over me."

He released a primal snarl that made my limbs wobbly and my pussy clench. "Fuck," he clipped. "Baby, if I were there, I'd be inside of that sweet mouth and then that tight little pussy."

"Bram!" I begged.

"Fuck yourself faster, Jadey. I want you to come now."

"Okay," I whined, writhing on the bed, my body ready to give in to the pleasure that was building.

"You close?" Bram's voice was a quiet grunt,

intermittent as he heaved breaths in and out.

"I'm so close!" I told him, undulating my hips faster, ready to let go. "Tell me what you look like right now." I let the words roll off my tongue. I was too far gone to be horrified by myself.

"I'm completely naked, holding my cock in my hand and the only thing I can think about is getting back inside of that perfect body. Spreading those gorgeous legs and plunging back in. Feeling that tight, wet cunt around my dick, thrusting in and out until I feel you come around me. I look like a man who needs you, who's so fucking desperate for you, he'll take you any way he can get you."

I gasped at his words. Then I shattered. I lost it. He had driven me over the edge, and I let out soft whimpers as I rode through my orgasm.

"Fuck yeah, Jadey, that's my girl." Bram growled as his breathing became more rapid right before he let out a series of rough grunts that turned into moans before his breathing slowed.

We were both silent. I closed my eyes and tried to ignore the wise little voice in my head that was telling me just how moronic this was. I was foolish for blurring lines and I knew if I kept doing it, I would only make things more difficult in the end.

"You still there, Jadey?" he asked after a few seconds of silence.

"Yes, I'm still here," I told him, my voice soft and relaxed.

"You, um. Are you okay?"

I laughed, and it felt like my first real laugh since I got into town. "I think so."

Bram heaved out a breath. "Damn baby, I missed

that laugh."

It didn't hurt this time, hearing that. It felt good, and that almost scared me more. "Did you?"

"Yeah. A lot."

I had to admit, the man was convincing. But even if I could be convinced somehow, I didn't understand. *Then why did you let me go? Why did you make me go?*

"I missed you too." It was the most honest thing I'd said in a while, the most unguarded and vulnerable. Here I was, once again, being reckless with my own heart.

"I think we need to talk," he said, his voice hesitant.

"Not now." I wasn't ready to talk to him. I needed to settle and gather my thoughts before we discussed anything, past or future.

"No, not now. But soon?"

"Yeah, soon," I told him, knowing full well that soon was relative, and I was still putting off the conversation I'd been avoiding for years.

"I want to keep talking to you like this."

I giggled. "By talking, you mean having phone sex with me?"

He chuckled. "Well yeah, I'd like that too. But I mean, I want to get to know you again. Don't shut me out because I fucked up. I know I don't deserve a second chance, but I'm asking for one. You were my best friend and I know that I threw that away, but I want you back in my life. I'll take anything."

It wasn't the worst idea, and maybe it would be a good start. I needed to feel him out and get to know him again before dropping bombs.

"That would be good, I think."

"Yeah?" His voice hitched, like he was surprised.

"Yes. Maybe we should not do this again though," I

suggested, half-heartedly, still feeling the intoxicating effects of my orgasm.

"Hmm," he grumbled. "We can negotiate terms later. The important part is settled for now. We're talking."

I smiled, some part of me glad that he didn't fully concede to my suggestion. "Friends," I told him.

"Call it what you want, baby."

I leaned my head back to stare at the ceiling. Yeah, I was so screwed.

****

Bram—Nineteen years old

Jules paced the length of my room, agitated and pulling at his black hair, which he'd grown out. Next to his new tattoos, he was starting to look like the scary motherfucker that he was becoming, and I was starting to wonder if letting him in my house wasn't the most reckless shit I'd ever done.

He hadn't even called to tell me he was coming, and I hadn't seen him in weeks. School was over and miraculously he'd graduated with honors, though I didn't know how since he didn't seem to give one fuck about school. But Jules had always just breezed through everything without having to work hard.

"Dude, what the fuck is going on?" I asked, the anxiety of his sudden visit and demeanor starting to get to me.

Jules stopped and stared me dead in the eyes. "Where's my sister?"

I shrugged. "I don't know, maybe at Ren's house."

"Good." Jules shook his head. "He fucking wants her back."

I furrowed my brow. "What? Who wants who

back?"

"Nathan," he gritted out, the name falling off his tongue with so much disdain.

"He wants who back?" I asked, still not understanding what he was talking about.

"He wants Jade home." Jules's nostrils flared, and I was suddenly filled with a protective rage that I possessed when it came to her.

I didn't hesitate and I wouldn't back down. "Fuck no!" I charged toward Jules. The dude could destroy me, but I couldn't think straight when it came to Jade. I grabbed him by the collar and shoved him into the wall, my words were a warning and my voice a threat. "If you came here to get her, I'm gonna tell you right fucking now that you'll have to go through me." My jaw tensed and I leaned in. "And with the way I'm feeling right now, I don't see that ending in a friendly sit-down, bro."

There had been a time, not too long ago, when I was outmatched by the strength and size of the burly motherfucker. But this year, I'd grown a few inches and spent a ton of time bulking up. I had never been small or skinny, but now, I had the strength to stand up to him and the will to win if I needed to.

Jules glared and then grabbed my hands before peeling them off him. "Back up, Bram. I didn't come here to fight you, man." He pushed forward into me, his chest up against mine. "But I will if you get in my goddamn face again."

I didn't move from my spot. With Jules, I had to stand my ground. "She isn't going anywhere. But most of all, she isn't going back to that shithole with you."

His eyes flashed and his jaw ticked before he spoke through clenched teeth. "Back. Up."

I swallowed my pride, loosening my grip, and shoving myself off him and away, still ready to fight if necessary.

"It's not gonna be pretty if she doesn't get her ass back there. And I mean the kind of not pretty where you end up in a shallow grave and she'll end up wishing she was in one with you. Do you understand what I'm fucking saying?" Jules's words landed heavy on me and all I heard were threats. Threats to Jade.

My skin crawled and anger burned through every fiber of my being. "Why? What does he want with her there now? It's been years. He hasn't even wondered where she's been or why she was gone. What's changed?" I asked every question that came to me, trying to focus, but my head was spinning and my thoughts were pure chaos.

Jules scoffed. "He needs free labor. The business is growing, and he got a taste of money. And now, he wants to keep all that money."

I looked down at Jules's clothes—his dark designer jeans and a pair of expensive motorcycle boots. I jerked my chin up at him, the accusation clear in my tone. "How'd you get here, Jules? Didn't see your car pull up."

His jaw flexed and tightened. He smirked, a wicked smile that held anything but humor. "Harley."

I nodded. "That's what I thought. Seems like someone else got a taste for money too."

I didn't get to finish my tirade before Jules was in my face.

"Don't run your mouth about shit you don't understand, brother." His words were a warning. One that had no effect, because all I could think about was Jade.

We were at a stalemate, but I knew one thing—he wasn't getting Jade. She wasn't going to be exposed and tainted by them. Jade was pure and perfect and if I knew anything, it was that she needed protection from the stain of her family.

"I'll do it," I told him, hoping that would be enough. It had to be. They weren't getting her.

Jules's head recoiled back a full inch and then he stepped back, his expression grim.

"You'll give her up?" he asked.

"Fuck no," I told him with a finality that I hoped he understood.

Jules smiled and then laughed deviously, before his laughter died down and I watched his face turn to stone. "Christ! I knew you were banging my sister, you piece of shit!" He charged toward me, pulling his fist back to lay a solid blow.

I dodged to the right and blocked, but not good enough. Pain tore through the side of my face when his fist collided with my upper cheek. My vision blurred, and I lurched forward on unsteady legs.

"What the hell?" I staggered in place, wiping the back of my hand across my face. "You asshole!"

I propelled forward, at the same time I cranked my arm back and clenched my fist, catching Jules's eye fast and hard.

Jules grunted and barely flinched. The guy had a whole other gear and if I wasn't pissed, I would've been impressed.

He tackled me to the ground and hit my ribs with a quick jab. We were grappling, each of us trying to get the jump on the other, neither succeeding.

"I'm not doing anything wrong with your sister!

And don't you ever fucking talk about her that way again!"

I pushed with the words, gaining some leverage, and getting his back to the floor.

"Fucking liar, I know you're with her. You think I'm an idiot? You think I can't see you two?" Jules pushed back, his arm wrapping around my neck from behind. "You forget that I know you! And my sisters been staying at your house off and on for years and you couldn't respect it, just had to get your fill!"

Jules released me from the choke hold only to shove me onto the ground, slamming me flat on my back. I didn't care. I'd keep fighting for her until I was beaten senseless if I had to.

Jules pulled his fist back, and I readied myself for lights out when I heard her screech.

"Jules! Stop!"

Jade ran toward him, and he turned, his fist still in the air, ready to strike. Except instead of landing on its intended target, me, his fist clocked her right in the side of the head as he turned. He hadn't swung, but he was fast and strong, and she went down.

I bucked up under his hold and managed to push him so far off me that his back hit the table on the side of my couch.

"Fuck!" Jules cried out.

I scrambled to get to Jade who was sprawled out on the floor, looking dazed.

"Jadey, are you okay?" She blinked, her eyes unable to focus. "Hey, hey, focus on me, okay? You're okay, you're okay."

Jade blinked up at me again and curled her fingers into my arm.

"Wha-what's going on?" she stammered, her voice airy.

"Don't worry about that. Let's get you up and into the bed." I gently wrapped my arm underneath her back and helped her up to a sitting position. "You good? This make you dizzy?"

Jade shook her head, and I noticed her eyes were on Jules, who was sitting on the ground, his back still to the side table, staring at us. "I think I'm okay."

"All right, let's get you standing then." I got her to her feet and guided her toward the bed. "Lie down. I'm gonna get you some ice."

I helped her lay back and ran my fingers through her hair. She flinched at the contact and my jaw turned to granite.

Jade's breath hitched, and I felt his presence behind me. Her lip quivered.

"You need to come home, Jade," Jules told her.

I kept my eyes on her when I replied to him. "The fuck did I tell you, man? What she needs right now, is ice."

I heard Jules heavy exhale before I felt the air shift around us. "Come on, let's get her some ice. Please." He bit out the last word like it pained him. I knew he loved his sister and up until today, I believed he'd do anything to keep her safe. And even though I wanted him out of my house right then, I knew I had to deal with him.

I knelt down to Jade and brushed her hair back before brushing a soft kiss on her forehead. "Be right back with your ice, Jadey."

Jade nodded, but her eyes shifted to Jules and then back to me. Her voice was a whisper when she told me, "I don't want to go home."

I got in close and interlaced our fingers. "You are home."

Her eyes shifted back to Jules briefly. "He's pissed."

"Yeah. But he'll get over it. Now rest and I'll be right back." I pushed up to standing and motioned to Jules.

We were silent until we got downstairs to the kitchen. Finally, Jules spoke.

"You'll do it?" He tipped his head in the direction of the stairs. "For her?"

I clenched my teeth and jerked my chin up. "I'll do anything for her."

"There won't be money in it for you."

I laughed dryly. Was he for real? "If you think I want that dirty money you've been rolling around in for the last year, you'd be wrong, brother. I'll do it for Jade and that's it."

"Fine," he muttered and pulled out a paper from his wallet. "Friday night, meet me here."

He handed over the paper and I studied the address. It wasn't anywhere near Brooks Falls. I furrowed my brow, looking up at him and opening my mouth to pelt him with a thousand questions, but he shook his head at me.

"You're either in or not," he said.

I jerked my chin up at him, giving him my assurance that I was in.

"You'll have a room at the Sheridan on Peoria. It's about ten miles from that address. Jade stays at your house and she knows nothing; that's the deal."

My heart was pounding in my chest. I was about to get in deep and once I did, I couldn't go back. But it was her or me. And I knew that if given the choice, I'd always protect her. And if not given the choice, I'd die trying.

****

"Bro! There you are." Cameron threw his arms out, a grin plastered on his knowing face. I'd made the mistake of telling him about my kiss with Jade, like we were two gossiping teenage girls.

"You bring anyone?" he asked, his eyebrows raised with the question.

I shook my head, because I hadn't. I hadn't heard from Jade in two days, and I figured I should give the woman some space and time to come around. It hadn't been easy to not reach out, but after the way we left things, I knew she needed time to process everything.

Thankfully, it was Friday, and everyone was actually here.

"Hey, handsome!" Raven stood up and extended her arms toward me. "I haven't seen you in forever!"

"It's been two weeks, baby," Cameron put in with a soft chuckle.

"Well, it feels like longer! I'm not used to going so long without seeing you." Raven made her way over to me.

"Hey there, gorgeous." I pulled her into a hug. "How's that little monster of yours doing?"

Raven enlarged her eyes. "Oh, a monster, no doubt! Completely head over heels in love, but she's good."

My eyebrows shot up. "In love?"

Raven giggled, and I noticed Cameron grit his teeth behind her before he added, "Yup, in love with Jet's kid."

I turned to look beyond the bar at Jet and then back at Raven and Cameron. "Well, damn. Isn't she too young for that?"

The two of them answered simultaneously, except Raven cooed, "It's adorable!" And clapped her hands together, while Cameron grunted, "Fuck yeah she is."

I tried to stifle my laughter. "See you two are on the same page with all this."

She nudged back on Cameron, who was now standing behind her. "Aw honey, relax, they're just babies." Turning back to me, Raven squeezed her hands together in front of her face. "Seriously, it's the most adorable thing. She follows him everywhere he goes and one time I even caught her trying to kiss him. God, Bram, you should've seen his face!"

Cameron rolled his eyes and then wrapped his arms around his wife. "Yeah, baby, it's real cute now. Just wait till Nash starts liking those kisses. And he will. That *baby* of ours is a carbon copy of you, so when I'm not jumping up and down and squealing like a schoolgirl in love, it's because I'm bracing myself to fight those little shits off with a stick one day soon. Including Nash."

Raven laughed and waved him off. "It's not that soon honey, she's four, not fourteen. And Nash is *not* a little shit, he's an angel!"

"Yeah, he is now, but don't forget who his father is," Cameron said before he shot me a look.

We'd all grown up together, and these guys were like brothers to me. So, I knew Jet, and I couldn't help but agree. The man had been a player for most of his life, and after a brief stint of commitment, one where he got royally screwed over by Nash's mom, he went back to his playing ways.

"Nash is seven, babe. And Z is four, but she's got an eye for boys already. Fuck, and older boys at that. Fuck." Cameron dropped his head back, the realization hitting him.

I laughed, and then shut my mouth when he speared me with a glance.

"Well, *you're* older than me, honey, and we work," Raven said with some attitude.

Cameron nestled his face into the back of her neck and murmured, "That's because you're a saint and you put up with me until I got my shit together."

She smiled then she leaned back. "That's true."

"Jesus, you two, want me to ask Jet if you can use his office or you planning to procreate in front of everyone?"

Raven giggled, and Cameron squeezed her tighter. "Hmm, that could work. I don't see anyone else when she's around."

My body tightened unexpectedly as his words sunk in. I got it. I got it on a level I couldn't even admit. That had always been true for me and Jade before I went and messed it up. Now, standing here, watching how happy they were together, I felt a sense of loss so deep, it was like I had torn my own heart from my chest the day I let her go.

Regardless of the pain, Raven and Cameron gave me hope. After all they'd gone through, separate and together, they had come out stronger in the end. Maybe Jade and I had a chance after all.

"Hey guys." Mika, my long-time friend and coworker, walked up, her arm slung over her wife, Tessa's, shoulder.

"Yes, hi," Tessa greeted, then wasted no time launching right in. "So, Bram, I uh, heard you have a new old flame in town?"

"Is that what you heard?" I asked, grabbing a seat

while I glared at Cameron.

Cameron shrugged. "You know I tell my girl everything."

I glanced at Raven, who was biting her lip, her eyes shifted to the side. "Um yeah, and you know I tell *my* girl everything."

Then Tessa tossed her hair to the other side. "So, yeah, I also tell my fiancé everything. Point is, we *all* know, so spill the damn tea, Taylor!"

"There's nothing to spill. She's back. She's got a kid." I hated the way I felt about Jadey having a child. I liked the kid, she was adorable, but I couldn't stop the feelings of loss, knowing Jade and I should've been a family.

"Okay, buck-o. Nice try, but back all the way up, take a left at the stop sign, and then back up some more. I saw her." Tessa's eyes got wide, and she pressed her lips together.

Mika bit her lip and fixed her eyes at me. "Uh yeah, we both saw her, babe. And I don't want to be disrespectful to my girl, and it's not disrespect because we discussed this and came to a consensus, but your woman is smoking hot."

I laughed, the sound both amused and painful. "She's not my woman anymore. I made sure of that a long time ago."

The table fell silent, all eyes on me.

"Wow, what happened?" Raven asked.

"Baby," Cameron warned gently, wrapping a hand around the back of Ravens neck, squeezing lightly.

"Sorry." She shrunk back.

I shot her a half-hearted smile. As far as they needed to know, I was still happy-go-lucky, easy to be around

Bram, when I wasn't okay at all, and I had ceased being that guy long ago.

"It was a long time ago, Rave. She's got a kid, and clearly she had moved on at some point. And I, well, you all know what I've been up to." I waggled my eyebrows like a douche. A non-committed douche at that, because if the sympathetic faces of my friends told me anything, it was that they weren't buying my bullshit.

"Hey guys. Are you all drinking the usual tonight?" Jet thankfully interjected.

Everyone gave their yeses or nods. All except for me.

"Not tonight. I'll have a double bourbon."

Jet smirked. "That bad, huh?"

"What the fuck does that mean?" I asked with a bite to my tone, stepping right into the trap. Jade had always been a point of contention between Jet and me. For the few years that Jade and I had been stuck in some limbo between friends and lovers, Jet tried to ask her out on multiple occasions, despite my best efforts to warn him off.

"Sexy as fuck Jadey not giving you the time of day anymore?" he asked with a laugh that held just a bit of animosity. Fuckin' Jet. Yes, he had always had a thing for her, but it was the kind of thing that I knew was just an itch he wanted to scratch. Get a taste of her and then move on to the next. But my Jade wasn't like that, and she didn't deserve that shit either, so I had done everything to protect her from it. Yes, I wanted her to be mine, but really, if there was one guy in that school even close to good enough for her, then I would've backed off. But Jet? He and I had come to blows over her before.

I felt my neck heat at his mention of her. Sure, he

was allowed to talk about her, but not like that. "Jade to you, man. And *my* Jadey is just fine. Really good after we went to the lake and talked on the phone a few nights ago. She's probably slept like a baby since." I kept my gaze fixed on him. His jaw ticked; my fists tightened. And then, before I knew what was happening, the asshole burst out into laughter.

"Fuck, man! Did you guys see that?" he asked the group but didn't wait for their responses. "Whew, Bram, dude you got it bad for the woman. I get it, I do. You know I always wanted *Jade.*" Jet waved his hand like he was pushing something out of the way. "But she was always your girl, even when she wasn't. I see shit ain't changed. Does she know that she's yours still?" He jerked his head back and looked at me, laughter filling the space between his words.

"What does that mean?" I asked, the curiosity winning out over my good sense, knowing this conversation with Jet was going to a place I didn't want it to go.

"It means that I saw what I saw when she was here," Jet said, his eyes now hardened and the tone of his voice matched his words. If he wanted to have it out, we would.

"Jet, come on bro, let it go," Cameron chided him like he used to do. The man had been managing Jet and I since the beginning it seemed. He was two years older than us and captain of the football team, so he took it upon himself to sort our shit out in high school, when he was around.

Jet tossed up a hand. "Let it go? Fuck, he threw—"

I slammed my fists onto the tables and stood up, face to face with Jet. I'd had enough listening to him spew about things he had no clue about. And we were nearly matched in size with him being maybe an inch taller to my six foot three. But pound for pound, we were matched.

"Don't talk about shit you know nothing about, *bro*." I spoke slow and clipped the words out as if it pained me to produce them. And it did.

Jet's eyes blazed and his lips were curled in disgust. I felt a hand land on my arm, and I flinched, pulling back and looking to the side. Raven was staring up at me, her eyes soft and sympathetic.

"Sit down, honey. Let's all have a drink and relax, okay?" Her lips hitched to one side in a gentle smile that effectively calmed me. I let it unwind the anger that was spinning me up. Cameron was a lucky man. She was equal parts sugar and spice, not to mention tough as nails and resilient too. And I trusted Raven. When she finally came fully into our circle, she and I had become close. The woman was like a sister to me. So when she gave me advice, I listened.

I ran my tongue along my teeth, trying to work out the rage, that, if I was being honest with myself, had nothing to do with Jet. He wasn't a threat to me and Jadey. In fact, the biggest threat to a "Me and Jadey" had always been me.

"Double bourbon," I muttered as I sat back down.

"Yeah bro, I got you," Jet replied, his voice disarmed, before he walked away.

And that was it. No one brought Jade up for the rest of the night. I could feel tension and the questions lingering, but no one said a thing. They didn't know what had happened with us. Not even Jade knew. And no one would ever know until it was safe. Sure, it seemed like she was safe now, but I still had reservations. Nathan's network had been far-reaching and even though he stayed fully off police radar after what happened with Jules, I knew if he could've taken me out without consequence, he would've. But Nathan had always been a selfish fuck, so he let Jules go and continued with business. In fact, what happened with Jules had only made Nathan's business stronger. As selfish as he was, he had become a shrewd businessman, learning from it so he didn't make the same mistakes twice.

I was sitting at the table alone, all my friends having left for the dance floor, when I felt a slap on my shoulder.

"On me, man." A glass of bourbon was placed in front of me.

I scoffed, still annoyed. I didn't bother to look at him.

"Come on man, look at me. I'm sorry. That was way out of line."

I lifted my chin, motioning to a chair. I barely heard the scraping of the chair legs on the floor over the music before Jet sat down in it.

"I was just trying to give you hell, but I took it too far." His head hung, and he peered up at me, the sheepish look in his eyes taking their effect. I inhaled and let my muscles relax.

"Yep." I took a sip of the drink. "It's all good."

I could feel Jet's eyes on me. I was sure it didn't take much for him to see that all was not good.

"I hate dredging up the past when I know it's painful, but with the way you look right now and have looked since Jade got back into town, I'm guessing that shit has already been dredged. So, forgive me for asking, but what the hell happened with you two? One day you were searching for wedding rings and then next day she was gone."

I took another healthy sip of the bourbon. "I did what I had to do at the time," I told him, the memories of the past and the pain I'd carried, pushing up to the surface. I shifted, fighting the urge to run, just so these damn feelings would stay buried.

"Had to?" he asked, his eyebrows raised, and his voice pitched with a new curiosity.

I looked him in the eyes with intent. "Had to."

Jet dipped his head down and tried again. "I know you loved her, man."

I kept my eyes locked on his. "I did. Still do. Never stopped. Why do you think I've been single all these years? It sure as hell isn't because I can't get a woman to look my way. Never had that problem."

Jet grinned. "You always were an arrogant motherfucker."

I smiled and nodded, glad we had slipped back to the easy place we usually operated in with one another.

"What are you gonna do, now that she's back?"

"I don't know. She's got a kid, a fuckin' life that has nothing to do with me."

Jet scowled. "So the fuck what?" Jet also had a kid and a nightmare of an ex that had left them high and dry the moment Nash was born.

"Calm down, I didn't mean it like that. I meant that it's different now. Jadey's got responsibilities and priorities, other than my bullshit, and I need to be careful how I go about it." I let my head fall into my hands. "But fuck, man, I want her back. I want her back more than anything I've ever wanted, except when I wanted her in high school."

Jet was nodding slowly. "Can I give you some

advice, as a single parent?"

My head snapped up to him. I'd listen to any advice that was going to help me right now. "Please."

"You don't go in unless you plan to be all in. *Especially* if the father isn't involved. Jade's not looking for a fling, she's looking for a man that can boss up and help take care of a child. If you're not gonna stick or if you're gonna drag her through the ringer again, just don't even bother."

His words burned in my chest. Drag her through the ringer? What did he know? I inhaled a breath, knowing he was coming from a real place. Jet was a single parent and after Nash's mother left, Jet only had one real relationship to speak of. One that ended painfully for both Jet and Nash. After that, he didn't bring women home. So, I got what he was saying, even if it pissed me off.

"Thanks, man. That's good advice."

"Yeah, well, I'm a real Einstein until I gotta figure my own shit out. Just remember me one day when you're happy and I'm still a bitter bachelor hooking up with barflies just so my dick doesn't forget how to work."

I laughed. "That sounds like a real hardship."

Jet's face turned hard, and he focused his eyes on me. "It ain't real man, none of it. It feels great in the moment until you feel like crap afterward. But you already know this; you're no different from me."

It was true and sobering. In all these years since Jade had been gone, I hadn't had one real relationship. Sure, sex was fun, but it was also lonely and not a single woman had ever come close to stacking up against Jade.

"All right, I gotta get back to help Rachel. She's going to chop my balls off if I leave her alone back there for too long." Jet caught my gaze and jerked up his chin. "We good?"

I jerked my chin up, giving it right back to him. "Always, man."

When he left, I pulled out my phone and checked my messages. I was disappointed to find that I had one message from Sierra and nothing from Jade. I didn't understand what Sierra's deal was lately. We had always been casual, bi-annual, and non-committal, so I didn't understand why she was texting me all a sudden. Whatever the case, I needed to get some, so I tapped out a text.

Me—*Hey, wanna do a repeat of the other night?*—

Chapter 6

Jade

I was comfortable, sunken into the oversized couch cushions in our small apartment living room. I looked at my phone, a goofy smile spreading across my face. Everything had been going great. Priscilla, my number one client, had finally texted the official party date. Priscilla Valdez was infamous—in her small, ritzy circle—for her out-of-this-world, knock-your-socks-off, indulgent anniversary parties. And fortunately for us, she had the money to match her eccentricity.

But that wasn't the reason for the stupid smile. It should have been—future work, and high-profile work at that, was huge. But no. It was a text that I had woken up to from the man that I had gone to bed thinking about. I'd only opened the text about ten thousand times and wrote a response that I deleted every single time.

What was I supposed to say to that? "Hell yes, please talk me into a self-induced orgasm any night of the week!" Or maybe I could beg him to get his fine ass over here, crawl in my window and do it to me himself? Yeah, none of those were options. I had been checking about once every five minutes, side-eyeing my phone like it had something up its sleeve, sitting on the table, mocking me with that stupid text.

And I was immature. I had written back the most

preposterous and vulgar things as a joke just for me, right before I deleted them and tossed my phone back to the table. I nabbed my phone and opened the text.

Me—*I'll only do a repeat if this time I can sit on your face, so I don't have to see the face of, or hear the voice of, the man who destroyed my life while he brings me to an earth-crumbling orgasm.*—

Backspace, backspace, backspace.

Me—Oh, *I'd love a repeat. Can you still do that delicious thing with your tongue?*—

Delete, delete, delete.

Me—*Yes, but I'm super into tantric sex now, so I'll only let you fuck me in the presence of a shamanic facilitator from here on out.*—

I was proud of that one and was snickering at my phone when Lex startled me.

"Hey, Mom!"

"Shit!" I jumped, dropping the phone, and clutching at my chest like I was having a heart attack. Lex tilted her head to the side and popped her hip, her lips twisted to one side with an accusatorial look. I sighed. "Sorry, honey. I'll toss a dollar in the jar."

Lex gleamed; no doubt she was happy she had caught me saying a swear. "Whatchya doin', mommy?" Lex craned her neck, leaning over to catch a glimpse of my phone, which was now face up on the floor. The kid was smart and nosy, and I was sure she could sense that my energy was off.

I snatched my phone up and let out a breath. "I was just writing back to Priscilla. You remember her, right?" I didn't wait for her response. "Well guess what? She scheduled the party!" I was rambling, feeling guilty and hating that my own kid had caught me doing something naughty.

"Cool!" Lex hopped on one foot in place, back to her usual happy self. "What's the theme this year?"

"We don't know yet, but knowing her, it will be amazing." I threw my arms over my head and fell back dreamily onto the couch.

Lex giggled and hopped over to me. She looked somewhat sleepy still, and I knew she had been having a tough time sleeping since she broke her elbow.

"You want some breakfast, sweety?" I asked, running a hand through her hair, avoiding the knots that appeared in her hair after a long night of tossing and turning.

"Yeah." She twisted her lips thoughtfully before she caught my gaze. "Bacon and scrambled eggs?"

"Sure. Why don't you chill on the couch and watch some cartoons while I make breakfast," I told her as I pushed up from the couch, my body still feeling heavy with sleep.

"Okay, mommy." Lex burrowed further into the couch. Reaching behind her, I grabbed the faux fur throw that sat on the back of our couch and placed it over her before I pressed a kiss to her forehead. Lex grabbed the remote from the arm of the couch and flipped through some channels until she landed on something she liked.

I had laid the bacon strips on a pan and was mid-cracking eggs and deliberating on the past when my phone rang. I rushed to answer it, wiping egg from my fingers onto a dish rag. Anticipation sprung, knowing it was Priscilla finally calling with a theme; I didn't want to miss her call. I needed to prepare and start ordering supplies as soon as I found out, because the date was rapidly approaching. So fast that I knew if she didn't tell me soon, I'd have to drive to one of the nearby cities to purchase supplies in person.

I swiped the phone in a hurry. "Priscilla! I got the date, and we are so excited for the theme. Tell me, tell me, tell me!" I squealed unapologetically.

The call was silent, and I cursed the mountain cell reception. I had never once had trouble in the city.

"Shoot. Priscilla, can you hear me?"

"Ummm." The deep voice pierced me and sent a series of jolts up from my spine, straight through my brain, mushing it up along the way before it settled somewhere in my stomach, releasing butterflies and curling my toes. I swallowed and held the phone out to look, even if I already knew. *Heartbreaker.* I had saved Bram's information this morning after ignoring his text, and I couldn't bring myself to call him anything else. Besides, it was a good reminder of exactly who he was to me every time he texted or called. It was supposed to keep me in the right frame of mind, except when I was reading and rereading his text, I didn't even notice the name.

"Bram?"

"Yeah, baby." My heart clenched. He had always called me Jadey when we were friends. It was sweet, something that had just been ours. It wasn't until we had crossed that invisible line that he started calling me baby. And that one word made my heart stop, cutting off oxygen to my brain so I couldn't think straight.

"What do you want?" I asked him, trying to sound cold, but sounding breathy instead. Ugh, I was overheated. It was hot in here. I stood up to look at the thermostat. How in the hell was it sixty-eight degrees inside my apartment, but it felt like a damn sauna?

"Who's Priscilla, Jadey?" Bram asked, his voice sounding slow and cautious.

"Huh?" I replied and god, was I panting in his ear?

"Is that your, uh." He cleared his throat before he said quickly, "Tantric sex advisor or whatever?"

The air was sucked from my lungs, and I bent over, passively observing the bacon sizzling in the pan, unable to breathe.

"What?" I managed to choke out on a whisper.

I waited. A long pause was followed by a long exhale before Bram asked again, somehow sounding more uncomfortable than he did the first time. "Tantric sex shaman?"

What the hell had I done? My stomach dropped, and I was pretty sure my spirit left my body. And it left, not because of anything other than the fact that my spirit was too ashamed to be a part of me anymore. I could hardly blame it.

"What did you say?" I whispered into the phone as if I said it quietly enough, this conversation would cease to exist.

"Listen, I'm down for anything if it involves you, but I need to know what I'm getting myself into. I spent the last ten minutes researching tantric sex online and I'm not gonna lie, I'm a little frightened. But I think under the right circumstances, I could also be intrigued."

I finally found my voice. "Oh my god. Bram. That was not. I. I didn't mean to."

He continued on like I hadn't just stumbled my way through a non-explanation. "I'll be honest though, I'm not that big on the idea of sharing you with anyone, so if we could skip the tantric festivals, I'd appreciate it."

Scowling into the phone, I hissed, "I didn't mean to

send that to you."

Bram said nothing. I could feel his agitation through the phone. Instantly I realized my mistake.

"No, I—" I stammered, but he cut me off.

"Who did you mean to send that to, Jade?" He emphasized my name, and I couldn't help but feel annoyed that he hadn't called me Jadey or, even better, baby.

I sighed. Any explanation was going to be humiliating, but nothing could be more humiliating than Bram thinking I only had sex in front of a shaman. So, I braced and pushed out a breath.

"I meant that I was replying to your message, but I didn't mean to send that. I was just being silly. I was writing and deleting stupid replies to a *stupid* question and apparently, I accidentally sent the last one."

I felt bad. I shouldn't have told him it was stupid question because that was a lie. I liked the question. It had made me feel all sorts of things all morning. I half-expected him to hang up on me or at the very least dole out some guilt. But all I heard was chuckling.

"What are you laughing at?" I snapped.

"Babe," he said through hearty laughter. "You." He kept laughing as if it was the funniest thing when it was embarrassing.

"Stop, Bram!" My face had been warm with humiliation, but now it was hot with anger.

"You, Jadey, Jesus, you haven't changed a bit." His laughter became louder, and if he hadn't reverted back to calling me Jadey, I might've gotten even angrier. "You're still that childish Jadey who does crazy shit for her own entertainment."

"I was just—"

"Damn, you have no idea how relieved I am. I think my balls retracted reading about all that tantric stuff. I'm all for free expression, but please, I don't want to do it in front of anyone else but you," he said through tapering chuckles.

His fear, and also his willingness, finally hit me and I giggled a little, picturing a terrified Bram reading about tantric sex. Then I stopped. Wait, he was reading about tantric sex, thinking that's what he had to do just to hop back into bed with me. Now I was the one laughing.

"Oh my god!" I was trying to keep myself together, but once it hit, it hit hard, and it all spilled out. "You were really going to do that?" I snorted, and I didn't even care because this was hilarious. "Have you not gotten laid in a while, Taylor?"

"What?" he replied as I turned off the burner and slid the pan of bacon to the side.

I laughed freely. "I'm just saying, if you were willing to get it on in tantric style in front of a shaman, you must really need some playtime."

The phone got quiet. I was all a sudden nervous that I'd struck a chord. Then Bram shattered my brain and my heart and everything I thought I knew to be true.

"Jadey, I'd fuckin' do anything to get you back in my bed." Okay, that was nothing special, just a man wanting to get sex. I'd heard that a thousand times. Then he cut himself wide open, gutting me in the process. "Permanently." *Tick, tick... BOOM.*

"Bram." I forced his name out with an exhale.

"No, don't say it. Don't dash my hope, Jadey. I know what I did, and I know what I have to do now. I'm not giving up until you're mine again."

My head fell. Did I tell him that I had always been

his? That I'd never stopped being his? That I'd probably die alone because never in my life had I once met any man that could be what he was to me? No, I couldn't say any of it. It was too dangerous. I wouldn't put myself on the line. Instead, I said the only words that I could say, the only ones that would protect me from reliving that nightmare.

"I can't," I whispered. I wanted to. Oh, how I wanted to.

He was silent before I heard his deep breath, followed by a lighthearted, but somewhat defeated sounding, "Not even with a sex shaman?"

I puffed out a relieved breath of air and smiled into the phone, loving that this part of Bram had stayed intact after all these years. That part of him that could bring levity into even the most difficult situations. "That might be the only way," I teased.

He scoffed into the phone. "Okay. I won't push you; I'll never push you. But I'll be waiting for the moment you decide that you can. And when you do, gorgeous, I promise I'll be right fuckin' here waiting to treat you the way you deserve to be treated."

"I—" I began to say, but he cut me off, and thankfully, because I had nothing to say to that. I was speechless. Again.

"Have a good day," he said softly. "I'll talk to you later, baby."

"Bye," I replied, my voice monotone and lost to everything this man was making me feel again. But he had already hung up.

I drained the grease from the pan and finished making the eggs as I reviewed the conversation in my head. Bram wouldn't push me, and that was good. Why then, if it was so good, did it bother me so much? I wiped tears from my eyes as I plated bacon and eggs. Peeking my head out of the kitchen, I caught a glance of Lex watching TV in the living room. She was my everything and I couldn't forget that.

"I can't."

"I'll be waiting for the moment you decide that you can."

Bram and I weren't done, but I knew that if I was to get through this next part, I'd have to stick to my guns. And after the last few weeks back in Brooks Falls, I realized that was going to be tougher than I ever imagined.

****

Instead of texting Bram that week, I texted Jake and made plans with him. I needed to put something in the middle of us, something cute and charming. I'd been around Bram again for all a month and I was already falling back into old ways. Jake had replied almost instantly, asking me to dinner at *Antonio's*, the only semi-upscale place in town.

Dinner had gone a direction that I really hadn't planned for. Jake was worse than I expected, but I tried to overlook it. Renata had only good things to say about him, and at the very least, he seemed like a good pediatrician who had a passion for working with children. That was about all I could give him, despite knowing *all* there was to know about Dr. Jake Jacobs. I sat in the booth of the dim restaurant, sipping Chianti, pretending not to have completely lost interest as the man talked about himself roughly ninety percent of the time. The other ten percent, he was checking out our waitress or any other good-looking woman that happened to walk by. If they wanted him, they could have him, though I doubted they'd find any more pleasure in listening to this man talk about everything from his workout regimen to his daily eating habits than I did.

When dinner was over, I was more than ready to go home. Jake and I had zero spark, but I had a sneaking suspicion that he was the kind of guy who was so far up his own ass, I wasn't sure he could find a way out to recognize when a woman wasn't feeling him. I made a note to self that a great doctor was not mutually exclusive with a great date.

When the check finally came, I had to hold myself from jumping up and running out. It was Dutch treat, which was completely fine with me. I was a modern woman and although I had gone on only a few dates since Lex was born, I didn't mind paying my own way. The more I held my own, the less men thought I owed them.

"Come have a drink with me at Shea's." Jake tipped up one side of his mouth into what I guessed was supposed to be a sexy smirk.

"Oh." I was caught off guard as I stumbled for an excuse. "Well, it's late and I've got to get back to my daughter," I lied.

His eyes fixed on me, that cocky smirk now fully plastered on his face. "One drink. I want to hear more about you and your business. Please?"

I worked my lips back and forth and looked at my phone. I didn't believe for a second that he wanted to hear anything about me, but it was only eight thirty and if I went home this early, after my first date in years, I had a feeling that Evie would never let me hear the end of it. I could have a drink, squeeze out another hour with this guy, drive around for another half hour and then head home at ten. Ten o'clock was an acceptable time to end a date.

"Okay, yeah, a drink sounds fun," I lied again.

Jake took my hand in his and I couldn't help the sinking feeling that overwhelmed me when we touched. It wasn't right and my entire body protested. It felt like cheating, and I hated that after so many years, Bram still held this power over me. Why couldn't he have gotten ugly?

My skin was crawling at the contact, and that was more annoying than anything. Sure, Jake was gorgeous initially, but now, not so much. I could've dealt with the cockiness, sometimes that's even attractive. But a man who thinks he's a gift to womankind *and* has a wandering eye on the very first date? Yea, no thank you.

I sucked in a breath and tried my best to be in the present with Jake. It was only an hour; I could at least try to enjoy it. The weather was great, and we decided to walk from the restaurant to the bar.

We stepped into Shea's, which was loud and lively. A wave of emotion passed over me and it suddenly dawned on me—Jet had built this. The player boy from high school, who hadn't been interested in much more than chasing girls, had built a successful business. I grinned, reminding myself to tell Jet how proud I was of him when I saw him again.

My smile evaporated as realization hit and I scanned the room, searching the tables anxiously for any familiar faces, hoping to avoid one in particular. After what felt like a thorough search, I was grateful that I didn't see Bram. My shoulders, which had been locked up in a defensive posture, fell, and I relaxed.

"Let's find a table," Jake said as he squeezed my hand. "Whew, it's busy."

"Sure is." My skin crawled at his touch as I tried to make my voice heard over the noise in the bar. It was pointless. Jake pulled me through the crowd, and I didn't miss his eyes taking in all the cute girls surrounding us. I didn't really care, though; this was the last time I'd be intentionally seeing him.

We found a table in the back, and it wasn't until we got close that I noticed them. Him. Bram. My Bram. I jerked at my own ridiculous thoughts. He wasn't mine.

My body went rigid when I saw that he was talking to a beautiful blonde woman who had the body of Playboy Playmate and the face of a model. Everything in me wanted to run. I wasn't sure if I was thankful or hurt that he hadn't seemed to notice me, but I figured that if I kept my head down and focused on Jake, we could avoid any and all interaction. Except, since I was keeping my head down, I hadn't noticed that we were headed straight for Bram's table.

"Where are we going?" My voice was frantic as I pulled back on Jake's hand.

"There's an open table." He pointed to the table right next to Bram's group. "I wanna snag it."

Noooooo. I curtained my face with my hair, as if that would do anything to shield me from him. My hair was my most obvious trait. It was a stupid plan, and I proved that fact when the curtains fell away from my face and I saw Bram staring at me. No, actually, he wasn't staring at *me.* I looked down to where his eyes fell—my hand in Jakes. I yanked my hand away, pretending to lift my purse.

"Here we go," Jake said as he pulled out a seat for me.

I was stiff as I forced myself to sit in the chair Jake had pulled out for me. "Thank you." I shot him a half-hearted smile.

"Not a problem, sweetheart." He reached out and squeezed my waist. I flinched, wishing I could disintegrate into the atmosphere at that moment. "I'll grab the first round of drinks. What can I get you?"

I blinked up at him. The first round? This was going to be both my first and last drink. There would be no rounds.

"I'll just have red wine, whatever house wine they have. I'm gonna run to the restroom while you get drinks." I shot up, proud of myself for hatching a plan so quickly. If I was in the bathroom while he was getting drinks, then I didn't have to face Bram and his friends. I tossed my purse on the table and kept my eyes forward as I scurried to the back. I'd felt Bram's eyes on me, but I didn't look. The tension in my body dissolved with each step away from that table. I got to the hallway, just a few feet from the bathroom, when I stopped to throw my head back in a "why meeeee?" pose. And then, I heard it.

"Jadey." The stern voice skewered me from behind, and I lurched forward before stopping dead in my tracks.

Two large hands wrapped around my waist, and I melted, right before I was pulled back into the warmth and familiarity of his body. The back of me hit the wall that was his chest, and I closed my eyes at the feel of him. I fit into him too naturally. Too right. My brain had ceased all rational thought and my body, well, it just rested further into Bram. I knew right then that after all this time, he still owned me. And I felt myself giving in.

My chest heaved with the closeness, pressed up against him like this, not understanding how I felt both fantastic and terrified.

"What are you doing?" My voice was barely a whisper as I turned my head to the side.

His body hardened against me as he bent down and whispered into my ear, his tone harsh, "Are you on a date?"

"Date?" I asked breathlessly, fully lost to the tingles against my skin that were causing my whole body to shiver.

"Hmm," Bram hummed before he pushed my hair to the side and ran the tip of his nose along a path from my ear to my neck.

I trembled through the question. "What are you doing?" I asked as I leaned into his touch, my voice nothing more than a whimper.

"I asked if you're on a date, Jadey." His voice was softer this time, and his tender tone worked its way underneath my skin.

My chest heaved, and I lost control, unable to stop what I did next. I let my head fall back and moaned as I rolled my hips, pressing back into Bram like we were all alone and not in the bathroom hallway of a crowded bar.

His grip tightened on my hips, and he rocked forward, moving with me. I nearly cried out in ecstasy when I felt his hard cock rub against my ass as I ground, shamelessly seeking friction. And then, I lost all sense of space and time.

"I don't like it," he bit out through what sounded like gritted teeth.

I writhed in front of him, not understanding. "You

don't like this?" I purred suggestively as I pushed my ass back, riding his hard dick through his jeans, ignoring just how public we were.

"You know you're still mine, right?" he snarled, and the only thing I could remember of the past was the delicious way this man had always made me feel.

"Mmm," I moaned as his nose brushed up the side of my neck to my ear. I gasped, falling deeper, memories that should have been in the forefront of my mind, fading away as I gave myself over to him.

Bram's lips fell to my neck, and he murmured, "I don't like seeing you with another man." His words struck that injured place inside of me and I retorted, doing my best to sound angry, but falling completely short of it.

"Another man?" I mewled. "I'm hardly cheating on you. We haven't been together in years." I said it, even though I felt the exact opposite. I did feel like I was cheating on him. I had been faithful to him for all those years.

"I know, baby," he said, some of the passion in his tone now replaced with distress. "You don't think I realize what I gave up?" he asked right before he sucked my neck, deep and hard. "Doesn't make it any easier seeing you with someone else."

"*You're* with someone else, Bram," I snapped back.

He wasn't fazed by my accusation as he continued to work my neck, his hands having moved from my hips, one hand at my belly and one sliding up toward my breast. "I'm not with anyone."

"Sierra?" I asked, a pang of jealousy hitting me with the mention of her.

"What?" he asked, still lost in my hair, in my neck,

his hand now cupping my breast.

"Sierra, Bram," I hissed, beginning to return to my senses.

Bram scoffed. "Fuck, it's not like that, Jadey. We aren't together, we just—"

God, it shouldn't have hurt. I knew he liked to play around. I'd tortured myself by imagining him doing it way too many times over the years.

"Please, spare me the details of your hookups." I tried to loosen from his hold, but his hand splayed across my stomach and his grip tightened, keeping me locked to him. My fake attempt to break free was a feeble one, because I knew that if I really wanted to go, he'd let me. This was Bram, after all.

"I haven't touched anyone since you got here, Jadey," he clipped.

I turned my face toward him, my nose scrunched, and I barked bitterly, "Wow, you're like the master of self-restraint, you may as well join the priesthood. It's been a fucking month, try not touching anyone for nine goddamned years!"

I knew my mistake right away before I ever felt his posture straighten behind me. "What did you just say?" he asked, his voice low and demanding.

"Ex-Except for one person," I stuttered through the words, wishing I could rewind time and go back to the Jade who wasn't dry humping her high school sweetheart in a bathroom hallway. I shouldn't be telling him all this, the man was driving me crazy, and I was losing my wits.

"And this fuck you're with? He's gonna be the one that gets to touch you?" He leaned into me as if there were any space left between us.

I felt my defensive resurface and my tenacity return

when I sassed, "Would you like me to find a group of men for you to choose from? Maybe one of them could fuck me proper and break the dry spell."

"Jadey," he warned. "Stop it."

But I wasn't going to stop it. I was pissed. "God, I can't believe that after all these years, you haven't changed one bit! You don't want me, but you don't want anyone else to have me."

"Please." His voice broke, and I heard a plea in it. "I do, baby. I do want you. Fuck, I've always wanted you."

I couldn't believe how easily the lies rolled off his tongue. "Is that so?" I sneered, no longer able to conceal my bitterness.

"Yes." He answered immediately. "Nothing has changed. From the day we met to the day I admitted I was in love with you, to now. You've always been the most important person in my life."

I froze, trying to gather my thoughts while my heart pounded so hard I thought it might jump right out of my chest. I couldn't take it and arguing with him was getting me nowhere.

"Stop. Please, I can't do this with you. Just let me get back to my date," I begged, just wanting this to be over.

Bram turned me around slowly. With both hands, he moved my hair behind my ears and then placed his hands on my hips. I gasped. It was one thing feeling his touch, but looking into his eyes while he did, it did me in. He pushed gently until I moved, allowing him to walk me back to the wall. I stared up at him and watched as he looked me up and down until his eyes finally settled on my lips.

"You look beautiful," he told me. "You always do,

but tonight you're stunning."

And seconds later, Bram crashed his lips to mine, his hard body pressing me against the wall, his large hands gripping my hips, keeping me in place while he ground himself into me. I moaned into his mouth. And my foolish hands found his sides so I could grab ahold of his shirt and pull him closer to me.

He pulled away to whisper, "God, Jadey, I want you. I want you so fucking bad."

"Stop talking and just kiss me." I yanked him back to me.

And that's exactly what he did. His hands roamed the tamer parts of my body while people walked by, in and out of the bathroom. His lips were so soft, just how I remembered them. It felt like kissing him for the first time, but also like we had been doing this for years. And we had done it for years before he sent me away.

Sent me away. He *sent me away.* The thought bounced around in my brain like a pinball, back and forth, back and forth, until it knocked some damn sense into me. I placed my hands on his chest in a very uncompelling bid to make him stop. My body didn't have the will to really put up any kind of wall, not when his mouth was on mine, and he was reminding me of all the reasons why we had always been perfect together. He finally pulled away for breath.

"Stop," I said solemnly.

Bram stopped instantly and his eyes opened. His face fell as he leaned forward to rest his forehead on mine while I came back down to earth. Actually, I fell to earth with a thud, the reality of what I had just done crashed like a meteorite. I was on a date with another man. Granted, Jake wasn't someone I would see again, but that didn't make it okay for me to make out with my ex when I was still on a date.

"I don't want to stop, Jadey." Bram leaned in for the kill, but I turned my head to the side.

"Why do you do this to me?" I asked. It was pain that erupted, springing up from the deepest, most empty parts of me. The hollow parts that he once filled before he completely drained me. It was a real question, one I wanted answers to, eventually. But not here, not now.

I shook my head. "I don't know why you're holding on to me after all these years. You didn't want me then and you don't want me now. You—" I wanted to remind him how wrong he had been about me. I wanted him to know how much he hurt me and that the years I spent away were because he wanted it that way, only to come back so he could jerk me around again. Instead, I pushed him off me because he didn't deserve it. He hadn't earned my truth and my vulnerability.

Bram moved to the side, and I walked away as the familiar, crushing feeling of leaving him hit me. I'd done it before and I'd do it again, over and over, if that's what it took to finally be free of him. I did it when I left Brooks Falls and every day since when I didn't call him or go looking for him, beg him to take me back and see who I really am.

I fixed my hair and hoped that my face and makeup didn't give too much away.

When I got back to the table, the situation was far worse than I'd left it. Jake was sitting at the table with Cameron and his friends. They were chatting and laughing. Well, Jake was chatting and laughing, anyway. I figured that man could entertain himself for hours.

I walked up to the table, ready to announce my

departure, when I felt hands at my waist, that warm, hard body back behind me again. He hadn't even bothered to stagger our arrival. Cameron's eyes widened as he looked at my face, and then he looked to Bram, a knowing smirk forming on his face. I put a hand to my mouth as heat spread across my cheeks.

"Hey, sorry, there was a line. Everything okay?" I asked Jake, eager to find out why we had merged tables with Bram's clan.

"Yeah, everything's great," he replied without looking my way, seemingly unbothered that I had disappeared for ten minutes. "I was just meeting one of your childhood friends." Jake smiled and laughed. "Along with everyone else."

I nodded and smiled as politely as I could, despite how uncomfortable I was. I waved to the other people at the table. "Hi, I'm Jade."

Bram leaned down, tugging me into his chest. My body quivered at his touch, and I huffed out a disbelieving breath. He spoke into my ear. "Jadey, this is Raven, Cameron's wife." He pointed to the beautiful black-haired woman who sat at Cameron's side. Her smile was warm and genuine as she sent me a small wave while she bit her lip, her gaze shifting between my eyes and Bram's hands on my stomach.

"It's so nice to finally meet you, Jade." The woman smiled warmly, easing some of my anxiety. "I've heard a lot about you lately. Welcome back to Brooks Falls. I hope you're feeling a bit more settled now." She laughed.

Bram's hand traveled from my stomach to my waist to turn me slightly. I should've been worried about Jake's reaction to handsy Bram, but he was too busy checking out Raven's boobs to notice his date.

"This is Mika. She works with me and Cameron at the station. And that's her girlfriend, Tessa."

He pointed to the two women.

"Fiancé," replied Tessa, whom I recognized as the blonde Bram has been laughing with, said, as she gave me a little wave. The other woman was just as beautiful, with a row of sparkly white teeth behind full lips and a perfectly coifed faux hawk that looked like it had just been freshly barbered.

"Nice to meet you, Jade. Bram tells us you just got back into town," Mika said. The woman was masculine, and she definitely had an edge to her, but her attitude was warm and her words genuine.

"It's nice to meet you all, too. And yeah, I've been here a few weeks now," I answered.

"Come on, baby. Let's sit down." Bram urged me forward. I looked back and scowled, sure he couldn't have possibly said it louder. I also couldn't help but notice that my date had no freaking interest in me, something I would've been grateful for had he not been a great reason for me to escape the clutches of my handsy ex.

Bram ushered me over to the chair next to him and pulled out a chair, only to shove me in. Once I sat, Bram threw his arm behind my chair.

"So, Jade, I heard you live up on Nathan Greene's property?" Mika asked me with a curious and knowing expression. If she worked with Bram and Cameron, I was sure she knew *all* about my father.

"I don't live there right now, actually—" I was about to explain when Tessa cut in.

"Oh, no? It's a huge house, how come you aren't

living in it?"

"My father and I were very different people," I said with some hesitation and a little exhaustion that Nathan Greene was dead, yet still somehow at the forefront of my life. "We hadn't really spoken in years, so when he died I decided it would be best to start fresh."

"You aren't planning to live there?" Mika asked.

"Oh no, I am. I'm just not planning to live in *that* house," I elaborated.

Raven smiled and admitted, "I don't understand."

"Well, I actually, um." I struggled with the words. "I actually had it torn down."

Cameron's head shot up and he jerked his head back. "That's a multimillion-dollar house."

I snickered. "Yes, it *was* a two-million-dollar house. Now it's a worthless pile of rubble."

Everyone shifted, sitting up straighter in their seats, but it was Jake that spoke up.

"You tore down a two-million-dollar home?"

"Um, yes, I did. I—" But he didn't let me speak, which at this point did not surprise me.

"Why would you do that when you could've sold it?" He scoffed. "Geez, women sometimes, so emotional! Damn, Jade, I wish we had been together a few weeks ago, I would've talked you out of it."

I blinked. Women sometimes? Together? Ugh, just when I didn't think this guy could get much worse.

I felt Bram's hand, which had been behind my chair, scratch lightly up my neck. My skin tingled at the contact. He leaned in to whisper, "Where'd you find this asshole?"

I narrowed my eyes at him, even though he was right.

153

"You clearly don't know Jadey very well, but she was never money hungry," Bram added in, skewering Jake with a look. The man appeared to be oblivious to Bram's insults, so I spoke up.

"It wasn't mine to sell, and I never wanted it." I was My eyebrows raised, and I some semblance of normalcy, but between this unwanted conversation topic with complete strangers and Bram's hands on me again, where they belonged for the past nine years, I was barely holding it together.

"Two million dollars isn't pocket change," Cameron's fiancé, Raven, spoke, her voice calm and soothing. "You must have had a really important reason for giving that up. I can respect that."

My eyebrows raised, and I stared back at her, grateful for the lifeline. "I did. And now I'm building something on my family's land that my daughter and I can live in. Something less, um, opulent."

Tessa laughed. "You mean something that doesn't say 'I own two tigers and a slew of exotic reptiles?'"

Mika nudged her girlfriend. "Tess!" she chided. "That was rude."

But I chuckled, thankful that Tessa had lightened the conversation. "No, it's okay, really." I put a hand up. "It's true, my father had a very unusual style."

"So," Tessa jumped right back in. "What do you do that you can afford to tear down a two-million-dollar home?" I was learning that Tessa was a spitfire. And while I appreciated a forthright personality, in that moment, it was making me spill tea I preferred to keep bottled up.

"Yeah, I own a patisserie with my friend Evie, who also moved here with us. We had a store in Charlotte, and we sold it to move our business here." I tried to wrap up the conversation quickly, when Jake decided now was the time to prove he'd actually listened.

"Jade, you're leaving out the best part," Jake urged, and I felt my eyes inflame and my face burn. Why couldn't he have just kept ignoring me?

I felt Bram's wandering fingers on my neck, teasing between my skin and my hair, before weaving through a thick lock.

"What's the best part, Jadey?" Bram asked, tugging lightly at the strand. I squirmed in my seat, prickles of heat from Bram's hair foreplay crawling down my spine. I wanted him to stop, but also to keep going.

I laughed dryly, positive that I was wearing a scowl. "We moved here to be closer to L.A. because our clientele is primarily based out of there."

"She's a chef to the stars," Jake slurred. I looked briefly at his drink. A nearly empty glass of Amber liquid sat in front of him.

"Jadey." Bram turned to me. "Is all that true?" His voice was strained, and his expression unreadable.

I gave him a slight smile. "I'm a Pâtissier, not a chef. But yeah, that's the gist."

"You didn't say anything about that." He sounded injured, like I'd owed him my life story after all he'd put me through.

I scoffed and kept my voice low when I sassed my response. "Well between you telling me to leave town the day I arrived, and kissing me, I didn't have much time. And also, you never asked."

Suddenly, my chair was turned to face him and my knees were stuck between his. I stared at our entwined limbs in fascination as his legs squeezed mine, locking me in place.

I felt eyes on us, but when Bram wanted my attention, he got it. Unwaveringly and unfortunately. It was a force of nature that I had zero defense against.

"I don't want you to go, baby." His hands were at my waist, and he was pulling me closer. He had no respect for my date. "And I'd like to keep kissing you." He pulled me in, his legs fully enveloping mine. "But I also wanna know about your life." He was inches from my face. My breath hitched.

I snapped out of his trance when I heard the faint ringing of a phone and recognized my ringtone for Evie.

"I need to get that." I glared at Bram, and he let me go. I stood up and walked to my purse, which had been sitting next to Jake's feet. Jake hadn't noticed a thing. He was deep in conversation with Raven's and Tessa's boobs and Cameron and Mika were deep in telepathic conversation with each other, most likely planning the murder of my date.

When I was in Jake's line of sight, he reached out for me and pulled me to his lap, the smell of alcohol strong on his breath.

"Umm." I froze, my eyes shot to Bram, whose jaw had suddenly turned rock hard. I tried to wiggle out of his hold. "I need to get my phone. It's my friend calling, and she has my daughter."

"You're on a date," Jake said, slurring into my hair. I cringed and tried to pull away.

"Yes, but I still have a child and she always comes first," I answered, suddenly feeling the air shift from playful to awkward and maybe a little annoyed. Playfulness coming from Jake, awkwardness coming from everyone else at the table, except Bram, who was full of rage.

"Isn't she with your friend?" Jake asked.

I didn't have a chance to answer, because Bram was up from his seat and digging in my purse. He yanked out my phone, swiped the screen, and answered it. Yes, he answered *my* phone. And right as he did, he ripped Jake's arm off me and pulled me up to him. I was plastered to his side, his arm wrapped around my waist.

"Hello," he clipped, sounding pissed. And why was he answering my phone and being rude to my Evie?

I stared up at him, stunned and unable to move to take back my phone.

"No, this is Bram." He paused. "Yeah, she was. She isn't anymore or ever again." His eyes sliced to me. No, they sliced *through* me. Why did he look pissed at *me*? "I'm with her, what's going on?" He paused; his eyes were still trained on me. "Shit, okay. We'll be right there."

That snapped me out of it. My head shook, and I felt fear widen my eyes. "What? What's wrong? Is it Lex?" I grabbed his shirt and clenched it in my fists.

"Yeah, Jadey, she's got a really high fever. Your friend wants you to come home, she's not sure what to do."

Jake stood on wobbly legs. "I'll take you home."

Bram speared the man with one single look. "No." My Bram, who had always been so easy-going and sweet, until it came to me. "You're not driving her anywhere." Bram turned back to me and glared. "Jadey, you're coming with me. Say bye to your *date*."

When I didn't say anything out of pure shock, he spoke up again. "Fuck, John or whatever, she had a mediocre time on your date, and she won't be calling you again for another one." Then he let me go, grabbed my purse, and interlaced our fingers together before hauling me out of Shea's.

Chapter 7

Bram

It felt great having her back in my arms. Her hand wrapped tightly in mine. It was the way we should've been for years. I'd fucked up. Now, I was going to find a way to make it right.

Jade wrenched her arm away from me, her beautiful face bright red. "What are you doing?"

"I'm taking you home."

"I didn't ask for you to take me home. I was on a date, a freaking date, Bram!"

"Oh, please, quit with the bullshit. You know you didn't like that guy."

Her green eyes lit with that annoyance and fire she'd always reserved just for me. "*That* is none of your concern, nor is it the point." She stormed off confidently, her head held high, that perfect ass swaying side to side.

I grabbed her hand and pulled her with me in the opposite direction. "My truck is over here, baby."

Jade spun and moved in pace with me. "You can't just take over someone else's date. You can't waltz in and kiss me and touch me like you used to, but *better*, and then just extricate me from the date because you feel like it!"

She was pissed and clearly had forgotten how much I liked her sassy attitude. But I couldn't think of that because I heard only one thing.

"Better, huh?" I looked at her from the side of my eye.

"What?" she asked, sounding distracted.

"You said I touched you like I used to, but better."

Jade whipped her head to the side and screwed up her face. "I didn't say that."

"Yes, you actually did say that." I placed a hand on her back and urged her forward. "And I'd like to hear more about it."

She snorted and rolled her eyes at me, but I swore I saw the faintest hint of a smirk.

"Right here." I motioned to my truck. "Now get your ass in my truck where you belong."

Once we were in and moving, I asked again, "So better?"

She ignored my questioning and instead focused on the road ahead. "Take the first right on Allen street and then a left on Evergreen Lane. It's the apartments on the left."

I turned down the street, and Jade craned her neck up and pointed. "Stop here."

I stopped, and I watched her frantically jump out of the truck without even a glance back. She closed the door and did a mad dash up the stairs to an apartment on the second floor that I could see through the breezeway.

If she thought she was getting rid of me that easily, she was dead wrong. I parked the truck and found her apartment, knocking lightly on the door.

The door flung open and that same woman who was with Jade the first time I saw her, was standing at the entrance.

"You." That was all the woman said as she narrowed

her eyes at me. I hadn't noticed the first time I met her, but she was beautiful. Her long, black hair was thick and shiny and framed her delicate features.

Caught off guard by her brashness, I stammered. "I, I just wanted to check on Jade and Lex. I'm Bram, by the way." I extended my hand to her.

She looked at my hand, one side of her lip snarled up, before she looked back up at me. "I know who you are." She pursed her lips to look me up and down. I let my hand fall, realizing that this was not going to be an easy interaction. "I shouldn't let you in, but since you delivered Jade home safely, you may enter. But if you piss her off, I'll have no problem tossing your ass back out."

I put my hands up in surrender. "I promise, no pissing her off."

"Okay then. They're down the hall, third door to the right." She pointed in the direction before sighing, sounding reluctant, when she said, "And I'm Evie. You may as well know my name since I have a feeling you won't be going away anytime soon." She rolled her eyes, her demeanor straddling the line between exasperation and mirth.

And she was right about one thing; I wasn't going away. Not tonight, not ever.

"Nice to meet you, Evie." The name didn't ring one single bell, but I just couldn't shake the feeling that I'd seen her before. I shifted my attention down the hall. I didn't really need instructions on where to go, because I could hear Lex crying and groaning in pain. I rapped on the door with my knuckles.

"Come in." Jade's voice was mild and gentle. I pushed open the door slowly. Lex was halfway on Jade, who looked up at me, anxiety in her features.

"Mom, my body hurts." Lex adjusted, squirming and squeaking with each movement, effectively cutting my heart in two.

"I know pumpkin, but I need you to be still so I can take your temperature, okay?" Jade coaxed.

"It hurts, mommy," Lex whimpered, tears pouring down her cheeks. That was all it took for me to spring into action. I stepped in, not sure if now was the right time to insert myself into their lives. But seeing Jade struggle moved me to action.

"Hey, Lex," I said as I took a step forward. "Do you remember me from Sunshine's?"

"Mmhmm," she whimpered, her eyes still spilling over with tears. "You're Mom's kissing friend."

I tried to hold back my smile, and I knew I'd failed when I heard Jade snort. I kept my eyes on Lex.

"Yeah, that's right." I moved her hair from her face. "Your mom told me you weren't feeling very good tonight, so I came over to check on you."

Tears poured down her pale cheeks that were streaked with red.

"Can I make you a deal?" I continued.

She nodded, her copper hair unmoving and matted to her face, reminding me so much of a young Jade.

"How about this? If you let your mom check your temperature, I'll buy you a big ice cream cone with sprinkles and fudge and whip cream and a cherry by the Lake."

Her nose scrunched up, and I thought she was going to reject the deal, but instead she came back with, "Two scoops?"

Caught off guard, I chuckled at her negotiation and

then quickly agreed. I looked at Jade, who was staring at me, her face soft.

When she noticed me looking back, she immediately broke our gaze.

"Okay Lex, you let your mom lift you up just a little and I'm going to put the thermometer under your arm, all right?"

Lex looked like dead weight and when she tried to shift Lex upward, Jade floundered. I extended my arms. "Here, let me?"

Jade nodded and I reached out for Lex and when I made contact with her arm, I snapped my gaze to Jade. "Jesus, baby, she's burning up," I whispered.

Jade's lip quivered. I propped Lex up very slightly on her back, her head resting on my legs, hair spread out across my lap.

Jade ran her hand through Lex's hair, and lifted her daughter's arm to place the thermometer. I watched in horror as the number rapidly climbed. Jade and I looked at each other, the calm that I had been holding onto disappearing when I saw the final number. Jade looked just as panicked.

"I need to get her to the hospital, Bram." Her voice was an unnerved whisper. "That's too high; something's not right."

She was right. I wasn't a parent and didn't know the first thing about caring for a child, but I did know that a temperature of one-hundred and five was not good.

"All right, Jadey. I'll take you guys."

She didn't even bother to argue. She just stood up and bent down to lift Lex. I placed my hand around Jade's arm. "How about I get her, babe?"

Jade looked up at me, her expression falling with a

sigh. "Okay, yeah. Good idea."

I lifted Lex in my arms and the three of us made our way to my truck. As bad of a situation as it was, I knew this was right. This was where I belonged. Where I had always belonged. And this time, I wasn't going to fuck it up.

****

Bram—Nineteen years old

Jade kicked her feet up on my dash and stretched out her arms. She was a far cry from the day I met her—quiet and shy and afraid to move. Tonight, especially, she was all laughs and light-heartedness. Something was different with her. She was seventeen now and not exactly a little girl anymore. She was gorgeous, and I fucking hated that I wasn't at school to protect her from the guys that were circling her like sharks. I was just glad that Jet graduated with me and I didn't have to keep my damn eyes on him anymore.

"It's a nice night," she said, her green eyes closed. And thank fuck they were because I couldn't seem to keep my eyes off her mouth tonight. Her lips were glossy and seemed fuller than ever. I knew I should look away, but staring at Jade had become an inevitability every time I saw her.

"Yeah. A lot of people out here tonight." I used my head to motion to the truck parked about twenty feet away from us.

"Who is? Wait, is that *Jet's* truck?" She slapped her hand over her mouth like this shit was some kind of scandal when everyone knew Jet was up here with a new girl every week.

"Yeah kiddo, it's no big secret. Why do you think I kept him away from you?"

She scrunched her nose at me. "You know, I really hate when you call me that. I'm seventeen, not seven. And you're two years older than me, not exactly sugar daddy territory, Bram."

"I know," I told her just as I reached over and gave her knee a squeeze. She rolled her eyes at me and yanked her leg away. "I just like to piss you off."

"Oh yes, the thing you excel at the most." She smirked, tossing her hair to the side. "How's school, by the way?" Jade asked in that biting way she did when she was trying to get to me. "Are you actually learning anything in college or just chasing girls?"

"Mostly learning." I raised my eyebrows. "And babe, you know I never had to chase shit. The girls always came to me. Still do."

"You're a man-whore. I honestly don't know how we became friends."

"Aw, Jadey, don't be mad." I laughed and crossed my arms in front of my chest, resting them on my steering wheel, and twisting my face in some animated pout.

Jade reached out and pushed one of my elbows, causing the whole thing to collapse and in the process sending one elbow to whack the steering wheel. The truck horn went off, the sound carrying through the quiet space.

"Shit! You trying to get us kicked out of our spot?"

Jade snorted. "*Our* spot? Oh please, you're a spot slut and you know it!"

"I am not. This is actually our spot, right here." And it was. We came to this spot all the time to look at the stars, and I never brought anyone else up here.

She looked at me with that "bullshit" look. "Oh, so

you got me on a technicality. What do you move, like ten paces away from this spot when you bring your conquests up here?"

"Jade—" I started, but she cut me off with a laugh.

"Do you tell them that the ground they are standing on is holy ground that is so sacrosanct that it cannot be fucked upon?"

"Jadey—"

"Or are you like lightning? Like you never fuck in the same place twice?" She giggled maniacally.

"Jesus Jadey, stop. This is the last thing I want to talk to *you* about."

And I meant that. Jade and I had been friends, best friends even, but our friendship teetered on the edge whenever relationships with other people came up. So, we'd avoided talking about the people we were seeing.

"Why? You're acting like I don't know you, Bram Taylor. I've known you for three years now. I know your ways." She leaned her head back on the seat. "And besides, everyone still talks. Even though you don't live here, I know you've brought girls up to the lake recently. Not that I care, but I'm just letting you know that I know."

I hated that she had to hear about it, and I also didn't know why I cared so damn much. Jade and I weren't anything now, and we never had been. We never even talked about it, even though half the people of this town thought we were something. I didn't have friends that were girls, I had girlfriends or girl I fucked. That was just how it was. Except for Jade.

"Doesn't mean I want to talk to you about it! You and I have a different kind of friendship."

She crossed her arms and huffed an exasperated,

cute little sound. "Yea, one where you bang every hot woman on two legs, except for me, and I don't get to date anyone because of *you* and Jules."

I stilled at her words, wondering if I'd really just heard that right.

"What did you say?"

Jade threw her head back and whined, "Ugh, nothing! I'm just having a bad day and you and Jules are pissing me off."

"You're gonna have to elaborate, Jadey."

"It's nothing. Besides, you said it yourself. We aren't *that* kind of friends."

The implication set my nerves on alert, and I felt the blood rush to my head. I was protective of her. Fuck it, I was possessive of her. Jealous even, but I kept that shit at bay because I couldn't go there, knowing it would ruin everything. But now, hearing this made me forget all that and set me ablaze.

"Tell me," I said sternly.

Her eyes turned to me, and a smile teased at her lips before she crossed her arms in front of her chest, pushing her everything up and out. I glanced down, and she shook her head at me.

"You can't intimidate me with your bossy attitude. Anyway, it's not that big of a deal, and it's definitely not your business."

"Tell me, Jadey," I gritted out through my teeth.

"Not going to happen, so get over it," she quipped, inspecting her nails. I knew she was pretending she didn't care about the fact that she had found a way to get to me. As evil as she was, Jade was still a horrible liar, and I could see it written all over her face how much she was loving this.

"I'll tell you one more time. Just one more. Fucking tell me."

"What are you going to do if I don't? You can't make me tell you!"

I got out of my truck, stalked to the passenger side door, and yanked the door open to Jade's surprised face. Pulling her out, I tossed her over my shoulder and stomped down to the lake.

Jade slapped on my back and whisper-screamed, "Put me down, Bram!"

"Nope. Not until you tell me."

I walked toward the lake. I had no problem throwing her ass in and keeping her there until she broke. And she would break, she always did.

"You're gonna get tired of carrying me around, so fine, enjoy having my ass in your face until your arms fall off."

I scoffed at her, knowing getting tired of carrying her tiny ass around wasn't going to happen.

"Nah, it'll be much easier to manage you when we're in the water."

"You wouldn't!"

"I would, and I will if you don't open that mouth of yours and start talking."

"Ha, I bet you've used a modified version of that line here on several occasions. Something to the effect of, 'why don't you open that pretty mouth of yours and *stop* talking,'" she said on a snort that told me she was proud of herself. When I didn't respond, she continued, "You know, because blow jobs."

"Yeah Jadey, I know what you mean. The people two cars over know what you mean. Now cut the bullshit before I toss your ass in."

I stood on the edge of a large rock that hung over the side of the lake. It was a good jumping rock, one we frequented. She knew how easy it would be for me to throw her in from here.

"You won't do it!"

I hoisted her off my shoulders and into my arms, swinging back to get momentum, but she hung on tight to me.

"Okay, okay, okay! Please don't. I'll tell you, I'll tell you, geez."

I held onto her, waiting for her to spill.

"It's a boy," she blurted out abruptly. My ears burned when confirmed with what I'd already guessed.

"A boy?"

She threw her hands up. "Yes, a boy. A very, very cute boy."

"Do I know him?" My words were clipped because all I wanted to do was tear some high schooler apart.

"That doesn't matter."

So, I fucking knew him and yeah, I'd be getting the name.

"Oh, it matters, Jadey. When all the guys I know are douchebags, I can guarantee he won't be good enough for you."

She rolled her eyes and shifted in my arms. "You can't keep sheltering me from everything and everyone, especially now that you aren't at the school! In fact, now that you've graduated, I've gotten asked out more than once."

"The fuck?"

"Yeah, Bram. I get to experience life without you breathing down my neck all the time."

"Who is it?"

She pressed her lips together and shook her head. "Who?"

"No."

"Who the fuck is it?" I growled at her and it wasn't lost on me that I was absolutely out of line and it also wasn't lost on me that I didn't give a fuck. Jadey was mine to protect. She had been since the day we met.

"Bram," she stammered and sounded just as confused as I was.

"Tell me."

"Geez, it's Austin Bradford! There, are you happy?"

No, no, I was not happy in the least. I closed my eyes for just the briefest second, remembering that prick. He was a year younger than me and a year older than Jade. He was also on the football team, so I knew him. Bradford was a player and not just a player, but one who bragged in the locker rooms to anyone who'd listen. He was the worst kind of shit. No way was I going to let that happen.

"Did you sleep with him?"

"What?" Jade screeched, sounding rightfully incredulous. She wasn't easy, and I knew that. I didn't understand the way I was acting any more than she did, but I definitely needed to make sure she and Bradford never happened. "Oh my god, you better put me down. I told you what you wanted to know, so put me down so I can get out of here. This isn't funny anymore."

Jade squirmed in my arms, kicking and writhing until I had no choice but to set her on her feet or drop her on her ass. So, I set her down, but put my hands on her hips, keeping her firmly in place.

"Jadey, he talks in the locker room. He tells everyone everything about whatever girl he's with and which one gives the best head. Jesus, tell me you aren't one of those girls." I gripped her hips tighter, and she shifted underneath my hold.

"No, you jerk!" Jade shoved my shoulder with a palm. "I would have hoped that you knew me better than that! That's why I had such a bad day." Her face fell, and she shifted her feet. I loosened my grip on her.

"My friend Renata, well, her boyfriend is Cooper, the tight end on the varsity team this year." I knew Cooper. He was a good dude and a good player. "Cooper knew from Renata that Austin and I had been talking, so he told Renata that he heard Austin going off about some chick who gave him road head and then of course Renata asked me, which is how I found out that we aren't exclusive. That's why I had a shitty day, because yesterday I learned the guy I've been talking to for a month and sometimes making out with is getting what he really wanted from other girls."

There was a lot to be dealt with, and Bradford was the least of my worries. He was a dick who couldn't keep the reins on his dick, so Jadey was better off without him. But this making out business, now *that* got to me. My nostrils flared. The thing was, I was known as the chill one, the guy who was always easy-going and I was, except when it came to Jade.

"Why are you making out with him?"

She stuck her tongue in the side of her cheek and grinned. "Oh, come on, I know you don't swing that way, but you can acknowledge a hot guy when you see one. And Austin is hot. He's a playing jerk, but a hot one. And obviously he knows it." She flipped her hair to the side and bristled her shoulders a bit.

"You shouldn't be with a guy like him, Jadey."

She scoffed at me and rolled out of my grip, taking a few large steps until she had made it around me before beginning the trek back to my truck.

"Yeah, I know, I know. You care about me blah, blah, blah and you just want me to be happy blah, blah, blah which means I should be celibate for the rest of my life while everyone and their mothers are out their getting laid, blah, blah, blah." She threw her hands up in frustration as she stormed ahead.

"Shit, slow down."

"I just wanna go home, I'm tired," Jade snipped.

"Are you mad at me?"

She stopped and whirled around. I didn't read the anger in her eyes, but there was something there.

"No, I don't care about you right now." Fuck, that stung. "I'm *angry* that the first guy I liked that liked me back turned out to not even like me. And I'm *embarrassed* that everyone knows, including you. But most of all, I'm *tired* of being the girl who everyone thinks is just trash."

"That's not true, Jadey."

"Oh really? Is that why all the good guys are throwing themselves at me, begging for a chance to be my boyfriend? Oh wait, they aren't. I'm trash and everyone knows I'll always be that, so why bother?"

"Jadey." My voice crackled under her harsh words.

"Don't. You know it's true. Just take me home."

I grabbed onto her arms, trying to force her to look at me, but she cried out in pain and bowed over, falling to her knees. My heard sped, and I got down in front of her. "Shit, are you okay?"

She bent her neck back to look at me. Tears were pouring down her face. "Yes."

172

I spoke softly. "You're not. What's wrong?"

"It's nothing." She threw herself into my arms and I held her while she sobbed.

I spoke as gently as I could, realizing that she was in a fragile state. "It's something. Please, you know you can tell me anything."

Jade pushed off me and pulled up the long sleeves of her shirt. My heart stopped dead in my chest and my jaw ticked. Motherfucker. I was going to hurt someone. I looked at the deep bruises, then back at her, then back at her arms. My nostrils flared and rage filled every cell in my body.

I tried to steady my voice for her, but I was fucking livid. "Did Bradford do this?" I didn't care if that little shit was younger than me. I'd beat his ass and gladly get slapped with assault charges.

"No, god no. Austin's a dick, but not that kind of dick."

"Who then?" I felt my entire face flare, and I knew it was true when Jade flinched.

"I didn't know them."

"What?" I asked, fear crawling across my skin.

Jade shook her head and looked down. "I don't understand, Bram." Tears fell down her cheeks, and I lifted her, carefully carrying her back to my truck.

"Tell me," I demanded.

"I don't know who they are, only that they said they worked for Nathan and came to bring me a message."

My world as I knew it came to a crashing halt as I stared into Jade's sad eyes. She knew that Nathan was useless, she just didn't know why. But at the end of the day, he was still her father, and I knew it hurt her.

My own voice came out as a disbelieving whisper.

Not because I didn't believe her, but I couldn't believe it. "What happened? What did they say?"

Jade looked at the ground, tears dripping from her eyes. "They came to my school today and waited for me. They said that Nathan wanted me back home and when I refused to go with them, they got mad. The shorter one, he was young, like your age maybe. He grabbed onto me and told me that I better get back home." Jade wiped her tears and continued, "If there weren't so many people in the parking lot, who knows what they would've done."

I heard it all. I heard every word she said, but my mind was laser focused on one single fact. *Back home.* Not a chance in hell was she ever going back to that place, and I'd see to it.

I wiped a stray tear from her cheek, running my thumb along the soft skin.

"Why didn't you call me immediately, Jadey? This is shit that I need to know."

"You're away at college. You should be having the time of your life, not worrying about some kid back home who can't get her life together. I didn't wanna bother you with all of it. It's too much."

I hated the way she saw herself and the way she thought I saw her. I lifted her chin and locked eyes with her. "Some kid back home?" I asked. "No, you're my best friend and you do have your life together. You can't control what Nathan does."

Jade pushed out a short breath between tears. "I don't understand him. He never wanted me, not ever. And now? I don't get it. I haven't lived there for over a year. Why, after seventeen years, does he all of a sudden want me?"

My jaw tensed as my body seized. I wanted to tell

her, but I knew it would crush her, or worse, scare her. I couldn't tell her the truth. She'd never forgive me, and I was afraid she'd never recover knowing what she lost her family to.

"You're never going back there. I won't let it happen, okay?" I promised, and I meant it. I'd do whatever it took to keep her safe.

She looked up at me, fear flashing across her vulnerable face.

"Do you trust me that I'll take care of it?" I asked and waited a few seconds until Jade nodded her head.

Thirty minutes later, I had dropped Jade off at home and was face to face with Jules and two other guys who stood a few paces behind him.

"Go," he told them, his voice in command as it had always been. The shorter of the two kids handed Jules a set of keys, before they both scurried away like rats. Jules turned to me.

"Don't fuck this up, man. You fuck this up and you know who's gonna pay."

I glared at him. "They came for Jade today."

Jules's head jerked back, his brow furrowed. "Who came for her?"

Relieved to hear that he had nothing to do with it and he was holding up his end of the bargain, I relaxed a bit. "Nathan tried to bring Jade home today"

His jaw flexed as rage formed in his eyes. "I'll handle that shit."

I lifted my chin. "We had a deal. I work for you and she's left out of it."

"I said I'd fucking handle it."

I stared at him, needing more.

Finally, he relented. "Nathan's been unpredictable

lately, man. Paranoid and worried about bringing in too many people from the outside. He still has it in his head that Jade will somehow be loyal to him. I'll deal with him; I promise you that. I want her kept out of it as much, if not more, than you do."

"She's got bruises."

"What?" His eyes flashed.

"They handled her, man. Rough."

"Motherfucker." Jules shifted his gaze to the side, trying to hide his guilt, but I saw it in him. I recognized it because I was feeling it too. We'd both failed to protect her, and it couldn't happen again.

I angled to look inside the car I was to be driving. Jules caught my gaze. "You won't see anything in there. It's stashed somewhere. I have no clue either and I'm sure as shit not wanting to find out. All you gotta do is drive it down, drop it off, wait while they unload it, and then head back. It's that simple."

"Am I bringing anything back?" I asked, knowing the drill.

Jules gave one short shake of his head. "Don't know. And neither will you."

I inhaled deep and then looked at him. "What do we do about Jade?"

Jules ran his hand through his hair and focused on me, studying me carefully as he said the words. "She needs to be far the fuck away from here."

His words hit me like an unexpected blow. "The whole reason I'm here is to protect her and you're telling me that's not enough?"

Jules scoffed. "It was a great fuckin' plan, but he wants her back. Fuck, man, even if he didn't want her back, you're in this life now and that makes her in this life too. Your bullshit and all that comes with you belongs to Nathan now and whoever the fuck else is up there making decisions. And now she's fucking in it, because *you're* in it. You fuck up, she pays."

His words rang true, echoing over and over in my mind as I started the car. *You fuck up, she pays.* Fuck.

As I adjusted the mirror, I noticed a small piece of paper taped to it. I pulled it off, scanning the words over and over, then looked around, before turning back to read them again. My heart raced and my hands shook. I pulled open the glove compartment and found the recording equipment. I drove until I got halfway down the mountain, then stopped to turn it on.

Chapter 8

Jade

Bram swung the truck around into an empty space in my apartment lot. I looked over at him. His hair was a mess of short, thick, sandy blond tresses on top of his head, and his eyes were heavy and dark with circles. He was always achingly handsome, but in that moment regardless of how rough he looked, after everything he'd done the past few days, he was the most attractive he'd ever been.

As for me, I was positive I looked as exhausted as I felt—like I'd hardly slept in days. Not only had the past few days been emotionally taxing, but physically as well. My back was still aching from sleeping in a hard and unforgiving hospital chair, and my neck was begging for a soft pillow.

Lex had spent two days in the hospital being treated for septicemia, which the doctor said had been caused by a pressure infection from her cast. It had started on her skin and had migrated to her bloodstream. And if we hadn't acted fast, Lex could've had an amputation. Or worse.

I still hadn't fully processed the situation, but I knew that we had been lucky and that was what I needed to remember. We caught it quickly and the emergency room staff took it seriously, diagnosing her fast. I knew that they had saved her arm, and quite possibly, her life, so I concentrated on that, otherwise, I would completely, and entirely, lose my shit.

As for Lex, she had been a trooper throughout the entire process. And Bram had stayed the duration, only leaving our sides to get us coffee or do Lex's bidding. He had made the mistake of taking a picture of the gift shop and showing it to Lex to cheer her up. After that, she was all sweet smiles and lovey-dovey eyes with him, asking for candy from the huge Jellybean dispenser or stuffed animals from the shelf. And he didn't say no, not once.

I turned to look back at Lex, who was still sleeping in the backseat of Bram's truck, surrounded by gift shop stuffed animals, and wrapped in the princess blanket that Evie had brought for her.

I felt a squeeze on my hand and looked back at Bram, whose lips were hitched up to one side in a small, sleepy grin. He kept his hand on mine, something that felt both weird and perfectly natural.

"How you doing, Jadey?" he asked with another squeeze of my hand.

I took in a breath, knowing I was so out of touch with my emotions at this point that I couldn't begin to answer that question with clarity. But I did my best to respond.

"I'm alive." I paused. "I'm drained." I paused again and looked up at the ceiling of his truck before rolling my head back toward him. "And." I took a deep breath. "I'm glad you're with us."

Bram's eyes softened when he said, "Yeah, me too," before he gave my hand a slight shake and said, "Come on, Jadey, let's get inside."

It seemed like the right thing to do was to tell him to

go home and sleep. I knew he needed it and he'd already done more than enough. But I was also aware that I couldn't carry a sleeping Lex and all her stuff up two flights of stairs.

I bit my lip and peered up at him. "I could probably manage Lex, but—"

He shook his head at me, releasing my hand, only to brush a strand of unkempt hair from my face. "Stop. If you think I'm going to let you do that, you really haven't been paying attention."

I didn't bother to argue because there was nothing to argue about. Right then, I needed him and he was willing.

Bram carried a sleeping Lex with ease and when we got to my apartment, he placed her in bed so I could get her settled before stepping outside to make a quick call to Evie and give her the update.

She answered on the first ring. "Hey honey, how's Lex?" Evie had been going back and forth from the hospital daily, but she was also managing everything for our business, and I knew she had to be tired as well.

"She's good, asleep in bed. We just got home." I started to choke up, my mind suddenly going to the worst possible place. "God, Vee, she could've—" I bowed over, the weight of that reality crushing me. "What if she hadn't?"

"Oh Jade," Evie said quietly, her voice mellow and calm. "Don't do that, hun. There's no point in going down that road. Lex is okay now, isn't she?" she asked, and I knew she expected an answer, one I needed to hear more than she did.

I nodded at the phone, my lip quivering with the sudden emotion. "Yes," I croaked out, losing what little control I had on my mental state and finally releasing three days' worth of tears.

Evie soothed me and I heard the love in her voice more than I caught any of what she said.

"Vee, but what if? I have to tell him, I have to. God, could you imagine?" My thoughts were chaotic, and I was becoming frantic.

"Shh," Evie shushed me gently. "Okay, yes, you do have to do that. But how about right now, you focus on Lex? She's safe, she's home, and that's the only thing that matters today, right?" She paused briefly before asking with hesitance, "Is he still with you?"

I inhaled and looked over at the door, as if I could see him through it. "Yeah, he's here with us like he's been the whole time. Vee, he." My voice cracked and I let out a stifled cry. "He did everything for us. For Lex, especially."

I swore I felt her smile through the phone when her voice went even softer. "I'm glad to hear that and—" She stopped abruptly and suddenly I didn't feel the smiles anymore. "Be careful, honey. Be careful with your heart. You gotta do what you came here to do, but don't forget to take care of yourself in the process. From what you've told me, he's all in, and then suddenly, he's all out. You deserve better than that and so does Lex."

I sighed into the phone, her words bringing me back to reality. "Yeah, you're right, Vee." I stood up straighter, readying myself to go back in. "Hey, I gotta go."

"Oh Jade, don't be mad at me, please. You're my best friend. I'm just trying to protect you, that's all."

I knew she was right, but it had been a tough couple of days, and I had reached my limit on what I could handle. "I know you are, and I love you for that. I just can't even think about any of it right now. We'll talk more about this in a few days when I can absorb it all, but right now I need a huge glass of wine and a good night's sleep in an actual bed."

"Okay, you go do that," Evie said, but then went on. "Real quick, before you go, I want to remind you that I gotta head to the city tomorrow. I didn't want to burden you with it when you were at the hospital, but we were supposed to meet with some vendors, remember?"

I pressed my eyes closed. It was just one thing on top of the next, and I really did need a mental break. "Shit, I completely spaced. I'm so sorry, maybe we should reschedule."

"Nah, it's fine. I can handle it. You focus on Lex, and I'll take care of the vendors."

I didn't like the idea of leaving her hanging like this and I really hated missing out on business meetings, especially when I had important clients to worry about. "That's a long drive into the city alone, hun."

"Oh please, I'm a big girl. If you want, I'll set up a video call so you can be there. And besides, even if we rescheduled now and went later, I'm not sure you wanna schlepp Lex to the city after all she's been through. The girl needs to heal and rest."

She was right. I didn't want to drag Lex around on another long drive for a while and she really did need to take it easy while her body fully healed. I eyed the wall like it could give me the answers and cure my indecisiveness. "All right, are you sure you're sure?"

Evie laughed. "Girl, this is why people have business partners. I can't count how many times you've stepped in when I needed you. It will be just fine. I was just waiting for you to get home before I headed out so we could touch base."

"Thank you, Vee," I said, letting some of the tension in my shoulders go.

"No problem, sweety. I'll give you a call when I get there and we can talk about tomorrow's set-up and anything we need to discuss before the meeting, okay?"

I smiled into the phone. "Sounds good. Drive safe. Bye."

"Bye hun."

When I went back inside, Bram was hovering over my couch, folding the throw blanket.

I grinned at him, helpless to withstand his pull. "What are you doing, Taylor?" I asked, with some of my attitude returning.

Bram shifted from one foot to the next. "Taylor, huh? After everything we've been through." It was nothing more than a tease.

I scoffed and sent him a smirk before I looked down at myself. "I need a shower." I curled my lips, suddenly feeling the layer of filth that had formed over multiple showerless days.

Bram lifted an arm and pretended to sniff. "Yeah, same," he said with a grimace.

"Ew." I rolled my eyes and gave his arm a playful shove. "You're gross!"

"Yeah, but you like me that way," he joked, a cocky smirk plastered on his chiseled jaw that was now covered in stubble that made him look more effortlessly handsome than disheveled.

"Please, I hardly like you at all," I scoffed as I pushed his arm again, but this time, he caught my hand and pulled me in.

"Mmm, is that why you keep touching me?" he asked as my body liquified into him.

"Bram. His name escaped my lips in a whisper. It was somehow both emotionally charged and raw. It was exactly how I felt when I looked at him. Except now, that guard I'd kept up all these years was beginning to come down.

His grin grew larger and hungrier and through it, our eyes stayed locked. It was hot, but mostly, it had to end before I did something stupid.

Thinking on my feet, I broke eye contact. "You really do smell, honey."

I flinched, the shock of my own words hitting me as I felt his body jerk slightly against me. I tipped my head back to look at him. His eyes searched me, and he was no longer wearing a grin. Instead, his jaw was relaxed and his eyes glimmering. Those beautiful blue eyes that I could get lost in.

"Hmm," he hummed, the simple sound hitting places it had no business hitting. "Yeah, I need a shower and a change of clothes," he finished.

His suggestion landed on me like a lead balloon. The idea of him leaving was a most unwelcome thought, and I told myself that it was because I needed help. If I were being honest, I knew I could do this alone—I just didn't want to. Not when he was around, anyway.

"Evie had to go out of town," I blurted out, hoping that he would understand what I was asking without me having to say it.

"Oh, okay." Bram raised his eyebrows. "Is everything all right with her?"

I backed away from him and waved my hands in the air, trying to appear carefree, but my movements were wooden. "Oh yeah, she's fine, but we were supposed to have a meeting with some suppliers in San Francisco tomorrow. I can't go, because well, you know."

He nodded and pursed his lips, and I could almost hear the "okay, and?"

"See, the thing is," I continued rambling. "I really, really need a shower. And I know you do too, so you gotta go and you're free to leave whenever, it's just that—"

"Jadey, stop talking." Bram reached out and ran his hand through my hair, settling it on my shoulder before moving to grip my arm. He gave it a light shake. "I'm staying right here. You can shower first. I'll watch for Lex and jump in after you." His sweet demeanor vanished, and his arrogant attitude returned. "Unless you wanna—"

I didn't let him finish. I knew where he was going and I knew in my current state, I might just say yes. "I'll shower first." I narrowed my eyes at him, attempting to halt my descension into pure lust and stupidity.

"Hmm. Okay, where's your room?" I shifted my gaze to the door right across from us. Bram spun me toward the door. "All right then, go on Jadey. And take your time, okay? It's been a long week. You need to relax a little. I'm not going anywhere."

I couldn't argue it. I was beat and stressed to the max. "Are you sure?" I made one final attempt.

"Go," he commanded, "I told you; I'm not going anywhere.".

At his words, the stress of the last two days finally caught up to me. My frazzled nerves unwound, and I broke down.

"Hey, hey, Jadey. All right, all right, let it out, babe."

Bram pulled me back into him and if I melted before, this time I attached myself to him, my cheek pressed firmly against his broad chest.

And I knew that this wasn't just any old cry—it was an ugly one. But I didn't care. I needed it. And he let me have it, holding me until the tears subsided and I was more drained than before.

"Come here, baby." Bram pushed me away from his body and within seconds, I was scooped up from the ground and we were on the move. I tossed my arms around him and buried my face in his neck, the wetness of my tears now plastered to his skin.

He pushed open the bathroom door, and I squeezed tighter as we neared the shower. I didn't even want him to let me go. I would've been perfectly content if he'd walked into the shower like this and just let the water run over me. As long as I didn't have to let go.

"Babe? You wanna get in the shower?" He tried carefully, and unsuccessfully, to pull me off him off.

I sniffed in his chest and shook my head, now pouting like a child and not a grown woman with her own child. "I don't want to let go."

"You wanna take a shower though, don't you, baby?" he asked, treating me every bit the child I was acting.

I shook my head. "No."

"No?"

I shook my head again. "No."

Bram moved, and I heard the crinkle of the shower curtain before he squatted down, me still in his arms, and turned on the water.

"At this point, you have two choices." He was still speaking to me gently, and it did nothing but spur my immaturity on. I hadn't been cared for like this since, well, him, and it felt nice. "You can either stand up and get in the shower or I'll make you a bath, so you don't have to stand up."

I didn't even think when I responded. "Bath."

"Okay, baby." Bram knelt down again and plugged the bath before he asked, "You ready for me to set you down?"

"Yes," I huffed, loving every second of this attention.

When he set me down, I turned to face him and lifted my arms.

"Jadey?" he asked with more than a little hesitation. "What are you doing?"

I sighed impatiently, digging into this helpless little act. "Waiting," I replied, looking up at him.

Bram's nostrils flared, and he let out a groan. I was about to drop my arms, thinking if he thought this was a bad idea, it probably was. But before I could, my shirt was quickly pulled up and off me. He flung it to the floor, reached around behind me, and expertly unhooked my bra. It registered how easily he disrobed me. I knew what it meant, because I'd known him and I was sure he'd had plenty of bra removal practice in the years leading up to, and following, him and I. So much so, he could probably write the manual on it.

"Fuck," Bram grunted, and I looked up at him, but his eyes were directed away from me, his jaw tight and focused intently on my sink. "Is this part of my punishment?" he asked, turning toward my pants buttons, his lips curled in disgust like they had personally offended him.

"What?" I asked, not catching his meaning.

"Nothing," he gritted out as he gripped my hips and said in a low voice, "Hang on to me." I placed my arms around his neck.

Suddenly, I was feeling something much different, and I was no longer sure this was a good idea. Bram flicked the buttons of my jeans and ordered me to let go. I let go, and he shimmied my pants down, his head turned completely to the side. Bram ran his hand through his hair as I kicked off pants.

"You're gonna have to, you know." He flicked a hand out, motioning to my lower half. I held onto him with one arm and with my other hand, worked myself out of the underwear.

When I was free of all my clothes, he lifted me back up into his arms. But this time, his face was in my face. "Tell me how in the fuck is it that you got more beautiful?"

I didn't stop to think about what was next, I just acted. I moved the few inches in and pressed a kiss to his lips.

"You're gonna kill me, baby. If my dick doesn't explode right now, my head might just from looking at you. And then you wanna kiss? Fuck Jadey, a man can only handle so much."

I giggled, the first real laugh in days. "Okay, honey. Put me down, I'm good now. I'll get in the tub, and I'll be okay."

I couldn't help but feel a little proud at how pained he looked. I didn't want to torment him, but the fact that I could, felt great.

Bram closed his eyes briefly before opening them back up, setting me down, and then scanning my body up and down. I bit my lip, never one to be shy about nudity, and he knew that all too well.

"Thank Christ," he said with a harsh exhale. "Okay, yes, good, that's good. I'll order us some food and you take that bath."

He was still standing in front of me, staring, not moving a single step to leave. I giggled and then took a step toward him, already feeling so much lighter than I did just minutes ago. My emotions were presently whacked, but I still had possession of myself. So, I knew exactly what I was doing when I wrapped one hand around the back of his neck and pressed my naked body to his fully clothed one. Breathing against him, my chest rising and falling, my body tight against him.

Bram placed his hands on my shoulders and then slid them down along my side, his fingertips grazing my ribs until they landed on my hips, where he squeezed.

"Fucking perfect," he whispered, watching me watch him. Then, his hands drifted around and down to my ass, where he gripped hard, pulling me close. My lower half jerked into him, and I felt his hardness spear into me. Oh my.

"This ass, baby. Wanna bite it." He squeezed roughly. "Wanna lick it." He lifted slightly, and I gasped. "Wanna *fuck* it." He slapped it, his eyes full of fire as he held me.

His hands were back at my hips as he slowly pushed me away and spun me around. I leaned back into him, grinding my ass into the erection I could feel through his jeans. Wanton and, at the moment, brainless.

"Bath, baby, now," he growled in my ear, making no effort to push me away, but instead, he slid his hands around and up to my breasts. He grabbed two handfuls and groaned as I arched my back, pushing my breasts

189

into his hands.

"Now Jadey, before I do something you'll regret," he roared.

I placed my hands on top of his and maneuvered them down, down, down along my belly, to the boney spot of my hips. I arched again, pushing my ass back and leaning my head back onto his shoulder, right before I smiled, righted myself, and stepped away.

Looking back over my shoulder at him, I couldn't help but revel in the pained, barbaric look on his face. I didn't hide my delight as I sat down into the tub. So much for being careful with him.

****

The bath was glorious, and I was already feeling more alive.

Bram took a shower after me, carrying a duffle bag in with him. I stopped myself from thinking too hard about why he had an overnight bag just sitting in his truck. I didn't want to be mad and ruminate on the past. I'd had nine years of that and right now, I just wanted to be with him and forget the rest.

I took his dirty clothes and threw them in the wash with mine. It all felt so domestic, the way the younger me had envisioned our lives going.

Bram had ordered Chinese food from *Dumplings* and nothing felt better than crashing my butt on the couch in front of the TV with some Kung Pao Chicken from my old favorite Chinese restaurant.

"I can't believe this place still exists and I can't believe you remembered my order." I nudged him while tearing into the paper bag that held my food.

He didn't stop what he was doing when he said with a smile, "Are you kidding me? We ate here every week for three years and you never once tried anything else, babe."

I rolled my eyes with a grin. He wasn't wrong, they had the best kung pao. And even though he teased me endlessly for never diverging, I didn't care. Why would I when I already knew what I liked? I was reminiscing when he proceeded to demolish me with his next words.

"Besides, I never forgot a single thing about you, Jadey." He glanced over, a sweet half-smile spanning one side of his now shaven face.

I swallowed hard, wanting so badly to believe that the earnestness I saw in his eyes, and intention I heard in his voice, was genuine. I glanced away from him and fiddled with my chopsticks.

From my periphery, I saw his head fall. There was so much unspoken between us and so much I had to tell him, with no clue where to start. Or how.

We ate our food in silence for a bit, unanswered questions and broken promises settling between us. Things I didn't know if we should stir up.

After a few minutes of silence, I couldn't take it. "Want to put on a movie? I have a few boxes of DVDs."

"DVDs? You're living in the dark ages, Jadey. Aren't you streaming?"

Annoyed, I didn't even bother to look at him. "Of course. I just haven't had time to get everything set up on the TV. If you'd like to watch something on my phone, go right ahead," I challenged him.

Bram snickered and got up to sort through the boxes of movies. "Your movie game is lacking," he informed me.

I sighed and accepted it, knowing it was true. Most of my movies were for kids and the ones that weren't were romances. I listened to Bram's grunts of disapproval while he rummaged through the unpacked box of DVDs. Suddenly a warm smile spread across his face, and he looked up at me, presenting me with an old copy of Les Mis.

"I don't wanna watch this shit, but damn, baby, remember this?"

Remember? Was he serious? I only cried every single time I watched it at his house.

I laughed, a gnawing feeling of regret and nostalgia over all I'd had and lost, ate away at my stomach. "It's still my favorite and I still cry every single time Fantine makes her sacrifice for Cosette." I grinned at him, a playful warning. "Except now that I have a daughter, it's much, much worse. And even if by some miracle you wanted to watch it right now, I'd say no because I am not in any frame of mind to be thinking like that."

"Right." His eyes softened on me, before he went back to searching. "Ah, you have Troy, now we're talkin'. That's a good movie."

I shrugged. "Never seen it."

"You bought it and never watched it?" he asked.

"Ummm, not exactly." I looked away, not wanting to explain that the one guy I dated had left it at my place.

Bram's body went still, and his jaw tightened just as his fingers flexed around the DVD, the plastic cover crinkling under his touch. "A boyfriend." It was a statement, and a pissed one at that.

"Yes," I answered him, pursing my lips to the side and tilting my head. It was a challenge. The man had no right to be irritated that I had had a boyfriend in all these years. I scoffed and got up from the couch and snatched the movie from him. "Calm your tits it was a long, *long* time ago."

"Right after us?" he asked, his face still hard as stone.

It had been right after us, like near immediately after us. I'd been lonely and hurt, looking for anyone to fill that void he had left in me. And the guy I'd dated had been just that and nothing more. A cute douche who only ever gave me one good thing.

"Yes, right after us. Right after *you* ended us." I glared at him and kept my eyes fastened securely on him. I wasn't going to back down and let him make me feel guilty, not after what he'd done to me. "Let's just put the movie on," I suggested, wanting to avoid this argument.

"Fine." He glowered at me as I loaded the disc. The movie played, and we both relaxed, the air between us settling soon after.

Bram flicked his eyes at my food, which I hadn't touched since I'd sat back down. "Not hungry, baby?"

I sighed. "No, not really. Still kind of freaked about Lex, I guess."

Bram set his food to the side and laid across the length of the couch. "Come here." He stretched out his arms toward me.

I chewed on my lip, memories flooding my mind and feelings filling my body. "I don't know," I said weakly, ready to give in to him if he said one more word.

"Jadey, get your sweet ass over here."

An unsanctioned smile passed across my face, preventing me from even trying to feign annoyance. I wanted to be wrapped up in those arms, laying across his hard body, his hands on me. So, I let my body make the decision and I moved, nestling myself between his limbs. And oh my god, it was like coming home after a long trip. I melted into his body as my head fell back onto him. Bram wrapped his arms around my middle, and he pulled me closer, until I was nestled between his long, muscular legs. I rested into him, allowing myself to feel every available ridge and muscle.

We were halfway through the movie when my phone pinged with a text.

Evie—*Hey, just wanted to let you know that I'm checking into my hotel. Hope you're getting some rest. Give Lex a hug from me.*—

Bram pushed up to lean over my shoulder. "Evie?"

I turned my head to the side, in profile to him, so I could see his face. "Yeah, she's in San Francisco for the business I was telling you about. She got there safe."

"Mmmm." My head buzzed with the tickle of his hum against my temple. "That's good, baby," he breathed his words along my cheek. My whole body shivered with it.

"Yeah," I whispered.

Bram ran a hand from my arm, up to my shoulder and along my neck until his fingers were running through my hair, except instead of sifting through, he glided to the middle of my head and then fisted my hair in his hands. I gasped at the familiar contact. Using his grip on me, he pulled my head to the side, exposing my neck to him. My lips parted and my breathing increased.

"I need to, oh, god. I need to text Vee back."

Bram's lips were hovering just above the soft flesh of my neck when he whispered, the words sending gentle vibrations across my ski, "I won't stop you, Jadey."

I swallowed hard and tapped out a response while Bram's lips brushed lightly on my skin, softly kissing my neck.

Me—*I'm glad you made it safe. Let's talk in the morning before the things. Tired.*—

"Liar." Bram nipped my shoulder, sending tingles down my arm, and I let out a whimper.

"Should I have told her that I couldn't talk because my ex-boyfriend is doing things to me that are making it hard for me to focus?" I asked and then followed with an "Ouch!" I squirmed when Bram sunk his teeth into my collarbone, my head being jerked back with a little more force. I felt the gush of moisture in my panties and oh my god, he was going to destroy me.

"I don't like that term," Bram growled into my ear. And at the sound of his deep, rumbling voice, my pussy throbbed with desire.

I heaved out a response. "Wha—what term don't you like?" I played innocent.

He nipped at my ear and then used his grip in my hair to yank my head further back so it was resting on his shoulders. "Ex." He drew out the words, like there was filth on his tongue.

I let out an unbridled moan, so turned on that I couldn't hide it if I wanted to. My phone vibrated and pinged in my hands.

Evie—*Ummm… You seem to be busy. Are you busy with something? Or… someone?*—

Dang. I reread my unintelligible text and rolled my eyes. Evie wasn't stupid, and more than that, she knew my history with Bram. And now she'd seen him.

"Jesus, give me that," Bram grunted, annoyance lacing his words.

"No!" I protested, but it was pointless. In seconds, the phone was in Bram's hands and he was snapping a picture of us in whatever precarious position we were in.

Then he sent it. He *sent* it. To Evie.

My mouth fell open as I watched the blue line extend until the not safe for my best friend's eyes picture said "delivered." I stared at the picture in horror, Bram's hands still in my hair, my head back, my eyes heavy.

"What did you just do?" I squeaked, still locked in the same position.

"Getting rid of your friend. We're fucking busy and she needed to go away."

"I can't, I, I mean, you can't just. That was so. God, Bram, you're such a—"

"Baby." His mellow voice stood out in contrast to mine, and it caught me off guard. I quieted when he said, "I'm fuckin' busy back here, do you mind?"

I scowled at him as he tossed my phone away. Secretly, though, I was in absolute heaven having this version of Bram back in my life. Bossy, sexy, needy when it came to me and *only* me. At least that's what I had believed for the longest time and what I was choosing to believe in that moment.

"Turn around, Jadey, and wrap your legs around me," he bossed, his eyes intent on mine, and that face. Oh god, that face was the face I fell in love with and had been in love with since the first moment I saw him. "I need to get back inside of you. Tell me you don't want it, and I'll stop."

My heart plummeted from my chest at his words. And he knew it, he knew what he had said, and he'd done it on purpose. It was everything we were and everything we still should have been.

I turned toward him, doing as he said, giving in without so much as a show of a struggle. A smile played on my lips when I told him, "I don't think I'll be tapping twice tonight, honey."

And that was all it took. He surged off the couch, my ass in his hands, my legs instinctually wrapping around him as he lifted up, carrying me down the hall, with his lips pressed hard to mine.

****

Bram tossed me onto my bed and I hit with a bounce. He wasted no time in getting to me. And when his lips crashed against mine, I opened immediately. Our tongues explored—sucking, licking, discovering each other again.

I lifted the hem of his shirt, and he easily took the hint, pulling the thing off over his head as fast as he could. And God, he was a man. *All* man. His body with a shirt was painfully sexy, but without one, I could see that he was all sharp ridges and shredded muscles. This was delightfully new.

Bram yanked off my shirt and unsnapped my bra, my breasts completely exposed to him as he took me in. His breaths were ragged as he ran a hand up my belly to my breasts. A shiver rocked through me at his touch. All thoughts except ones of Bram left my head. His fingers found my nipple, and he lightly tugged, squeezing gently, before taking both my breasts in his hands. I arched into his touch; the feeling was so exquisite that all I could do was seek more.

When Bram's blue eyes found mine, I was near gone. When he grinned and lowered his face to my breasts and took my entire nipple in his mouth, I was finished. I whimpered at the sudden act, bucking my hips up into him.

"Baby," he said between sucks, not even lifting his head to look at me. "Look at this perfect body. You are so beautiful." He ran a hand from my calf up to my thigh. "Your soft skin feels so good to touch again." He moved his hand up, sliding it past my waist to the top of my belly. "And this sexy stomach, I could stare at it all night." He rubbed his thumb along the spot on my stomach before pressing a kiss on it. "And these tits," he growled, running his hand up further and cupping my breast. "How have you gotten more beautiful?" He asked the same question that I'd been wondering about him.

I pressed my eyes closed and smiled, giving him the truth. "I keep thinking the same thing about you."

"Fuck." He rolled his hips into me, the hardness pushing into my leg, completely winding me up.

Bram dipped his hands into the waistband of my sleep shorts, hooking his thumbs into my panties as well. And when he pulled down, he took everything with him, leaving me bare to him. I lay, staring up at him, allowing him to get reacquainted with my body. A body that had always belonged to him, even in our separation.

Bram ran a few fingers along my thigh, making a trail to the center of my thighs. And when he got there, he nudged them apart with his hands.

"Perfect," he said as he lazed a finger along the outside of my pussy, taunting me with his touch.

"Mmm," I moaned, the needy sound leaving my lips as I bucked up and toward his fingers, realizing suddenly how long it had been since I'd been touched by a man. Panic rose up in me and I grabbed Bram's hand.

"Bram, wait," I squeaked out.

He raised his eyebrows at me. "Wait or stop?"

I grinned, not wanting him to do either, but knowing I had to tell him.

"Just wait." I kept my hand on his.

"What is it, Jadey?" he asked with a lazy smile, his eyes half-shut and his hair mussed. I was in danger of forgetting any of what I wanted to say if I looked at him. I focused my gaze to the side, away from his eyes and definitely away from his body.

"I haven't done this in a really long time," I admitted, embarrassment creeping up my neck as little flashes of heat.

"Done what?" he asked, taking my jaw in his hand, and turning my face toward him.

I widened my eyes and gestured with my head, hoping that he would understand without me saying it. Bram just watched and waited.

I inhaled and held his gaze when I replied with a whisper.

"Sex."

Bram nodded, no reaction evident on his face. "Am I still waiting?" he asked, working his hand out of mine.

I shook my head and instantly his fingers slid just inside the entrance of my pussy. I let out a sharp gasp and ground into his fingers.

"What constitutes a long time, Jadey?" he asked, slowly working his fingers inside of me.

I didn't want him to know, but as humiliating as it was, he needed to understand what my life had been. But mostly, in the present moment, I really wanted him to be easy on me. I was terrified that I'd forgotten how to even move my body, to give someone else pleasure, and chances were, I was going to screw this up.

"Nine," I mumbled beneath my breath, my heart now pounding in my chest. I wasn't sure if it was the anxiety of intimacy or the admission of celibacy, but either way, if I didn't calm down, I was going to pass out.

"Nine what?" Bram asked with a shrug of one shoulder before he pressed his fingers deeper into me. I exhaled a shaky breath, the feel of him to exquisite, I could hardly process it. "Nine minutes?" He tweaked one side of his lips into a sexy smirk and looked up at me. I shook my head at him. Bram lowered his lips to my belly, and I felt the buzz of his "Hmm" rumble along the surface of my skin. I shivered.

"Nine days?" He looked up and asked on an annoyed growl, his eyes flashing with something dark. I bit my lip and gave a single head shake.

"Weeks?"

My shoulders fell as I finally spoke up with a "No".

Bram raised his eyebrows at me. "Ah. Months." He said it like it was a fact and a sad one at that. My face heated and I could feel the humiliation radiating through me. I could've crawled right under a rock and hid if I wasn't about to finally get laid.

"Nine months is a while, but nothing to be ashamed of." He dipped his head down, breaking contact and focusing back on the work he was doing with his fingers.

Reluctantly, I replied, "No, Bram." I pressed my eyes closed, wishing he would just understand. After all this time, he didn't get that he was still the only one I ever wanted. That if at any time he had come back to me, I'd have thrown myself at him, held on so tight that he'd have no choice but to never let me go. He had always been the only one.

"Jadey, what are you saying?" he asked with a tilt of his head.

"Years," I murmured. "It's been nine years."

That stopped him dead. Bram pulled his hands, his

oh so capable hands, away from me and looked down. I expected him to be stunned, shocked, surprised, I didn't know, anything but the way he was looking at me. His expression was somber and I could almost feel the regret pouring out of him. I wanted to reach out and tell him it was okay, tell him that it wasn't his fault. But I was no liar.

Bram wasn't saying anything. I was starting to feel nervous, like maybe I should have just lied. Then, without warning, his fingers, which had been paused at my entrance, pushed into me. Two thick fingers slid through my wetness and my breath hitched as he pushed in deep, his body moving down to hover over me.

"I'll make it good, baby. I'll make you remember. I'll make you fucking feel what he had and we're going to have again. Do you understand me?" he growled, his voice slightly unhinged, his eyes lit with so much fire.

My heart splintered and my pussy convulsed with the memories. I squeaked out my "Yes, I understand." And I did. I knew that no other man could make me feel the way he did.

"We have to be quiet. Lex is asleep, but if she wakes up, I—"

Bram leaned down, his fingers going deeper as I felt my face twist with exquisite pain. His lips brushed against mine and he held my gaze when he pulled away, his free hand sliding up to my throat where he grabbed, tilting my head back, forcing eye contact.

His voice was a snarl and his grip on my throat tightened when he said, "You'll be quiet then, won't you baby?" He framed it as a question, but I knew it was a command. My chest rose and fell, his grip on me a reminder that he hadn't forgotten precisely how I liked it. "Now, no more talking for you, Jadey." Bram's hand slid off my throat up to my face where took hold of my jaw, compressing me between his hands as he bent down to my face. "Answer me," he demanded.

"I'll be quiet," I whispered, the anticipation coursing through my body, feeling a lot like pleasure.

"Good."

Bram moved back and released my jaw, but continued working me with his fingers, his movements were slow and filled with intent as he built me up until he found that spot that he had always owned. My entire body tensed and I pressed my legs together as I tried to catch my breath.

"Mmm, there it is." Satisfaction flashed across his handsome face, his eyes glinting even through the darkness I saw in them.

"Bram, god honey, don't stop doing it like that, please," I begged, my voice whiny and pathetic. I didn't even care. I needed this. I needed him.

And he didn't stop. Bram fucked me with his fingers, while his thumb circled my clit. And I was gone with his touch, undulating into his hand, shamelessly trying to get more of what he was giving me.

"I want you inside of me," I told him, nabbing his wrist and holding it in place. I wanted it all and right now.

"I will be, but not yet Jadey."

I held fast to his wrist, pressing down on the finger circling my clit, desperate for more, craving release. Bram's eyes were heavy as he worked me, watching me writhe and buck beneath his touch. I felt my orgasm building, tearing through my body like an uncontrollable tidal wave. I arched into his hand. "Don't stop, honey!"

I pleaded, as if he was going to take it away from me at any moment.

He kept moving his fingers deep inside me while he bent down and buried his face between my legs.

"I need to taste you," he rumbled and then ran his tongue along my pussy, sliding his free hand up to my breast to roll my nipple in his fingers.

"God, yes," I whispered, holding onto his hair as I rolled my hips into his face. His tongue felt so good running along my pussy. He lapped and licked, the sounds emanating from both of us becoming more primal with each stroke of his tongue. Bram pressed his two fingers deeper into me, the tip of his tongue now working my clit as he hit that spot inside of me that he had always known.

"Ah!" I cried out quietly, as my hand in his hair clasped, my pussy pulsating around his fingers, my hips thrusting up, riding the high of my orgasm that sent shockwaves of pleasure through my entire body.

I threw my head back and released his hair while his movements inside of me became languid strokes. Bram pulled his fingers out of me on a downstroke and fell to the bed beside me. My eyes were closed when he pulled me into him, my hair whipping around to cover my face, before he moved it away with a sweet caress.

"Fuck. I missed you, Jadey."

I pressed my closed eyes even tighter, the pain of his words splitting me in two because just for a little while, I wanted to forget the loneliness of the past nine years. Just for tonight, I didn't want to think about all I had lost.

"Don't," I charged, my voice breaking. "Please, I don't want to do this right now. I just want you to make me forget how much it hurts. I want you to remind me how good it was before."

He heaved out a large gust of breath. "Fuck," he said on a whisper so quiet, I wasn't sure I was meant to hear it. "Okay, baby. Let's forget it all tonight."

Bram rolled us over so he was hovering over me. I tugged on the waistband of his gym shorts and he smiled wickedly, before pushing himself up off me.

"What are you doing?" My voice was desperate and frantic. I wanted the main event, or else I was fairly certain my vagina would stage a coup against me at this point.

"I need a condom, baby."

"Oh god. Right!"

Bram snickered as he left the room, returning quickly with his wallet. He pulled out a string of condoms, his reason for having so many stowed away something I decided not to allow myself to think about. He tore one off and tossed his wallet and the rest of the condoms to my bedside table.

I bit my lip, afraid to ask, but feeling brazen enough to do it. "Are we going to need all those?" God, I hoped so.

Bram smiled as he pulled his shorts down. Immediately, my brain scrambled, and I had already forgotten what I'd asked when he answered me.

"Oh yeah, Jadey. Might not be enough by the time I'm done with you baby."

"What?" I asked the hard length bulging from his boxer briefs. My eyes surveyed the rest of him and I paused to admire his thick, muscular legs that were testing the durability of his boxer briefs. I didn't have much time to ponder this before those came off too. My mouth went completely dry, all moisture leaving my lips, all oxygen leaving my brain. Maybe I just didn't remember what he was like, maybe he had always been this perfect. I didn't know or really care, because right now, standing before me in all his glory, he was a god. His cock stood upright, fully erect, thick, and long and I just admired him, mesmerized, fully hypnotized by all the things I remembered he could do to me.

Bram stroked himself, his hand running leisurely up from the base of his cock to the head, where he squeezed. The crinkle of a condom wrapper pulled me from the spell and my head snapped up to his to see him tear the wrapping with his teeth. He sheathed himself with the condom and rolled it down his length. That sight alone sent shivers through my body and my pussy throbbed with desire.

I leaned up on my elbows to get a better view and then without warning, I was on my back, being yanked down the bed toward Bram. I screeched, the carefree sound followed by a giggle. It was the most lighthearted I'd felt in years, the burdensome weight I was carrying all but forgotten under the gaze of the man who had been the source of both my joy and my unending pain.

Bram wrapped one of my legs around his hip and paused. Looking down on me, he shook his head. "You're so beautiful, sometimes it hurts to look at you Jadey. I can't believe I ever—" He cut himself off and shut his eyes, inhaling a deep, labored breath. When he opened them, they were darker than they had been. In seconds, he'd gone to the place I was at, a place where our past and future simply didn't exist, a place where we could just be without all the bullshit that came with us.

He lined himself up at my opening, working the tip of his cock through my wetness. I thrust my hips up, impatient to feel him inside of me again. When the tip of his cock was in, we both let out a heavy sigh. Did he feel it too? Did he realize this was always how it was supposed to be? I forced the sorrow out of my mind, determined to focus on just this moment.

"Jade." He moaned out my name before he drew back and thrust in slowly, his thick length pushing me open. "You're tight, baby. Is this okay?" That self-restraint he had always worn around me shone through. It was the only thing that had continued to confound me all these years later. This man, the one who had destroyed me was the very same man who had protected me all those years.

Bram continued to work himself inside of me at a pace that was both necessary and driving me completely mad.

"I need more, baby, can I give you more?" he asked on a groan as he slid his cock halfway inside of me.

"Yes, please, give me everything. I need all you, Bram, and I need it now." I lifted myself up and pushed onto him, forcing him deeper inside.

With that, he grunted. "Oh, shit, you're so tight. Fuck, it feels too good, you feel too fuckin' good."

"More," I pleaded, all too ready to absorb more of him, feel more of him, remember what it was like to be connected with him in this way.

Bram thrust a little harder as I urged my hips forward, meeting his thrust, pushing him all the way so he was completely buried inside. "Ah, fuck!" he gritted out, his jaw tense, his muscles contracting as he held me in place. "Jadey, I'm gonna fuck you, I'm gonna fuck you hard baby, can you handle that?"

My knees shook under him, the fullness of my sex

making me powerless to speak. I shut my eyes and breathed through the pain, letting the pleasure engulf my senses. When I opened them, I locked eyes with him. "Fuck me."

I didn't need to say it again. Bram released a deep rumble that I would've found terrifying if I wasn't so desperate for the man. He moved in me, pumping in and out, never with too much force. He held my leg behind him, angling himself so he could get deep inside. I was ready. I squeezed my leg around his back and bucked my hips forward, knowing he understood that I wanted him to let go, that I was ready.

His eyes widened with fire, nostrils flared with his restraint. "You ready for more?"

"Yes, more!"

With that, he lowered himself down, leaning into my body, putting his mouth on mine to draw deep, passionate kisses from me as he stilled, his cock filling me completely. Bram plucked a soft kiss from my lips as he pulled out nearly all the way and pressed my face to his shoulder. And I knew why when he charged forward, plunging all the way in so hard I lost my breath. I bit down onto his shoulder, muffling the moans that escaped me. I ran my nails along his back and when I reached around him as far I could, I dug in.

"Give me more."

"Jesus, I forgot how fucking greedy and demanding you could be." As he said the words, he pulled out and thrust back inside, faster than before. I bit down again. This time he didn't stop, slamming into me with a fervent energy that I matched whole-heartedly. Bram grabbed my ass and pulled me closer, somehow seating himself deeper inside of me.

"Full, honey, I'm so full," I uttered into his shoulder, wrapping my legs around him, holding him there, the feel of completely taking him something I never wanted to forget. We rocked against each other in place, with him bottomed out and me pulling tight. He took my breath away, and I scrambled to catch it.

"Jadey, I need this, I need you. I need you every fucking second of every day," Bram whispered into my neck, our bodies practically one. "Tell me something true, Jadey. Give me something real."

And that was all it took for me to lose my mind and drop my guard. I went running toward danger and threw myself off the cliff when I whimpered, "I still love you."

"Fuck yes, tell me again, baby." He was relentless as he fucked me, the veins in his neck protruding, his muscles flexing with each movement of his beautiful body.

"I still love you," I mewled like the idiot I was. And at the stupidity of my statement, Bram jerked inside of me with a grunt, a movement that sent me spiraling further down the rabbit hole of my unwelcome emotions. "I've never stopped loving you," I admitted, foolishly caught in the heat of the moment, no longer able to hold myself back.

Bram shut me up when his mouth found mine and he took me in a deep kiss. My orgasm climbed as my walls fell. And my body was full with him as my mind filled with emotions that I hadn't allowed myself to feel in years. And then I lost it. My pussy throbbed around him as I lost complete control. I let out a desperate sound as I came, burying my head in his chest to avoid the pitfall his eyes.

But Bram was never one to let me get away with

anything. His hand slid up my scalp and he grabbed a handful, using it as leverage to pull my head back.

"Fuck yes, Jadey." He forced eye contact, and that was all it took for me to lose whatever bits of myself I'd been holding back. I rode hard beneath him, rocking my hips into him as I moaned through my orgasm. "That's right, let go for me, baby. Squeeze my cock with that tight little pussy. Fuuuuck."

And I did. I let go, and it felt real. It felt honest. Bram grunted and pushed up to his hands. I caught hold of his waist as he drew back before plunging in deep. This time he wasn't slow or careful about it. When he pulled back, he grabbed my leg and tossed it over his shoulder. Bram's bucks were hard, and his face was wild as he fucked me into oblivion. I held on, trying to give him back just as much as he gave me.

"Ride my cock," Bram commanded, just as he flipped us over. "And turn around so I can see that sweet ass when I cum inside of you."

I shivered. He was a man who got what he wanted and tonight, I would be the one giving it to him. I turned around and Bram groaned as I lowered myself onto him.

"God your body is so fucking perfect." He squeezed my ass cheeks and held onto them as I bounced on his cock. I was working hard as my motions went from rhythmic to reckless.

"Fuck yeah, Jadey." Bram's hands drifted to my hips, and he thrust up into me as I bounded down on top of him. Sweat beaded on my brow, my core tightened, and then just as Bram bucked up, I lost it and threw my head back, my orgasm releasing on a whimper. He thrust one last time and then held me in place, groaning before he jerked into me on a muted roar that I felt more than heard. I convulsed around him as his dick throbbed inside of me.

I looked back over my shoulder, fully expecting him to be laid back with the relaxation of release. But he wasn't. He was watching me, surveying my body carefully.

"My girl."

I stilled, struck by the way two single words had the power to possess me. Bram's fingers pressed into my sides when he told me, "Hop off, babe. I gotta take care of this condom."

I dismounted slowly, both loving and hating the feel of his thick length sliding out of me. Without delay, Bram rolled on top of me and pressed his lips onto mine. I couldn't stop the way my body reacted to him. I reached around to yank him closer and lifted up to kiss him deeper. I was still just as affected by his charm as I had always been.

He kissed the corner of my mouth and pushed off the bed. His body was a dream, the muscles of his back flexing as he walked away.

When he came back, I tossed his boxer briefs toward him. Bram caught them with a smug grin.

"That was, um, fun." I shrugged.

"That was." Bram smirked and raised his brows, before he sat down on the bed, boxers still in hand.

"And thanks for everything this past few days." I settled my eyes on him. "I mean it. It's been rough and having you there meant a lot to us."

"You're welcome." His eyes fixed onto mine as his lips tugged up on one side.

"Your clothes should be dry now," I reminded.

Bram dropped his boxers to the floor and sat down

on the bed. "Okay, thanks."

"Sooooo," I drew out, looking at him from the side of my eyes as he settled deeper into the bed.

"What are you doing?" I asked.

He didn't even look at me when he replied, "Getting in bed with my woman," like it was an everyday occurrence for us.

I jerked my head back. "Your woman? Are you insane? We had sex, that hardly makes me 'your' anything." I tossed my hands in the air and looked at him. "You can't stay here, Bram."

His face looked stricken when he asked, "Are you telling me to leave?"

I didn't hesitate to answer. "Yes, I want you to leave."

He scoffed. "But we just—"

"I know we just, and now I want you to go." My voice wavered right along with my resolve to get him the hell out of there. "*That* was a mistake, and it can't happen again."

Bram searched my face, silently staring for a few beats before he chuckled, grabbed my arm, and pulled me in. "Still a fucking liar, Jade Greene." My head landed on his chest and I immediately melted into him. "That was cute though, baby. A valiant effort." He gave my arms a shake.

I rolled my eyes at him. "Thanks."

"I think we need to—"

His words were cut off by a sharp cry followed by a sad little whimper, coming from the hallway.

"Mommy, mommy." Lex's fragile voice cracked. "My tummy aches."

I shot up and threw the covers over Bram.

"Do not move!" I pointed my finger at him and glared, before throwing on my clothes and running out of the room.

Lex was standing in the hallway, a puddle of vomit at her feet. "Oh no, honey, what happened?"

"I threw up," she whined. "My tummy hurts."

I felt her head and much to my relief, she was cool to the touch. "Come on, honey, let's get you cleaned up."

"But mommy, I made a mess." Lex pointed to the floor.

"Don't you worry about that. I'll get it later." I ushered my little girl to the bathroom and spent the next thirty minutes getting her washed up and back in bed.

I grabbed some towels and carpet cleaner, exhausted, but ready to scrub the floor. But when I got to the spot where Lex had gotten sick, there was nothing to clean. I sighed, smiling as I looked at my bedroom door.

I opened the door to my room, ready to throw myself at Bram, but he wasn't there. My heart fell. I could hardly blame the man. If he wanted someone with a simple life, I surely wasn't the one. I went out to the living room, a few tears rolling down my cheeks as I deliberated over drinking wine or eating ice cream. Maybe tonight it would have to be both.

"Is she okay, baby?"

I jumped at the sound of his voice and threw my hand over my heart. "Oh my god, Bram, I thought you'd left." I swiped at the tears and tried to turn my head away from him.

It was no use. He spun me around and pulled me into him. "Why are you crying, Jadey? Is Lex all right?"

His gentle voice only made it worse, and my voice cracked when I said, "I think so. I mean, the doctor said that the antibiotics could cause nausea, but I don't know." I peered up at him and I could feel my lip quiver. "After what happened." I paused to inhale, trying to control my thoughts from spiraling down into the "what if's". I cleared my throat. "After what *almost* happened. I just, I should call."

Bram's eyes swept over me as he reached out to swipe a stray tear with his thumb. "How about I call Raven, babe? She's a nurse, maybe she can give us some advice before we call the doctor."

"Yeah?"

"Yeah, do you think that's a good idea?" Bram's soothing voice was enough to calm me, but when his hand ran along the back of my head, my anxiety dissolved, and I relaxed into him. "Maybe sit down and relax, drink your glass of wine," he suggested as he reached back and grabbed a filled glass from the counter. Handing it to me, he asked, "Where's Lex?"

"She's in bed," I replied, taking the wine glass from him and having a sip, before setting it back down.

Bram said nothing as he planted his hands at my waist and lifted me onto the kitchen counter. I landed with a squeak and a giggle. After brushing my lips with a kiss that I felt all the way down to my toes, he pulled his phone from his pocket and scrolled through his contacts.

He put the phone to his ear as he pushed himself between my legs. I wrapped a leg around his waist to pull him further in and giggled when his eyes widened and mouthed the words, "Call or fuck?"

I could already hear the phone ringing, but I answered anyway, "Call please."

"Rave? It's Bram. You got a minute? Great, hang on

a sec, I'm gonna put you on speaker." Bram switched the call to speaker and put it between us.

"Hey, you still there?"

Raven's soft, sweet voice floated through the phone like a song. "Yep, I'm here. Is everything okay, hun?"

"Well, that's why I'm calling you. I'm with Jade right now. You got my messages about Lex, right?"

"I did. Oh, I'm so sorry to hear that Jade, I hope she's doing better."

"Thanks, Raven. She is doing better and we're all home now," I responded like we were one big freaking family.

"Oh? Oh." That last "oh" had a knowing spark to it that was flinch-worthy. When I did, Bram smirked and looked at me with those gorgeous arctic blues that relaxed me instantly.

"Yeah, Raven. *Oh*." I narrowed my eyes at him. "Anyway, Lex is on an antibiotic, what is it called, baby?"

"Um, cip, uh, hang on, I need to get the bottle."

"Is it Ciprofloxacin?" Raven asked.

"Yes, that's the one." I smiled into the phone, like she could see me.

Bram took over again. He seemed to be concerned, but still clear-headed, something I desperately needed to ground me.

"So she's taking that at home and she woke up about thirty minutes ago throwing up. Said she had a stomachache."

"Hmm. Did you take her temperature?"

"I did," I told her. "Her temp was normal, ninety-seven point eight."

"Okay, well that's good. Cipro can definitely have

that side effect, especially if she took it on an empty stomach. And how is she now?"

"Go get Lex, baby." Bram lifted me off the counter as easily as he'd set me on it.

When I returned with Lex, I was jolted when she squealed in delight. "Bram! You're still here!" She dropped my hand and charged toward him, wrapping his leg in a hug.

"That sounds promising," Raven laughed.

"I sure am, sweetheart. Are you feeling all right?" Bram knelt down and brushed her untamed locks back as he placed his hand on her forehead.

"Yeah, I threw up though. 'Member how that doctor said the medicine could make me sick? Well, I think it did because I woke up and I puke right up. All over my bed and the hallway. It was so gross."

"Your bed?" I asked, confused. I had put Lex back to bed, and she hadn't seen a thing.

Bram turned to look up at me. "I already got it, baby. Her sheets are in the wash. I took care of it while you took care of the most important thing," he said that as he looked at her and my heart fisted, pulsing and racing and floundering around in fluttery little circles in my chest.

Bram's hand fell from her forehead. "Are you hungry?

"Mmmm, maybe a little. My tummy still feels a little yuck though."

"What do you think, Rave?" Bram asked into the phone.

"I think she sounds fine, but if the vomiting and nausea persists, I'd go ahead and take her in. If she develops any fever, go right in. But right now, it seems like normal antibiotic ickiness, so I think you should try and give her some food. Try something mild like crackers, soup, yogurt, toast, things like that, and see how she does. Does that sound like a plan, Lex?" Raven asked.

"Yes. Are you my mom's friend?"

"I am. And I hope that I get to meet you soon. I have a daughter as well. Her name's Zara and she's younger than you, but I bet she'd love you."

"Cool! I like little, little ones and they usually like me because I can come up with a lot of fun games for them. Mom says that I'm gonna be a real good babysitter one day, so keep that in mind, okay?"

Raven giggled, and I also heard a deep laugh in the background. I tilted my head and Bram shook his.

"Hey, Cameron."

"Hey, man."

"Who's that?" Lex asked.

"That's my best friend, Cameron. He's Raven's husband and Zara's dad."

"Am I gonna meet them soon?" Lex wasn't even looking at me when she asked Bram.

"I think so, as long as your mom says it's okay."

Lex looked up at me with those hopeful eyes.

"Of course, honey. Gotta get you healed up a bit, but definitely as soon as possible, okay?"

"Yay!" Lex did a sad little jump. A feeble thing that reminded me I needed to get this girl some food.

"Thank you so much, Raven. I'm going to make Lex some food now, so I'm jumping off, but seriously, I owe you one. I was kind of freaking out and I feel a lot better about it now."

"Absolutely, Jade. Anytime. You two call me if anything else comes up, any time of day or night, okay?"

God, she was the best. "Okay, thanks."

"Bye, guys," Bram said. "And thanks, Rave. I'll text you updates tomorrow."

"Sounds good. Night."

"How does soup and crackers sound, honey?" I rummaged around the pantry, hoping we actually had soup and crackers.

"Okay," Lex answered, less than enthused.

Bram tugged a strand of her hair. "How about you and I go put on a movie while your mom gets that ready?"

"Yes!" Lex said, already heading to the living room.

It was at that moment that I realized he wasn't wearing a shirt. I sidled up to his front and shamelessly ran my hand along his abs. "Bram, where's your shirt?"

"Seriously, Jade?" His eyes roamed the length of my body and I followed them, looking down at what he was looking at. My shirt, or I supposed, *his* shirt.

"Oh. Oops?" I lifted one shoulder and smiled my most innocent smile.

He narrowed his eyes at me. "Yeah, oops. I couldn't exactly wear one of yours, babe."

"No, I suppose you couldn't, even though with these abs," I ran my hand along his stomach, "You could definitely rock a mean crop and I've got plenty of those."

"Plenty of crops, huh? I'd like you to get your fine ass out of my shirt and go put one of those on, Jadey."

I bit my lip, our flirtation easy and comfortable, but still exhilarating. "Fine. I'll be right back then."

I began to walk away, but was yanked back when Bram caught my hand. He pulled me into him, my back flush against his front. With his hands at my waist, he rolled his hips into me and oh Lord, I felt it everywhere.

"Bram, you. I have to."

"Is that right?" he asked and I could feel his smug grin without even looking at him.

"I need to change. Remember the conversation we had two seconds ago?"

He leaned down so his lips were at the shell of my ear. "Mmmmm." A chill rocked through my body from fingertips to toes as I laid my head back on him.

"Now that I know you still love me, I'm not going anywhere, Jadey. So you can try and push me away babe, tap twice, bite me, I don't give a fuck. I'm staying right here."

My eyes widened and my lips tipped up at his words. It was the second time he'd mentioned *that*, and it still did things to me. But now that I'd had him again, I was remembering much, much more vividly. I turned my head to the side to look at him and searched his eyes for a sign that I was being a fool. I found nothing, only the eyes of the boy who'd once loved me. But he hadn't said it back to me.

I was a fool. Still that dumb girl completely in love with a man who wanted her to want him, but would never fully give himself. I peeled myself off him and tried to gather my thoughts.

And thankfully, the rest of the night was drama free. Lex had soup, and we watched a mouse who became a chef until she fell asleep, head on my lap, feet on Bram's. He made her bed with the fresh sheets and carried her to it. Then, I wrapped myself around him in my bed and slept like the dead. When I woke up alone with a note, I smiled as I read the words.

Chapter 9

Bram

I hadn't felt this good in years. I spent that night in Jade's bed after both she and Lex fell asleep on the couch. After carefully carrying Lex to bed, I picked up Jade and brought her to bed, laid her down, and held her in my arms all night. We didn't have sex again, and it didn't even matter. Being close to her was a second chance that I never thought I'd get in my lifetime.

I wasn't surprised at all how quickly Jade and I fell into lockstep with one another, moving about like we were still one unit. We had always understood each other, connected on a deeper level that I wasn't sure I even grasped as a kid. What shocked the shit out of me though, was how fast I fell for Lex. She was an incredible kid and everything about her screamed "Jade". Except over the past few days, I learned that Lex and I had a very similar sense of humor, one that involved lots of ribbing and teasing. She wasn't dry wit like her mother—she was talkative, bubbly, and easygoing.

Despite the difficulty of the past few days, they had still been some of the best days I'd ever had. Spending time with Jade and Lex, doing mundane shit, was something I never realized I needed or wanted. I had grown up with a great family, the best really, but after Jade left, I'd never recovered. I hadn't let myself consider the possibility that I'd have that, so I never went searching for it, knowing that not a single person could replace what I'd lost. I shut those desires out, aware I had closed the door on my chance for that life.

I hadn't been to my house in a few days, not wanting to leave the girls alone for a single second. I wasn't planning to stay here long. What shocked the shit out me, and head to work so I could finish my day and get back to them. The air around me felt dense and heavy as I got out of my truck—a familiar feeling that set me on edge. I opened my door and looked around. Everything was in place.

Just as I closed the door, I was caught off guard when an arm wrapped around my neck from behind and I was pulled back and whipped around. I grasped at the arm, trying to loosen it as I fought back as best I could.

I was a big dude. Over six feet tall, and strong. But this guy was huge. I could see his shadow looming over me as I was drug further back into my house. I reached back for my concealed side-arm when I was released and pushed forward into the wall. I turned quickly as I reached back, finding no weapon for me to grab. Fuck. But my whole body went stiff when my eyes landed on him. All fucking six foot five of the bastard, tatted up to the max, wearing what looked like the same goddamned heavy motorcycle boots, and more scars than he'd had the last time I'd seen him, and he'd had a few then.

"Motherfucker," I mumbled, gaining some traction back, the blood and oxygen returning to my head as he stepped back from me. He was holding my sidearm loosely at his hip, studying me with those dead, unreadable eyes.

"What the fuck are you doing in my house, man?" I

asked, irritated, running a hand through my hair, avoiding eye contact, because I knew why the fuck he was here.

He took two long strides toward me, lifting his arms and shoving my chest with them until I hit the wall. I took the blows, knowing I deserved this shit.

"What the fuck did I tell you to do?" he shouted on a push. "Did I say to fuckin' move in with them?" he asked with another shove. "Or did I say to get rid of them?" he asked again, this time his face close to mine, his eyes lit, that intense look that only this guy could use to slice through a person.

"Did you know she had a kid?" I accused, feeling aggravated with him.

"Grow the fuck up, of course I knew. I've been keeping tabs on her for nine years."

"Yeah? Then you know she's got a life, a business. She's moved everything up here. She's not the same girl, man. She's a woman, a mother. She doesn't give a shit if I want her here or not. What do you expect me to do? She's uprooted her goddamned life. We aren't kids anymore, bro. I can't just destroy her all over again and she'll go running. And I'm not gonna fucking try." I pushed off the wall and stood as tall as I could, not backing down, thinking of my Jadey and now, my Lex. "Do what you need to do to get this shit figured out, but they aren't going fucking anywhere." I pushed back on him; the man was a wall, but I didn't care. When it came to Jadey, I'd always found a way.

"Man, he's not gone, and he's not going to give up until he has everything he wants. And that everything includes the shit Jade fucking destroyed and sold." He shook his head low, almost like he was defeated, something I'd never seen from him. "He won't stop until he's bled her dry, and he's so far fucking gone, he won't give a shit about the kid."

At his words, my heart fell to the fucking floor. *He'll bleed her dry. He won't give a shit about the kid.* Memories I'd suppressed for so many years came rushing back, and I knew he was right. I knew Nathan wouldn't stop at anything to get what he wanted. He never had, not even at the expense of his own children.

"Fuck. We need to figure something out." He shifted on his boots and grimaced before getting up in my face again. "But you better not take your fucking eyes off them." The man was callous and cold as they came, dead inside, but when it came to Jade, he'd always done anything to shield her from all the shit.

"I haven't, you know that. And I won't. Not ever again, man." I stared at him with intent, sending my message, letting him know that this time, I wouldn't be driven away. I caught his empty eyes and didn't even get a reaction. He just lifted his chin.

"One more thing."

"What?"

"There's a small safe where Nathan kept all his shit. You're gonna wanna find that before anyone else does, for your sake and Jades. Shit doesn't matter to me, but I'd like to have it when you find it."

My skin crawled, imagining what could be in there. "What'll I find in it?"

"Evidence," he said, before turning to head for the door.

"Jules."

He stopped, not looking back. "Hm."

"Find that motherfucker and take him out. And if

you don't, I will."

Jules's back straightened as he grunted and shot me a backward glance that was more like a grimace.

"Take care of yourself, brother."

Jules flicked two fingers behind him as he walked away. The guy was as tough as they came, a real fucking piece of work. But at the end of the day, I'd known what made him, and what it had cost him to get it. His life had been dark. A darkness he'd protected Jadey from, throwing himself into the fire to give my girl the chance she deserved. And for that, I knew I'd always owe him.

****

It was still early by the time I got to the station for work.

"Morning, Mika."

"Hey, you," she said with a knowing lift of her brows. "You've been gone a few days. Everything okay with Jade's daughter?"

"Yeah, she's all right. The kid spent a few days in the hospital, but she's good. They're home."

Mika pursed her lips and tipped her head back. "Oh yeah? And where were *you* that whole time?"

I grinned and shook my head. "You know I was with them."

She smiled and laughed a little. "Yeah, dude, we all know. You know how that chain works."

"I sure do. Now, what's going on today?"

"So far, all is quiet in town. A quiet day is a good day, right?"

"Damn straight. Guess I'll do a patrol, check in on the good folks at the Blue Rose. Anything I can grab you while I'm working hard out there?"

"Psh, patrolling the tough streets of Brooks Falls to

get to the Blue? You gonna be okay out there?"

I chuckled, shifting the gear on my hip. "Tell me what you want, babe. You know I don't go to the Blue without getting my number one work woman something."

Mika's desk phone rang, and she tipped her head up at me. "Usual. And when you come back, be ready to dish on the new girls in your life!" she demanded, before answering and transforming from friend to professional in the span of a breath.

I tipped my head to her and headed back out, trying to ignore the sadness that hit me suddenly and heavily. The new girls in my life. It shouldn't have been that way. I couldn't help but beat myself up over how much time I had wasted being a fucking idiot who was too much of a coward to go find Jadey and try to start a life with her again.

Shit, and how many times over the years had Mom asked me about Jade, begged me to go find her and bring her home?

Mom had been hit the hardest, after me, of course, when Jade left town. Both of my parents were devastated. Jade had not just become a fixture in their lives, she'd become like a daughter to them, and they'd loved her. They still loved her. When she left all her shit behind and ran out of town, they didn't understand and I couldn't make them.

I pulled out my phone and hit the speed dial.

"Hello?"

"Mom, hey."

"Bram." Her voice came alert. "Honey, is everything okay?"

"Yeah Mom, everything's fine. Can't a son call his

mom at eight in the morning?"

Mom snickered into the phone. "Well, he *can*, but he usually doesn't. I'm not complaining sweetheart, I always love to hear from you."

I decided to jump right into it. "Jadey's home."

The phone went silent.

I looked at it to make sure the call hadn't dropped. "Mom, can you hear me?"

I heard a choked sob on the other end of the phone. "Shit, Mom."

Her heavy breaths were replaced by a "Son?" as my dad's voice came through.

"Hey pop."

"What's going on? Why's your mother crying?" Dad asked frantically. "Is everything okay? Are you okay?"

"Yes, yes, I'm fine. Everything's fine. Jade's home, pop."

Dad's worried questions were replaced by silence. I ran my hand over my face, wishing that we could've done this in person.

"She's home?" Dad's voice cracked.

"Yeah."

"And she's, um, she's not, you know? She's good?"

I didn't know what he was asking, so I just covered all bases. "She's not married. She owns a really successful business, and she has a kid."

"A kid, but not married?" My parents weren't really old-fashioned, not at all, but I could read in my dad's tone that his concern was for Jade, not her marriage status.

"I want you guys to come up soon if you can. I know she'd love to see you."

I heard rustling on the other end of the phone. "Bram, it's Mom. Sorry honey, I'm back. I just had to gather myself."

"I get it. Are you okay?"

"Oh yes, I'm fine." I could tell she was trying to sound flippant, but her voice was strained. "So, you two are talking again, then?"

"Yeah, we are."

"Are you an item again?" Her voice pitched, and I hated that I couldn't just give her a straight answer.

Mom had always loved the idea of me and Jade and despite the fact that she'd been living with us for two years, my parents didn't seem to suspect that we were together until much later.

"We're figuring that part out. But that's what I'm hoping for."

I heard Mom sigh into the phone. "When should we come? Oh, I would come now if we weren't across the country. I miss that girl so much."

"I'm sure Jadey would love to see you guys anytime you can get out here." I pulled into the parking lot and lied to my mom. "Gotta get to work, Mom."

"Okay, sweetheart. Tell Jade we say hello and I'll let you know when we're heading your way, all right?"

"Okay Mom, love you."

"Love you too, sweetheart."

****

Later that day, Gray and I got called out to a crash outside of town. Nothing major, but when the people behind the wheel were over seventy, the whole of Brooks Falls emergency services went out.

Gray and I waited on the side for the EMT's to finish checking the couple out.

"Heard I missed meeting Jade at Shea's the other night."

"Yeah, you did. Where were you off to?"

"Had a thing in Sacramento."

"A thing?"

Gray's body jostled. The guy was usually pretty chill, even more than I was, but something about his demeanor told me not to ask questions. I shifted the topic.

"You still seeing that woman from Grass Valley?"

His posture wound down. "Nah, she turned out to be kind of a stalker."

"Never find anyone good again after Raven?" I jabbed, trying to lighten the mood.

Gray had been intent on dating Raven when she first got into town and even when it was made clear that she and Cameron were exploring a relationship, he still held fast to those feelings. We all felt sorry for the guy. He'd had it bad for her.

Gray chuckled. "She's a good woman, not sure there are many better out there."

He was right. Raven was good, one of the best even. She was a fucking smoke show, sure, but on the inside, she was one of the kindest women I'd ever met and a fucking phenomenal mother. Just like my Jadey.

"Bram, hey!" The bubbly voice of Sierra pitched from behind and I turned around to find her and another EMT walking toward us.

"Hey Sierra, those folks all right?" I tipped my head toward the couple who were standing by their car, looking a lot less frazzled than when we'd first arrived.

"Yeah, we checked them. They look fine and they're ready to give their statement."

"I got it," Gray volunteered. He nodded to me and made his way to them.

When he was out of earshot, Sierra focused her attention on me. "How've you been, handsome?"

"Been great, you?"

"Not bad."

The woman standing beside Sierra cleared her throat. "I'm Mary, by the way." She smiled at me, her face turning red as soon as we made eye contact.

"Nice to meet you, Mary. I'm Bram." I shook her hand and tried not to chuckle at her reaction to me.

"So, we never got to finish our date the other night," Sierra put in.

"Our date?" I flinched. Was she talking about the pre-hookup drinks at Shea's?

"Yeah, at Shea's."

Okay, she was talking about that. Sierra and I had never dated. We never referred to what we did as dating, and we never discussed dating. And that was okay with me, because I didn't fucking date.

"Yeah, you know I wasn't feeling well," I lied, feeling like a piece of shit as I did it.

"I know, poor thing." She bit her lip and tipped her chin down. "I want us to finish that date and then, um, maybe go on another one?"

Fuck. I looked at Sierra, her face soft and vulnerable, and then I looked at Mary, whose hands were bunched underneath her chin like she was watching the love match of the century form right in front of her eyes. I wanted to tell Sierra that I had a woman; even if it wasn't true now for me and Jade, it would be. Jade and I were always an inevitability, and now was no different. But I couldn't bring myself to shut Sierra down like this, not in front of someone else.

"How about I call you later?"

Sierra's eyes lit and fuck, I was a dick. She was a nice girl, always had been, but she and I had an agreement. Our relationship had never been more than friends with benefits and that's the way we both had wanted it for so long.

"That sounds perfect." Sierra smiled. "We better get going. Good to see you, Bram. Can't wait for the next time." She winked as they both headed to the ambulance. And I resolved to call her later and clear things up.

Chapter 10

Bram—Twenty years old

Mom was high octane today, ecstatic because we were finally celebrating Jade's eighteenth birthday, a day that had happened mid-week, but Jade and I agreed we'd wait to do anything until I got home from school that weekend. Mom was also energetic because she got this way around the holidays. She was a holiday fiend and my poor dad had to suffer for it, lugging decorations up and down the attic for four months straight, beginning with Halloween. That was until Dad said I had come of age, which was around fourteen. Then I was the one who lugged them, aiding and abetting Mom in her aggressive effort to bring holiday spirit to the neighborhood. I hated it until Jade moved in and I realized she loved the holidays at our house. Then, I was the one initiating decoration mode, just to get my best friend to smile.

Jade was never big on her birthday since it was so close to Thanksgiving and sometimes fell on the day. She once told me that it wasn't because she had to share the spotlight with a holiday, but having her birthday on a holiday was "a double depression whammy" as she termed it. Nathan didn't exactly go all out, or even make a goddamned effort to give his kids holidays, but add on top of that Jade's birthday, and it sucked for her. Jules had tried for a while to do right by Jade, but he was long out of her life like that and preoccupied with other things.

"Hey there, honey!" Mom was always cheery, but around the holidays, she was even more so. Her chipper voice was no surprise as she bounded in from the kitchen carrying a huge cake.

I jerked my head back at the ridiculous sight.

"Holy shit, Mom. Where did you get that thing?" I laughed. It was cool as hell. I knew my mom hadn't made it. She was an excellent cook and even a fantastic baker, but when it came to decorating, she had the skills of a kindergartner who ate paste.

"Watch your mouth, Bram! I know you're an adult now, but I'm still your mother." She gave me a sharp look as she scolded me. "And I got it from this talented woman in town." Mom beamed, something glinting in her eye.

"Damn. I didn't know there was anyone in town that could do *that*."

The cake was crazy for a birthday cake, but didn't surprise me in the least. Mom would go all out for any birthday, but she definitely would for Jadey's. It was one smaller cake stacked on top of a larger cake. The white frosting on it looked smooth and there were flowers on top, but not those standard flowers you'd see on most cakes from the grocery store. These appeared to be Birds of Paradise, a flower we didn't get in the mountains, but I knew were Jade's favorite.

"There sure is, hun," Mom put in with a huge smile.

"Ah, perfect timing," Dad said as the side door into the kitchen swung open and Jade walked in. "Aha, here's the woman in town with all the talent." Dad slapped my shoulder.

I looked at him, confused, before it dawned on me.

I snapped my head to Jade, who face was one brilliant shade of red as she bit that bottom lip. Fucking hell, she had somehow become more beautiful than she already had been.

"Jadey? Did *you* make that?"

She shrugged and avoided my eyes as she pulled a chair out. "It's not a big deal. I just had fun with it."

I scoffed. "Fun?" I wrinkled my brow and gently shook her shoulder. She was always way too modest and horrible at accepting compliments. She smelled sweet, she was a straight-A student, but constantly downplayed anything she did well. I didn't usually push, but this was insane.

She laughed and shoved my shoulder. "Yes, *fun.* Anyway, it's not like it's hard to make a cake. People do it all the time."

"No, people do not do *that* all, or any, of the time, unless they're a pro."

"I just practiced a lot." Jade shifted her eyes down and I knew she was done with the compliments. I reached for her hand under the table and gave her a light squeeze. She looked at me from the periphery and smiled this cute, tight-lipped little smirk.

Dad grabbed his belly, which wasn't really a belly at all. He was a tall, lean man and had been fairly built in his day. "She sure has, son. I think I've gained five pounds in a month just eating all those delicious things she makes!"

Jade laughed and interlaced our fingers under the table, holding my hand in place at her leg.

"Sorry, Mr. Taylor. I know you prefer flax eggs and turkey bacon." Jade winked at Dad as she and Mom both burst into giggles.

"What the hell are flax eggs? And what am I missing?"

Jade's thumb broke free from our hold and started making little circles in the middle of my hand. I shivered and gave her a curious look. The woman was beaming and fuck, it was good seeing her like this. She looked happy in my family, comfortable even. And even though my parents had told her to call them Anita and Bill, she insisted on Mr. and Mrs. Taylor.

"Your mom went through a health kick about a month ago and decided that she would take all the joy out of food by buying rubber versions of real food." Dad sighed.

"Oh, I did not!"

"Turkey bacon, Nita?"

Jade giggled and moved her chair closer to me so she could lean in. "Your dad says that the reason healthy people are so skinny isn't because their food is better for you, it's because their food is so gross that they don't want to eat it."

Fuck. I breathed her in. She smelled sweet, and I tried to ignore the way my body tightened in reaction to her. That shit was new.

"Well, there may be some merit to it after all," Mom said as she arranged the cake in front of Jade. "It's so pretty, honey, not entirely sure we should put candles in it."

Jade smiled up at my mom, a warmth passing between them. "This is perfect."

We sang the birthday song to Jade and then cut into the cake. I'd had fancy looking cakes before and they never tasted the way they looked. The best cakes had always been the ugly homemade ones, but holy shit, this one was good.

After cake, Mom and Dad left to get her present ready while we cleared the table. Jade hopped up on the counter and watched me do all the work. I tried to ignore just how fucking gorgeous she looked tonight. She was beautiful all the time, but tonight she was fucking glowing. She was wearing this tiny sundress that tightened at her slim waist and then rested delicately on her hips, falling down her gentle curves. The pale yellow complimented her skin tone and her copper hair, all wild the way it was. It had grown out to the middle of her back and looked like the sun bursting around her. I stopped myself. Jesus. The fucking sun? What the hell was I doing? I shook off the thoughts and tore my eyes away from the freckles going down her long legs.

"Jadey, fuck, that cake was good. You're talented, babe." I placed a clean plate in the cabinet above where she had parked her ass and leaned in to nudge her. But when I went to pull away, I had a leg wrapped around my back, holding me in place.

I swallowed, ignoring the feeling of being close to her because this was just Jade and I, it wasn't a big deal. We were affectionate, we'd always been that way. Jade wrapped herself around me, a warm expression settling on her beautiful face as she rested her head on my shoulder. I let my arms fall and held her to me.

"Thanks," Jade whispered in my ear, her voice soft and inviting. Her lips were still at my ear as she sighed.

I stayed in place, unable to tear myself away from her. "Did you have a good birthday?"

She nodded, her lips running so slowly against my ear as all that hair bounced around me. "Mmhmm."

Fuck, was I in hell? Was I finally being punished for

all my shit?

"It was the best, Bram. I love your parents and I love you, too."

Jade pulled away and smiled at me, her eyes searching mine, before moving in and leaving a lingering kiss on my lips. Shit. Her lips were wet and tender and fuck. My body reacted on its own as I leaned in closer, putting pressure on her.

I pulled away, placed my hand on her cheek, and rested my forehead on hers. "My parents love you and you know I do."

She perked up a little. "Where'd they go?"

I closed my eyes and sighed, knowing I should back away from her. "They ran upstairs, probably pretending to do something so we'd get all the cleaning done."

"They'll be gone for a bit?" she asked, biting her lip and peering up at me through her lashes.

"Maybe." My heart pounded in my chest like a warning, or anticipation.

Jade's leg tightened around my waist, pulling me deeper into her. My body stilled, and I studied her. Her eyes were heavy, and she licked her lips.

"Kiss me again then."

"What?" I was stunned, stuck in my head at the idea of taking what I wanted from Jade. My Jadey.

"Kiss me, Bram. Please." Her voice was pleading, and it broke something in me. "You're the only thing I want for my birthday."

Fuck me. Fuck me. My head spun, my dick twitched, and I knew that I was screwed. I swallowed hard, placed my hand on her knee, and watched it glide slowly up her thigh. I bunched the hem of her dress in my hand and pushed it up further on her thigh. Jade gasped, and I shot my head up in time to watch those beautiful lips part. I didn't hesitate to lean in and draw a deep kiss from her mouth. And if I wasn't lost in her before, I was now. She whimpered into my mouth, fisted her hands in my shirt, and kissed me back. I felt it everywhere. I pulled back and moved my hand at her waist up along her side until I grazed the side of her breast. Jade's leg squeezed and my now hardened length pressed into her.

"Fuck, Jadey," I mumbled right before I crashed my lips to hers. Jade was jolted back on impact, but I wrapped my arms around her, my hands gripped firmly on her lower back, tugging her body as close as I could get her. Our lips worked together in unison. I licked across her lips, teasing her with my tongue before drawing her back in deeply. Jade tilted her head to the side and deepened the kiss. My hands were on her thighs, pushing the dress up until I saw what she was wearing underneath. My mind came back to awareness, and I launched myself off her. Jade fell slightly forward, slamming her hands down to maintain her balance on the kitchen counter.

"Bram, don't stop."

"Jadey, I. Fuck, I can't."

Hurt flashed across her face, and her whole body stiffened as I rushed to amend the statement. "My parents are going to walk back in here any second, and I really don't want to explain that to them." Shit, I wasn't sure I could explain that to them, considering I didn't understand it myself.

"Right, okay." Jade's eyes became alert. "I guess that's probably smart. Later than." She nodded in understanding as I reviewed my shitty fucking luck.

Seriously? Now? *Now* she wanted me?

Jade hopped off the counter and smoothed her dress. Walking over to me, she ran her hand up my chest and around to my back before sliding it down lightly and pulling herself into me. She got on her tiptoes and there was no way for her to kiss me unless I bent down, so I fucking did it and let her kiss me. I wanted her to do so much more. This was bad, really fucking bad. I needed to talk to her. And soon.

"Later," I whispered like a fucking tool and then watched beautiful Jade as she sauntered back to the counter, leaving me damn confused.

A few minutes later, the kitchen was cleaned and my parents called us out to the dining room. They were carrying a small box wrapped in bright yellow wrapping paper with a white bow on top. Mom stepped up to the table where Jade sat and placed the box in front of her. Jade stared at it, like she didn't know what to do with it. Then she looked back up at Mom and tilted her head. Mom smiled that compassionate smile that she always wore. It was a smile that communicated love and care, one that couldn't be mistaken for anything else.

"The three of us wanted to get you something special, but also something practical that you could use. It was Bram's idea, of course, that boy's always thinking of you."

Jade stared at it some more, like it was some kind of cruel joke.

"Well, go ahead, open it child," Dad put in gently, his hand placed on Jade's shoulder as he stood behind her. I was leaning against the table, needing some space from the girl who had just turned my world upside down. My phone pinged and I read the text. Yep, I was fucked.

My mind was racing a mile a minute and panic was setting in as I realized that I had no fucking time.

Jade tore into the paper and all I could think was how much of a tool I was. She opened the box and then looked up, scanning all our faces. Her face was so fucking adorable when she was processing something, I could nearly see the gears turning as she tried to make sense of things.

"You got me a key?"

Mom smiled and Dad shook his head in laughter. I forced a smile, but didn't have much in me at the moment.

"Come out to the garage, dear." Dad extended his hand for Jade and she took it, standing up slowly and appearing to be in some sort of daze. We all walked her to the garage. Dad hit the switch to open the door, lighting up the place and illuminating a red car with a big bow on it.

Jade scanned us, her eyes narrowing before getting wide as she threw her hands over her face. I had prepared for this reaction, because I knew my Jade. I went to her side and wrapped an arm around her. Jade turned to me and buried her head in my chest. Mom and Dad looked at me and smiled softly. I had prepared them for the eventuality that Jade wouldn't know how to accept this gift, warning them that she would probably freak out. Jade was bawling in my chest, clutching onto my shirt with a death grip. I peeled her off me and pushed back the wet hair from her face.

"Happy birthday, Jadey."

"I, I can't," she stammered through the words.

"You can, babe, and you will. You don't reject a gift from people who love you."

"It's a car, Bram," she whispered, as if we were the only two in the garage. "It's not a gift, it's a *car*. What's next, a house? Oh wait, your parents have already given me that! No, no! I can't take anything else from you. I'm holding on, trying to wait out the rest of this year so I can get out and stop being a burden to everyone. And this? This is too much. I can't take it. I won't." Jade shook her head with a vehemence, like she could somehow shake away this gift.

Like a fucking idiot, I ran my fingers through her hair and pulled back, positioning her so my lips were at her ear. "Jadey, you can take it and you will take it. It's a gift and you know we love you." I stroked her back as I held her and fuck, she felt so good in my arms.

Jade tilted her head back to look up at me and her eyes explored.

"Jade, honey, are you okay?" Mom cocked her head.

"Yes, Mrs. Taylor. I just, I don't really know how to accept a gift like this. You guys have already done enough for me and—"

Mom cut her off. "Oh dear, come here, please." Mom stretched out her arms and I released Jade.

She collided with Mom and I knew by Jade's resigned nodding that words were being passed between them. Soon enough, Jadey ran to Dad and threw her arms around him. She pulled back and smiled sweetly. "Thank you, Mr. Taylor."

Her smile was captivating, and I was lost in it when she threw herself at me. The impact of her body pushed me back, but I was a seasoned pro when it came to Jade's hugs.

"Thank you." Jade whispered in my ear, her arms pulling us close, her body plastered to mine. And it felt good, too fucking good.

****

Jade—18 years old

Oh lord, being in Bram's arms felt like a fantasy come to life. And I had missed him. I'd seen him plenty, but not every day like I was used to. It was my eighteenth birthday, and I'd spent a full school year trying to convince myself that the hole I felt in my chest had nothing to do with Bram. But deep down, I knew it did. We loved each other. He *loved* me. A person didn't do the things he'd done unless they loved someone, and Bram had inserted himself in my life and single-handedly changed the course of it.

I drew back from him, wondering if he felt the very same agonized torture that I felt in his presence. I wanted to be fused to the man and in that moment, after our kiss, it was even harder to pry myself off him. But his parents were there and Bram and I weren't a *Bram and I* yet.

But god, it felt good to be back in his arms. He had been at school and for the past month, I'd hardly seen him, except maybe once. We still talked or texted almost every night, but it wasn't the same. So by the time my birthday came around, I knew what it was. I knew that I was missing my best friend, but more than that, I knew that I wanted more. And based on our kiss in the kitchen earlier and what I had felt behind his jeans, he definitely wanted it too. We shared a brief look as I glanced into his handsome face, those arctic blue eyes piercing my very soul to its depth. And then, in one very unexpected moment, I was knocked right on my ass.

"Bram! Hey, baby!"

A high-pitched voice smacked me from behind. It hit like a series of explosions and her words were a bomb detonating all over my dreams. *Baby?* Boom. I turned my head toward the voice, my arms still wrapped around his neck. Boom. She was gorgeous, with long legs and a perfect model physique. Her skin was tan and glowing and her hair was a silky, shiny mass of carefully constructed blonde waves. I blinked at her, confused.

Bram unhooked my arms from around him and reluctantly, I let go for fear of looking even more pathetic than I felt. I stared as it all happened in slow motion, like watching a tragedy occur before your very eyes. You don't want to see it, but you can't look away.

Bram stepped away from me and moved toward her. Her wide smile showcased a row of sparkling white teeth that looked even whiter behind her bright red lips. I couldn't tear my eyes away until I came to and realized just what I was seeing. Lips locked, arms wrapped, nails dug in. And there it was, the last boom. The final detonation in a string of soul-crushing events that I wasn't sure I'd ever recover from.

The kiss ended after what seemed like an obscene amount of time, even though I knew it had only been seconds. They turned toward us and Bram opened his mouth to speak, but the woman, and oh yes, she was a woman, got there first.

Her voice was all cheerleader pep, and I was positive that she was exactly that.

"Hi ya'll," she drawled, like a freaking southern belle. "I'm Hailey, Bram's girlfriend. It's so nice to meet you, Mr. and Mrs. Taylor!" She asserted her perfectly manicured hand toward them.

"Hi, dear." Mrs. Taylor sounded almost weary when she said it. I knew that I was projecting, hoping everyone found her as annoying as I did. "It's very nice to meet you. We hadn't been expecting you, but what a nice surprise."

Bram cleared his throat. "Yeah, sorry about that Mom. Hailey was driving by to see her folks in Glenwood and texted me last minute."

"No, no, not a problem at all." Mrs. Taylor's eyes flashed to me.

Oh sweet Jesus, was that sympathy? I panicked. Oh god, she felt sorry for me. She *knew*. Who exactly did I think I was fooling? With the way I had been throwing myself at him all day, I was sure the entire town somehow knew I'd just faced the rejection of my life. I felt the blood drain from my face. I had been throwing myself at him. No, it was much worse. I had been *pushing* myself on him.

I smiled back at Mrs. Taylor, giving her the fakest shit I'd ever smiled, trying to reassure her that I was fine. I was most definitely not fine. I was all kinds of jumbled and I had a sneaking suspicion that once I had time to process all this, I'd be decidedly heartbroken. But I didn't have time for that now. Now was the time to save face. Now was the time to strike first and strike hard, just as my brother had taught me. And no, I wasn't going to punch her, even if I really, really wanted to.

"And you must be the famous Jade!" Hailey turned to me, her smile quite possibly just as fake as mine, but way prettier and way more convincing. "Bram has told me all about you. It's so nice to finally meet you." She moved in closer and closer until I felt like I was crashing. Devastation was about to happen and I was powerless to do fuck all about it. Her perfectly toned and tanned arms wrapped around me for the hug and I felt my already stiff body go wooden. "It's so nice to meet Bram's little *sister*!"

Whoosh. Instantly the air in the room went from uncomfortably thin to full on oxygen deprivation. And surely that's what caused this series of delusions. It had to be, because she called me his *sister*. Rage or pain? How to choose.

"We aren't actually related," I fumbled out the words in a mumble, shrugging my way out of her hold.

"Oh yes, honey, I know *all* about it." Her mouth formed a sympathetic frown. My eyes twitched.

I smirked and took a step away. I had been so happy just minutes ago, before college mountain cheerleader waltzed in and tossed a wet blanket over my birthday plans.

"That's sweet," I replied, monotone. And god, it wasn't sweet. It was actually disgusting considering he just had his tongue in my mouth and his hands up my dress, but I was certain he didn't want *her* to know that and I was even more certain that his parents didn't want to know that. "Well, Bram and I have been close for a long time now. I suppose that makes me like family." I grimaced, trying to cover the wistfulness in my voice with a biting tone that just made me sound childish. Great.

I looked at the Taylor's, feeling the self-pity melt away as it was replaced with love. "Gosh, thank you guys so much. I can't thank you enough. I'm not even sure I deserve any of this, not after all you've done for me." I felt my lips raise on one side, the thought of Jules bringing me sudden and unexpected peace. "But my brother always told me not to reject kindness from the people who love you, so." I shrugged. "Thank you, and I love you so very much." Tears brimmed, and it was all

243

I could do to hold them back.

"Oh sweetheart." Mrs. Taylor reached out, and I knew what it was. Shit. She was feeling all kinds of sorry for me. And I didn't even care. I really needed that hug. I fell into her arms and melted into the squeeze. I went to pull back, but she held me tighter. And I knew she knew when she whispered, "Never settle for less, sweety. You deserve everything this world has to offer. You're talented, bright, and beautiful and anyone who can't see that, doesn't deserve it."

I pressed my eyes closed, because, oh yeah, she *knew*. Pity. I lifted my head, a few small tears falling down my cheeks. "Thank you."

I made my way to Mr. Taylor, who held out the key for me. I took it in my hand before I threw myself at him. He let out a small grunt upon contact and then a chuckle. "Happy birthday, dear."

Mr. Taylor released me, and I stood up straight, thrusting my chin in the air, determined not to let any of this ruin my eighteenth birthday. I mean, I just got a car. I had nothing to be mopey about. Sure, the boy I've loved since I was thirteen had a girlfriend, and that shit hurt. But it wasn't the end of the world. Damn, it hurt, though. Yeah, I needed to get out of here.

"I think I'll take it on a test drive," I told Mr. Taylor. And if the look on his face didn't tell me that his parents had known all along, then I don't know what. His expression said it all. *Hang in there, Jade. It'll be okay. You'll find someone.* I imagined platitude upon platitude, said out of pure love, but it would be no less painful to hear.

"That's a great idea. It has a full tank of gas already, so no need to make any stops."

I shook my head in disbelief. "You guys are too much."

I turned around toward my car, which was unfortunately directly behind Bram and Hailey. I kept the smile plastered on my face, even though it was dimmed under the heavy weight of Bram's tense posture and apologetic gaze. I avoided his eyes. It was all too painful, and I was sure that if I looked him in the eye, I would lose it.

"Thanks again, *big bro*." The words came out as an unveiled accusation. Liar, cheater, jerk! "It was really nice to meet you, Kirsten."

"Hailey," she corrected.

"Uh-huh. Bram has told me so much about. It's nice to put a beautiful face to a name."

I was doing my best not be a raging bitch. It wasn't her fault Bram was stupid. I made a bee-line for my car, got in, and drove straight to Renata's, because, of course, I had to show her my car. That lasted all thirty seconds before I was in her arms crying and confessing to her all things Bram and I. I told her everything and was surprised when she *wasn't* surprised that I had loved him all this time.

Once I was all cried out, I drove home and tip-toed in the door, shutting and locking it behind me as I tried to be quiet. Bram's truck was parked out front, and I had no clue if Hailey was still here. I didn't want to know. Tomorrow, I'd wake up early and go to the gas station for coffee, so I didn't have to find out if she was still there.

The stairs creaked under me and I flinched. I heard a toilet flush and noticed Bram's light was on. *Fuck. He's awake. Fuck, fuck.*

I hurried down the hall, hoping to avoid any awkward conversations with anyone really, but especially Bram's perfect ten of a girlfriend.

I made it to my room just in time and managed to shut my door without a sound, then left the lights off for good measure. I went into my closet, flipped on the light, and stripped myself of my clothes, laughing at my own stupidity as I tore off my dress. It was fall, and it was freaking freezing outside. The dress hadn't been cheap, and neither had the panties that I'd bought to seduce Bram with. I hung my head. God, I was so stupid. Looking in the full-length mirror at myself, I shook my head in disgust. My hair was extra wild from driving with the windows down, so I could sob into the night, and the heat up, so I didn't freeze my ass off doing it.

I surveyed my body; I was all pale skin and pitiful curves. And then there was the underwear. God, the freaking underwear. I had worn a tiny satin thong that I'd also bought for Bram. A thong that he seemed to approve of, right before he remembered he had a fucking girlfriend and still didn't warn me. "So stupid," I mumbled as I tried to tame my mess of locks.

"Of course he doesn't want you!" I whispered to the mirror. "Did ya see her, Jade? Get your shit together!"

I did my nighttime routine and got my bethonged ass into bed. Fuck pajamas and fuck Bram and fuck Hailey.

I had just gotten settled when I heard it.

"Jadey? Are you awake?"

I pressed my eyes closed. For him, I was not awake. I kept silent and still, hoping he would buy the act and just go away. I didn't have the energy to deal with him. And I still wasn't clear on who I was more pissed at—him for being so stupid and hot and perfect? Or me, for being just plain stupid?

I heard the door close again, and I breathed out a sigh of relief. I was definitely waking up early and getting the hell out of dodge until he went back to school. I could stay at Renata's for a few days or sleep in my damn car. Hell, anything to avoid him right now.

Except, he wasn't gone, and I knew it when I felt the covers lift off me right before a large, warm body lay next to me. A mostly naked me.

"Shit." Bram cursed under his breath when his hand brushed against my bare back. I tried to even out my breathing and maintain the sleeping act, but once he made contact, I was wheezing out breaths. His body was so close to me and all I wanted to do was push back into him and feel him. Pathetic.

"I know you're awake, Jadey. We need to talk."

Was he serious? I didn't want to talk to him and I especially didn't want to do it naked in my bed with his girlfriend sleeping next door. I loved him, but I wasn't a cheater. I tore myself away from him and shot up to my knees, pulling the blanket up to cover me.

"Are you kidding me?"

"Jadey, come here." He reached out his arms, and I glared at him.

"Your sister?" I hissed, still pissed about that.

"Jadey, *come on.*"

"No! Hell no! Don't *Jadey* me! You have a girlfriend, a tiny detail you failed to mention to me before you slid your tongue down my throat! So if you would please get out of my bed and get back to her, that'd be great," I snipped at him, my voice wavering..

"Jesus Jade, she isn't—"

I cut him off. I didn't want to hear his excuses. "Oh

no, she isn't?"

I was mid-sassy head toss when Bram grabbed my wrist and pulled me down. I gasped, hovering over him, my face so close to his.

"She's *not* my girlfriend."

"Ha!" I threw my head back, more irritated than before. "Really? You should probably let her know, *baby*. But you know what, Bram? I don't even care, because whatever she is, you might as well get back to her because I don't want you in here."

I felt cool air hit my breasts and in one horrifying moment, realized the blanket had fallen down.

His eyes skimmed over my body and his throat was tight when he told me, "Liar, Jadey. You're lying."

What? God, were we ten?

"Get your ass back over here and I'll fucking explain."

What was there to explain? He kissed me. He had a girlfriend.

"Get your ass over here."

I shook my head. "I'm pretty much naked, so no."

Bram smirked as he pulled off his shirt and his sleep pants, tossing them to the side of the bed.

I stared at him in his boxer briefs, my mouth agape.

"Now we're even." He reached out and pulled me into him and I didn't fight it, I fell into him. We were skin to skin, something we'd never been, and god, it felt so good.

"Fine, now explain." My voice warbled, and I knew he heard it when his body relaxed and he brushed the hair from my face, pulling it back so I was exposed. His lips fell to my ear as his hands wound around me.

"Do you know how many times I've thought about

this, Jadey?" he whispered into my ear and my entire body shuddered. I shook my head.

"More than I can count."

Bram's lips moved and I could feel his breath lingering along my neck. Goosebumps formed, and I nearly whimpered when he began trailing kisses along my neck.

"Please, Bram. Explain."

"Mmm," he hummed, and I felt the vibrations tickle my skin. "I broke up with her almost immediately after you left. If I had known even a little how you felt, I would've never, Jadey, never. Shit, even when I didn't know how you felt, it was hard."

"Is that why you didn't tell me?"

"Yeah, that's why."

"And why did you tell her that I was like your kid sister?"

He sighed out a breath, his gorgeous blue eyes softening on me. "She had concerns about you, Jadey. The way I talk about you and I, the history we have? I guess I was trying to downplay it all for her, but fuck, Jadey, also for me."

"Did it work?"

Bram scoffed. "What do you think?" He looked down at our bodies intertwined and smirked.

I giggled, unable to hide my glee any longer.

"She knew her fears were justified when she saw you tonight and after you left, we had a long talk. But she already knew. The moment she saw us together, she said she knew."

"I've spoken to you every day for a month while you've been gone and in all those conversations you never mentioned her. Then tonight, I finally see you, I throw myself at you, and you let me. Not once, until she showed up, did you mention her."

"Babe." He said it like it explained everything.

I pursed my lips and narrowed my eyes.

"Okay. I felt guilty being with someone else, even if we weren't together, so I never brought her up. As for tonight, yeah, you did throw yourself at me," he said with a huge grin that made my heart sputter. "And I tried to stop you as best I could, but damn babe, it's you and me. A man can only resist so much. I've always wanted you, even if I didn't fully understand it. It's always been you." His words healed me, soothing the pain that had been eating away at me all evening, as his hands ran the length of my back.

And right then, I made my choice. "I don't want to talk anymore, Bram."

"Jadey, I said I was—" He stopped talking when I launched myself over, landing astride him, my breasts and body bared to him. Nothing about it felt unnatural.

"Jesus," he exasperated, staring up at me, his eyes working up and down, taking all me in.

Without further thought, I ground down on him, hypnotized by the feeling of his hardness growing underneath my body. I didn't have the first clue about what I was doing, not even a little, but my body knew what it wanted and so did his. He thrust up into me.

"Do you feel that, Jadey?" he asked, his voice harsh and strained.

I nodded.

"That's what you do to me every second of every fucking day. That's what you've been doing to me for years. Shit, I've wanted you for too long."

"I don't know what I'm doing," I quickly confessed.

"I'm not experienced, other than kissing," I warned him, trying to make him understand that I wasn't going to be like the other girls he had been with. Sure, I'd kissed boys, but I'd drawn the line there. It was the reason my dates had dried up in high school once the word got out that I didn't put out.

"I just want you the way you are, that's all I've ever wanted."

Bram lifted me and spun me onto my back. Before I could even release a yelp, his mouth was on mine, kissing me with a hunger that matched my own, an unrestrained need that hadn't ever been present between us, until now. My heart beat wildly in my chest. Fear and excitement buzzed within.

"What do you want, Jadey?" His voice was deep and needy.

"I want you."

"How do you want me, baby?"

I arched my back, lifting my hips off the bed and pushing into him, as my answer.

"You want me inside of you?"

"Yes."

"Yes what?" he grunted as he pushed his hips into me.

"Yes," I whimpered. "I need you inside of me. Please."

"Fuck," Bram groaned. "You need me, baby?" His words were like talons, digging into my skin and tearing back any fear that laid on the surface.

I wound my arms around his back and pulled him close. "I've always needed you, Bram. Always."

He tore his briefs off, but it was too dark. I wanted to see his body, and I needed to show him me, the parts of me that were only for him.

"Can I turn on the lights?"

Bram stopped moving and let out a small breath. "Fuck. Yes."

He stood up and took a few steps to my wall where he flicked the light switch on. I patted myself on the back for a decision well made when I saw him standing in the light. He was beautiful. Long, muscular limbs and a great ass. I didn't get to appreciate the back of him for very long before he was turning around.

My jaw dropped to the floor. Oh my. I'd never seen a dick up close, so I wasn't exactly sure if they just looked bigger in real life, but this was something.

I came to when he was standing in front of me, sure that what he saw was me panting like an animal in heat. I bit my lip, not bothering to hide a lusty gaze. I was feeling bold and somehow, very comfortable. I got up to my knees, so we were face to chest, and looked up at him.

"Touch me," I pleaded, doing nothing to mask my need.

Bram's jaw tightened as a growl rumbled out of him. "Shit," he cursed, closing the distance between us. "Fuck, Jadey," he breathed out on a harsh exhale. "You're perfect, babe. You don't know how long I've wanted you like this. But not just sex, that's not what this is. It's always been more with us, Jadey, and it always will be."

His words were said with deference as his hand slid between my thighs. He watched with fascination as his fingers moved across me, his eyes locked on what he was doing.

"Bram." His name fell from my lips. It was an

appeal for more and I knew he understood when one finger went inside of me. I heaved out a sigh of relief at the contact. "More." His eyes darkened slightly as he pushed another finger in and I melted into his touch.

"That good, baby?" Bram asked in a throaty, restrained voice that I'd never heard before. "Don't want to hurt you.

"It doesn't hurt. It feels so good," I whimpered at his chest, my lips running along his tanned skin. At that, he nudged my head up and his lips fell to mine to draw out a deep, wet kiss as his fingers worked inside of me. His thumb moved to my clit where he made slow circles. I bucked into him, the sensations nothing I'd ever felt before.

"Fuck yeah, Jadey." His words were nearly incomprehensible as he spoke at my lips, before diving back in and moaning through our kisses.

My core buzzed with the pleasure he was giving me. It built slowly, bringing me higher and higher, closer and closer to an invisible ledge and oh god, I wanted to dive right off it into the unknown with him. I was thrusting into his hand when my core tightened around him and I spasmed, a loud moan that was muffled by his kiss. His Movements slowed, and he stopped when my hips jerked wildly into him.

Bram smiled hazily as he rested his forehead on mine and slowly removed his fingers from me.

"Jadey, we don't have to do anything else." He was heaving breaths in front of me. "We don't have to do anything you aren't ready for. You say the words and we'll be done, okay baby? I don't care, I'll wait for you, for as long as you need."

I smiled at him and bit my lip. The boy who had

protected me for years had become the man that still wanted to protect me, even from himself. But that was the thing. He was the only person I trusted.

"I don't want to be done. I want you. I want this."

"Okay," he scratched out. "I'll go get a condom."

I reached out and grabbed his forearm. "Top drawer of my nightstand." I dropped my gaze to the bed as I said it, watching him from the side of my eye.

His eyebrows raised. "You have condoms? I thought you said you haven't had—"

"I haven't," I interrupted, shaking my head and staring at the ground while pinpricks of shame crawled up my neck. "You are my first, for um, everything. Well, you will be, when we do the other things," I mumbled the last, suddenly wishing I had some experience.

"Oh." Bram ran his hands through his hair and worked his jaw back and forth. "You bought these for—"

"Us, yes, I bought them for us."

God, what did he want from me? I had already cut myself wide open for him and now I was standing stark naked in front of the man. How much more of myself could I give? I was studiously watching the bed like it was the most interesting thing in the room, when Bram's hand came to my jaw and he turned my head toward him.

"I love you, Jadey."

My heart pulsed as butterflies released in my stomach. "I love you too," I confessed in a whisper.

Bram pulled me to his chest and his fingers sifted gently through my hair. After a few moments, he put his hands at my waist, lightly pushing and urging me to lie down. Bram got on my bed and hovered over me, his face so soft and loving that I felt a fullness in my heart, even in the deepest parts of me that had been hollowed out and empty for so long.

He reached over to the top drawer of my side table and with large eyes he turned toward me. I blanched, suddenly remembering what was in there.

"Fifty condoms, babe?"

My cheeks heated as he pulled out the box of fifty assorted condoms and scoffed. "Fuck, okay, yes, I'm down for it. Or up for it." The side of his lips twitched, and I narrowed my eyes at him. "But you can just throw out the small dick ones, won't be needing those. Donate them to Austin Bradford or something."

I giggled, loving that he even remembered Austin Bradford. "Are you jealous?" I teased.

"Ha! I was never jealous, babe. I knew he wasn't good enough for you."

"Right," I mumbled, but I was too focused on the condom Bram had pulled out after searching through the box. I peeked at the wrapping and my lips formed an "O."

"What?" He asked.

"Nothing, I was just looking so I know what to buy next time." I felt my cheeks warm.

Bram chuckled and bent down to kiss me. "Next time, huh? Well, first, with fifty condoms, we should be good for at least a week."

My eyebrows shot up, and off my forehead.

"A joke, babe. At least two weeks." He winked. "But secondly, you don't buy condoms, I'll take care of that."

"XXL?" I asked.

His lips quirked, and he didn't answer, instead he looked down at me as he tore the wrapper. I watched with curiosity as he rolled the condom over himself. He did it a little good. I squirmed when he stroked himself.

Bram pushed my hair back from my face. "You need me to stop, just tell me. And if it hurts too much, tell me, Jadey, and I'll stop right away. Just say stop or tap twice."

My core spasmed just thinking about him inside of me. I nodded and bit my lip. He was so concerned about me that he was forgetting that I wanted this just as much as he did.

He ran the tip of his cock along my opening before pushing just a little of himself inside of me. He worked his way in gradually, staring into my eyes, his jaw ticking and his fists clenched at the sides of my head.

He was halfway in when I had the inclination to move. I lifted my hips into him and he gasped and closed his eyes, before moving one hand to my hip and pushing it down.

"Don't, Jadey. Let me go in slow," he said through gritted teeth.

I stayed down as he kept working himself inside of me. I pressed my eyes close, adjusting to his length.

"Jadey, are you okay?" Bram asked, his voice panicked.

I placed a hand on his cheek. "Yes, I'm good. Please don't stop."

His hips gave a final long push as he fully seated himself inside of me. My breath left me on a high-pitched mewl. "Oh my god, Bram."

"Breathe baby, just breathe," he soothed and didn't move as he held himself over me.

I did. I breathed in and out slowly, because the feel of him all the way inside of me took my entire breath away. He moved slowly in me, barely pulling himself out before going fully in again. He did this for a while until finally it started to feel a little good.

I placed my shaky hands on his abs and let them move with him. I lifted my hips up into him on a down thrust and his eyes went wide, before he closed them tight, his nostrils flaring.

"Let go a little, please," I implored with a needy whimper.

Bram's eyes shot open. "I can't, Jadey. I'll hurt you."

"You won't. You'll never hurt me."

"Jadey," he admonished.

"No, I need more."

"Fuck. Okay."

He worked a bit faster and harder, keeping his eyes closed the entire time. I didn't understand why he wouldn't look at me.

"Bram, why are your eyes closed?" I reached out and touched his cheek.

Opening them, he inhaled deep before he spoke. "If I look at you, Jadey, I'm gonna fucking lose control. I can't look at your goddamned perfect body without losing my mind."

"Tell me then."

"Tell you what?"

"Look at me and tell me what you see." I was brazen and lost in our moment.

He lurched forward and dropped his head to mine. "Are you trying to kill me? You want me to be embarrassed that my first time with you is faster than the first time I had sex? Because that's what's going to happen." He could barely get out the words as he spoke with harsh breaths.

"Tell me."

"Jesus, Jadey. I see your round tits bouncing as I fuck you." He lowered his head and sucked one nipple into his mouth.

"Ah!" I released a puff air and my hips bucked up.

"I see your beautiful stomach flexing as you lift up those curvy hips to get more of me." He thrust in, the hardest he had given me yet. It hurt, but it also felt so good. I moaned through it, all the while watching him, begging with my eyes for more.

"I see your perfect, long legs below me and I want you to fucking wrap them around me and never let go."

I felt everything clench around him, my body reacting on its own to his words. Beautiful, beautiful words that I only ever wanted to hear coming from his mouth. I shifted under him and wrapped one leg around his back and stuttered through a breath.

"Let go, baby," I told him. "Give in to us, I need to see you want me as much as I want you."

And that was all it took for him to lose control. The fire in his eyes blazed and the groans and grunts escaping his lips did wicked things to me as he fucked me harder.

"Jadey, I, I'm close."

"I want it Bram. Give me you." I wasn't entirely sure what I was asking for, only that it was him who I wanted. I wanted to be the only one to do this to him, with him.

Bram's speed increased and soon after, his hips were jerking as he grunted through an orgasm. I watched in utter fascination as he pulsed and jerked inside of me. His movements slowed to a stop before he slid out of me, watching my face the entire time and flinching when I gasped at the end.

He rolled over onto his back and pulled off the condom before tossing it in my trashcan. Bram turned to me, our sweaty bodies still on full display. "I love you so fucking much, Jadey, sometimes it hurts."

I placed my hand on his face. "It hurts me too and I don't want to hurt anymore."

"I'll never hurt you, baby. Never. I'll always love you and I'll always take care of you."

We lay in the light for so long, cuddling and laughing, reminiscing about the years we shared together and sharing the secret times we lusted after one another. I was so safe, I was so cared for. And I knew, beyond a shadow of a doubt, that this man would never hurt me.

Chapter 11

Jade—Present Day

I didn't really know what to expect from Bram at this point. He said he'd check on us, but I wasn't sure if that meant he'd call or come over. I didn't have time to think about him, though. I was due to video chat into a vendor meeting at five and I also had to head to my property and talk to Andrew about his progress on the house. He'd designed a beautiful, updated version of the two-story home that I'd spent the better part of my teen years in—Bram's house. It was the only house that I wanted and when I thought of my best childhood memories; they were all in that house. And when I envisioned giving Lex the life she deserved, that's the house I wanted to raise her in. That house had been my safe haven from the moment I found myself at their door right up until the moment I left it.

Even though my family's land had been a stain on my childhood, I wanted to reclaim it and putting a modern replica of the Taylor house on it was like merging two parts of me, the two parts that made me who I was, the good and the bad, the beautiful side of my upbringing and the rough parts.

I was in the middle of cleaning the kitchen when the doorbell rang. I was being lazy this morning despite all I needed to get done and instead of making lunch, I'd ordered pizza.

My hair was still wrapped in a towel and I was wearing sweatpants that I had tied high on my waist and a tiny bandeau that left my stomach exposed. I looked down at myself, deciding I didn't care if the pizza delivery person saw me like this.

I rushed to grab my purse and then swung the door open, my face buried in my purse, searching.

Two pizza boxes floated in the air, smelling like pure heaven. "Hi! Thank you, let me just grab your tip and I'll take those from—"

The man pushed into my house past me and I balked in surprise until I realized just who it was.

"Why are you delivering my pizza?"

He set the pizza down on the dining room table and whipped around to me. His eyes flashed as he looked at me, but then, as they made their way up and down my body, they darkened.

"Why are you answering the door like *that*?"

I looked down at myself, confused. Sure, I was showing some skin, but this wasn't the nineteen fifties. "I just got out of the shower." I stuck my hand on my hip and popped it out, suddenly annoyed with him. "I wasn't expecting my police officer pizza delivery guy for another fifteen minutes, so I thought I had time."

Bram's lips ticked, and he licked his lips as he moved, his darkened eyes fixed on me. All my sass and confidence disappeared into thin air as my knees wobbled and I was sure I'd melt into a puddle on the floor. I had no time to react before he lifted me. I wrapped my legs around his waist on instinct as he carried me to the kitchen, then planted my ass on the counter.

I squeaked and pushed his shoulder playfully, like the giddy high school girl I reverted to whenever I was around him. Though, in high school, I think I actually had more willpower. But a nine year dry spell and the love of your life coming back into your life was bound to do that to a woman.

"What do you think you're doing? Lex is awake!" I scolded him quietly.

"I'll be quick."

Oh lord. The tip of his index finger dipped just below the waistband of my sweats and he ran it along the inside, teasing me. I wasn't entirely sure who he was torturing more, because his face looked just as pained.

I didn't wait for him to kiss me. Instead, I leaned forward and stole a kiss from his lips. His eyes closed, and he groaned when his finger left my waistband and became two firm hands planted on my hips. He drew me forcefully into him, my center pressing against him between my legs. Our kiss became heated, and it took everything I had not to lose my wits. I broke our kiss and pushed him away, smiling at the look on his face. It was hunger. For me.

Bram stepped away and pulled me from the counter, setting me on my feet. "Can I request that you wear this only for me?"

I laughed and shook my head at him. "I only wear this for the house when I'm doing all my hygiene and self-care things."

"And the pizza man," he grumbled.

I ignored him, enjoying his jealousy a little too much. "What are you doing here, besides delivering my pizza? Which, by the way, I didn't get a chance to tip my delivery guy."

Bram pulled me in, his hands at my lower back, my head tipped up to look into his beautiful blue eyes. "Don't worry, Jadey." He kissed me. "I tipped him." Another kiss. "Ten dollars to get the fuck off my woman's doorstep." Kiss.

His woman. *His*. I pushed away, needing to put a fortress between us before I did, or said, something stupid. Well, okay, something more stupid than all the stupid I'd already done. This was moving fast, and *this* wasn't even what I came here for.

"You're back!" Lex materialized from the hallway and ran straight for Bram. "Are you here for lunch? We ordered pizza! Mom said I could have pizza because it's the only thing that sounds good to me and I haven't really eaten much in the last few days but you already knew that because you've been with us... want some pizza?" It was a string or words thrown at the man in one long run-on sentence.

Bram smiled at Lex and knelt down. "You seem like you're doing better today." His voice was tender and full of care as he placed a hand on her forehead. "You get sick anymore this morning?"

"Nope! I just woke up. Mom and I were lazy this morning because we didn't sleep very good last night after I threw up." Lex bounced on her toes, beaming brightly at him. "Thanks for doing the yucky job, so my mom didn't have to do it. She always has to do all the yuck things alone. Want pizza?"

His smile got bigger, and he stood up and gave Lex a singular nod. "Pizza. What kind did we get?"

"I have pepperoni and cheese, because that's the best pizza." Lex scrunched her nose in disgust and launched in, "Mom always gets her pizza with these really salty, purple olives and tomatoes and other weird things. It's gross."

I threw my hand over my heart and gave her an expression of feigned hurt.

"What? It is, Mom."

"It's called a Mediterranean pizza, and it's delicious!"

Bram scrunched up his nose and looked at Lex. "I'm with you, kiddo. That stuff belongs on a salad, not a pizza."

"That's what I tell Mom!" Lex yelled and gave a tiny jump that was enough to get her off the ground.

"Are you staying all day?" she asked, as I grabbed plates from the cupboard and handed them out.

"No, I have to go back to work, but I couldn't get through the rest of my day without checking on my girls."

Lex beamed, those light green eyes aglow beyond all that unbrushed copper hair. "Are you gonna come back after work? Mom has a meeting and—"

"Lex," I scolded. "Bram has things to do, honey. He hasn't been home in three days."

She dropped her head. "Okay, sorry."

"It's okay, Jadey. I'll come back. I stopped at home this morning, grabbed some clothes and stuff."

That put a smile back on Lex's face and a frown on mine. He shot me a grin and shoveled a slice of pizza into his mouth.

"Honey, why don't you put on a movie and we will be right out."

"Okay!" Her eyes brightened before she left for the living room and set her pizza on the coffee table. I waited until she looked busy with other things before I turned to

Bram.

"*What* are you doing?"

He furrowed his brow and looked down at his plate. "Eating pizza? You should do the same. Your salad pizza is getting cold." He smirked and I speared him with a look.

"No. What are you doing in my life?"

It was a fair question. A heavy one, but fair, and I expected him to consider it a moment before he answered. But no, it took him not even two seconds to produce an answer.

"Being in it. Getting you back," he said, and then took another bite of pizza, as if he didn't just drop a bomb on me.

"Bram." I set my hand on his chest and shook my head. He set his plate down and walked forward with my hand still on him, pushing me back into an alcove of the kitchen.

"Jadey."

I stumbled over my words, losing traction as he got closer to me. "You, you can't just come back into my life like nothing happened between us. We have stuff we need to talk about."

"I know and I want to talk about all it, but in the meantime, I'm going to be right here."

"I need time to think. There's too much to say."

And it was true. I had things to say that had been stewing in bitterness for nine years. I had so much pain that I didn't even know how to communicate to the man the depths of what he had done to me. And then, what would happen when he finally knew the truth about what he'd done? What I'd done? Would he leave me again? This time, it wouldn't only be me. And from the moment she entered this world, I'd sworn that I'd do everything I could to protect her from the same kind of pain I endured as a child.

"Okay, baby. Take time to think." Bram ran the back of his knuckles across my cheek, wiping at a tear that had gotten loose. "But can I come back tonight and at least help you with Lex while you have your meeting?"

I bit my lip, knowing that I should let him come. He ran a thumb across my lip before dropping it to the cleft in my chin and pulling my lips apart so he could kiss me softly. And dammit, I breathed him in so deep.

"Yes, you can come back."

"Mmm, good." His mood shifted, and I knew it when he pressed up against me. "This is fucking torture, you know that, right? I can't look at you when you're wearing normal clothes without getting hard."

I squirmed under his gaze, trying to keep my composure. "I'm wearing sweats and a towel on my head," I dismissed. "This isn't sexy."

He groaned as his eyes raked over my body. "I better finish my pizza and get back to work before I do something stupid. I get off at four thirty. I'll bring dinner."

"No, it's okay, I'll make something. I'm getting kinda tired of eating out." We had been eating out for three days straight and I needed a home cooked meal.

"Okay then, I'll cook. You get ready for your meeting and do whatever it is to make yourself hotter than you already are, and I'll make dinner. Deal?"

I cast a glance at the tiled kitchen floor, knowing I was going to give in. "Fine, deal."

"Good. All right then, I've gotta go back to work. I'll see you tonight."

Then he turned on his heel and left, giving Lex a ruffle of her hair and letting her know that she and him were cooking dinner tonight, thus leaving me realizing that me and my plans were completely and utterly fucked.

****

Bram

I knew how to make one thing and because I wanted to impress Jadey and Lex, I stopped at the store to grab the ingredients for Mom's famous Chicken Divan. When I texted her to tell her I was making it for the girls, I swore I could hear her screech through the phone.

I got to Jade's fifteen minutes before her meeting started. When she answered the door, I had to clench my fists to keep myself back. She'd always been beautiful since the first time I saw her standing at my doorstep. But grown-up Jade was magnetic.

Her look was all business. She was wearing some form fitting pink skirt that went down to her knees and hugged every last torturous curve. And the silk blouse she wore. I wanted to rip every last button off with my teeth. So yeah, I was feeling animalistic around her and it didn't help that her hair was tied up in a long ponytail, that made it hard not to fantasize about what I could do with it.

"Shit, Jadey. Look at you."

"Thanks?"

"Yeah, babe. I meant you look fuckin' amazing. Professional, but sexy as all hell."

At my words, her cheeks turned red and damn, I missed that too.

"Thank you. Hey, so, I'm just finishing getting ready for my meeting. Lex is in her room video chatting with a friend, but she knows you're getting here soon, so she'll probably be out in a few and if she's not out in like twenty minutes, can you just check on her?"

"Course."

"Okay, great." Jade shuffled around some papers that were spread across her dining table. "You've won that girl over, you know? She really likes you. Wouldn't stop talking about your plans all day. I believe she has a few movies picked out, so I'm sorry to tell you, but it looks like you'll be enjoying pony marathon tonight." Jade assembled her papers and looked up at me with a smile.

"Well, I was always curious about Bronies. Who knows, maybe I'll join."

Jade's shoulders shook as she stifled laughter. "They aren't organized, Bram. I don't think we have a local Brony chapter." Her stifled laughs became giggles.

"Maybe I'll start my own."

"You're ridiculous. But Lex will appreciate your enthusiasm for the ponies."

"She's an incredible kid, you know?"

Jade smiled brightly. "Yeah, I know." She craned her neck to see in the bags as her eyebrows raised. "What do we have here?"

I put the bags behind my back and shook my head at her. "You'll just have to wait and see. But I promise you won't be disappointed."

****

"Are you my mom's new boyfriend?"

I was in the middle of shredding chicken when Lex asked. I'd learned the kid was no holds barred, say what you mean, mean what you say kind of kid. And I liked it. Until right then.

"Uh, what?" I stalled. Shit. I had no idea what to say here. I wasn't Jade boyfriend. I knew that much. I wasn't going to stay out of her life, I knew that too. "Your mom and I are old friends. You know that."

Lex cocked her head to the side, her face stone-cold seriousness that would've made me laugh if not for the words that followed.

"You better not hurt my mom. I like you, but if you hurt her, I won't like you much anymore. My biological father hurt her real bad."

At that, my jaw clenched. I knew I'd done it, I'd fucking caused it, and I had no right to be jealous. But the idea of someone's hands all over my Jade sent the blood rushing straight to my head and suddenly I wanted to tear some fucker in half.

"He did?" I gritted out.

Lex's eyes fell. "Yeah. He didn't love her because she was havin' me, so he left us. Or something like that. But Mom cries sometimes when she thinks I'm in bed and I think she's still missin' him."

It was like a spear to my heart. Missing him. Fuck. "I'm sorry Lex." I didn't know what to say to the kid. "You know, sometimes people just cry because it feels good. I wouldn't worry about your mom. She's a tough woman."

Lex looked up at me and smiled. "I know." Her smile faded, and she went back to what she was doing. "I hope you and Mom stay kissing friends because I like you and I don't want to not like you."

"Your mom's lucky to have you, kiddo."

"She knows. She tells me all the time!"

Lex and I were in the middle of an episode when Jade appeared, looking cute as hell in sweats and a tee.

269

She slumped down on the other side of the couch, way too far from me.

I reached my arms out, motioning her over. Jade bit down on that plump bottom lip as she looked at Lex and then shook her head at me. I got it and after my conversation with Lex, it made sense.

"What smells so good?"

"Hmm, why don't you come to the kitchen, and see?" I didn't care one shit about the food. I just wanted Jade alone for a few minutes.

I stood up and pulled her off the couch, then placed my hands on her waist from behind to push her forward. Jade's hands fell to mine, and she held me in place as we walked to the oven.

"Counter," she demanded when we were standing in the kitchen.

"Counter?"

"Yes, counter. Put me on it." Her lips hitched up at the side and fuck, she was perfect.

My dick twitched in my pants at her words and I didn't hesitate before I grabbing her, putting her on the countertop, and pushing her legs apart with my hands so I could shove my body between.

"Thanks for helping me out tonight."

"Mmm, anytime baby." I kissed her lips and Jade moaned into my mouth as one leg wrapped around my back and dug in, drawing me closer to her center. Her hand ran up the back of my neck.

"And that for helping me at the hospital," she said breathlessly between kisses.

I rolled into her. "Again, anytime, but hopefully that'll never happen again."

"Agree."

We both shut up when Jade fisted her hands in my hair and pulled me close. I sucked in her bottom lip, biting it gently with my teeth.

Jade's eyes were heavy and her lips swollen.

"Do you need me, baby?"

Jade hesitated before answering quietly. "Yes. I've always needed you."

Fuck. I pressed into her while pulling her even closer, erasing any space between our bodies.

"Do you need me, Bram?"

I didn't have to think about it. "I've always needed you, Jadey. Every second of every fucking day, I've needed you. And now that you're back, I'm not letting you go."

I saw the questions written in her expression. But this was not the time. Eventually, I'd have to explain it all, but for now, we'd enjoy each other for a little longer. was forced to tear myself away from her. Eventually I'd have to explain it all, but for now, we'd enjoy each other for a little bit longer.

Chapter 12

Bram

"Dinner was really, really good. I forgot how much I loved Chicken Divan."

"I'll tell my mom it worked out. She'll be happy. She was happy to hear that you're back."

Jade turned and gave me a half-assed, half-smile. "I miss her. I've missed her for years, actually. Your dad too."

I reached out and grabbed her hand, interlacing our fingers together. "I know."

"Are they still mad about how I left?"

"What? Mad at you?" I laughed, because she couldn't be fucking serious. Jade stared back at me, guilt in her eyes. Fuck me. "No Jadey, they aren't mad at you. Believe me, they never blamed you for anything that happened between us."

"How could they not, with the way I left?"

"Because they were pissed at me, Jadey. They knew what the fuck I'd done and I'm not entirely sure my mom ever forgave me after I lost you. Pretty sure she always loved you more than me, anyway."

We were both silent, neither of us making an effort to talk about all the shit we needed to talk about. I wanted to explain it all, make her finally understand why I'd done it. I wanted to ask her about Lex's father. Jade yawned. I replayed the last week over in my mind and yeah, now was not the time.

"You tired, baby?"

She sighed and let her head fall back. "Yeah, it's been a long few days and I haven't slept much. I've been so worried about Lex, I can barely think straight, let alone sleep."

"Come over here and lie down." I motioned to her, and she didn't hesitate to crawl over and lay her head on my lap. "How about this? You get some sleep and I'll be right here in case Lex wakes up."

"Bram," she protested, but stopped when my fingers sifted through her hair and ran across her scalp. Jade moaned. "Oh god, that feels so good."

My cock instantly sprung to life, thinking those words were for *him* and it was playtime. Down, boy. I shifted, trying to make sure I didn't jab her in the head with my erection.

"Oh, god. I might be able to fall asleep like this."

"Good. Get some rest babe, I'll be here."

I waited for her to fall asleep before I carried her to bed, doing my damn best not to wake her up. I needed to find that safe, and I had to do it without Jade finding out.

****

Jade

"Goodness, I forgot how awful it is to wake up this early," Evie whined at me while I fought with the keyhole, trying to open the door. I swore last week when I came to look at the place, the real estate agent had opened it with ease.

Last week, the previous owners had finished moving out, but with Lex's hospital stay and Evie travelling to San Francisco, we hadn't been able to come by for any amount of time, other than a quick look. Everything had been in order and I was excited for Evie and Lex to see it.

Evie was resting her forehead on the brick and holding a very sleepy Lex's hand. I rattled the lock, hoping that if I shook it enough, it would open. I also worried that if anyone else shook it enough, it would open.

"Something wrong with the key, mommy?" A sleepy Lex sidled up next to me and perused my struggle.

"I don't know, honey, I sure hope not. Otherwise Evie might go on strike."

"What's a strike?"

Evie groaned, and I stifled a giggle. I had forgotten how much she hated waking up early. I liked the mornings, even though I could do without five a.m. wake ups, I also could survive them with a cup of coffee, or two. Even so, I didn't have coffee, and I was way too tired to give a lesson on workers' unions.

"It's when people who work together form a group and push for better working conditions."

"Is that real?"

I rattled the handle and turned to Lex. "It sure is." Luckily, she was too sleepy to demand more details. I made one final play at the damn door and was pleasantly surprised when I finally finagled it open with a loud "Aha!"

Evie startled and shot to standing, mumbling, "Are we there yet?"

Lex grabbed Evie's hand and pulled. "We've been here silly. You were sleeping! Come on, let's see the store."

I followed closely behind, searching for the light

switch, tripping over no less than two something's on my search for the switch, which was odd, considering when I saw the place last week, it was sparkling clean. I flipped it on and a very, very dim light filled the room as we all let out a collective gasp.

"Holy fucking hell!"

"Whoa," Lex mumbled.

"Oh my god." I threw a hand on my forehead. "I, I just saw it last week," I stammered, trying to make sense of what the hell I was looking at. "It, oh god!" My eyes centered on the long wall behind the display cases, which had been pristine and beautiful last week, but were now nothing more than empty, broken shells of cases where they sat. Glass littered the floor in front of them, along with scattered trash. But that wasn't what caught my attention. It was the red spray paint that had been sprayed across that wall in long, cryptic lettering.

"Evie, get Lex outside!" My head spun as I reached for the phone in my purse with shaking hands. I hit the contact and waited, staring up at the wall, my lip quivering as it rang. After a few rings, I heard his sleepy voice.

"Jade? Is everything okay?"

"No," I choked out and then proceeded to say nothing as I hyperventilated into the phone. I wasn't poor, and I also had insurance on the property; I could handle some vandalism. But it wasn't the work that was going to have to be done or even the money to do it. No, not all. It was the words. Words that called a thousand other emotions to mind.

Bram's voice sounded much more alert when he spoke again. "Jade, what's wrong? Where are you?"

"Store. I'm at our new store." I exhaled the breath I

had been holding. "Bram, it's, it's bad. It's destroyed. I don't understand. I don't understand." The memories collided into me, and that was all it took for me to lose it.

"Okay, okay, it's okay Jadey. Where are you at? Is it the old bakery building?" His voice was sharp, and he spoke with calm authority.

"Yes."

"Okay, hang on, sweetheart. You stay on the phone."

I hung on and listened while Bram made another phone call. "Sheriff, it's Taylor. I'm headed to Lou's old bakery. The new owner is there, and she says it's been vandalized. Yes, sir. Okay, thank you, sir. Yeah, will do. Later."

I heard muted cursing, and the phone rustled. "Baby, you still there?"

"Yeah, I'm here."

"Cameron's on his way. He's on duty and I'll be there as soon as possible, okay? I'm leaving right now, but it'll take me thirty minutes to get there. I need you to get out of the building. Don't touch anything more than what you've already touched. Is anyone with you?"

"Evie and Lex."

"Fuck!" His cool waned. I heard a faint "Motherfucker," before he was back. "You all get back in your car and lock the doors. I'll tell Cam where you're at, but you don't unlock those doors for anyone, except for him or me. Do you understand?"

I nodded, suddenly feeling even more terrified. What was happening?

"Baby, tell me you understand."

"I, I do. I understand."

"Are you still in there?"

"Yes."

"Get out, Jade. Get out now. Stay on the phone with me and walk out. Don't touch the door handle or lock the door, just shove out with your shoulder and get out. Now, Jade."

His final words jolted me and I jumped to. "Okay, I'm leaving right now."

I glanced back one final time at the words. Something sick and twisted in me needed to see them, to affirm them, to remind me of that confusing day. The day my world completely fell apart. I had thought it was a mix-up, a mistake, that someone had gotten the wrong girl. But now, I was sure that those words and that knife had always been intended for me. I just didn't know why.

Too pretty of a face.

My entire body shivered and shook as I scurried out the door, slamming into it with my shoulder. A few minutes later, Cameron arrived. The three of us waited in the SUV while he and another officer went in with flashlights. Twenty minutes after that, Bram arrived, but he came to me first, knocking on my window, motioning for me to come out.

I turned to Evie. "Can you take Lex to Sunshine's while I deal with this? I'll get a ride over when I'm done."

Evie looked around, then back at me. "Are you sure? I can stay and deal with it while you take Lex."

"I'm sure, hun. I need to talk to Bram."

Evie nodded and took my place in the car. I waited until they were out of sight until I turned to Bram.

"Cameron sent me pictures." His face was stone as he spoke through gritted teeth.

"How bad is it? I only saw the front."

He worked his jaw from side to side and angled his head a bit. God, even angry he was handsome. And even terrified out of my head, I still wanted to kiss him.

"It's bad, baby." He narrowed his eyes a bit and studied me. "Did you read what's spray-painted on the wall?"

I nodded, trying to hide any recognition of that old memory, but it was fruitless. I felt it dripping off me, supplanting my face with the new knowledge that what happened to me that day was not a coincidence.

"That mean something to you?" he asked, studying me closely.

"No, I, I don't think so." *Bury it Jade, bury the memories.* I had mentally covered them in dirt, knowing that if I buried them, I'd never have to re-live that pain— the pain of what he'd done, that guilt over what I'd done. After all these years, I'd been so hurt by him, but I had my own secrets to hide, sure that if I could keep myself from thinking of them, they'd cease to exist.

Bram pulled me into him. "It's going to be okay. I'm going to make sure you and Lex are protected. Do you trust me with that, baby?"

Did I? Did I trust him now? Did I have a choice not to? He was a cop, and by all accounts, a good one. He was also the man who'd broken my heart. But I had to trust him because I had no one else.

I nodded and heard his audible sigh of relief. I rested my head on his chest and closed my eyes, breathing him in, letting the comforting feel of being in his arms wash over me.

Chapter 13

Bram—Twenty-one years old

"We're completely fucked if we don't get this information to PD, man!" I ran my hand through my hair as I paced like the nervous wreck I was. This had been our meeting place for the past year. We'd collected as much information as we could on Nathan's network and operating procedures. I'd been the one to wear a wire to every single pickup and drop-off, hoping that if we had enough audio, we could help nail these guys.

"Calm the hell down. It ain't gonna help shit if you're acting like you got something to be nervous about. Man, I told you we needed to go about our business as usual, act like fucking everything is normal, otherwise it's gonna be both our asses. And to be frank, I don't give a fuck about our asses, but you know who'll get dragged into this because of you." Jules stood, like everything in the world was all right, like we hadn't potentially got caught. All we could do was hope that his pay-off was enough to buy silence.

I stopped and stared dead at him. Me? He wanted to blame me? "Right, like your plan of bringing Jade in to work with you was better?"

Jules snapped to me and answered right away, "No asshole, not better. But you've taken her place, you kept her close, and now you two are fuckin' together. Your plan would've made sense had you gotten her out like I fuckin' told you to."

"I love her, Jules."

"Nah, man. If you love her, you'd do everything you can to keep her safe. You're selfish, that's what you are."

I gulped back the reality check like a thick sludge pouring down my throat, choking me and poisoning my insides. Jules studied me.

"Yeah, you see it now, don't you?"

I gritted my teeth, annoyed at how right he was. No. I wasn't getting rid of Jade. Besides, she'd never leave me. What would I tell her? *I've been working for your father for years and I need to keep you safe?* That would destroy her. If she knew the entire story, she'd never let up. She'd never leave me.

"It's not that simple and you know it. I've made her promises that I intend to keep. We've made plans for our life together, man." I slumped down on a tree stump and let my head fall into my hands.

I had told Jade that I wanted to marry her. As soon as school was over and I started working as a sports trainer, I'd save money so I could give her the ring and the wedding she wanted. We planned to stay in Brooks Falls and I could work in White Oak, get a job at the university's football team, while Jade worked on building a small business for her cakes and other shit she made. We had our lives planned: two kids, maybe a dog, and if we could, buy the house my parents owned when they retired to Arizona or Florida. All of that was swirling around in my head when Jules broke through my thoughts.

"You're not gonna make a single one of those promises from the grave. Or worse, if she gets caught up in this, you won't have a Jade to make promises to." His voice was solemn, sad and distant, not like typical Jules.

I had always known growing up that Jules loved his sister and looked after her from day one. When he started working at the local grocery store in town, I knew he gave his sister money for clothes and food. He wasn't a brother; he was a parent.

"I know you love her, but—"

"I'm not breaking up with her." My response was definitive. "She has no one, Jules. She has you and me and my parents. She gets out of this town, she's completely fuckin' alone. Do you really think that's better?"

He hung his head, looking defeated. "I think it's better than dead, man. She'd at least have a fighting chance in hell to do something with her life. Jade's always been the talented, smart one when it came to school, but so fucking I and innocent with life. You know this. And fuck, she already knows Nathan and I are fucked, so doesn't even have me anymore. You know that the less she knows, the better. And the farther away she is from this when shit goes down, the better."

It was true. She finally understood what Nathan and Jules had been up to when town gossip reached her ears. Jade didn't give a final fuck about her father, but she loved her brother and finding out he was dealing, had almost destroyed her. She couldn't find out about me. She couldn't know anything that would get her wrapped up in this shit.

I knew Jules was right, that I had to get her away from this, but I couldn't bring myself to do it. And she wouldn't go easily.

****

Jade

I was terrified and I couldn't settle. Bram and I finally made it to Sunshine's after filling out a lengthy police report, and being grilled by Bram on every single detail. He was on edge, more so than I was, which didn't surprise me. He'd always been protective, but something about this energy was different.

When we got to Sunshine's, Bram went immediately to Lex, and I followed, hot on his heels, prepared to calm my sweet girl. But before I could get there, she had thrown herself in his arms, full of tears, asking him if he was going to protect me. My heart broke at the sight of it. She already trusted him so much and he already cared about her so much. His hands ran through her hair as he lifted her up and held her as she sobbed.

I joined them and he pulled me in, but Lex didn't come to me. She only begged over and over for him to protect me. My heart splintered at her words. I'd never seen her so afraid.

"Honey, I'm right here and I'll be just fine. Lex? Will you look at me?" I pulled her thick hair back from her eyes, which were by now red and sparkling with tears.

"Mom, I, I'm scared. I don't want to lose you," Lex choked out through wails.

"Let's go home, baby," Bram whispered to me, as he held Lex with one arm and took my hand.

I looked at Evie, trying to catch her eyes, but she was a million miles away and trembling. I pulled out of Bram's hold and reached for Evie. She jumped at the contact, but I held her attention.

"Vee, hun, are you okay?"

"What?" she snapped to me, like she hadn't seen me

standing right in front of her. Her dark eyes widened in surprise and a look of fear flashed across her beautiful face, before she shook her head and sighed out a small breath.

Evie smiled, a sad smile that I wasn't buying for a second.

"Are you okay?" I asked again, realizing that she didn't hear me the first time.

"Of course. I'm just worried about you and Lex. Are *you* okay?" She turned the focus back on me and I ignored the gnawing feeling in my gut that told me to press. This was Evie. She was happy-go-lucky and this probably just shocked her.

"Yeah, we'll be all right. It was probably just some kids," I lied, knowing that after what I'd seen and what I felt, it was so much more than that.

Evie and I looked at each other and I swore that I saw suspicion in her eyes, but then she smiled again.

"Right. You're probably right." Evie locked arms with me and we followed Bram to my SUV.

****

We spent the rest of the day together and tried to get our minds off what had happened. Lex was much more at ease with Bram around and I knew it was because she felt safe in his presence. I could hardly blame the kid.

It was a good day and effectively took our attention away from the drama. We played games at the apartment all day and at night, Evie made dinner for us. It felt easy and comfortable, which was exactly what we'd all needed.

"Let me give you a ride home," Bram offered to Evie, who'd just finished tucking in Lex.

Evie scoffed. "I'm in walking distance, like literally

right across the street. Why don't you guys watch me get in the house and that'll be good enough." She patted Bram's bicep, and then made wide eyes at me.

Bram shook his head at her. But I had to agree. Those arms were something.

After watching Evie get home safely, Bram and I went to the small balcony of my apartment that was facing trees. The darkness shrouded us except for a few candles that we lit. He had popped open a bottle of beer and poured me a half glass of wine. It was peaceful and private and watching him in all his mountain man cop glory was enough to make my knees knock.

"What is that face?" Bram asked with a smirk as I tipped the glass of wine up to my mouth, allowing my eyes to fasten securely on his lips.

"What face?" I feigned innocence as I pointed at my chest. "My face?" I put the glass down and ran my tongue across the top lip and looked to the side.

"Yeah, babe, your face." Bram shifted, and narrowed his eyes. "That face. Those fuckin lips. That tongue," he said darkly as he focused on my mouth. His eyes were at half-mast when he looked at me and shook his head. "What am I gonna do with you?"

"I don't know what you're gonna do *with* me, but I have a few ideas about what I'm gonna do *to* you." Bram gaped and I stood up from my seat across from him and shot him a sexy grin.

"What are you doing to do me?" he asked with a strangled laugh.

I didn't answer as I moved toward him. His hands were instantly at my hips and mine at his shoulders as I ran my nails down the length of his arms, dipping and rolling across every muscle. I was in the middle of worshipping his rugged arms when I was brought back to the moment by a groan. That did it, unlocking something inside of me, something that I had buried. Something that had only ever been for him.

I pulled away and lowered to my knees in front of him. Bram's posture straightened as he shifted in his chair.

"Jadey, what are you doing?" His voice was strained, and his body was so rigid. "It's been a difficult day; you shouldn't do this."

I ran my hand along his thick thighs. "That's funny, because I feel the exact opposite." I peered up through my lashes and I knew I was a goner.

"Fuck," he drew out, looking tortured and conflicted beneath my touch.

"Do you want to watch while I suck you?"

"You can't fucking talk like that right now. I'm gonna cum just thinking of those lips wrapped around my cock."

I lifted my shirt and tossed it to the floor. His eyes darkened as they roamed over me. I unhooked the lace bra and let my breasts fall. He swallowed hard and reached out a hand. I leaned into his touch and watched as his eyes momentarily closed, his hand kneading my breast before he rolled my nipple between his fingers.

"Ah!" I bucked at the sudden sensation of his hands on me and let my head fall back. "Feels good." The wetness gathered at my center, and I looked up at him. "Shirt."

Bram ripped his shirt off, and if I wasn't wet enough before, I was now. How one man could be so perfect, I didn't know. And that small trail of hair on his hard stomach led to places I was ready to explore. I reached out and ran a finger along the inside at the waist of his jeans, teasing him with my touch. I needed him to want me so badly that he snapped and let himself go. He'd always been gentle with me, but the times I'd stretched his restraint so thin that he snapped like a band? Well, let's just say that those were the times I fantasized about when I was taking care of myself.

I undid his jeans, flicking the single button and unzipping his fly slowly while I watched him watching me. I hadn't forgotten how much he'd loved to watch the things we did to each other. I placed my hands at his sides and then ran my fingers down, latching onto the waist of his jeans and pulling them off. His body shivered. When I saw his boxer briefs, I licked my lips, remembering what was in there. I'd seen him and felt him when he fucked me in my bed, but nothing could replace being up close and personal with him like this. His cock was beautiful, long and thick, and the tip was glistening with a dot of pre-cum.

I bent my head down to kiss a path along his stony abs and his hips jerked at the contact.

"Do you like that?" I asked, widening my eyes in feigned innocence, knowing I was tormenting him.

"You're being a tease." His dark eyes glinted. "What are you trying to do to me?"

"I told you. I'm trying to suck you." I pouted my lips, digging in with my nails, quickly unraveling his restraint.

His hands pushed into my hair and he fisted it in the back of my head right before he yanked it back and to the side. He bent down to my ear.

"Is this what you want, baby? You want me to lose fucking self-control?" he gritted out through tight lips.

I whimpered, feeling my pussy pulse, knowing I was dripping. "What, what would make you think that?" I asked, trying to catch my breath. Hell, I was trying to maintain my control, but the man was undoing me quicker than I was him.

He pulled my hair again, this time gripping tighter. I gasped, my arousal almost too much to contain.

"Just like old times, huh?" Bram leaned in and growled into my ear.

I nodded, unable to find words good enough to express my desire.

"You make me fuckin' crazy. If you don't get that filthy mouth on my cock, there's no telling what I might do."

I grinned, feeling my eyes get heavier. This was where I had always liked us best, some place between desire and desperation, pain and pleasure, a place he and I had spent so much time playing with one another and testing our limits.

"You want it?" Bram asked.

"So bad," I whispered, and then licked my lips.

Bram let go of my hair and leaned back with a dark smile. "Suck then, baby."

My heart was racing. It was almost too much. I pulled his boxer briefs down, pressing my thighs together at the sight. I sighed. His cock sprang free, hard and long and thick and all for me. I lowered myself to him, starting at his balls, gently licking and sucking them, before moving to his base and licking one long path up to the tip.

"Fuck," he ground out quietly.

I let his dick leave my lips with a pop, but didn't give any time for a reaction when I took him deeper in my mouth until he hit the back of my throat. He breathed out a heavy breath as I sucked him, my mouth wrapped around all his hard, as I reveled in the moment and forgot everything else that had happened that day.

"Jesus, Jadey, fuck!"

I gripped the side of his legs, pulling him closer and going deeper.

Bram grabbed onto my hair and pulled me off him, before shoving me back down. "Yeah, you like that, don't you?" he asked, holding my head in place.

I nodded and moaned around him.

"I'll give you what you want, but you remember the rules, right?"

I nodded immediately. Oh, I knew the rules. We'd established them early on when we both realized he liked to give it rough just as much as I liked getting it that way. All I had to do was tap him twice, and he's stop. I'd never needed to tap, but I appreciated how concerned he was for me, even during our more passionate moments.

"You want this cum?" He pulled his cock all the way out. I shook my head up and down and watched as his eyes narrowed. Bram pulled my head back, and through gritted teeth, demanded, "No. Say it. Tell me what you want."

I could hardly think straight, let alone speak, so I answered him with a simple and somewhat breathless, "Yes," then marveled at the sight of his intensity kicking up from ten to ten thousand. The corners of his eyes crinkled, and his brow furrowed when the hand he was using to pull my hair slid around to my face and squeezed.

"I said, tell me what you want." His voice was quiet and low, laced with his weakening self-restraint. "If I didn't know better, I'd think you were trying to provoke me."

He wasn't wrong. This was my favorite game. Feign innocence and stupidity in exchange for his delicious punishments.

"I want your cum," I whispered. "I need it."

"Mmm, that's right. That's what I need from you." Bram pet my hair and the gentle gesture in the midst of all this nearly took me out.

"Move back," Bram told me as he pushed to standing. I moved and straightened until I was face to dick.

"Open your mouth, baby," Bram commanded, and I quickly obliged, ready for him to be back inside me.

It took no time for him to find his stride, pumping and bucking into my mouth as I took every inch.

"Jadey, that's. Fuck. What are you trying to do to me? Ah yeah." He grunted out the string of words, rushed and desperate, and I knew he was close. I cupped his balls and pressed my thumb gently beneath them.

Bram thrusted harder and I felt his body tense and tighten beneath me, his powerful hips bucking up as warm liquid shot into my throat. I tapped twice on his leg and my hair was immediately freed as I jerked back and let him watch me swallow his cum. His beautiful blue eyes were dark with lust as he watched me. I bent back down and licked the tip of his cock to ensure I hadn't missed a drop.

At the contact, he moaned. "Look what you do to me," he said tenderly, cupping my jaw with one hand."

I smiled and bit my lip. "Look what you do to me," I replied, half teasing, half wishing he had any clue what he did to me.

"Then I guess it's a good match." He grinned, then reached out a hand and pulled me up to standing so he could plant a kiss on my lips. He pulled up his pants but left them undone. "Bed?" he asked.

"Bed," I answered, and we walked inside and went to straight to bed and didn't get a lick of sleep that night.

Chapter 14

Jade

For the next few days, Bram stayed with us, refusing to leave our side except to go to work. Evie and I had spent what felt like seventy-two straight hours on the phone with the insurance company.

With Priscilla's party hot on our heels, I knew we weren't going to be able to get the store in order with enough time. The only thing we could do was turn Evie's kitchen into ground zero and hope that it would have enough space to work with.

The only positive that week was when Andrew called to let me know that he wanted to go over the house interiors with me. He offered to come to me, and I easily accepted. With Lex in her final week of the cast and everything else going on, I was exhausted.

I opened the door to my apartment.

"Hi Andrew!" I swung open the door and motioned for him to come in. "Thanks so much for coming to meet me here."

"Not a problem at all. I understand you're busy and this is a small town, so I, uh, I heard about what happened with your store."

I smiled weakly at him, mostly because I really was sick of talking about it. After recounting everything to the police and then discussing in detail with insurance, I was all talked out. Not to mention Bram was on edge anytime it was mentioned in his presence, so I avoided the topic as much as possible.

"Yeah. Probably some kids or something." I shrugged, looking to the side.

"Right. Well, I hope they figure out who did it."

"Yep. So, I was thinking dark hardwoods for the floors." I pivoted harder than a politician in a debate. "But only in spaces with lots of natural light!" I added, hoping we could move on.

"Oh, uh, yes." He pulled out a notepad and started scribbling down my answers on it. For the next two hours, we went over design details, interior options, and paint colors. It felt fun and light, and was a welcome distraction from everything else going on.

At five o'clock, the door swung open and in walked Bram, all smiles and carrying a big plastic bag. Lex jumped up from her spot on the couch and ran right to him.

"Bram! I didn't know you were coming over today!" Lex exclaimed as she hugged his leg.

"It was a surprise, kiddo," he answered, the smile quickly disappearing from his face when he looked my way.

"Hey." My voice cracked under the pressure of his glare.

"Hey, baby," he replied to me, but he was staring at Andrew. "I didn't know anyone else would be over."

I licked my lips and shifted in my seat. Bram and I hadn't exactly established ourselves as anything and I was still not sure what to make of him in my life.

"Bram, this is Andrew, my *builder*," I emphasized as I turned to Andrew. "This is Bram, my—" I froze. My eyes shifted to Lex, who was paying way too much attention to this conversation. I panned to Bram, whose lips pressed into a thin line told me all I needed to know. "My friend, Bram Taylor," I finished.

The word hung in the air like a storm cloud, and I felt Bram's mood quickly shift from annoyance to pure anger. His eyes blazed as he turned them on me.

"A word, Jadey." It wasn't a question.

"Ms. Greene, I can—" Andrew began to say, but I cut him off.

"Actually, Bram, we're kind of in the middle of something. We've been at it for two hours and I'm sure Andrew would really like to finish so he can get out of here. We can have a word later." I dismissed him, knowing it wouldn't help, but what choice did I have? I wasn't going to be rude to Andrew, and I also wasn't going to leave Lex alone with a man I barely knew.

I flinched when his face hardened, and I heard the plastic bag being crushed in his fist. That's when I noticed that the bag was from the Blue Rose, and with all the awkwardness, I'd completely missed the incredible smell wafting around my house. My stomach grumbled.

Bram nodded slowly and patted Lex on the shoulder. She'd been attached to his leg since he walked in, something that had not escaped me. "Let's bring this food to the kitchen, huh?"

"Oh, I can help. I know where Mom keeps the good plates!"

I couldn't help but smile at how cute the two of them were together. They walked to the kitchen where Bram put the bag down and instructed Lex to "wait here, kiddo" before he stalked over to me. The man towered over me and if I didn't know better, I'd be terrified. And just when I expected him to make some snide remark, he bent down, grabbed a strand of my hair and gently put it back. "Hi my Jadey." His voice was butter, smooth and delicious and probably not that good for me. I swallowed, barely hanging on, when he bent down and planted a soft kiss on my lips.

"Ew, you guys are kissing again!" My eyes were wide open, fixed on Bram, whose lips were still pressed to mine. His eyes were narrowed. Then I heard Lex sigh and say to whoever was listening. "They're kissin' all the time now. They sneak away like I can't see them, but I'm eight, Mr. Andrew. I'm not dumb."

My eyes enlarged and Bram's kissing scowl became a kissing smile as he chuckled into my lips. When he let me go, he smirked, way too self-satisfied when all I wanted to do was smack the arrogance right off his handsome, stupid, chiseled face.

"I'll wait until you have a minute, baby." Then he turned to Lex, who was still waiting in the kitchen. "We can get that food ready later. What are we watching?" He gestured to the TV with his head.

"Ms. Greene," Andrew spoke up again. "I have a six o'clock appointment, so now would be good a time to close this out. I have more than enough to get started." He smiled, his face warm and genuine, and I hadn't missed that he was no longer calling me Jade.

I smiled back, grateful for his kindness. Besides, I was ready to turn my brain off for a few and eat whatever it was that Bram had brought in. "Okay, that sounds great. I can email you with anything else I think of."

"Absolutely," Andrew replied, and then turned to Bram. "Very nice to meet you," he lied, before looking at me. "You should bring Bram out to the site sometime and show him the progress. Maybe bring your friend too." He suggested with a wink and damn, the guy was good.

I followed Andrew to the door and saw him out, waving goodbye as he left the apartment.

I was all smiles until I shut the door behind me and shot Bram a death glare. Before I could dig into him, Lex interjected.

"Mom, it's almost five thirty!" She pointed to the clock. "I'm supposed to go to Liam's house. My bags are all packed and I'm ready. Can we go early? Please, please?"

I looked at the calendar on my phone and saw that she was right. I was supposed to drop her off in fifteen minutes. I also noticed that I had another event named MEETING WITH PRISCILLA!!! scheduled right on top of it.

"Oh, crap." I moved quickly around the house, gathering my purse and keys, hoping I could get Lex there and get back in time for my call.

"Jadey, what's the matter?" Bram asked, as I frantically threw my stuff together.

"I gotta get Lex to Renata's and I have to go now so I can be back for my planning session with Priscilla in fifteen minutes." I tossed my wallet into my purse and was stopped when Bram curled his large hands around my waist from behind and pulled me in.

"All right, baby, calm down."

I was tense and even though being in his arms was just about the best damn thing ever, I wiggled out, needing to get going.

"I can't calm down. I have things to do," I replied, grabbing Lex's overnight bag.

"Yeah, and you also have me." Bram snagged the bag from me.

"Hey! I don't have time for this." I gripped the bag handle so both our hands were on it. I could feel the clock ticking and the last thing I needed was to piss off my best client by showing up to our meeting late, when I was already going to be under-prepared.

"I can do things other than kiss you and feed you, you know?" Bram scoffed and then used his other hand to peel my grip from the bag. "I'll take Lex to Renata's, and you stay here and prepare for your call, okay?"

"But—" I went to protest, but Bram interrupted.

"No. Now say okay and go get ready for your meeting."

My jaw fell slack. "Okay?" I asked, confused, bewildered, and definitely smitten.

"There you go, babe, you did it," Bram teased, then focused his attention on Lex. "Looks like it's just you and me. That okay with you?"

She jumped and did a small spin. "Yes! Can we ride in the truck, though? I want to look really cool when I pull up to Liam's house."

Bram and I shared a knowing look while I stifled an amused snort.

"Yep, I've got the truck," Bram told Lex, then looked at me. "Be back, babe. After your call, we're gonna talk." He leaned in and placed a kiss on my lips. It felt great, but I really melted when he and Lex sauntered out the door, hand in hand. I stood in the doorway watching them descend the staircase, chatting and laughing the entire way.

****

I leaned on the kitchen counter and sighed before I

took a big sip of wine. I'd just gotten off the call with Priscilla and was ready to relax. Unfortunately, Bram was more interested in arguing about Andrew.

"He's building my house. I really don't see what the big deal is. You're acting like you walked in on us making out."

Bram's nostrils flared. "Pretty sure that's what he wanted."

I scoffed and rolled my eyes. "He was here to perform the job that I hired him to do. You're way overreacting."

"Overreacting?" Bram took a step toward me. "Seriously, Jadey?" He bent down so we were nose to nose, and I could feel his anger. "Three days ago, you walked into your new store to find it completely destroyed with a message that I still haven't been able to make sense of." He studied my face, and I glanced down, knowing I should tell him. I didn't understand why he hadn't pressed, but I was glad for it.

"Then, some guy that I've never met, and you barely know, invites himself over to your apartment without me vetting him, or at the very least, being here to make sure you're safe. How am I supposed to protect you if you're letting strangers in your house?"

I threw up my hands. "He's not a stranger! I hired the man," I hissed right into his face.

"Tell me what the fuck it meant, Jade!" Bram yelled, the question throwing me off so much that I stumbled backward.

"Wha—what?" I stammered.

"You know what, Jade. Tell me what it meant."

"You don't deserve the truth!" I broke, my calm snapping like a stretched rubber band. My heat beat wildly as my breaths came heavy and the memory of that day flooded in.

****

Jade—19 years old

I was on cloud nine driving back into town, and I couldn't wait to see Bram. My meeting with admissions at Le Cordon Bleu in San Francisco had gone great, and the school was amazing. The patisserie courses were exactly what I'd been looking for, and I felt like I was finally finding my footing and my path.

Bram and I had hardly talked while I was gone. He had been stressed, working overtime to recover some of his college grades that had slipped because he'd been working so much. And I was busy trying to do something with my life that was worthy of the man who somehow loved me.

It was eleven thirty when I got back to Brooks Falls, so I decided to wait in the park across from the Blue Rose, where I was meeting Bram for lunch.

It was beautiful outside, and I got lost in the smell of the storm heading in over the mountains. A cool, crisp breeze blew in, rustling up not only the leaves but also, all my hair. I giggled and hopped on a swing, letting the clean mountain air relax me as I swung back and forth, daydreaming about my future with Bram. I was mid-swing when I felt a pair of calloused hands grab my shoulders. I let out a shriek as I fell back, landing on my side in the wood chips.

I pushed up with my hands, ready to yell at some asshole kids, but a kick to my ribs sent me fully to the ground. I cried out and immediately curled up in a protective posture. I was glad that I did, because the next kick landed on the arm that was guarding my belly.

"Please, stop!" I begged, ready to please for mercy, when a hand on my hair yanked me up. I was set on my knees when I felt lips at my ear. I shuddered and fear paralyzed me.

"He has two days to deliver," a raspy voice warned.

"Wh—what? I don't know what you're talking about. You have the wrong person!" I stumbled around the words, but the man's grip got even tighter.

I felt the cold edge of a blade hit my cheek and I froze in place. I closed my eyes, wondering if I'd ever see Bram again. Panic surfaced as the blade was lowered to my chest and then to my exposed shoulder.

"Too pretty of a face," the voice rumbled in my ear right before the cool, sharp edge of the blade sliced across my shoulder. I hadn't even felt pain, only the cold steel of the knife, followed by the wetness of blood.

"Two more days," the man clipped out right before he shoved me forward.

****

I drove as fast as I could to the emergency room in White Oak, trying to ignore the blood that had splattered all over my seat and clothes. I'd called Bram several times, but to no avail.

It hadn't been too deep a cut and thankfully, stitches weren't necessary. I hadn't been able to get a hold of Bram the entire time. But finally, as I was leaving the hospital, I received a text from him.

Bram—*Change of plans. Couldn't meet for lunch, come to my school. Student Union where we normally meet.*—

Me—*Okay, I'll be there in five.*—

I parked and pulled my hoodie on to cover the huge pad of gauze that was plastered across my shoulder. I didn't want to lead with that. I knew how Bram could be, and it was better to ease him into whatever the hell had happened.

Walking up to the huge lawn in front of the Student Union building, I squinted, looking for him in the spot we normally met, but I only saw couples. I did recognize one of them as Bram's friend, so I made my way toward him when I stopped dead.

The air left my lungs on what felt like one final exhale. I heaved, wheezing and gasping for breath. The wind had been knocked out of me and all I could do was gape at the sight of them.

Long locks of wavy, blonde hair fell down the muscular back of the boy I'd recognize anywhere. Her perfectly lined blue eyes caught mine and she pushed away, whispering something in his ear. I was frozen, certain that my knees would buckle right underneath me, certain that my heart had stopped altogether.

Thunder boomed overhead, and I felt the first drops of rain as he walked toward me. He was different. I saw it before I felt it and at that point, I didn't think I could handle his explanation. I wanted to run, but I was stuck in place.

"Jade. I'm glad you came." He lifted his chin and peered down at me, his stony eyes condescending in their descent to meet my own gaze. He cleared his throat.

"I, um, I can't do this anymore. I've pretended long enough with you. I've tried to feel about you the way you feel about me because you've been in my life for so long and I've just. I've always felt sorry for you, Jade. But you've gotta know with who I am and who you are." He motioned between us, and I tilted my head, still stuck in a daze. "This will never work. You're trailer trash and my family, Jade, we have class. I can't keep this up and honestly, I'm tired of taking care of you."

I swayed to the side, feeling as unstable on the outside as I did internally. Bram reached out to touch me, but I jumped back, gaining my footing and stumbling back.

"Jade, I—"

I let out a whimper and turned a palm up, watching the raindrops fall faster and harder than before. Then, I did what I should have done from the start—I ran, knowing that I would never see him again.

Chapter 15

Bram

I carried Jade to the couch, her body shaking, tears falling onto her legs that were barely covered by a pair of tiny shorts.

"Baby. I, I didn't want to do it." I sat down on the couch, Jade still cradled in my arms.

"You didn't, you." She stumbled through the words as she pushed up and moved to the other side of the couch. "You didn't want to do it?" Jade's chest heaved as her green eyes lit. I opened my mouth to speak, but she cut me off.

"Don't tell me that!" She shook her head vehemently. "After all these years, all the pain you caused me, and you wanna start with that?"

Her voice was trembling, getting louder with each word. "We planned a future together. *You* told me that you wanted to marry me and never gave me any indication otherwise! I never asked for any of it." She threw a hand out, her face red and wet, before she finished me. "I would've been happy without any of it, so long as I had you in my life."

"I didn't know what else to do." My voice cracked. It was all I could manage to say.

"The only thing you knew how to do was to *destroy* me?" she asked, but I knew it wasn't a question.

"Jadey." I reached out, but she slapped my hand away.

"Don't touch me!"

"Fuck!" Tears welled in my eyes as I felt the anger rise up in me. I'd kept it down all these years, shoving it deeper down, ignoring the pain, the loss of control over the life I'd wanted to give her. That was it. I was done living afraid. "I have always loved you, Jadey. Fucking always."

"You're lying! Why are you doing this to me?" She was shaking her head, sobbing uncontrollably.

I reached out and interlaced our fingers together, keeping them tight so she couldn't get out of my grip. "Do you trust me, baby?"

"No!" She yanked her arm, but the hold I had on her only served to pull her in toward me. Jade collapsed into me, and I breathed a sigh of relief when I felt the tension in her body ease in my arms.

"You do, I know you do," I spoke into her hair, desperate to make this right. "If you didn't trust me, you wouldn't let me be here with you, with Lex."

"I hate you," she said, her voice weak and tired.

"No, Jadey." I gave her a light shake. "You love me," I whispered. "You still fucking love me."

She gasped, still shaking her head no. "Please, stop!"

"Never, baby," I told her, just as I grabbed her hips and moved her so she was straddling me. "You love me. You have to love me, Jadey," I croaked out through tears. "And I've never, not once in all these lonely years, stopped loving you, Jade Greene. You are my life and even if you never take me back, I'll fucking love you until the day I die."

Jade let her head fall forward, so we were forehead to forehead when she whimpered. "I don't want to feel this way. I'm so tired, Bram."

"What don't you want to feel?" I pressed, needing to hear her to say it.

Her voice was barely audible when she spoke. "I've never stopped loving you, never. I can't. I'm too weak. God knows I've tried to let you go, but I've always loved you."

I breathed for what seemed like the first time in nine years. I gripped her face with both hands and looked into her eyes. I needed her to know, to feel, to understand how I really saw her.

"You are a lot of things, Jade Greene—an incredible mother, a successful businesswoman, a strong person, and the fucking love of my life. You have *never* been weak, Jadey. Your strength is the way you love."

"Bram," she whispered, putting one hand over mine that still held her face. With that, I couldn't take it any longer. I released her face, sliding one hand around the back of her head and pulled her close, pressing my lips to hers in a deep kiss that was sensual, until it became heated,

I pulled away and told her breathlessly, "Tits, give me your goddamn tits."

Jade took no time in pulling her shirt off and unclasping her bra. Her full, round breasts fell, and I was momentarily hypnotized by the stiff, pink nipples that stood at attention in front of me.

"Fuck, baby. You're so beautiful," I said before I bent down and sucked her nipple into my mouth, rolling my tongue over the hard peak. Jade moaned, arching her back, pressing her breasts into my face. I didn't want to let her go, but I had to hear her say it again, so I tore myself away.

"Tell me again, Jadey. I need to hear you say it."

"I love you," she replied on an exhale. "But I'm scared, Bram. What if you—"

"I won't," I said definitively. "I'll never hurt you like that again, I promise."

"I don't trust you," Jade whispered, and her words sliced through me. I deserved them, I'd earned them, but fuck, they hurt.

"I know, baby." I gripped her ass and stood up. Jade wrapped her legs around me. "I did that to us, but now I'm gonna make it right. Everything I've ever done has been for you," I told her as I walked us to her room.

I lade Jade down on the bed. Her creamy skin looked like a gift and her wild, copper hair was flung freely across the bed. I caught her gaze. Those green eyes were long gone, hooded and filled with lust.

"Enough talking for now," I growled, pulling her shorts down and staring at the small strip of fabric covering her. I fingered the lace at the crease between her pussy and her thigh. Jade whimpered and moved her hips toward my finger.

"No," I gritted out.

Her jaw fell and her eyes clouded over. I pushed her panties aside and bent down to her center. Jade gasped, heaving breaths.

"Bram." She said my name in a tremulous pant, but I was already between her thighs, my tongue on her pussy, licking one long slow path up, until I reached her clit. I sucked it gently into my mouth and she cried out, bucking up into me. I hadn't forgotten how to make her feel good.

"Need more, baby?" I asked.

"Yes, please!" she begged, looking down at me, her eyes barely open.

I grabbed her panties and worked them down her legs before tossing them to the side. Jade sighed when I slid one finger inside of her and continued to lick her. She tasted like heaven, and I could feel my dick pulsing inside my jeans with each lick.

Jade gripped my hair and pushed my head down into her with a moan. I put a second finger inside of her and could feel her knees shaking at the side of my head. I slid my fingers in and out, her pussy so wet I could hear my fingers move in and out.

"Bram, I—" Jade gasped, and I knew she was close.

I lifted my head to encourage her, because damn, I needed this as much as she did. "Let go, baby. Come for me. I wanna taste you. I want all of you, baby. Give me what's fucking mine!" I growled and plunged back down into her right as she fell apart all over my mouth. I lapped up her juices like I was desperate for the woman, because I was.

When I was satisfied that Jade had been satisfied, I pushed off the bed and ripped my shirt off, before pulling my pants and boxer briefs down in one motion. Placing my hands on her thighs, I pushed her knees apart.

"Condoms," I said, sounding impatient, because I was. If I didn't get inside of her right then, I was going to lose my mind.

"The pill," Jade replied. "I'm on the pill and was tested recently."

"What?" I asked, annoyed and fighting images of Jade with someone else.

"Bram!" Jade scolded. "You wanna do this right

now?" she asked, matching my annoyance. Except she was right, because no, I definitely had better things to be doing than arguing about Jade's sex life.

"Tested last week, Jadey. All good," I told her and grinned when she raised her brows,

"Ambitious," she replied.

"Just hopeful, Jadey." I kissed her soft, swollen lips.

"Then fuck condoms and fuck me."

That was all she needed to say before I was back between her legs. "You want me to fuck you or love you?"

Jade's lip quivered as she lifted her forehead to mine and pulled a deep kiss from my lips. "Love me, baby." I felt her words everywhere.

I rolled my hips, letting the tip of my cock graze her pussy before pulling away.

"I said love me, not torture me!" she said on a breath.

I smiled into our kiss before I pushed up onto my knees above her. Grabbing my hardened length, I gave it a few strokes.

"This what you want, Jadey?"

Jade licked her lips and panted out a, "Yes!"

I ran the slick tip of my cock along her pussy and pressed in when I got to her clit, swirling the tip around. Jade dug her nails into my back and pulled me closer, whispering into my ear, "Stop teasing me and give me what's *mine*!"

It had never taken much for Jade to weaken my resolve. But when she demanded, I give her what she needed. I couldn't deny her. The teasing was over.

"Fuck. Jadey, it's all yours. I'm all yours," I told her, lifting one of her legs over my shoulder and lining my dick up with her opening.

"Bram." She sighed as I slid in, giving her only a little before I drew back and thrust slowly forward, inch by inch, until I filled her. We moved in unison, like we had never stopped being a part of one another.

"Oh god, it feels good. Too good. I can't." Jade jerked and bowed under my touch, but I didn't relent.

"You're gonna come for me again, baby," I told her as I rolled us over, managing to stay inside of her. I looked up at my beautiful Jade, who was now straddling me. "Can you still come like this?" I asked, needing to see her ride me.

"I don't know, but I'm willing to conduct the experiment," she said with a smirk.

"Mmm," I groaned, grabbing both Jade's ass-cheeks and moving her on top of me. "More," I commanded.

Jade obliged, swirling and undulating on my dick while I thrust up into her, barely able to contain myself as I watched her breasts bounce over me.

Jade moaned, rubbing her finger over her clit, her eyes going wild.

"Oh fuck, come for me, baby," I begged, ready for my own release.

"Yes!" Jade whipped her head back, crying out as she found another orgasm. I gave her a few moments to ride it out, watching as her face transformed from desperate to serene.

When I was certain she'd enjoyed every last moment, I planted my hands on her waist and told her through a growl, "Now you're gonna get fucked."

"I said I wanted you to lo—" I didn't let her finish when I lifted her off me and rolled her to her hands and knees.

Jade let out a small giggle and looked back at me. "Well, okay then."

"Stay down," I ordered before I grabbed the back of her hair and pushed her face down into the bed.

I heard Jade's muffled, "Yes, sir," which was the green light I needed to keep going with her this way.

I lifted her hips and aligned myself with her pussy before sliding back in. I'd just been inside the woman, and she still somehow felt better than she did ten seconds ago, and she'd felt phenomenal then.

She whimpered as I fully seated myself inside of her.

"Tell me who you belong to, baby!" I pulled out and thrust back in.

"Ah!" Jade cried out, clasping the bed sheets in her fists. "You, honey. I belong to you!"

I pulled out just to plunge in again, only this time she pushed back meeting my buck.

"Fuck! Tell me whose ass this is," I whispered harshly into the shell of her ear.

"It's yours, all it is yours," she ground out through heaving breaths.

"That's right," I said, bucking wildly, moving in and out of her, losing myself more and more with each passing second. "Tell me that you'll always be mine, Jadey. No matter what."

Jade turned her head to the side, speaking so clearly when she said, "No matter what, my love."

"Fuck!" Her words unraveled me, and I couldn't hold it any longer.

Jade pushed back into me. The feeling of her and I with no barriers in between was so all-consuming. My head was spinning, and my cock was throbbing with my pending release. My balls tightened, and I felt my orgasm building. I was going to explode inside of her. I sped up, panting and pushing my way in and out, watching her ass bounce as I fucked her. I couldn't hold on anymore.

"Ah yeah, Jadey," I moaned, my dick draining inside of her. "Look what you do to me," I grunted, still thrusting, letting her pussy milk my cock until I was spent. And I was fucking spent.

We fell to the bed together with Jade beneath me, the two of us still connected.

I lifted off her and moved her hair to one side, placing a soft kiss behind her ear.

We spent the rest of the night in each other's space, touching and kissing and holding each other every chance we got. It was everything. It gave me hope for our future. And this time, I wasn't going to let anything ruin us.

****

I looked over at my gorgeous Jadey, copper hair blowing in the wind coming in from the open windows of my truck.

I could hear the high-pitched voices of Gabby and Cece, Lex's favorite animated ninja-monkey duo, blaring from her smart tablet in the back.

We were on our way to the lake to spend the day with our friends. The sun was out and ever since Jade and I had solidified our relationship, we'd been getting closer and closer.

It had been a month since the incident at her store and since then, nothing more had happened.

I'd stayed close during that time, barely letting Jade and Lex be alone, be without my protection. Lex had finally gotten her cast off and her elbow had set and healed nicely. Jade's house was coming along, with Andrew projecting another month of work before they were finished. He'd promised Jade it would go up fast, and he definitely delivered.

I still hadn't heard back from Philips on the status of Jules' prison sentence, and I was starting to get worried. In fact, I hadn't heard shit from anyone, and that set me on edge. I had no clue what to worry about—did I worry about Nathan or someone else?

When the explosion at Nathan's happened, I'd reached out to the one remaining contact I had in Nathan's organization. I'd first heard from him when Jules got locked up and we'd communicated periodically since then. I'd never met the guy, so I didn't know what to believe, but he had given me the notion that someone on the forensics team was dirty, so when the official report said that Nathan was dead, I'd had my doubts.

All of that was on my mind as I tried to keep things moving forward with Jade.

We pulled up to the lake around one and everyone was already there.

Jade had made beignets for the adults and cake pops for the kids. The beignets, she said, were for practice for Priscilla's party and damn, they were the best things I'd ever put in my mouth, other than the woman herself.

Evie met us at the lake, and we all walked to the canopy that Cameron had set up.

"You're here!" Raven ran up to us with a huge smile. "Jade! I'm glad you could make it. It's so nice to see you again!" Raven turned to Evie and smiled brightly. "And you must be the bestie business partner!"

Evie grinned and held out a hand. "Evie Nakamura."

In true Raven fashion, she ignored the hand and went right for the hug.

"It's nice to meet you." Raven beamed as she embraced Evie. "Bram has told me all about you! And he's been bragging non-stop about your shop." She released a still grinning Evie. "I, for one, cannot wait to gain ten pounds at your bakery!"

Raven barely took a breath before she knelt in front of Lex. "And you must be the famous Lex that I keep hearing so much about!" Raven offered Lex a hand and in true Lex fashion, she went in for the hug.

"Oh my god, a kindred spirit," Raven cooed, giving Lex a light squeeze. "Does everyone tell you that you look just like your mama?"

Lex pulled back from the hug and nodded. "Yep, everyone says that," she said with a casual shrug. "Everyone is always saying how pretty Mom is, so I don't mind it."

"Smart girl," Raven replied with a laugh.

"But don't you remember me?" Lex asked, but launched back in before Raven could answer. "I remember you! We talked on the phone when I was sick. You told Mom and Bram that I was going to be okay when I threw up from that gross medicine."

Raven's eyes lit up. "I do remember, and I'm glad you do, too. Would you like to meet my Zara?"

Lex bounced and looked up at me, searching my eyes for approval, before I tipped my head to the side and motioned to Jade. But I'd felt it in my chest at that moment, the weight of the responsibility, the split decisions that Jade had been making for Lex since day one. It felt important, but more than that, it felt right.

Jade smiled and gave Lex the go ahead before she

skipped away excitedly, following Raven's lead.

"Hey, glad you all came," Jet said as he and Cameron walked up to us. Jet tipped his head at me, then reached out and gave Jade a hug that was too fucking long.

"That's good enough." I tugged on Jade's hand and Jet laughed.

"What? I haven't seen her in weeks and before that, years." He shrugged with mock innocence, before he raised his brows and turned to Evie. "Hey, I'm Jet. You must be the business partner."

We finished the introductions and got settled under the canopy where Mika and Tessa had been stationed. Raven had returned from taking Lex to the meet the other kids, and was now leaning on Cameron, watching the kids play.

"So, Mika and I have decided to start trying," Tessa blurted out abruptly as everyone, except for Raven, turned their heads to look at her.

"Try?" Gray asked. The man was smart, but he was younger than the rest of us, and it was pretty much always obvious.

"Yeah, man. For a baby," Mika said with a smile. "We think we're ready and we both want a child."

I looked over at Raven, who did not look at all shocked. "God, finally! It's been killing me keeping this in!"

Cameron's face turned a very subtle shade of red as he woodenly smiled and threw his arms out. "Yes! Wow, what a surprise! I'm so excited for you both."

Jet put in, just as awkwardly, "Yeah, same. So surprised! You two will be amazing parents."

Tessa narrowed her eyes at Cameron, then turned to

Raven. "Oh my god, you dirty little secret teller!"

Raven grimaced. "What? Nooooo." She shifted her eyes upward and then tried on a smile. "He's my husband, babe. He has ways of extracting information from me!"

"Mmmhmmm, oh I know he does! Don't forget, we used to be roommates, and I spent a lot of time listening to his 'ways of extraction'." Cameron laughed and Raven blushed.

Mika cleared her throat. "You knew too, didn't you?" she asked Jet.

"Yeah, Cam told me." He shrugged.

"Thanks, dickhead!" Cameron said, just as the kids ran up to the canopy.

"Ooo, Uncle Cam, that's a bad word," Jets son, Nash, added as he baseball slid into his dad.

Cameron rolled his eyes and murmured to Jet, "Like he's never heard that, and worse."

"What's a dickhead, Daddy?" Zara tugged on Cameron's shirt.

Cameron pressed his eyes together and glanced at Raven, who was giving him the stink eye.

"It's a word that adults say as a joke sometimes," Jade put in. "Not everyone uses it as a joke, so it's better to just not say it," she added with a smile. And fuck, I loved her. The woman was quick and sharp and in total control.

"Yeah, in my house, if Mom or Evie say a bad word, we have a swear jar. I've made a lot of money since we moved here and especially because Bram stays over now and he pays me a lot of money!" Lex said dramatically, her eyes bugging out.

"Hey!" I teased, snatching her by the waist and

pulling her in for a hug. Lex giggle as I told her, "You're making me look bad, kiddo."

Lex was still laughing when she continued, "And even sometimes when he comes home from work he walks right to the jar, puts in ten dollars, and asks me how many bad words that buys him!"

Jade turned her head to me, her mouth agape. "We are going to have a conversation about *that.*"

I smirked, knowing exactly how that conversation would go.

"You know, this is ya'lls fault," Mika joked. "We're surrounded by the cutest kids all the time."

"True story," Tessa added.

"I mean, for real," Mika continued. "Zara was enough to make me want babies, but then Nash, and now Lex?"

We all laughed at Mika's sweet words, but I couldn't help the jealousy that rose in me. Even if it was my fault, it still fucking hurt.

I decided that was a good time to head to the bathroom and relieve my bladder. I needed a minute to clear my head, anyway.

"Bram, hey!" I heard Sierra's cheery voice before I saw her trotting toward me in short shorts and a bikini top.

"Hey, Sierra. How are you?" I hadn't seen or spoken to her since the failed date.

"Good. Well, better now that I've finally caught up to you," she said with a playful shove.

I was silent, caught off guard by her forwardness and unsure of what to say.

"I was hoping we could maybe talk about that date we missed?" she asked.

"Oh, actually," I responded, grateful for the opening to explain my situation.

"Wait!" She put up a hand. "Before you say no, because I know that's where this is going, just hear me out." She didn't give me a chance to say anything else. "I know we only did a once in a while thing and it was never serious, but I've been thinking about it, and I want more. We have great sex, we like each other, we're both hot." She laughed. "It just makes sense."

Great sex was an overstatement, but I wasn't about to hurt her feelings. Sierra had always been kind, but that spark was just never there.

"Sierra, I'm—" I tried to say, but before I could finish, her mouth was on me, lips pressed to mine, her tongue sliding across my lips for access. I put my hands on her hips and pushed her away gently.

"Sierra, I'm with—"

I heard a gasp from behind me and then immediately following that, a choked sob. I whipped around and saw nothing but streaks of red hair flying in the wind as Jade did a mad dash away from me.

"Fuck!" I cried out.

"Oh my god." Sierra slapped a hand over her mouth. "Are you two together?"

I turned my head and growled at her, "Probably a question you want to ask someone before you kiss them without warning!"

She slunk back and I could see the tears forming in her eyes. At that point, with the thin line I was walking with Jade, I didn't give a fuck about offending Sierra.

I stalked back to our set-up and everyone was staring at me with varying degrees of disgust and annoyance. I didn't give a fuck about them either.

"Where's Jade?" I demanded more than asked.

Tessa pointed to the parking lot, and I saw Jade loading Lex into Evie's car. I jogged over, fear and anger building with each step.

Jade got in the car and slammed the door shut right as I got there. Her face was red and streaked with tears. I looked beyond her at Evie. Her eyes were squinted, and she was shaking her head.

And she was right, now was not the time. Not in front of Lex. So, I stepped back from the vehicle and watched numbly as they drove away.

Chapter 16

Jade

I laid in bed, restless and unable to fall asleep as I read and reread a text he'd sent hours ago. *You didn't see what you thought you saw*. The man had a big ol' pair of balls. I'd give him that. After everything he'd put me through, he still had the audacity to gaslight me. After reading that, I couldn't even cry anymore. I was pissed, angrier than I'd ever been.

Needless to say, the rest of my night had sucked. After convincing Lex that everything would be fine so she could get some rest and stop asking about Bram, I did nothing but stew in self-pity and, eventually, anger.

"Ugh, damn him!" I raged to myself as I tapped my phone.

"Hey hun, you okay?" Evie asked, her voice sympathetic.

"Not really," I replied. "I need a favor," I admitted, feeling guilty. Hadn't the woman done enough? "Can you come over and stay with Lex for a while?"

"Jade," Evie warned, and I could feel her judgement.

"I know, Vee, but I—" I what? I didn't have any explanation. I was compelled by what I was certain were dark forces beyond my control, because why else would I keep doing this to myself?

Evie sighed and agreed to come over. By the time

she arrived and I'd given her the quick briefing, it was ten o'clock when I was pounding down his door.

The door swung open, the light from inside illuminating a face that was just as puffy as mine. Bram's shoulders fell when he saw me and he reached out.

"Baby, fuck. Come—"

I pushed past him, shoving his arm out of the way, and walked straight into his house like I owned the place.

I spun on my heels and stared right into his blue eyes, ready to have the fight that had been a long time coming.

"What you did to me, that cut deep," I started. "It cut so deep that my wounds never healed. Hell, they never even scarred over." I tossed out a hand. "For nine years I've been walking around just fucking bleeding because of you."

"Jade." His voice came out in a whisper, and I did my best to ignore the sadness written in the lines of his face.

"No, let me talk." I wiped away a few tears and inhaled the courage to continue, because before the end of this night, I was going to need to get this out. All of it.

"Imagine, Bram. The only person who I trusted, the only man who never let me down, makes *me* come to him." I laughed bitterly, the half-smile on my face anything but amused. "He gives me no good explanation of what I've done to deserve any of this and then tells me he's with someone else, someone better. And silly, naïve, little me had *zero* indication that it was coming because I thought we were happy."

"Jadey, baby." His voice came out on a crack, sharp edges lacing his words.

"All the noise that I'd fought so hard to tune out. All

the judgement that he himself told me was bullshit. You built me up." I placed a hand on my chest, trying to keep my heart in place as everything poured out of me.

"You made me believe in myself." I pointed to him. "You did that." His shoulders slumped and tears streamed. I didn't care. "I didn't ask you for it. I didn't ask you to take me into your home. You did that!" I screeched. "You wanted it. And then, after all that, all those years, you take everything I fought against and used it to destroy me!"

By now, my tears were flowing freely and I didn't even give a fuck. "You gutted me, Bram. I was still bleeding from being assaulted with a goddamn knife and even that paled in comparison to what you did to me."

I watched as his eyes transformed from sad to furious in the matter of seconds. His body was tense before, but now it was rigid. He had no clue that it would be the first of many blows.

"What the fuck?" he hollered, and I jumped back. I don't know what I had been expecting from him, but it wasn't that.

I spent the next several minutes recounting the events of that day while Bram paced around his living room, looking completely unhinged.

"Why the *fuck* am I finding out about this now?" he growled.

Oh hell no. He was not about to turn this around on me. I leaned forward and threw my hands out. "And when would I have done that? When you were making out with some dumb bitch? Or when you were telling me I was trash and that you never wanted to see me again?"

"No, fuck!" Bram yelled, turning away from me, hitting his wall with an open hand.

"Yes!" I cried, confused by his anger. The man had no right. "You did it, and now you have to deal with the consequences." I fell slightly forward, my will to fight leaving with the words I knew I had to say. "I have loved you from the time I first saw you, and somehow, even after what you did to me, you still have a hold on me. So much so I wonder if I just think I deserve to be miserable for my entire life, in love with a man who could do something so terrible to me over and fucking over!"

He moved to me and grabbed my hand. "No baby, it wasn't like that!"

I pried my hand away and glared at him. "It was like that, because you did what you did. And maybe you had your messed up reasons, but you destroyed me."

He was shaking his head, standing in front of me, trying to convince me or himself of his innocence. I didn't know.

"All those years I knew you and I had never known you to be so hateful, so cold. That's who I have to remind myself you are, that man. I will *never* forgive what you did to me, Bram. Never. What happened with Sierra today, it doesn't matter, I should've expected it."

"Goddamnit, Jadey! Fucking listen to me!"

"I don't give a shit what you have to say!" I screamed into his face, losing control. "I was pregnant!" I screeched and then stepped back, realizing what I'd done.

Bram stilled, and I watched as the color drained from his face. He blinked, and we were both silent, the air thick with the reality of what I'd said.

"I drove to Charlotte," I carried on. I had to finish this. "And I don't think I stopped crying, not for a second, Bram. I drove nearly straight through. I spent two days just fucking driving, not having the first clue where I was going. But I knew that I had to get as far away from you as possible."

Bram fell to his knees in front of me, his spirit broken.

"It should've been the happiest time of my life. Of *our* life." I choked out some fragmented whimper that came straight from my soul. "I had just found out at the ER and I couldn't wait to tell you. We were too young, I knew that, but I loved you. And I left the doctors so sure that you loved me and we'd find a way to make it work, just like everything else we did together."

"No," he sobbed, his head hanging. I wanted to go to him, comfort him, tell him it was all okay. But he needed to know the truth. My truth, and his.

"I was homeless, pregnant, and nineteen. I had nothing, Bram. Nothing but the clothes on my back and whatever few hundred dollars I had in my bank account. I knew I couldn't raise a child."

"No," Bram whispered, and I couldn't do it any longer. I couldn't pretend that seeing him like this wasn't breaking my heart. I sat down on the floor next to him.

"I went to the abortion clinic two weeks later. I knew it was the right thing to do. I couldn't give my child the life they deserved. I had no way to do it. I was a month along at that point and it was now or never."

He choked out a sob, and I didn't know if my next would hurt him more or heal some small part of his wounds.

"But I couldn't do it," I whispered.

His head shot up; his eyes locked on me.

"For the first two years of Lex's life, I didn't have much." I laughed humorlessly. "Mostly just depression and food stamps. It didn't help that I was back in a damn trailer, but this time raising a child, trying to make ends meet on a librarian salary."

"She's, she's?" Bram shook his head, struggling with the words.

"Lexa Taylor Greene was born on a beautiful fall day." I smiled listlessly, remembering both the pain and joy I felt at that time. "She came early. Two weeks, to be exact." I shook my head, lost in the memory. "I remember holding her tiny little finger, telling her how anxious I had been to meet her."

"She's mine?" Bram asked in a croak.

"Ours," I replied.

Bram nodded for a few seconds before he shot up to standing and slammed a fist into the wall as he screamed, "Motherfucker!"

I didn't even flinch. If anything, I could relate. I'd lived with this knowledge, this pain, this loneliness for years. And now he knew what he'd done to our family. And these were the consequences for all of us.

****

Bram

I pulled my fist out of the wall and stared at the bloody mess of flesh that was on the outside what I felt on the inside. Fuck, I had a daughter. I wanted to celebrate and rage all at once.

Jade was silent behind me, still on the floor, somehow looking less pained than all the weeks since she arrived in town. I walked over to her and bent down. Her body stiffened at my closeness, but I scooped her up anyway and lifted her in my arms. She rested her head on my shoulder and let out a heavy breath.

"Jadey, please," I begged. "Please listen to me,

baby."

Jade looked up at me, her eyes wide.

"I didn't kiss her, Jade. You need to know that. It's still my fault. I didn't make it clear that you and I were together. She didn't know."

"I know," Jade whispered weakly. "I saw you push her back. I just reacted. It was almost like I was back on that grass all those years ago and I couldn't stop the way it felt."

I brushed a kiss on her forehead and murmured into her hair. "I want to explain to you what happened that day. Can you just trust me that I did what I thought was best for you at the time?"

Jade lifted her eyes, and I saw a softness and vulnerability in them that I hadn't seen since we were kids. I certainly hadn't seen it since she'd been here. "Yes." She gave it to me freely, without question.

All my breath left me instantly at her one simple word. It gave me hope, and that was all I needed.

"I have a kid."

Jade nodded and gave me an exhausted grin. "An amazing kid. But I think you already know that."

I did. I grabbed my keys and wallet and headed out the door, still carrying Jade in my arms.

"What are you doing?" she asked, completely collapsed in my arms.

"Taking us home. I'm not spending another day away from her, Jade." And I wasn't. I would fight for what was mine, what had always been mine. And never again would anyone take it away.

Chapter 17

Jade

I rolled over, feeling Bram's arm beneath my head in the bed. We'd gone back to the apartment and immediately crashed. I'd woken up a few times throughout the night, still wrapped in Bram's arms, the anxiety of the next step looming over me.

"Morning, baby." Bram rolled over so half his body was hovering over me before he bent down and brushed a kiss on my lips. His beautiful blue eyes locked with mine and he shook his head slowly.

"What?" I asked, feeling slightly on edge.

Bram sighed, and I would've been nervous if he didn't look so relaxed. "I just can't believe I'm a father. I woke up yesterday as just a dude, and now I'm a fucking dad. To *our* kid."

I inhaled and touched his cheek with my hand. "I know it's a lot, but we can take it really, really slow."

Bram jerked his head back, and I dropped my hand. "Slow?" he asked. "Jadey, I've missed so much time with Lex. The last thing I want to do is slow roll this and miss anything else." He shook his head, looking a little more frantic. "I'm a dad," he said, eyes wide.

"Yes, you are a dad," I reiterated. "But don't you think maybe you should take time to process this before we jump into anything?"

"Absolutely not," Bram returned immediately. "I've wanted to be a family with you since we were kids."

His words stung, even though I knew he didn't mean them to. He still hadn't given me any explanation, and I hadn't forgotten. But I also knew that we needed time, and the most important thing in all this, Lex still didn't know that she had a father.

"How should we tell her?" I asked, completely out of my depth with this one.

Bram ran a shaky hand through his hair and I watched what I assumed, or at least hoped, was him forming the solutions to all our problems.

"Lex is smart, but she's also only eight," Bram put in. "She doesn't need to know about Nathan, or that you were ever in danger. It'll only worry her, and I really don't want our daughter walking around in fear."

My heart leapt. *Our* daughter.

"We need to explain to her in a way that she can understand. Maybe we tell her that—"

His idea was interrupted by the sleepy voice of Lex. "Mom?"

I perked up and looked toward the door, grateful that we'd been too exhausted to even get out of our clothes last night.

"Hey, sweetheart," I spoke softly. "Why don't you go out and make some cereal and we'll be right there."

Lex poked her head in further, her sleepy eyes becoming alert when she spotted Bram. "You're here!" Her whole face had lit up and my heart melted.

"Of course I'm here, kiddo," he replied. "Where else would I be?"

"You could be at work," Lex sassed back. "Or you could've been on your way back from Sunshine's with donuts," she said with a tease.

Bram chuckled. "I guess I know where I'm going this morning."

Lex beamed and bounced in place before I caught her eyes and motioned for her to go to the kitchen. I grinned at the sound of her light hums as she skipped away.

Bram and I both got out of bed. Me, to actually put on my pajamas and him, to put on his shoes so he could make good on his promise of donuts.

****

We sat on the couch, the three of us, watching cartoons and eating donuts. Lex had fused herself to Bram in a side cuddle the minute he'd sat on the couch.

She took a bite of her jelly donut and looked up at Bram. "I was sad when you didn't come home with us last night."

Damn. Lex's words pierced, and I looked over at Bram, but he was staring back at Lex, his blue eyes warm, the edges of his lips curled just a little.

"I'm sorry I made you feel sad, kiddo." He leaned down and tapped his forehead on hers.

"That's okay," Lex's voice had gone from sad to peppy in the matter of seconds. "Are you gonna stay for good?"

Bram gulped back some air. "I am gonna stay. I could never leave my two favorite girls."

"You're gonna stay all the time?" Lex tilted her head, her eyes so hopeful, I felt a pang in my chest.

Bram looked at me and searched my face. I knew what he was asking, and I knew that there would never be a good time to have this conversation, so I nodded.

"Lex, can we talk to you about something?" Bram

ran a hand through her long hair. God, he was already so good with her.

As for me, my heart was pounding and I could feel the sweat beading on my forehead.

Lex shrugged. "Sure."

Bram smiled and pulled her hair to one side, gentle and loving, just as a dad would do. "Well, you know your mom and I have known each other for a long time, right?"

"Yeah! Before you lost her number." Lex rolled her eyes and then looked over at me. "Boys," she said, and I couldn't help but giggle, grateful for any amount of levity at that point.

Bram laughed. "Well, to be honest, we really used to be boyfriend and girlfriend before she moved to North Carolina."

"I knew it!" Lex straightened and narrowed her eyes at Bram, then lifted a pointy finger. "I never saw Mom kissing anyone before you."

I giggled, rolling my eyes dramatically. "Okay, detective." I reached over and tickled Lex's side. She squealed and wiggled in place for a few seconds. Bram let the laughter die down before he got right back into it.

"The truth is that we loved each other."

Lex furrowed her brow. "You loved her?"

"Yes, kiddo, and I still *love* her. I've always loved your mom."

"Are you gonna move in?" Lex asked, and I could tell she was trying to appear casual, but she couldn't hide the anticipation in her eyes. "Because I had a friend whose dad found a new wife and when they got married, she moved all her stuff in. But she didn't call his new wife Mom because she already had a mom. She just called her 'Melanie'."

Bram grinned. "I am gonna move in," he announced, and it was news to me. "But this is a little different from your friend and Melanie."

"How?" Lex asked, her face now serious.

Bram lifted a shoulder. and it was the first time I'd seen him at a loss for words. I jumped in, happy to take the reins from here.

"Well, first of all, there are some things you need to know." I inhaled a large breath, knowing that what I really needed was some courage to get through this next part. "Bram told me that you overheard a conversation between me and Aunt Evie."

Lex's eyes fell, and she bit her lip. "Ummm."

"It's okay," I reassured. "You aren't in trouble. I just want to explain, because what you heard wasn't exactly true."

"What do you mean?" Lex scrunched her nose and waited while I gathered the confidence to finish this.

"Well, your father didn't know about you," I started, but guilt and fear bubbled to the surface. All these years I had believed that I'd done what was right for Lex, and now, I wasn't so sure. "And I had my reasons for that, and your dad had his reasons for not finding me. He was protecting me, kind of like a hero does."

Lex was fully attentive and alert and the confusion on her face was killing me. "A hero?"

"Yeah, a hero. Like the kind of heroes that give up everything to protect their family."

Lex tilted her head back and looked up at Bram. "Is Bram a hero?" Her lip quivered with the question, deepening the pit that was growing in my stomach.

I took a few breaths, knowing that it was now and

there was no longer any never. "Yeah, Lex bug. He's *our* hero."

Lex wiggled out of Bram's arms and ran to me, burying her head in my chest. I looked at Bram, my heart breaking even more when he dropped his head into his hand, tears welling in his eyes.

Lex sniffled, and I didn't know what to say. I was about to say something when Lex whispered, "Is he, um, is he my?" She paused, shrinking back, unable to complete the question.

"Yes." I replied softly. "Bram is your dad, Lex."

She pushed her head deeper into me and I felt her whole body shake. Oh god, it hurt. It hurt too much. Bram's face was crestfallen, tears flowing freely. I knew with time we'd get through it, but damn, it hurt.

After a few painful moments, Lex lifted her head and looked up at me. "I wanted him to be my dad," she whispered so quietly I barely made out her words.

The energy in the room shifted. "Lex" Bram's deep voice cracked, and it was all I could do to hold myself together at the thickness of emotion I heard in it.

Lex lifted her head and looked over at him.

"I want you to know that I love you and nothing has to change for us, okay? You can call me Bram if you feel comfortable with that, and I'm going to keep being in your life. We can still watch movies and play video games and be as silly as we want."

Lex nodded and then turned back around to bury her head in my arms. It had been a heavy two days and no doubt, this was only the first of many tough conversations. But we were moving forward in truth and honesty, and best of all, we were doing it as a family.

Chapter 18

The next few months were busy and highly eventful. We'd finished the renovation of our shop without any further incident, opening right on schedule with much local success.

We'd managed to secure several standing orders from businesses in and around Brooks Falls before we even opened our doors. Between the shop and events, we were doing more business than ever.

Lex had started school, and it was by luck that she and Liam were in the same class. They'd become the best of friends, Lex's cheery presence lightening Liam's anger over what he had lost.

And with all that going on, the builders had finished the house on my family's property, and we'd moved in a week ago. And by we I meant me, Lex, and Bram.

Bram had wasted no time in breaking the news of his fatherhood to his friends, something that set off a whirlwind of barbecues and get-togethers that only served to solidify us as a family.

Lex still hadn't called Bram "Dad", but he was unbothered by it, happy to just be in her life, picking her up from school and taking her to do fun things every chance he got.

We made quick work of moving into the house and getting set up so it would be somewhat presentable by the time Bram's parents arrived. I'd not seen Mr. and Mrs. Taylor in nine long years and today, that finally changed.

I was standing on the porch, sipping a cup of tea and trying to enjoy the view of my property, now that everything was just so. But really, I was bouncing on my toes, nervous as ever, when I heard tires roll across the unfinished part of the driveway. Even though I'd been expecting this visit, my heart flailed around in my chest like a windsock during Santa Ana season. It had been nine years, but more than that, I'd left without so much as a wave or even a "hey, thanks for taking me in and oh, I don't know, saving my entire life."

Bram must've sensed my unease, because I felt his arms wrap around me from behind, before he leaned down and whispered into my hair.

"Don't be nervous, baby. They're as excited to see you as you are them."

I watched as Mrs. Taylor exited the car first and then, as if driven by unknown, and way more relaxed, forces, I was out of Bram's arms and on the move, jogging down the porch steps, toward the woman who had changed my life in more ways than she'd ever know.

"Oh!" Mrs. Taylor's voice broke with her exclamation, but her face brightened. "My sweet Jade! You're home."

No sooner did the words leave her mouth than I was in her arms, crying through our overdue embrace.

Mrs. Taylor pulled back and held my shoulders as her eyes swept over me. "You and Bram, finally. And my." She inhaled a shaky breath. "My granddaughter."

Ashamed, I cast my eyes down. I'd never wanted to keep Lex from them and right then, I felt as if I was

starting into the consequences of my choices. "I'm so so-
." I shook my head and began to search for worthy
enough words to apologize for what I had done.

"No," Mrs. Taylor said, just as I saw Mr. Taylor
appear in my periphery. "Bram told us everything," she
said, then dipped her head down to catch my eyes.
"*Everything.*" She repeated.

I glanced over at Mr. Taylor, searching his face for
any clue that Bram had actually told them everything.
Mr. Taylor's smile was warm as I'd remembered, but
behind it was pain that hadn't been there before.

"So good to see you again, kiddo," Mr. Taylor
finally spoke. "You wipe that sad face off now, you
hear?"

I cracked a small smile. "I'm sorry we hurt you both,
too," I finally said. It didn't matter if they knew or there
were explanations. We'd hurt them, that was that.

Mr. Taylor pressed his lips together, his gentle
expression bringing tears to my eyes already. "It's the
natural burden of a parent to carry the weight of your
children's pain and mistakes, dear. But now you two
come back together, you see, we also get to carry the
joy." With that, I fell into his arms. I was nothing but a
puddle of tears and gratitude.

"You're here!" Lex's high-pitched screech was all I
needed to hear to know that she was excited, not nervous.

We'd explained to her that they were coming to
meet her and she could call them Grandma and Grandpa
if she liked, but that there was no pressure. Lex had been
inscrutable for that entire conversation, telling us that she
would take the week before they arrived, to think on it.

"Oh dear!" Mrs. Taylor threw a hand over her heart
as she beamed in the direction of Lex.

My little girl bounded down the porch steps, skid to a stop when she got us, and jumped in place. I smiled when I heard Mr. Taylor snicker next to me.

"You must be Lex," Mrs. Taylor said and offered a hand.

Lex giggled, then straightened her spine. "And you must be Grandma," she said in a deep voice that intimated she was being silly. Lex took Mrs. Taylor's hand and gave it one exaggerated shake.

I looked over at Mrs. Taylor, who was absolutely glowing now. "I sure am. Grandma Nita," she said with an official nod. Lex grinned.

"I like you! Can we hug now?"

Lex had hardly finished the words when she was in her grandma's arms and I was back to crying.

"This is your Grandpa Bill," she said to Lex, and then turned back to her husband. "This is our granddaughter, Lex, honey."

Mr. Taylor smiled at Lex, and then he bent down to give her a hug. "You're just as beautiful as your mother, child."

"Bram doesn't really look like you," Lex said, and I was glad we'd briefed them beforehand. She still hadn't settled into calling Bram, "Dad." It was a big change, and we both had wanted to give her plenty of space to adjust.

Mr. Taylor laughed and brushed his eyes with his forearm. "No, I suppose not. But I used to be really handsome when I was a lot younger."

Lex scrunched her nose up. "I didn't say you weren't handsome, Grandpa! It's just that he has blue eyes and yours are brown."

I heard Bram snort behind me and then whispered in my ear. "Already buttering up the grandparents."

Lex grabbed onto Mrs. Taylor's hand with her left hand and Mr. Taylor's with her right, then began slowly walking them toward the house. "Let's go inside! Do you wanna see my room and my stuffies and all my books?"

"I absolutely—" Mrs. Taylor stopped dead and Lex and Mr. Taylor stopped with her. Mrs. Taylor looked back at me. "Jade," she said breathlessly. "Is that our?" She paused and looked back at the house. "*That* is our house!"

I felt the tingling warmth of embarrassment travel from my neck to my cheeks as I answered her unasked question. "It is," I offered. "It's kind of a replica of your house," I said.

"I see." She swiped at a tear.

"I know it sounds strange, but I just wanted to feel like I was home again." I tried to explain, feeling dumber with each word. "And I wanted Lex to experience something close to my childhood home," I admitted, wiping away my own tear.

"You lived with Bram and my grandparents?" Lex asked.

Bram grabbed my hand, and we both walked toward them. When we got to them, I let go of him and bent down to my daughter. "Yeah, baby. We grew up together, and I didn't have a family," I told her, hoping to get away with the abbreviated version of this story.

Lex let go of her grandparents' hands and ran to Bram, jumping into his arms with a leap and a squeal. "Thank you for taking care of my mom," I'd find out later that was what she'd whispered to him.

And then we proceeded to have the most relaxed, laughter-filled visit.

Chapter 19

Bram

Jade had been right about that damn huge window in her bonus room. We'd been moved into the house for weeks now and every clear night, we'd sat in front of that window, looking for constellations and shooting stars.

It had been Jade's idea to build a library around the room and have the loveseat right in front of the window. And usually the three of us piled on the couch together, but tonight Evie was over for dinner and an impromptu planning session with Jade. They'd been waiting for one of their clients to call, deciding to stargaze before a serious and intense planning session with Priscilla. It was a name I'd heard uttered almost more than my own in this house and I'd known from all that Jade has told me, she was important.

I'd been cuddled on the couch with Jade, but Evie and Lex had been wrapped up in a serious game of candy blackjack.

Jade's phone suddenly vibrated on the table next to the loveseat. She picked it up and before she answered, looked at me and then Evie. "It's Priscilla. I'm gonna head up to the office, hun. Our first agenda item is the special diets desserts, if you wanna plan to join us in thirty for the logistics." That was all Jade said before the phone was to ear. "Priscilla, hi!" she answered and her voice got quieter and quieter as she left the room for her office upstairs.

"Who's winning?" I glanced over, surveilling the mix of chocolate bars and hard candies that served as the betting chips, and I couldn't help but laugh at the dark glasses Lex was wearing. The kid had seen five minutes of a James Bond movie with us, and now she was a hustler.

"She is," Lex mumbled, pushing a pink sucker and three chocolate bars forward.

My phone pinged in my pocket and when I pulled it out, it was a text from Jade. "Can you come help me with something? It's urgent."

I laughed and shoved my phone back in my pocket. "I'll be right back. Jade needs help."

Evie stopped and looked up at me. "Do you want to finish my game and I'll go check on her?"

I waved her off. "You keep taking candy from my kid." I motioned between Lex's near-empty pile and Evie's mound of candy. "And I'll check on my Jade."

Evie nudged Lex with a grin. "She knows her auntie don't let anyone slide," she teased.

Bram chuckled. "Woooow!"

Lex giggled, lowering her glasses and leveling Evie with a pout. "I can't believe you'd take candy from a *baby*, Auntie!"

"Pshh." Evie rolled her eyes, moving her head back and forth with each petty word. "Oh, now you're a baby? You weren't a baby when you told me to stop pushing you on the swings yesterday because, and I quote, 'I'm almost nine, I can do it myself.'"

"Lord," I laughed. "Well, now I'm not sure which of you is the baby.".

"Her!" Evie and Lex replied in unison, before they

both broke out into laughter.

I shook my head and turned to leave the room. Had I known what was waiting for me, I would've looked at my little girl one last time.

****

Bram

I made my way upstairs and down the hallway to Jade's office. It was colder upstairs, almost chilly, and I noticed that the closer I got to Jade's office, the colder it got. Maybe she was having issues with the heater, I thought, trying to stay quiet so as not to disturb her meeting.

A shiver raced down my spine as I neared, the room eerily silent, with no light peeking out from under the doorway. On instinct, I felt around in my pocket for my hunting knife, satisfied to clock it before I pushed the door open and stood outside the doorway.

"Babe?" I stared at Jade, who was sitting perfectly still, her phone sitting on the desk in front of her, her face drained of color.

"Can you come in?" She asked, her voice robotic.

With a single, long stride, I was in her office. I didn't have to look hard before Ice shot through my veins and my jaw hardened at the sight of the gun pointing at Jade.

"Bram." His throaty, deep voice was as indicative of his lifestyle as the sores that lined his face. "Glad you could make it, boy. Looks like the gangs all here." He tipped his head. "Well, you'd all be here if my foolish son hadn't gotten his ass thrown in prison!"

I swallowed hard. "What do you want, Nathan?" I asked.

Waving the gun in Jade's direction, he said as if he were amused, "Too collect my shit of course." Then he got serious and added, "You wouldn't know anything about that, now, would you, Officer?"

"How?" Jade's voice broke through my rage. "How are you even here?" She asked. "I thought you were dead."

"Well girl, had you stayed to join the prolific family business, you'd know that your dear ol' Dad has friends in all kinds of places. Clean and dirty and everything in-between. Ain't that right, boy?" He motioned toward me with his head but kept his eyes on Jade.

I felt the air shift, and Jade's eyes were on me. "Bram?" she asked. My name was the only question she needed to ask.

Now wasn't the time for this explanation. "I know how you're here, motherfucker," I told him. "What I don't know is what you have to collect."

Nathan's eyes got wild, and he threw the gun-free hand in the air. "Not much, it seems, seeing my idiot daughter sold all my shit and built the fuckin' Cleavers' house on my empire." Then he settled and turned back to Jade. "Then, if you wanna see your kid ever again, you're gonna come work for me. Both of you." Then he looked at me and emphasized, "Again."

"Again?" Jade whispered and looked over at me. I could see her in my periphery and could only imagine what she was thinking.

I kept my eyes fastened on Nathan, disgust roiling in my gut when a smirk spread across his face.

"You've always been just like your mother, girl." He said, his nose scrunched like Jade was the stench in the room. "And you always thought you were too good for us, didn't you?" he asked, but didn't wait for an answer. "Turns out you can take the girl out of the trash but you can't take the trash outta the girl," Nathan laughed and gestured toward me with his gun, before the grin on his face disappeared and he focused on Jade.

"I know you got my safe, girl. And after you give me that, you're both gonna do the time to build back up what you destroyed!"

Safe? I thought. What safe and how had I let this happen?

Jade scoffed. "You can have your safe and anything else in this house, but I will *never* work for you!"

"Jade, stop," I warned.

"What's he gonna do? Shoot me? My own father?"

Fuck. She didn't know the half of it and it was my damn fault. I'd seen what he was willing to do to his own children.

I took a small step forward and instantly Nathan straightened and held the gun steady.

"No, no, no. Don't you move another inch. I think you know what I'm capable of."

My jaw tightened, and I stopped.

"Where's the safe, girl?" he asked Jade.

"Under the desk," she replied, and I inhaled. Fuck. I had hauled that damn thing in. Had I known it was his, I would've dropped the thing at the bottom of the lake.

"Good. I'll be needing some help with this."

"I'll help," I offered.

"How stupid do you think I am, boy? Don't worry, I have help," Nathan grinned, his wicked smile growing with my realization.

I froze right before my heart was crushed into a million pieces.

"Daddy!" Lex's screech filled the house.

"Lex!" Jade screamed, and I turned my head in her

340

direction. She was on the move. "Please, don't—" were the last words I heard Jade scream before the sound of gunshots rang out.

****

Jade

My head was pounding, and my ears were ringing. I was weighed down, unable to move, and everything felt like a blur as I tried to blink my eyes open. Where was I?

"Hurry the hell up, Bud!" A man's voice buzzed in my ear, the noise of his holler faint and distant.

I groaned, pushing against the heaviness on top of me, trying to force my eyes open. When I finally did, the light assaulted to them, and I whimpered, before I pressed them closed again.

"Bud!" The man's voice was clearer this time. The man? Why was there a man?

No sooner had the question entered my mind, before I was answering it. Almost with a jolt, I came to and gently tugged and what I now realized was an arm draped over me.

"Bram," I asked, my voice shaking.

"Jesus Christ, can't even get good help around here!" Nathan, I remembered.

"Lex," I finally managed to force out, blinking my eyes enough that I could begin to make out the figure standing over me, his back toward me.

"Where's Lex?" I whispered, but not loud enough. I needed help. I needed Bram. "Honey?" My voice cracked, and I shook his arm a little harder. Nothing. I slid my hand between Bram's body and mine, thinking I could shove him off of me first. I went numb when I felt the warm wetness that had pooled beneath him. "No," I cried out, the forcefulness of the word causing my head to throb.

"Don't worry, girl." Nathan turned around so that he was looking down at me. "No one hurt the kid. Can't say as much for him and your friend, but that's the price you pay for everything you've taken from me, huh?"

Tears streamed down my cheeks, helpless while I stared back at the man who had only ever created anything just to destroy it. Including me. I couldn't speak. I could hardly feel anymore.

I heard heavy footsteps approaching, the sound getting louder and louder. Nathan turned toward the door, and I did my best to look around him, needing to see Lex.

A massive shadow darkened the entrance before a large man stepped in the doorway. The air in the room thinned, and I watched as Nathan's spine straightened, his body going rigid.

The man in the doorway came to light, and I gasped. He wore motorcycle boots over jeans and a tight gray tee that showcased sleeves of tattoos. His black hair was shiny, tinged with gray, and scooped up into a bun on top of his head. Green eyes whose spark had long been snuffed out flashed to me, while at the same time I muttered, "Jules."

"What the fuck?" Nathan yelled, and on instinct, I closed my eyes. A single gunshot filled the room before everything went black.

Chapter 20

Bram

I woke to the sound of a slow, steady beep pulsing in my ears. I was laying down. My eyes were heavy, and I tried to move. Hell, everything was heavy.

"Daddy?"

Lex. My daughter. She was here. And she'd called me Dad. Instantly, I rustled, the beeping sounds getting louder and faster.

"Honey, calm, I'm here." Jade told me, her voice so soft, and I barely heard her through my panicked breaths. "Are you awake? Can you hear me?" Jade asked, and I worked extra to force open my eyes.

"Is Daddy awake? I wanna see him, Mom."

That was all it took. My heart fluttered violently as I forced my eyes open. I looked around, trying to grasp onto something, anything, that would keep me focused. My eyes settled on Jade. Her face was red and puffy, and leaning over me.

I motioned to my hand with my eyes and then wiggled my fingers a few times. Satisfied when Jade carefully worked her fingers between mine, I searched for our daughter.

"Lex Bug." The words scratched out from my throat painfully and as soon as my eyes landed on her. Her hair was a mess, but that wasn't out of the ordinary. I scanned her from head to toe, and everything else appeared to be okay. "Lemme see," I muttered, trying to push up from the bed and get a full view of Lex.

"She's all right, honey." Jade whispered and squeezed my hand as she did. "Gentle, okay Lex?" Jade said just as I noticed Lex hop onto a chair sitting next to the bed. I turned my head.

"Daddy, you're awake!" A few tears streamed down her face and my heart clenched.

"I heard your voice, and I had to wake up and see my favorite girl," I rasped and flinched when a sharp, yet muted, pain shot down my side.

"Be careful, Daddy." Lex said gently, the way you'd talk to a child. Daddy. I wasn't ever going to get sick of hearing that. "Remember when I had to be really still because of my elbow?" She carried on in that exaggerated voice. I nodded, unable to speak, but this time because the kid had left me speechless. "It's like that, okay?"

I cleared my throat. "Okay," I told Lex, before I let my head fall back onto the pillow.

I listened as Jade spoke quietly, saying something about how I was awake and coherent. It wasn't more than ten seconds later when a team hospital staff filed into the room. I kept my eyes on Jade and Lex, who had left the chair reluctantly when Jade had called her over, but not before saying, "you're okay, Daddy."

I was feeling a lot of emotions and I wanted nothing more than to see my girls. But instead, I spent the next hour and a half being moved and prodded and tested and questioned.

"Is this a hospital or a prison?" I asked Jade when I was finally free of the last nurse. "You'd think I could figure out where the fuck I was before-." I stopped grumbling when I heard a small snicker.

"Sorry, Baby," I told Jade, then looked at Lex, who was standing behind and to the side of her mom. "Sorry, Lex Bug."

Lex grinned, a wide smile that nearly touched her eyes, before she popped out from behind Jade and bounced to the chair beside me.

"We brought you something, Daddy," Lex said proudly, a smile on her face that reminded me of a young Jade.

I turned to Jade, whose eyes were glistening. "Is it a wheelchair to get me out of this place?" I teased.

Lex giggled, and Jade tugged at my hand slightly. "No, silly," Lex bopped her head back and forth with each word. "We got you these!" She announced, then produced two stuffed animals.

I chuckled, but my eyes watered and I did my best to hold it together.

"Do you remember these, Daddy?" Lex wiggled the animals in the air.

"How could I forget, baby girl?" I felt a stray tear fall.

"This little cutie was the first one you got me when I just got to the hospital! I named her Katie." She handed me a small stuffed giraffe that had wings and was wearing a purple tutu. I smiled, remembering that day, thinking how unaware I'd been, walking around in that gift shop, carrying a tutu-ed giraffe for the kid of the woman I loved. The kid who'd turned out to be mine.

"Katie is a faerie, Daddy!" Lex grinned. "That's why I brought her."

I swallowed, and it felt like I had gravel in my throat.

"Do you remember what I told you about Katie?" I asked. "Remember that she-."

I was cut off by Lex, who launched in. "She is a faerie, Daddy. That means that she has magical." Lex waved her hands in the air dramatically. "Mystical, supernatural, curative properties!" Lex stood up on the chair, delivering the same grand finale I'd delivered when I'd presented the giraffe to her. I wasn't sure if I was going to laugh or cry, watching my daughter reenact one of our memories.

"And this one I named Bingo, because I couldn't think of anything better." She shrugged, plopped back down on the chair, and presented a round, stuffed ball with little felt spikes jutting off of it.

"Hey now, justice for Bingo the Bacteria," Jade cut in, snatching the toy from Lex, who giggled and made an exaggerated pouty face at her mom.

"Bingo has been a very educational hand-washing tool and I still stand by my choice!" Jade huffed.

"It's okay, Mommy," Lex teased. "Daddy just has better stuffy taste."

"Slim pickins' at the gift shop that day, Jade?" I taunted.

Jade smirked, and she rolled her eyes before muttering, "Well, Mr. Save-the-Day got all the good ones before I got there."

My girls laughed, and I watched, taking it all in.

"Bram?" Jade whispered.

"How did I get so lucky, huh?" I asked, not expecting an answer.

"It's not luck. You're a hero, Daddy." Lex said matter-of-factly, and I felt my jaw quiver.

"She's right," Jade whispered, laying her hand on

346

my chest. "You're our hero. You saved us."

I shook my head. She had no idea. "No, baby, you both saved me."

****

Jade

"Careful babe, wait, wait, wait! Cam's here, he's gonna help you get out," I scolded because damn, the man was not a good patient. He'd been impatiently waiting in the hospital for three weeks while he healed, getting grouchier by the day.

The only good news had been that Andrew heard what had happened and rushed the final touches on the house, wrapping up early so we could come back to a home instead of a crime scene.

Bram rolled his eyes and flung open the door, mumbling something about being able to get out of his own goddamned truck and why did I have to drive, because I never drove his truck, not once.

"Can you just get home in one piece, honey?" I asked. "I want to know you're settled before I head back to the hospital to Vee."

Bram had taken just one shot, but it had gone through his arm and grazed his side. It had taken two surgeries to repair his arm, and he was in for months of physical therapy, but he'd fully recover.

Evie hadn't been as lucky, but she'd been just as brave. She had protected Lex by shoving her in the closet while she fought off one of Nathan's armed goons. She'd taken a gunshot wound to the abdomen before Jules stepped in. But I'd passed the man on my way to the ambulance, so I'd knew that Evie just might've won had the man not had a gun. Sure, Jules had knocked him out with a single blow, but he was covered in scratches and bruises before that.

But she was still in critical condition, having nearly bled out from the bullet that had just missed her stomach.

Cameron rushed to the truck and gripped Bram's good arm to help him down.

"You too?" Bram asked, sounding irritated.

"Bro, you just got shot. Cut the bullshit and let me help you."

"Oooooooo, Daddy, you said a real bad one! A really big, bad word. Mama, you heard it too, right?" Zara squeaked from the side of the truck and looked up at Raven with big eyes.

"Oh, I heard it!" Raven said, her voice light and her face stern. "I'll make sure Daddy goes in a really big timeout."

Cameron winked at her. "I bet you will, baby."

"Be careful with my dad, okay?" Lex walked to the side of Cameron, micromanaging the process.

With that, Bram's face softened and he let Cameron help. When I got him situated in our new bedroom, I gave him a few pain pills and left so he could sleep and I could prepare for my drive back to the hospital to see Evie.

"Where are the girls?" I asked Raven as I sat down at the dining room table.

She turned her head and smiled at me, before she placed a cup of coffee in front of me and sat down. "Lex wanted to show Zara her room, so they're playing upstairs. Don't worry, Lex told Zara they had to be quiet." She grinned. "She sure does look out for her dad."

"Jade." Cameron walked into the kitchen and took a seat at the table. "I have some news." I searched his face for a clue and sat back when I noted the seriousness of his expression.

I sighed, readying myself. "What is it?"

"I wanna talk to you about Nathan's safe."

I exhaled the breath I'd been holding. "Sure, but I don't really know that much."

Cameron nodded. "Do you know what he had in there?" he asked.

"Sorry, but no," I shrugged. "I didn't have a way of opening it, but I just assumed it was money."

What I wanted to discuss was my brother. I'd seen him, I know I had, but no one was talking about the man who'd saved our lives.

I'd told Cameron about it in the official police report, and he'd seemed very interested then. And why wouldn't they all be? He was there, witness to a crime.

"Did you find Jules?" I asked, my heart falling at the mention of his name.

Cameron sighed. "I called the penitentiary," he said, then dipped his head to one side. "They said there is no way he could've been in Brooks Falls that night because he was asleep in a prison cell."

"What?" His words hit me like a slap to the face. "No, Cameron, I saw him. I know I did!" I turned to Raven, starting to feel desperate. "I'm not crazy," I told her.

"Oh honey, no one is saying that!" Raven placed a hand on my arm before she focused on Cameron. "Babe, can you be a little more clear?"

I looked at Cameron and waited for him to do just that.

"Bram told me some things about your brother and his *situation*." Cameron took a breath, and with a loud sigh, he went on. "He's never been to prison, Jade. Not once."

I shook my head, unable to speak.

"I don't know the details, but I do know that whoever is protecting Jules is way above the pay grade of anyone who could potentially prosecute him." Cameron finished, and I finally came to when Raven squeezed my arm.

"Prosecute?" I whispered. "Jules saved my life. He saved all of our lives!" I didn't understand. "Prosecute him for what?"

Cameron cleared his throat. "Well, back to the safe, Jade."

It finally hit me. "What did you find?"

Cameron cleared his throat and looked slightly to the side of me. "Extensive documentation, pictures, who drove which routes and what they transported."

I scoffed. "That's surprising. Nathan couldn't manage his own home, but he kept *extensive* records of his business?" I shook my head. "Well, that's great then. You should have enough evidence to put him away for good, right?"

Cameron nodded. "Oh, yeah."

"Good?" I questioned, my unease building.

Cameron shook his head. "Not the best, Jade. Both your brother and Bram are implicated in the records they found."

Bram? Implicated? My head became fuzzy, and suddenly all I could think about was losing Bram. Again.

"Is he facing jail time?" I stammered and mindlessly clasped onto Raven's arm.

"No, nothing like that." Cameron shook his head, but his voice was still low and foreboding. "The statute of limitations on felony drug charges has long passed."

"Okay," I drew out. "So then, what's the problem?"

"What he did was illegal and while he may not be facing drug charges, he's been placed on administrative leave."

I blinked. That stupid safe. I should've thrown it off the nearest cliff.

Cameron continued on. "Sheriff Riler is not happy with how this looks for the department."

I swallowed hard. "So, is he out?" I asked, not sure I even wanted the answer.

Cameron nodded before he answered. "Yeah, Jade. He'll be out."

I let the information settle. Financially, we would be fine on my income alone, but I didn't know how Bram would take it, and after all he'd been through, I didn't want to deliver him one more piece of bad news.

"Jade, honey, are you okay?" Raven put her hand over mine and searched my eyes. "I'm so sorry.

I nodded and wiped a tear. "Yeah, I'm okay. I just, he's." I stopped because I wasn't okay. "Will you just let me talk to him first?" I asked Cameron.

"Of course." Cameron gave me a curt nod and before I could struggle my way through another sentence, I heard my phone ringing.

"I better get that." I stood up from the table and headed to the front of the house, where I'd left my purse.

I pulled out the ringing phone to look at the screen, except it wasn't my phone. A tiny sticky note was stuck to the phone that read, "For Jade." I looked around, not really sure what I was looking for, before I swiped the screen. "Hello?" I said anxiously.

"Jade." My brother's voice set my heart at ease. "I'm glad you answered."

"J—"

"Nope. Don't say it. You're talking to Evie," he said matter of fact.

"Hey Vee," I said through tremors. "How are you feeling, honey?"

"I heard about Bram, that he lost his job," Jules said, and I looked around. How the hell did he find that out?

"Yes," I replied. "Do you need anything else?"

"There's an opening with the agency I work for."

I exhaled sharply. "No, sweetie," I emphasized. "I don't know where that is."

Jules sighed. "Jade, just hear me out."

"No," I replied more adamantly. "I don't think you left it at the store."

"It's not anything like what I do, I promise. He wouldn't be in any danger. We just need someone to help rehab our injured." He paused and then said slowly, "Employees."

I looked over my shoulder, then stepped outside, placing the phone back to my ear.

"I don't even know what you do or who these employees would be!" I hissed. "He's been through enough. We've been through enough." I felt the tears well in my eyes.

"Jade, he went to school for this shit. It was all he ever wanted to do. Sure, it's not sports therapy, but it's pretty damn close and he'd be helping people who are making a difference." Jules was silent for a beat. "He gave everything up for our family, Jade." Jules's voice was solemn and his words tugged at my heart. "He gave everything up for you. I just want to help him get a sliver of something good back. He's got you and Lex now. Let me help him."

I inhaled slowly. "Okay, I'll talk to him about it."

"Good. I'll call him, too. Later though. All right, Jade, bye," Jules clipped.

"Wait!" I said before he could hang up. "Just bye? I haven't spoken with you in years. Can't you at least talk to me for a minute?" There was only silence before I asked, "Jules?"

"I'm here."

"I miss you," I told him, wishing so badly I could see my brother again. "I've missed you for a long time. I didn't even get a chance to thank you for saving our lives."

"It's not a big deal, Jade," he said, like it actually wasn't.

"Bram told me what you did for me for so many years." My voice cracked as I thought back to that painful conversation. Bram had been one week in the hospital when he finally told me. I'd cried for the rest of the day, struggling to make peace, landing somewhere between gratefulness and guilt.

Jules cleared his throat. "Yeah." That was all he said.

"So, are you married, or do I have any little nieces or nephews terrorizing the world?"

For the first time in a long time, I heard Jules laugh. "Not even close."

"Girlfriend? Fiancé? Anyone?" I pressed, curious, but also not knowing what else to ask him.

He scoffed. "Just one woman, but I'm invisible to her."

I rolled my eyes. remembering the sight of my brother. "I find it hard to believe that you could be invisible to anyone," I teased. "What are you, eight foot three?"

Jules laughed a second time, something I counted as a win. "Well, it's true. That shit ain't for me, anyway. My, um, lifestyle isn't conducive to a relationship. Hasn't ever been and I don't foresee a change. It is what it is. I get to give other people an opportunity to live their lives. That's my sacrifice, my penance."

I said nothing, only pressed my eyes closed. What did he have to pay a penance for? The sins of my father? I hated what he'd done to Jules, what he'd made him believe about himself,

"I gotta go, Jadey," Jules said, his voice once again serious. "And you get back to the hospital and take care of Evelyn. She shouldn't be alone."

I jerked my head back. "Evelyn?"

"Or Evie, whatever you call her. I put something on your porch for her. Bring it to the hospital for me?"

"What?" I looked around. And sure enough, on my porch was a small, blue bonsai tree. "A tree?"

He chuckled into the phone. "Her favorite tree."

What the fuck was going on and how did Jules know so much about Evie?

"She can't know about me, Jade. Just give her the gift, okay? It'll cheer her up, I promise."

"Sure," I assured him, desperately wanting more answers, but knowing I wouldn't get them. Not now anyway.

Jules cleared his throat. "Keep this phone on hand and tell Bram to answer his when I call. Bye, kiddo."

With that, he hung up, not even giving me a chance to say goodbye. I picked up the tree and headed inside.

Chapter 21

Bram

If someone had told me when I was twenty-one that in nine years I'd have a family with the love of my life, I would've laughed in their face. Nine years ago, when I lost Jade and committed my life to protecting her and burying my secrets, I thought my life was over for me. Fuck, just two months ago when I found out I'd lost my job at the department, I felt like my professional life was over.

Who knew that such a kick to the nuts could be a damn blessing in disguise? Not long after Jade told me the news that Cameron had delivered, wanting to prepare me for the meeting I'd scheduled with Sheriff Riler, I'd received a call from Jules about a job.

The organization that he, and now I, worked for operated completely in the shadows. And the thing was, the area surrounding Brooks Falls was the perfect place for injured mercenaries to hide out and recover.

I didn't hesitate to take the position and even agreed to go back to school to get my masters in exercise science. I was doing it all online, while renovating my house into a tucked away training center. With me not living there anymore, it was the perfect place for employees to stay and recover.

I was learning a lot about what Jules had been up to

since he got recruited and because I was now fully immersed in his world; he confided some other things to me. Like the woman he'd been pining after for years and how they met and the many reasons they could never be together. It was a shock when he told me, but I accepted it quickly and I didn't have to make promises or agree to keep my mouth shut, because it was just expected. That was the world I was living in now.

And our little family was thriving. Every night, we put Lex to bed together in our new home. A home that looked near identical to the home I grew up in. Jade had said it was the home that I'd given her, and now she was giving it back to me.

I headed up the stairs after a long day at my old house, putting up drywall and building out additional rooms. It was midnight and Jade was leaving for Los Angeles tomorrow for Priscilla's party, so I didn't expect to see her awake.

I pulled back the covers and slipped into the bed next to Jade. I felt the brush of her bare skin on my hand and I shivered at the touch. Fuck, she was perfect.

I moved in close and wrapped my arms around her. And fuck, she was also naked. I lifted the covers just to see her and my cock took note of everything I saw, instantly hardening and straining in my sleep pants.

She was wearing this tiny emerald colored thong and her back was to me, showcasing her perfectly round and grabbable ass. "Fuck," I groaned, lifting the blanket just a little more.

"See something you like?" Jade's sleepy voice barely cut through the lust induced haze.

"Sorry, baby. Go back to sleep." I ran my hand along her spine, coaxing her back to sleep. She had an early flight and needed the rest.

"I'm not gonna see you for a long time, honey," she mumbled, rolling over so that she was facing me.

I laughed. "You'll be gone for four days. It's not exactly an extended absence."

Jade pushed up and narrowed her eyes at me. "Excuse me? Are you saying that you're totally fine with four days away from me, Bram Taylor? And are you also saying that you don't want to fuck me before I leave?"

"Don't," I warned, knowing if she said fuck me one more time, I'd lose control.

A half-smile quirked on her lips, and she fluttered her lashes. "Don't what? Don't ask you a simple question? Four days, babe. Four days you won't have me, and my pussy is so wet right now. I need to be fu—"

I didn't let her finish. I flipped her on top of me, propping myself up on the headboard of our bed. I had Jade's legs on either side of my body, straddling me, wearing nothing but that tiny thong.

She moved back, hooking her thumbs in my sleep pants and pulling them down slowly with my boxer briefs, letting her lips graze my cock as she worked them off me. I hissed at the contact of her lips on my dick.

"Mmm," she moaned. I felt it in every part of me.

Jade tossed my clothes to the side and ran her hands up my legs as she moved back up my body, cupping my balls lightly before wrapping her hand around my cock at the base and squeezing. I bucked up into her hand and then her mouth was on me, wrapped around me, sucking.

"Jadey, baby. Fuck yeah, god your mouth feels so damn good on my cock. You like when I fuck your mouth, baby?" I asked as I thrusted up into her.

Jade lifted her eyes to me and nodded, her mouth still on me, her tongue making circles around the sensitive head of my dick. "Jesus!" I threw my head back, enjoying every fucking second of what my woman gave me.

"I need you to stop, Jadey. I need to be inside of you when I come." I latched onto the back of her hair, not pushing or pulling, just keeping her in place on my cock. "Yeah?"

She nodded, the only movement she could make with my hands on her. I pushed her forward to take more of me, unable to pull her off just yet. Jade groaned around me as I slid further in, burying my cock deep in her mouth. Her sounds set something off in me, just as they always did. I drew back my cock and then bucked back into her mouth. Jade let her head fall forward as she kept her lips tight, and I thrust in, eliciting a whimper from the back of her throat.

"Fuck!" I ground out, quickly spiraling out of control. "Get up here, baby."

Jade slowly pulled back, licking my cock in her mouth as she did, and releasing me with one final suck to the head. I jerked, cursing and groaning through the pleasure.

"Get on my face, baby." I pushed off the headboard so I could lie down on my back and didn't wait for her to move. Instead, I grabbed her by the hips and yanked her to me. She landed with a squeal. "Lift your ass up. I like the panties, but they gotta go."

Jade made sexy little noises as I worked her panties down her legs and threw them to the side and lifted her up onto my face.

"Baby!" she cried out as I plunged my tongue inside

of her. Jade circled her hips over my face. "Yes, just like that. Oh god, that feels so good!"

She was so damn wet, and I was fucking dripping with her, knowing I'd be tasting her on my tongue for hours afterward. I sucked in her clit, enjoying the way her ass pushed back away from me when the sensations became too much.

With one hand at her belly and one on her ass, I moved her, forcing her to ride my face as I tongue-fucked her. When I felt her knees squeeze gently at the side of my face, I knew she was close.

Jade's fingers tangled in my hair as I licked her up and down, sliding a finger into her, pushing her closer and closer to the edge.

"Bram, I'm, I'm gonna come. Don't stop! Please, don't stop!" she pled as if I could ever stop.

As quickly as she announced it, I felt her release on my tongue, her pussy pulsing on me as I continued fucking her with my mouth and hand. She squeezed around me as she moaned my name into the night.

I didn't let her come down slowly. Instead, I lifted her off me and hovered over her, lining my cock up with her entrance, and charged forward, needing to be inside of her as fast as humanly possible.

"Bram!" she cried out, and I felt again as she squeezed around me.

"That's right baby, give me another one," I gritted in her ear as I pumped into her perfect little pussy.

"You cock is magic," she whined, barely intelligible.

"Fucking cum all over my cock, baby." I flung one of her legs over my shoulder and pounded ruthlessly. She knew the rules, I knew the rules, and unless one of us tapped out, it was a fucking free for all and right now, I needed to be rough.

Jade arched her back, pushing up into me as I buried myself in her. Fuck, she felt good, and I was sure she would always feel this way for the rest of our lives.

I rode her harder, and the leg over my shoulder became a leg wrapped around me, pulling me in as I charged forward, forcing my cock as deep as it would go inside of her. When I felt my body tightening and the sensation wound up straight to my balls, I slammed into her, fully seated myself, and watched her lose her mind as we both came.

"Jadey, baby. Fuck, I love you. God, I love you so much," I rumbled out as I continued to spill into her. My hips jerked one final time as I dropped my forehead to hers and then placed a soft kiss on her swollen lips.

"Honey." Her eyes fluttered open as she stared up at me. "You're a sex god," she said in that sleepy voice of hers.

I chuckled and sunk my teeth into her bottom lip. "And you're my sex goddess."

Epilogue

Jade

Priscilla's party went off without one single hitch. My four days in Los Angeles had been fun, but it had felt long and by the time I was done, I'd been ready to get home for three days.

I missed Bram and Lex. Most of all, I missed our life together. It was hard to believe that just a year ago, I'd be coming back home to Evie and Lex, wondering if I'd ever find love again. And back then, I was positive that I wouldn't.

As I drove back through Brooks Falls, I let the calm settle around me. I found it odd that this place had brought me so much pain and turmoil, yet it was the only place I'd ever felt at home. It defied logic, but it just was. And for all that it was, I was grateful. And knowing what I knew now, that people had given up so much for me so that I could have it all, so I could build a life and find success and happiness, it made this place all the more magical and solidified its spot in my heart.

When I made it past town and to our property, I beamed at it. The fence, that ugly security fence, had finally come down, and we were in the process of replacing it with a simple wood fence meant for nothing more than to define the edges of our property.

I parked, relieved that I was finally home. I opened the door with the security code and walked into the house. It smelled of warm apple pie and cloves. The house was dark, and I guessed with the nights getting darker earlier, everyone was asleep earlier. I noticed a very dim light in my favorite room was on.

It was a beautiful place, surrounded by windows and on clear nights, you could see the stars. A fireplace sat on the edge of one side, rounding out the utter coziness of the room.

More often than not, the three of us would do our nighttime reading in that room, with Lex bundled up on her dad's lap in one of the comfy chairs that set askew of the fireplace, while I watched them like I was I was reliving all my best daydreams.

The closer I got to that room, the more I noticed. Candles made a trail from the living room through the kitchen leading to the room. I followed the path, smiling at the sweet welcome home of Lex and Bram. I got to the steps leading down to the room and stopped dead. My heart suddenly pounded, and my breath left me. My knees wobbled with anxiety as I stared into the face of the only man I'd ever loved.

"Jadey," he said, on bended knee, holding a closed, deep blue, velvet box that reflected the light from the candles. "You are the first and only woman I have ever loved. As kids, you stole my heart and you've owned it ever since. When you delivered yourself on my doorstep, I knew there was something special about you."

"Bram," I whispered, tears streaming down my cheeks.

"And the closer we got, the more I realized that I'd do anything to keep your light shining bright in the world."

Bram motioned for me to go to him. I glanced to the

side, finally seeing Evie and Lex. Evie was sitting on the loveseat in front of Lex, who was bouncing gleefully. Evie placed a hand over her heart and pressed her lips together. I took the few steps down into the room.

"Back then, we were kids," Bram continued. "Making decisions about tough things the best way we knew how. We've made mistakes, we've lost time, and we almost lost each other. In all that, we managed to make the most beautiful human being that I have the honor of calling my daughter."

Bram looked over at Lex and winked. Lex beamed, giving him the thumbs up. "Keep going Daddy, you almost did it!"

I laughed through tears and managed to wipe a few from my face.

"In all that, we found our way back to one another. I don't know how I lived for all those years without you, and looking back, I realize that I wasn't really living. I never want to be without my girls again."

I exhaled, trying to control my breathing, knowing the last thing I wanted was to pass out mid-proposal. Bram took that moment to open the box.

"Jade Greene, will you do me the honor of marrying me?"

I stared down at the open box, eyeing the pear cut, aquamarine stone set in a white gold band.

"Bram!" I threw my hand over my mouth and nodded, trying to will the words to come.

"Say yes, Mommy!" Lex hollered from the side, and we all laughed.

I cleared my throat. "I have something to say first, if that's okay?" I asked.

Bram looked up and grinned. "I would expect

nothing less, Miss soon-to-be-Taylor."

I stared back at the man who had changed the course of my life. He'd given everything up for me. "Bram Taylor, you have been my family since the day I walked into your house. You've proposed to me a thousand times before and sure, they were all in my mind and yes, when I was fifteen you proposed to me at school, in front of the team of very disappointed cheerleaders."

Bram smiled and shook his head.

"Of all the times you proposed to me and all the ways I could've imagined it, not a single one of them was better than this. All you've done in my life is surround me with love, with cushioning, and family to get me through. I've loved you since the first time I saw you and I know I'll love you to my dying day." I looked over at Lex.

"How much is a swear?" I asked.

"One dollar!" she returned. "Inflation," she said to Evie with a shrug.

I nodded and turned back to Bram. "So, hell yes, I'll marry you!" I hollered that last part and then leapt into his arms as he stood, planting a thousand kisses on me.

Bram smiled against my lips and murmured, "Mine, all mine, Jadey."

And I was. I was all his. I'd always been and that would never change.

A word about the author...

Sonnet Harlynn lives in Raleigh, North Carolina where she spends her time writing the stories she dreams about all day. Her incessant writing is fueled by a coffee addiction and a determined drive to bring the characters in her head to life.

http://golddustliterary.com

Thank you for purchasing
this publication of The Wild Rose Press, Inc.

For questions or more information
contact us at
info@thewildrosepress.com.

The Wild Rose Press, Inc.
www.thewildrosepress.com